ITHACA LOST

KIRSTEN MCKENZIE

SSP

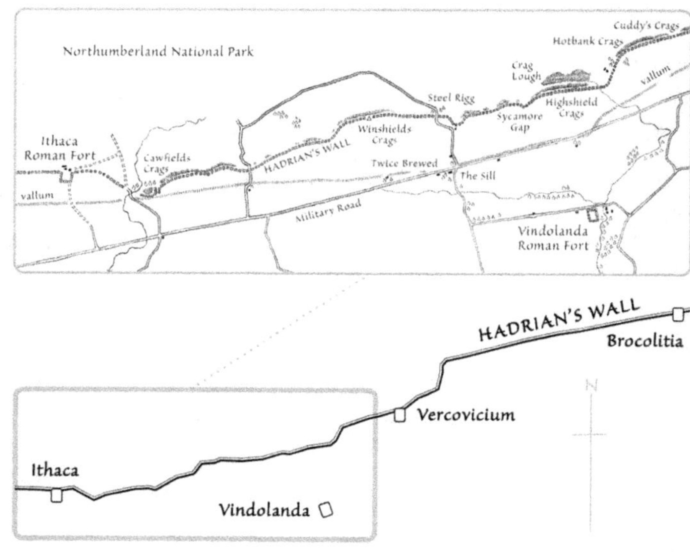

Northumberland National Park
Cuddy's Crags
Hotbank Crags
Crag Lough
vallum
Steel Rigg
Highshield Crags
Sycamore Gap
Winshields Crags
Ithaca Roman Fort
Cawfields Crags
HADRIAN'S WALL
Twice Brewed
The Sill
vallum
Military Road
Vindolanda Roman Fort
HADRIAN'S WALL
Brocolitia
Vercovicium
N
Ithaca
Vindolanda

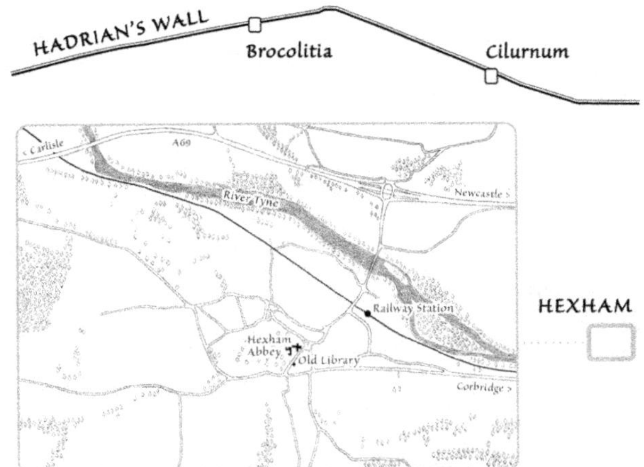

HADRIAN'S WALL
Brocolitia
Cilurnum
< Carlisle
A69
River Tyne
Newcastle >
Railway Station
Hexham Abbey
Old Library
Corbridge >
HEXHAM

Published 2024 by Squabbling Sparrows Press

ISBN 978 1 99 115769 0 (Wingspan Pocket Edition)

Illustrations by: **Mark Richards**

ALSO BY KIRSTEN MCKENZIE

The Ithaca Time Travel Trilogy
ITHACA BOUND
ITHACA LOST
ITHACA FOUND

The Old Curiosity Shop Time Travel Trilogy
FIFTEEN POSTCARDS
THE LAST LETTER
TELEGRAM HOME

Standalone Paranormal Thrillers
PAINTED
DOCTOR PERRY
THE FORGER AND THE THIEF

Short Story Anthologies
LANDMARKS
NOIR FROM THE BAR
REMAINS TO BE TOLD: DARK TALES OF AOTEAROA

This book is dedicated to the staff of Vindolanda.
Past and present.

PART ONE

MADNESS SPEAKS

'Everything. I want everything. What part of that word is difficult to understand?'

Mayor Jane Badrick's aide hurried off like a wounded puppy, his tail between his legs.

'How much do we pay him?' the mayor asked the man in the leather club chair opposite her. 'Don't bother answering, it's too much, that's what it is. He should pay me for the privilege of working in my office, learning from me.'

If Jane Badrick noticed her companion's discomfort, she made no mention. Instead, she rifled through the stack of papers on her giant mahogany desk before locating the document she needed.

'We can try compulsorily acquiring the place,' she suggested.

'It is unlikely to succeed,' Darren Saunders replied, legal training dripping from his words.

'I'm paying for your advice, not your opinion,' Jane snapped back. 'You handled her inheritance of the place, so I expect you to find the loophole I need.'

Jane's obsession with Ithaca Farm and, by extension, its new owner, Lillian Arlosh, had occupied her every waking moment since Jane had been rescued from Ithaca Farm. Her foolish husband wanted her to take time off from her role as Hexham's mayor, to relax. But then he had been a fool since the day of their wedding, and before that too.

She had married Matthew Badrick to make her parents happy. Now that they were long gone, she would have divorced him and carried on living her best life, if not for her goal of winning a seat at the next general election. Voters preferred married members of parliament. It didn't matter if they were unhappily married and having rampant sex with strangers on the boardroom table at Downing Street, as long as a convincingly loving spouse appeared on their arm at every photo opportunity. And that was the one and only reason she stayed married to Matthew Badrick.

'The genealogist found no other living members of the Arlosh family. Lillian Arlosh is the sole heir of William Arlosh. Their family tree is exceedingly narrow,' Saunders explained as he adjusted his Eton tie, loosening the Windsor knot a fraction of an inch, the heat in the office almost unbearably high.

Jane noted and enjoyed watching the perspiration on the lawyer's forehead. She preferred the heat and wasn't personally responsible for paying the utility bills, so she kept the thermostat up as high as possible.

'Go back through these documents, and the ones that fool of an aide is out there searching for, and find a way for Ithaca Farm to pass into council hands. I guarantee that there will be a way we can acquire it.' She tapped her manicured fingernails on the leather desk pad. 'Alternatively, a mortgagee sale would also suit.'

With the lawyer dismissed, Jane sank back into her seat, her thoughts turning inwards. Had it only been six weeks ago that she had stood beside two Iceni warriors, gunning the engine of her Land Rover, facing down a cohort of Roman soldiers? It felt both like a lifetime ago and mere moments ago. Either way, she had much more to achieve before she returned to that time, but unfettered access to Ithaca Farm was the key. Until that happened, Jane planned to stay in the here and now, stockpiling everything she needed for her next trip back in time.

'Excuse me, Mayor?'

Jane jerked out of her reverie.

'What?'

'Anson Darby is on the line for you, from Tyne River University.'

'Put him through,' Jane waved her assistant away, motioning for him to close the door.

Jane smoothed her blonde hair, annoyed at the few wisps escaping from the concrete-like hair spray she used to hold it in place.

'You took your time,' she said, holding the phone a good inch away from her ear and her oversized gaudy diamond studs.

'It hasn't been easy,' Anson Darby replied.

Jane imagined him sitting in his pokey office at the university, sweating like the lawyer had before him.

'Your challenges don't interest me. Tell me you've done what I asked.'

'Not quite—'

'Then ring back when you have,' Jane said before disconnecting the call. Idiots, she was surrounded by idiots.

Jane's eyes swivelled to a framed photograph on the wall. She had commissioned this piece from the acclaimed photographer Peter Savin in her first week out of the hospital, raising more than one eyebrow amongst her family and staff — a bird's-eye view of Ithaca Farm. Taken by drone, Savin had captured an eery mist, taking the shot as it swirled around the newly exposed Roman ruins on Ithaca Farm. After paying him handsomely, an enlarged print now hung in the centre of the wall, replacing the faded photos of Queen Elizabeth and Prince Philip. Given that they were both dead, she didn't think that they would care that she had relegated them to the skip outside.

Those ruins were the door, and she had the key. She just didn't have access yet.

WHAT WOULD EDGAR ALLAN POE SAY?

Apple Collings sat to the left of Henry Neumegen, one eye on the cafe's doorway, and the other on her new friend.

The pair made an odd couple — Apple with her milk-coloured skin and pink-rimmed eyes, and Neumegen in his long overcoat and dated three piece suit. His gold pocket watch and fob chain worth more than most people earned in a week.

'Lillian will be here soon, and she'll know,' Apple offered.

Neumegen only nodded. Apple had learnt that he was a man of little words, mainly to protect his secrets than for any other reason. She suspected he would be quite voluble around his close friends, in an environment safer than that of the Mooreeffoc cafe in the heart of Hexham.

'Have you tried the eggs? You should. They're from Lintz Hall farm in Burnopfield. Free range,' Apple enthused, waving the laminated menu, filling the silence.

The appearance of Lillian Arlosh saved her from any further discomfort.

'What did the coroner say?' Apple asked, her pale eyes shining.

Neumegen leaned forward, his slender face almost as excited as Apple's.

'It's treasure,' Lillian said.

'So you're rich!'

'It's not as easy as that.'

'You would have been better off if they hadn't declared it as treasure,' Neumegen offered. 'I think I will have the eggs.'

Apple threw her head back. The man was an enigma.

The three unlikeliest of friends bent their heads low together as they waited for their breakfast to arrive. Upon Apple's unrelenting badgering, Neumegen had moved out of the Twice Brewed Inn, and was now staying with Apple and her father, a far easier solution than staying with Lillian, who could not move without an army of reporters or town gossips commenting on her every breath.

Neumegen and Apple's father had more in common than her father did with the other thirteen-thousand residents of Hexham, despite having lived there all his life. Apple had overheard the two men discussing the merits of the Hexham and Allendale Railway and how it was a crime the smaller lines were closed. They'd both spoken as if they had frequented the line daily, regardless of the fact that the passenger service had been discontinued back in the thirties.

Apple watched Lillian from under her eyelashes. Despite almost owning a loyalty card to the Hexham Hospital, Lillian still refused to discuss her last trip, but Apple knew something dire must have happened, or was about to happen. Shadows lurked behind Lillian's eyes, and not even the undivided attention of Badger during Lillian's hospital stay had been enough to banish them.

Her pulse quickened at the thought of Badger. Or more precisely, thinking of Badger's mother. The woman was a menace, and she was the purpose of today's meeting.

'What will the mayor do now that the coins have been pronounced as treasure?' Apple asked, with her knowledge of the 1996 Treasure Act more than a little hazy.

'She has no say over the coins. It's up to the Treasure Valuation Committee to decide what they are worth, and which museums get them, or something like that. No, what concerns me the most is whether the ruins at Ithaca

Farm will be designated as a scheduled monument,' Lillian said.

Neumegen coughed politely, and the girls swung their heads towards the opening door. Jasper Fletcher, the Hexham Herald reporter, filled the open doorway, his red hair in desperate need of a trim by a good barber.

'He won't leave me alone,' Lillian hissed.

'I'll deal with the man,' Neumegen said.

'That'll make it worse. He already suspects you're involved somehow,' Apple said, shaking her head. 'Leave him to me. I'll distract him, and you two can—'

The waitress appeared, balancing all three plates with unequalled dexterity.

'Thanks, Pauline,' Apple said.

Pauline replied in her unintelligible Northern accent, sending Apple into fits of laughter.

'Yeah, you should,' Apple replied, still laughing. 'I'll explain later,' she said to Lillian and Neumegen's confused stares. 'But don't worry about Jasper. Pauline used to change his nappies. She'll sort him out for us.'

True to her word, the diminutive blonde waitress seemed to dominate the reporter as he slunk further and further into his seat at the counter, his attention diverted from the threesome.

'Let's go,' Apple said, wiping her mouth, her food disappearing faster than a summer fog. 'We can chat at the library.'

Neumegen threw some crisp pound notes onto the table, and they slipped out of the café like a group of truants skipping school.

Back at the makeshift library behind St Mark's Church, with Pramod Sharma's absence still very much filling the air, Neumegen, Apple and Lillian each pulled up a battered dining chair to their command centre — an old post office desk, scarred with decades of ink and gouges made by overly enthusiastic pen nibs. The desk boasted piles of photocopied papers and brittle original documents, all related to Ithaca Farm. Apple recognised early on that Lillian didn't have the funds to pay a lawyer to fight her battles, but she had her friends. And Neumegen seemed to have an exceptional understanding of arcane English law, despite spending most of his time in a small pawnbroking establishment on Auckland's Queen Street, in the 1860s... He put his knowledge down to a partial law degree he'd walked away from in his misspent youth, but had given no further details.

'If you sign this, then you're signing away any opportunity you might have to monetise the ruins,' Apple said, passing a sheaf of papers to Lillian.

'I can't sign those. I need all the money I can get to help rewild the farm. It should be easy enough to work the ruins into my plan. That seems like the right thing to do. But I can't even think about it when really I should go back to J... They, they need all the help they can get,' Lillian replied. 'Besides, if I don't go back, signing or not signing those documents probably won't be an issue. Probably none of this will even be here,' she said, waving her arms around the cramped church hall, filled to the rafters with books.

Apple watched her friend. She knew why Lillian wanted to go back, even though Lillian had never admitted it. And she admired her for her commitment. It wasn't your average person who went back in time to prevent something they had seen in a vision, especially when visions were traditionally unreliable.

'Come on, Lillian, we've talked about this so much. We agreed we'd wait until the traditional period of Saturnalia.'

Apple watched Lillian nod, and Neumegen check his pocket watch. They both did her head in, and she wasn't even a time traveller. Time travel was wasted on these two.

According to every online article Apple had read, Saturnalia began in two days. It was Lillian's best opportunity to pinpoint an arrival time, so everything they had prepared revolved around the festival. The poet Catullus called it "the best of days". But as far as Apple could work out, Saturnalia was no different to Meditrinalia. Both involved copious amounts of alcohol, but with the addition of gifts.

'You need to sign the ruins over,' Neumegen counselled. 'Let English Heritage shoulder the cost of managing the ruins and protecting them. We can negotiate a split of the proceeds or a bequest upon your, ah, passing...'

Lillian took the pen Apple held and scribbled her signature across the bottom of the legal papers.

'Dad would never have signed,' Lillian said.

Although Lillian whispered the words, Apple heard. Nothing in the past can be undone. So there was no point in living what ifs or if onlys. What was done was done, and no amount of wishing, or time travel, could bring back the dead. Pramod Sharma had at least explained that to her.

'He'd be so proud of what you've achieved,' Apple said. 'And I'm sure that one day, you'll get to meet him and he'll be able to tell you.'

Lillian wiped her hands, her eyes on the desk. And Neumegen had fallen silent. Whenever their discussions veered off into family, Neumegen clamped his thin lips shut, and busied himself by tidying stacks of paperwork, or disappeared to the kitchen with their dirty cups.

'Did you get the dice?' she asked, changing the subject. Breaking through the complex layers of Neumegen's defences would take more time, and that was something they had little of.

'The Vindolanda gift shop had replica Roman wooden dice. I thought they'd do. What do you think?' Lillian replied.

'They should be of an age,' Neumegen said. 'But they could work. I'm not sure.'

Apple tried hard not to scream, but she let his indecisiveness pass without comment, only adding, 'I bought some mead from the Holy Island, Lindisfarne. The website said they'd been making mead there since Roman times. It was the closest I could get without bidding at Christie's fine wine auction. The last ancient bottle of mead sold there for twenty-thousand pounds, and I wasn't asking my father for a loan.'

That cracked the ice.

With the replica dice and the mead already in hand, a Roman coin was the last item they needed. And their largest hurdle. Lillian's gold coin had gone missing when she was in Hexham Hospital. And after the media frenzy around the mayor's disappearance and the discovery of the hoard of Roman coins, asking the hospital where Lillian's coin might be had not seemed like a good idea.

'What about that archaeologist? The one who let himself into your house? He's involved in the study of the coins. You could ask him.'

'I don't trust him,' Lillian replied. 'There must be another way. Can't you go back and get one from your time?'

Apple knew Neumegen wouldn't. From his explanations, and those of Sharma, it seemed like the men followed complicated rules around their time travel. Apple thought that those rules were pretty stupid, and didn't understand why Neumegen didn't just slip back in time and buy an old coin from somewhere on his expansive timeline. After all, Sharma was supposedly Neumegen's best friend, and it would save them all a lot of angst. Unless there was something he wasn't sharing with them...

Surprisingly, Neumegen responded with, 'What about the man with the metal detector?'

Lillian straightened. 'He could have picked up a coin or too before I chased him away. It's worth a shot.'

'That's an option. We could try tracking him down. I should have thought of that,' Apple added.

'You've had other things on your mind.'

'I'll make some of my own enquiries,' Neumegen said.

Apple frowned. The Hexham population would no more talk to Neumegen about their sex lives than they would about any illegal metal detecting along the border of Hadrian's Wall. The weather and the price of cheese were standard conversations with strangers in town. Nothing more or less.

It was as if the man had read her mind.

'My sources are quite different to yours, Apple.'

'Jasper Fletcher wrote about the local metal detecting clubs not so long ago. I kept the article, probably because my subconscious knew we'd need it. I'll start there,' Lillian said.

'Any word from your antique dealer friend?' Apple asked, remembering the woman from London who had proven her weight in Roman gold at the time of Lillian's last disappearance.

'She's coming back up, and she's been invited to the Saturnalia festival at the Bellingham. Paige Spencer thought it would be nice for her to come back to help celebrate the official reopening of the Bellingham.'

'The Saturnalia party,' Neumegen exclaimed, 'is where it has to happen.'

'At the Bellingham?' Lillian asked.

'It's a genuine festive event, with the right ambience, and crowds, and feasting. It's the perfect combination for us to travel back to the right time. But we'll need some small gifts. Things like...'

Apple watched him cast his eye about the room, and knew what his answer would be.

'Pramod's carvings.'

Whilst the shelves in the room were stuffed full of books, every minuscule gap sported a beautifully carved animal. Tiny wooden wolves and tigers and elephants peppered the shelves, together with badgers and beavers and moles. A menagerie of wildlife stalking each other across books penned by Follett and King, Carver and Gillespie, Ross and Christie. All carved by the delicate hand of Pramod Sharma.

'Which ones?' Apple asked.

'All of them,' Lillian replied.

Neumegen nodded, his deep brown eyes disguising his thoughts.

One by one, Pramod's tiny animals left their bookish enclosures, joining their wooden companions in a cardboard Noah's Ark.

'I'll ring Paige to tell her we're all coming and that we're bringing gifts for Saturnalia,' Apple said.

'Will you tell her that Nicole will be there too?' Lillian asked. Whilst Nicole had seemed to accept the goings on during her last visit, she had not been quite the same after her experience with the other worldly man at Ithaca Farm, barely discussing it, and paling at any mention of the night. Even on the phone, weeks later, Lillian could tell how unsettled she had been. 'She's coming back to the farm to finish packing the stuff she left behind, and I asked her to stay for the festival.'

'And what about the other altars? Will she take those?' Neumegen asked.

'No, not them. They'll stay with me. Having them close to the farm feels right.'

'It is sad that someone had been moved in the past,' Neumegen mused. 'It must have angered the gods at the time.'

No one replied. Now and then he threw a comment which sent shivers down Apple's spine, and Lillian's too, she suspected. Apple no more believed in the gods than she did time travel. But then again, and look where that had got her.

'I'm going to drop these off, so I'll see you both tomorrow. Does anyone need a lift back?' Lillian asked.

Apple and Neumegen both shook their heads. Travelling in Lillian's beat up Land Rover was best saved for life and death emergencies.

As the three unlikely friends left the church hall, with Neumegen loading the box of carved animals into Lillian's car, the painted face of Holly Corben stared at them through the office window across the road. She tapped a quick message into her phone and hit send. The melodic ping of the delivered message sending a smile to her face. There was more than one way to rid herself of a rival, especially one as tiresome as Lillian Arlosh.

GUNS, GERMS AND STEEL

'Mother, you wanted to see me?' Badger appeared in the open doorway of his mother's home office.

'Andrew, how lovely to see you,' Jane Badrick gushed, the smudges of mascara under her eyes marring her normally perfect presentation.

'I'm only here because you messaged, asking to see me urgently.'

'You're here because you love your mummy, and you'd do anything for her,' Jane laughed. 'Come into the kitchen and have a drink. It feels like gin o'clock, and that new distillery has sent me a lovely bottle of Sloe and Hawthorn Hepple gin to try.'

'Why are you being sent bottles of gin?'

'Influence, darling. Isn't that what you young people call it, being an influencer?'

'You're the mayor. I don't think voters look fondly on their elected representatives having a side hustle. I mean, bribery is illegal, yes?'

Jane snorted, pulling her son into a bear hug on her way to the kitchen, the pungent fug of liquor lingering behind her.

'Two gins, darling,' she instructed her husband, who was already at the bench, bottle in hand.

'Andrew, I didn't hear you come in.'

'I came in through the backdoor,' Badger replied.

'Will you be eating with us?'

'Of course he will,' Jane declared, swallowing a large mouthful of the drink she was already halfway through. One which was more gin than tonic.

'Why did you want me here when you've barely spoken a word to me since they found you? I mean, it's not like anyone has actually told me what happened to you. The papers said it was a car jacking.'

'Your father and I decided it was better not to worry you.'

'Cut the bullshit, mother. I'm an adult. I don't need to be protected. I need to know what happened and if you were hurt?'

'Have a drink, Andrew,' Jane said, the lightness vanishing from her tone.

'I'm not thirsty.'

'You mother offered you a drink,' Matthew said from behind his cellphone.

'Thank you, Matthew, but I'm handling this,' Jane said. 'Perhaps it would be best if you retired to the front room, whilst Andrew and I have a wee chat?' Jane's voice warning that no was not an answer she expected from her husband.

With just the two of them in the kitchen, Jane checked her reflection in the polished copper pots handing above the Aga stove, before tidying an errant hair and turning towards her only child.

'Tell me about your friend.'

'Which one?'

'Do not play coy with me, Andrew. I do not have time for your petty word play. You know who I mean, the Arlosh girl.'

'She has a name.'

'She shouldn't even own that farm. She's barely a relation. What do you think it would take for her to walk away from Ithaca Farm?'

Jane laughed as her son's jaw dropped. She had heard the rumours about his infatuation with the girl, as evidenced by his visits to the hospital, the coffees in town, and numerous sightings of his Fiat on the road out to Ithaca Farm. And the reports from Holly Corben. Holly was such a nice girl, and far more suitable as a future partner for her son. Just the thing to keep him tied to Hexham, to support her next election campaign. A successful election relied on strong family ties.

'She won't walk. Lillian has a dream to rewild the farm, like they did at Knepp Home Farm.'

'She will walk, and you will help her reach that decision sooner rather than later.'

'No, Mother, I will not.'

'This isn't a debate, Andrew. That girl is out of her depth, and seems to be experiencing frighteningly similar delusions to William Arlosh, before his family packed him off into care. Although they left *that* a little too late. The man was becoming a menace in town, ranting about soldiers and barbarians. They should have institutionalised him years ago, but your father wouldn't let me make the call. He said he would help him. A fat lot of good that did.'

'Where did you go when you disappeared?'

'Don't change the subject. I want that girl gone.'

'Apologise to Dad for me. I won't be staying for supper. I'm sure he'll understand,' Badger said, leaving his unfinished drink on the counter.

Jane watched her son leave. He would do what she asked. He always did, despite his false bravado. Young men often flexed their muscles with their parents. That was nature's way. But a son did what his mummy told him. *Her* son, at least.

WITH A THIRD GIN under her belt and her office door locked, Jane trawled the internet. Her husband may be an idiot, but it would not do for him to see her online shopping cart. Where once she would have ordered handbags and shoes and expensive elixirs of youth from Christian Dior or Chanel, now her cart bulged with pistols and pepper spray, and tactical vests. She did not have enough for an army, but then she wasn't kitting out an entire platoon, only herself.

Jane smiled as she considered her new car, the replacement for the one she had left with Gar and Bricius. The insurance money had appeared her in account much faster than she'd expected. It is amazing what the threat of negative publicity could achieve. For her replacement vehicle, she had selected a Land Rover Defender — for the versatility and boot space. The rest of the features were irrelevant. By tomorrow afternoon, the Defender would be in her garage. And then she just needed to deploy her husband elsewhere so she could pack the car in blissful solitude.

The warm buzz from the gin faded as she caught sight of the stark white invitation on her desk. The distinctive royal blue logo on the invite filling her with rage. A party at the Bellingham. Not securing ownership of the old building had been the one loss she had faced during her tenure as mayor, and it made her sick to her stomach knowing that an outsider now owned it. Those feelings were made even worse when the new owner had remodelled the interior of the historic Bellingham Tea Rooms, and was now pimping out the rooms like cheap Ibiza holiday packages.

The card promised a Saturnalia celebration, reminiscent of the ancient Roman festival honouring the god Saturn. Normally, Jane had no time for gods or festivals, unless they suited her reelection goals. But this event? This one suited her perfectly.

Jane dialled the number on the invitation, punching in the numbers with her exquisitely manicured nails. Would she miss her weekly manicures in Rome? She filed a mental note to pack a gel polish kit amidst her deadly arsenal.

The phone was answered at the other end.

'Ms Spencer? It's Jane Badrick. Your invitation has arrived, and I am delighted to accept. My calendar is blessedly free that night.' An audible layer of vile coated every word out of Jane's mouth. Smoothing her eyebrow with a practised hand, Jane muttered some meaningless platitudes before hanging up. Paige Spencer was another person who needed to leave Hexham. They did not need her sort in town. It wouldn't surprise Jane if the Bellingham proprietor was sleeping with half the married men in the district, and the single ones. Not that there were many of those. Which reminded her of another call she needed to make, and this phone number she knew by heart.

'Darby? It's Jane. I need that delivery by the 17th … yes, of December … That was our arrangement. My husband will see to your promotion … There will be no impediment, I can assure you … Yes, and oversight of the Ithaca excavations, as agreed … The 17th, Darby, and not a second later.'

Satisfied with the call, she poured another shot of gin into her glass and downed it straight. Things were coming together nicely. Now she had some study to do before bed. Carrying her gin to her vintage Chesterfield leather wingback armchair, she curled her legs up underneath her, and opened her book — The Twelve Caesars by Suetonius (and Robert Graves). Jane was well known for her comprehensive preparation before going into battle in the council chambers, and so preparing for this next battle would be no different.

FINANCIAL MISMANAGEMENT

John Revell pulled his belt one notch tighter. It was the second time this year he'd shrunk. Normally he would be strutting around like Kate Mosse, flaunting his newly svelte figure, and splashing out on a shirt from Peter England. But not this time. He only wished that the pounds of flesh he had lost would somehow magically appear on his balance sheet.

Revell ran his finger down the expense column of the Hexham Herald accounts, seeking something else to cut. If they fired Sue the receptionist, the Classifieds team could answer the phones, and his wife Gail could cover things on busy days. She would hate it, but she was the one who got them into this fix. Her, and her lofty dreams of being Northumberland's premiere accommodation provider.

He rubbed his face. *Hell,* even the skin on his face felt thinner. He'd never been much for the accounting side of things, preferring to lower his gold handicap wherever and whenever he could. But that was now an impossibility. The green fees at the Royal Hexham Club had increased another twenty pounds. They were trying to bankrupt him one hole at a time. For the past fortnight, he had claimed he was suffering from a slipped disc to avoid showing his face at the club and having to explain why his green fees were still in arrears. He'd almost had a heart attack when his accountant had explained, in explicit spread sheeted detail, just how much money Revell and his wife had frittered away on golf trips and beauty treatments. Gail still wasn't talking to him after he had refused to pay for any further nail treatments. If he could not play golf, then she could paint her own damn nails.

With no further savings identified at the Hexham Herald, Revell moved onto their other business — the Hexham Holiday Cottages. What had seemed like a profitable idea had since morphed into something more akin to building the Death Star, with money pouring out of their accounts. Far more than came in. First, Gail had begged for two modern replica gypsy wagons. They were cute; she had said. And easy to move around. And more flexible for group bookings. Like a fool, he had believed her, without doing his own research. He had been sucked in by the glossy brochures provided by the slick fox-faced sales agent, and before he knew it, they had signed on the dotted line for ten of the things, each with its own fireplace and ensuite. Ten! All clad in Siberian Larch for god's sake. To fund it, he had mortgaged the Hexham Herald building, and he would never forgive Gail for getting them into this mess.

Revell left his chair and stood at the window. Hadrian's Wall glowered at him through the skeletal trees in the garden. In summer, the green branches obscured his view, but in winter the leafless trees framed everything so beautifully he could spend hours staring out his window and not be bored. He knew everyone thought him oafish and gauche. But he'd always appreciated a fine view. If only more tourists would come and experience the incredible vista from his ten, very expensive but generous sized, balconies and fitted French doors. At least the caravans were hidden from view on a piece of land much closer to the wall. Land they co-owned with Jane Badrick. Which was a whole other expense.

Thinking about Jane made his heart skip a beat, then another. A chill crept over his body, and his forehead felt clammy. His hand involuntarily closed, crumpling the horror accounts in his fist. His heart skipped another beat. Christ, was this it?

Revell gulped down some air, forcing his hands to relax. *Slow your breathing*, he told himself. Deep breaths. Do not let Jane rob you of your life. Do not even think about the blonde harridan. Let it go. Breathe.

His body responded, with his heart settling into a more normal rhythm, but how long that would last was anyone's guess. He had been summoned to a meeting with Jane this afternoon, which had the real capacity to see him into his grave. But it was unavoidable, as was everything with Jane Badrick, mayor of Hexham.

'Sit down, John.'

'Hello, Jane, how are you feeling?' Revell replied, perspiration blooming behind the glasses frames as he lowered himself into the leather armchair.

'I've had better weeks.'

'Is there anything we can help with?' he asked, his brain churning through a thousand potential reasons for the mayor's bad mood. 'Is it the Hexham Hub?'

'That is the one bright spark on my horizon. Turning that useless library into a visitor centre and a commercial hub is *bringing* money into the council coffers, instead of bleeding it out. No, John, I think you know why I called you to this meeting. There's an unaccountable deficit in my personal budget. I'm interested in hearing why I can't see any deposits from you this month?'

Not depositing their share of monthly mortgage payment for the site of the holiday cottages had been a risk, but after weighing up the pros and cons, Revell had used what money they had to pay other, more pressing debts, like their overdue utility bills, and wages at the paper. Debts which could not be offset by any other means. The other means crackled ominously in the folder in his clammy hands.

'We're suffering a temporary shortage of funds this month. The weather, you see...' he started.

'The weather, the weather, if one more person tries using the English weather as an excuse for the lack of tourists, then let me draw your attention to the latest report from the Office for National Statistics. They posted that nineteen million people visited Britain last year. Nineteen million. So do not tell me that it's the weather keeping the tourists away. It shouldn't be difficult to book ten people into your cottages every weekend.'

Revell did the maths in his head — ten people, at a minimum, every weekend, meant at least five hundred and twenty guests. His accountant would have danced a little jig at the annual Hexham Time Travellers Flash Mob if that were true. As it was, they had barely seen a hundred people over the past summer, with no one booked for December. November had seen a pair of siblings from Australia staying — Joe and Lucy. And whilst both were completely entertaining, they'd complained of the terrible exchange rate, and had shared a cabin. Their bill had barely covered the cleaning fee.

'And the pandemic—'

'Do not mention that word. Where is my money?'

'Our finances are stretched, and we were hoping, what with the friendship between us, that you'd understand that we can't pay this month. Let's not forget the Christmas spirit, and all that...' Revell petered off as he clocked the look on Jane's face, which was devoid of anything resembling Christmas cheer or friendship.

'I have expenses that need paying before I next see you at the Bellingham's Disneyesque attempt at celebrating Saturnalia. Are we quite clear?'

Revell swallowed. It was now or never. This was not the first time he had wielded the power of his paper for personal gain, but it was the only time he had used it against someone as powerful as Jane Badrick.

'I understand. But there is one other thing, an article I want to run past you before it goes to print.' Revell handed the manilla folder to Jane, before fishing a handkerchief out of his pocket and wiping his classes.

'What's this?'

'An article one of my reporters has worked on—'

'You only have one reporter, John, that red-headed imbecile, Jasper Fletcher.'

Revell shrugged. Jasper was many things, but he was not an imbecile. Revell had worked damn hard to keep to Jasper's byline buried so he would not lose him to one of the bigger publications. He had lost too many good reporters to his competitors. So he did whatever it took to keep Jasper. Which included not always letting the lad write what he wanted to, apart from this one article... Revell watched Jane's face as she read the typed pages and tried not to smile.

Although Jasper hadn't shared the article with his employer, Revell had found it on the paper's server easily enough. The boy had been working on it for years, documenting every one of Jane Badrick's dubious decisions, detailing an almost infinite number of potential instances of bribery whilst in her role as Hexham's mayor. Revell would have signed his own death warrant if he had printed it in the Hexham Herald. Too many of his advertisers were so far down Jane's pockets that they were practically in her underpants. No, this was more a threat to release the article to someone outside of Hexham. To someone unconnected to the golden-haired Jane "Her Highness" Badrick.

'And what, John, am I meant to do with this?' Jane asked.

Revell flinched as Jane threw the pages at his face. He had too much at stake to back down now. He pulled his gut in and squared his shoulders.

'It's a good article, some of his better work. Jasper has been with me a long time, and I know he's looking at moving to the city. The rumour is that the Chronicle has a vacancy for a senior reporter. This could be his way in.'

Revell held the mayor's gaze, his heart racing.

'My money, John, and reflect on your position before

you say, or do, anything else. My connections run deeper than just with the members of the Rotary Club and the Hexham Wine Appreciation Society. They will make your life miserable.'

Frozen to his seat, Revell stared at a page on the ground, resting against the mayor's designer shoes. Shoes his wife had told him were handmade. He could only guess at the price of handmade shoes. And he knew in that instant that no matter how many adverts for fibreglass roofing materials he ran, or how many advertorials for the Save Mart furniture sales he wrote, he was no more likely to wear handmade shoes than he would be invited to visit Buckingham Palace.

'John?'

'Gail has some visitors booked into the cottages this weekend for the Christmas tournament. I'll pop by tonight with my golf clubs and persuade them to stay a little longer. I'm sure the Bellingham wouldn't mind two more guests at their Saturnalia event.'

'A good answer, John. And I think it's time for the local paper to run another story about the risk to our way of life by city people moving in and buying up all the land. The people need to know.'

NIGHT TERRORS

Lillian opened her eyes, terror filling her mouth as she tore at the sheets strangling her body. Sheets or hands? It took a monumental effort not to scream, to not draw any further attention to her madness. She blinked away the darkness, persuading herself that there was no half-crazed druid in her room. Just moonlight and the shadow of the monstrous wardrobe in the corner.

After moving to Ithaca Farm, she had thought the wardrobe quaint, reminiscent of the magical wardrobe in CS Lewis's books. But now she found it terrifying, lurking in the corner of her room; a repository for monsters, the sort which only ever emerged on the blackest of nights. On a night like tonight.

She reached for the lamp, the bulb restoring reality with its ordinary light casting ordinary shadows. Perhaps the antiques dealer from London would take the hideous thing? The only beautiful part of the oak wardrobe was the rosette motif above the carved panels. A feminine touch to a purely masculine piece of furniture.

Although she knew the wardrobe was void of any threat — she had checked it before going to bed — she still threw off her bedcovers and crossed the freezing floor to fling open the doors. Coat hangers rattled on the metal pole but revealed nothing more exciting than old robes, jackets, and a woollen cape.

Lillian pulled the cape from the hanger, the rough fibres warm in her hand despite the chill in the night air. It still smelled of Julius, and the night of her first vision.

With the cape in her hands, she crossed to the dressing table, the sturdy mate to the wardrobe but less imposing, less sinister. Somewhere in her jewellery box there was a brooch, the one that had been attached to the cape. Her hand closed around the heavy fibula brooch, which was shaped like a leaping dolphin, its pin still needle-sharp.

With the cape around her shoulders, Lillian pinned on the dolphin brooch, and stepped back to check her reflection. Would this cape help her blend in? It was from the right period, and not her imagination. She rubbed her head. Her scrapes had long since scabbed over, and the bruising had disappeared, but some wounds did not heal as fast. And her heart ached for a phantom, for an anomaly in time.

Lillian had tried talking to Nicole Pilcher about the man they had seen in the hallway that night, but Nicole refused to engage. She knew Nicole had seen him, the man who had spirited Lillian out of this time and into another. She remembered Nicole's face reflecting the same terror Lillian had felt at the sight of the skeletal man with wild unkept hair. His bare feet knotted with bulging veins ripe for eruption, and a mouthful of teeth like the jagged rocks beneath the Dunstanburgh Castle cliffs. She would never forget the icy grip of his hand against her flesh. But then he had vanished, leaving her alone in a time that was not hers. Everything else made sense, at least as far as travelling back in time could make sense. But he did not fit. And Lillian needed answers.

After checking the inside of the wardrobe for a second time, and twitching the curtain to survey the shadowy landscape, Lillian climbed back into bed, wrapping the woollen cloak tight around her body. Tonight she'd dream about Julius, imagining the cloak as his arms around her, holding her close to his chest.

'Stay alive,' she whispered to the empty room, hoping that her words would somehow reach Julius.

❄

WITH THE SUN struggling to rise and the cloak in a tangled mess on the floor, Lillian chastised herself for her foolishness the night before. But still she collected the cloak, returning it to its hanger in the wardrobe. The fibula brooch went back into the jewellery box.

She stirred through the other pieces in the box, which had also come with the house. The jewellery box contained an assorted of 1950s costume jewellery — pairs of clip-on earrings, Edwardian style paste brooches, long strings of coral beads and faux pearls, a diamanté choker with a silver clasp, and a handful of cocktail rings. Nothing of any great value from what Lillian could determine, but all of them were beautiful in their own right. She had meant to show the contents to Nicole from the Old Curiosity Shop. But after what had happened, she had forgotten. She must remember to give it to Nicole once she arrived later today.

She'd not had the time nor the inclination to sort through the box before, spending most of her days at the farm either clearing invasive weeds, tearing down fencing, or being carted off to hospital. So it was a surprise to find a gold ring, inset with a red stone etched with a delicate rendition of a peacock, nestled in a corner.

Outside, a dog started barking, drawing Lillian's attention away from the ring and towards the window. A pair of hikers were crossing the field, their long walking sticks protruding like strange appendages, almost spider-like.

Lillian shook her head, the gold ring forgotten for the moment. The dog's howls had died away as the hikers disappeared from sight. She didn't mind people crossing her land. If her rewilding plans were successful, she hoped people would visit to experience the lush regrowth of the ancient woodlands, like what rocker Brian May had done with May's Wood over the past ten years. She might not have his funds, but she had the will. He had planted one-hundred-thousand trees. She would be happy with a thousand, but there were too many hoops to jump through first. From what she could remember from her time in Roman Britain, the Roman's had cut down most of the trees in the vicinity, both for heating, and to deny their enemies any chance of cover. Then the Victorians and the more recent mega farms had finished the rest off, save for a few special specimens. She wanted to change that. But first she had to prepare for a visitation from Rewilding Britain, the only organisation prepared to support her efforts to rewild Ithaca Farm. It seemed like the government and every other heritage organisation was against her. Against her and nature.

THINGS THAT GO BUMP IN THE NIGHT

Nicole dried the last blue Denby mug and hung it next to the other mugs swinging from old hooks screwed into the hutch dresser. With the kitchen finally immaculate, she slumped into the nearest chair and dropped her head into her arms. Normally the client would have offered her a cup of tea by now, but to be brutally honest, she preferred coffee, although she'd yet to find a single coffee bean in Lillian's kitchen. She had found plenty of other items, all of which she'd either washed and dried, or polished and buffed, or stacked and packed. Lillian's kitchen now looked like a show home instead of a hoarder's hovel.

She could not wait for Lillian to return from town to show her everything she had already achieved. It was a shame that they had missed each other this morning. Nicole suspected they had probably driven past each other on the Stanegate, but she had been so busy thinking about Mel that she'd probably missed Lillian's rust bucket clanking past. It didn't matter; she knew what she had to do. So she had carried on boxing up everything Lillian had said could go. Half a dozen cardboard boxes now stood like Lego blocks in the front hall, waiting for the weather to clear before Nicole loaded them into her van. She'd agreed to go to the Saturnalia Festival at the Bellingham with Lillian, but she could not wait to leave the inhospitable north for the more temperate climes of the south after that. After driving through the snow on her way up to Hexham, she doubted she would ever complain about the weather in London again.

Whilst awaiting Lillian's return, she had tried to pack as much as she could without acting like some prize winner given ninety-seconds to grab as much as they could for free from Fortnum & Mason the day before Christmas. But when the sun disappeared behind the horizon, and Lillian still hadn't returned, Nicole retreated to the library with a blanket and a book. Nothing would induce her to go upstairs alone in this house. Nothing. Not after what had happened last time she was here.

She had only returned to the house to resume packing the treasures she'd paid Lillian upfront for before the incident with the... She tried not to think about that experience. Part of returning was because she wanted to prove to herself that she was braver than she remembered. Besides, she had Mel on speed dial if she needed him.

Every creak and groan of the farmhouse made her twitch. She tried telling herself that it was just her overactive imagination, but the feeling of there being someone else in the house with her grew with every passing minute.

Nicole rubbed her eyes and glanced at the grandfather clock ticking in the corner. Lillian should be here any minute now. She stifled a yawn and stretched her stiff limbs. Another long day of packing awaited her tomorrow, and then an evening at the Saturnalia Festival in town. After that, she'd head back to London for that curry Mel had promised her for their third date.

A gust of wind rattled the windows and Nicole cast a nervous glance at the dark windows, her imagination conjuring sinister figures lurking outside. She was a grown woman, and there was nothing to be afraid off. But still, she should just check...

Taking a deep breath to steady her nerves, Nicole pulled open the front door, her senses on high alert. The chilly night air rushed in as she peered into the inky darkness outside, but the snow lay undisturbed, and her only companions were the silent trees looming like ancient sentinels.

The cold seeped through her shoes and into her bones as she searched for any signs of an intruder from the safety of the doorway, but the desolation remained unbroken save for the eerie squeals of a nearby barn owl.

Nicole's breath came fast and shallow as she slammed the door shut. Regardless of the evidence, she could not shake the feeling that she was not alone. Returning to the library, she wrapped her arms around herself, feeling the cold despite the layers of clothing she wore. To take her mind off her nerves, she reexamined the contents of the bookshelves. The books were mostly old sets of Readers Digests, early pulp fiction paperbacks, and ancient reference books, all well out of date. But she spotted one which looked promising. Bound in leather, with gilt lettering and a worn silk ribbon dangling from its centre, its pages were crinkled with age. Nicole flipped through the brittle pages, her fingers tracing the elegant script. The book definitely belonged to another era. She handled old things every day, but this felt very special.

Turning to the copyright page, she drew in a sharp breath. Volume I of a first edition of Jane Austen's final published work — Northanger Abbey, with a biographical note from Henry, Jane Austen's brother, with a publication date of 1817.

Then the sound of a car outside. Lillian was finally home.

Nicole laid the book on the arm of the chair and checked that the room was spotless. She caressed the warm leather bindings of Northanger Abbey and wondered if Lillian even knew what she had in her bookcase. Nicole was not a rare book dealer, but even she knew that any Jane Austen first edition was worth a pretty penny.

While she waited for Lillian to come inside, she ran a finger across the other books in the bookcase on the off chance that the rest of the set was there. But it was in vain. Only one volume of the set existed.

Nicole looked towards the library door. What was taking Lillian so long?

WHEN NICOLE REALISED it was Anson Darby who had let himself into the house, and not Lillian, she hadn't been overly concerned. After all, she'd met him — a respected archaeologist working on the altar site in the field behind the farmhouse. Perhaps he'd arranged to meet Lillian tonight?

But after watching him caress the altars she and Lillian had spend so long moving from the barn into the house, she knew something wasn't right.

ANSON DARBY HAD BEEN SO busy imagining the international acclaim coming his way that he did not hear the floorboards creak behind him.

'What are you doing in here?'

Anson froze, his long fingers tightening against the ancient stone.

'I think you should leave.'

Torch light bounced across the room until it settled uneasily against Anson's head. He fancied he could feel the light infiltrating his thoughts. He could not let that happen.

'Hear me out,' he said, standing up, his long frame towering over the detritus of the room.

'I'm not listening. I want you to leave or I'll call the police. You can come back when Lillian is home.'

'Ring the police then, but you'll have to explain what you know about these antiquities. They'll be very interested, I'm sure. Especially given how the local community feels about Lillian as it is.'

'I said, get out. It's none of your business what's inside this house. Until Lillian returns, I'm its custodian.' Nicole Pilcher's tiny frame filled the doorway.

Anson grasped about for a suitable response. 'I'd wager that Lillian needs money for her schemes, you know, to plant trees or to import a family of beavers or whatever it is she plans to do. And I bet that doesn't come cheap. I came here to tell her we found more coins while we were excavating the altar, and those coins match those found at the site where the mayor went missing.'

'Coins?'

'Gold ones. The Coroner declared it as treasure, and they will pay out Lillian, as the landowner.'

'Get. Out.'

The smile fled from Anson's face, and was replaced with a visage of anger. The pounding in his ears drowned out whatever it was the bitch was saying now. He deserved the fame for finding the altars. Him and him alone. Ithaca Farm should have been his, but like everything else in his life, Lillian had rejected him. The same way he missed out on funding again and again. He would not be overlooked again.

Anson walked towards Nicole, grinning, his manic eyes glowing in the torchlight.

'Oh, I'm not leaving until we've moved these altars to their rightful position—'

'You can't know where that is. The police will be here any minute.'

'They haven't rung. I didn't fall off the back of the last lorry. Have you seen the weather? No one's coming. It's just you and me, moving altars.'

NICOLE THOUGHT back to the time some years ago when she had witnessed a mugging, but had been too scared to intervene. When the police had turned up, she'd felt their silent judgement for not intervening. Since then, she had read up on adrenaline and what it made you do; fight, flight, or freeze. She had frozen. And on the night Lillian was snatched by a man in the filthy white robe, she had frozen again, and Lillian had vanished, leaving only a lingering odour of decay behind. Nicole would never forgive herself for that.

So, she had learnt her lesson. There would be no more freezing. Now she would fight.

'Where do you imagine you're going to hide them?' she demanded of the archaeologist.

'Not hide, find,' Darby replied, his eyes shining with a religious fervour.

'Who's going to believe that you stumbled across a dozen Roman altars?' she asked.

'Everyone.'

Nicole laughed. She had heard some preposterous stories in her life, but this one took the cake. Swallowing her fear, she asked again about his plans.

'You wouldn't understand,' he replied, shifting his eyes from hers, sweeping them over the other items in the room. 'She doesn't need them. Look at all the stuff in here. No one's ever left me a house, and everything in it. I've never won the lottery. The only luck I've had is the bad sort. The kind that sticks to you like mud.'

'You're an archaeologist. You're living the dream of millions of people around the world. So don't talk rubbish,' she replied, emboldened by his misery.

'You don't know what it's like, always begging for money, kowtowing to every potential wealthy benefactor. Ensuring that the university remains politically neutral. The glory that will come from the discovery of these altars cannot be taken from me.'

Whilst Darby talked, Nicole edged backwards. He had been right about the weather, and with the farmhouse's remote location, there was nowhere to run to for help. But she would not allow herself to remain in a room with no potential means of escape.

'Don't even think of trying to escape.'

Nicole ducked to left. Darby grabbed her. They tussled. Nicole's slight build hid a well developed set of muscles — honed through lugging cartons of crockery, heavy oak furniture, and awkwardly shaped ceramic crocks, amongst a thousand other items on a near daily basis.

'It's my treasure,' Darby growled. 'My glory.'

Nicole wiggled out from underneath the man, grinding

her elbows into his shoulders as she flipped herself over, her knee landing heavily where she knew it would hurt the most.

If only Lillian had alerted the authorities when she had discovered the altars in the old barn, none of them would be in this situation.

Nicole's mind scrambled for options. If she ran upstairs, she risked facing the same wraith who had taken Lillian. If she stayed downstairs, then she would have to contend with the mad archaeologist. Perhaps she should have stuck with being a hotelier, like her family had wanted. But where was the fun in dealing with entitled tourists prone to vomiting in the decorative pots and peeling away the expensive flocked wallpaper?

'Don't touch me,' she yelled, backing away from the man writhing on the ground.

A collection of walking sticks languished in the ornamental umbrella stand. The large brass face of an English Bulldog beckoned, and she grabbed it, brandishing it like a sword.

Darby lunged for her and Nicole swung the bulbous head of the walking stick towards the side of his head, and he fell to the floor, either unconscious or dead. At this point, Nicole didn't care. She dropped the stick and ran.

The lights flickered once, and then twice, before vanishing all together. She froze. Somewhere on the kitchen bench was her cellphone, her lifeline to the outside world.

Inching across the flagged floor, her arms outstretched, Nicole groped for the bench and her phone. Every footfall echoed as if magnified by a loudhailer. Would it wake Darby?

The bench. Nicole cast her hands across the worn surface. Papers scattered. She bumped a rough-cast bowl, moving it nearer to the perilous edge of the bench. Another inch. Then another, and her hand fell upon the reassuring rectangle of her mobile phone.

As Nicole lifted the phone from the bench, her sleeve

caught the bowl's lip, sending it and its contents crashing to the ground.

Pandemonium.

A banging and crashing from the other room was evidence enough of Darby's health, and his anger.

Nicole's sense of direction had always been poor, but she knew her way upstairs. With a fraction of a second to decide, she took her chance and ran, stumbling her way through the kitchen, into the formal entrance way and up the stairs.

Should she turn right towards her bedroom? Or left towards Lillian's?

Left.

Opening the door as quietly as possible, she eased into Lillian's room, closing the door behind her.

With no signal on her phone, her only options, other than running outside into the snow, were to face the madman downstairs, or to hide and hope for the best. There was one other option which might materialise, literally one which did not bear thinking about...

Panicking, Nicole threw herself into the giant wardrobe, burrowing beneath mouldy jackets and plaid dressing gowns. *Surely these items did not belong to Lillian? They were at least two decades older than Lillian to start with, if not older.*

Curled into a ball, Nicole held her breath as she listened to Darby's footsteps stampeding up the stairs. Lillian's bedroom door creaked, followed by what sounded like gunfire outside the wardrobe. She visualised Darby yanking the drawers from the dressing table and dumping them onto the floor. The shattering of what she presumed was a crystal trinket dish tinkled across the floorboards, followed by swearing worthy of a dockworker.

Then silence. Darby *had* to know she was in the wardrobe. Nicole squeezed her eyes shut, her beating heart reverberating off the oak panels. And then, just as suddenly as he had appeared, Darby disappeared, abandoning his search.

Nicole waited for what seemed like an eternity before

unfolding her cramped limbs and emerging like a butterfly from its chrysalis. The house sat eerily quiet. Nicole tiptoed through the carnage on the floor, straining for any sound of Darby.

Somewhere downstairs, the house phone began ringing as the lights flickered back on.

With a surge of adrenaline, Nicole leapt towards the doorway, towards salvation, flinging herself through the open door, and straight into Darby's arms.

Darby grabbed her and slammed her head into the doorframe.

Nothingness followed.

THE PAWNBROKER'S SHOP

Neumegen paced the worn carpet at the Twice Brewed Inn, oblivious to the torn wallpaper and the tatty furniture. He was out of place in this world, in a century he did not altogether enjoy. The last time he had seen Sharma, they had argued about Metella, and Sharma's plan to bring her back to the twenty-first century. Love always found a way, though. Even through time. He should know.

He noticed the barman's eyes following him. He'd have to be careful. People of this era were not fond of strangers, no matter how innocent their intentions. It might be more prudent to go into Hexham instead of wearing a path in the carpet. He knew he would not stumble upon anything at the Twice Brewed Inn that could help rescue his friend.

He stepped out into the overcast morning and snared a taxi disgorging its passengers. The taxi driver looked like he was having an internal debate with himself about taking him, but the fact Neumegen was holding a leather satchel and wearing an expensive-looking overcoat must have outweighed any misgivings.

'Hexham,' Neumegen instructed.

The driver mumbled something incomprehensible, and they set off, taking the narrow country roads at a crawl, the driver concentrating on not hitting anything, or anyone, the winter roads still busy with brave wall walkers. Neumegen looked out at the rolling green hills, the vista marred by the ugly additions of industrial chimneys, wind farms and cellphone towers.

He did not have long to wait before the taxi stopped in front of a Georgian townhouse, long past its prime.

'You sure that this is the correct address, mate?' the driver asked, his voice dripping with disbelief.

Neumegen nodded, spying the pawnbroker's symbol on the small sign swinging in the icy wind.

Handing over a ten-pound note, he clambered out of the car, his lanky frame unfolding like a jack-in-the-box.

A strange feeling of anticipation swelled, and after a moments deliberation, Neumegen entered the pawnshop with an eagerness he had not experienced since he had left 1860s Auckland. The thrill of the chase was afoot.

Old leather and tobacco smoke flavoured the air, with the faded green carpet muffling his footsteps as he wandered around, taking in the array of items for sale.

'Can I help you?' A battled-scarred boxer-like man appeared behind the scratched glass counter, his eyes narrowing as Neumegen drew nearer.

Neumegen paused, almost certain he had seen that face before. He could not shake the uneasy feeling he had also been recognised.

'I'm after something quite particular,' he started.

The man cocked his head to the side, the movement so abrupt that his pugilist's ears seemed to take on a life of their own. 'I've got all sorts in here. If I don't have it, I can get it for you,' he boasted.

'It has to be from a very specific time period,' Neumegen explained.

The man placed his fists on the counter. 'Go on then.'

'I'm looking for a Roman artefact. It is of the utmost importance to me.'

'You a collector?' the pawnbroker asked, his eyes darting to the door and back again.

'No,' Neumegen shook his head. 'It's for personal reasons. A replacement for something lost by a dear friend.'

The pawnbroker raised his bushy eyebrows. The sound

of a ticking German cuckoo clock the only accompaniment to their awkward silence. He leant forward, his forearms resting on the counter, his hands fiddling with a dog-eared exercise book.

'You look familiar,' the man finally said. 'Have you been in here before?'

'No, it's my first time. You were recommended by the barman at the Twice Brewed Inn.' That was partially true. The barman had also said to be careful not to flash too much cash as the proprietor was known to amend his prices, upwards, based on how much he thought his clients could afford. Which would explain why nothing that Neumegen could see had a price sticker.

The explanation seemed to pacify the man, and he stood up, the exercise book still in his hands, but clearly ready to do business.

'If I had a penny for every person who wanted to buy a chunk of Roman history, I'd be sipping cocktails on the beaches of Ibiza, instead of being stuck in this damp ruin of bricks with a heating system that only works if there's a full moon. You're going to have to be more specific. I'm not a mind reader.'

'A coin of Decimus Clodius Albinus, around 193 to 194, with the goddess Minerva on the obverse.'

'You're asking for miracles, mate.'

'Merely a coin, one coin,' Neumegen said, before adding, 'price is no object.'

'You might as well be asking for a pot of gold at the end of the rainbow, but I might know someone who could help. She'll be in town for the Saturnalia festival.' The pawnbroker pointed a bulky finger at a poster taped to the counter advertising the upcoming festivities.

Neumegen's eyes lingered on the poster, taking note of the date and location. 'A Saturnalia festival? It's been a long time since I attended one of those,' he mused before turning his attention back to the pawnbroker. 'Can you introduce me?'

The pawnbroker leaned in conspiratorially. 'Her name

is Loretta. She's a bit of an oddity, but she has a knack for sourcing specific artefacts. Just don't get on her bad side.'

Neumegen nodded, taking heed of the warning. 'I'll bear that in mind. Can you tell me where I might find her?'

The pawnbroker scribbled an address on a scrap of paper and handed it over. 'She'll be staying at the Bellingham Tea Rooms. Ask for Loretta Hambly. She won't be hard to spot. Just look for the wool.' The pawnbroker laughed, amused by some private joke he didn't share.

Neumegen thanked the man and tucked the paper into his waistcoat pocket, where it nestled comfortably next to his pocket watch. He still couldn't shake the feeling that he'd met the man before, either in this life, or in a past one. It was getting hard to keep up.

Emerging from the Georgian villa, Neumegen stepped into a world shrouded in shadows. An unusually dense winter fog wrapped itself around him like a blanket, emptying the streets, save for one passing police car, its flashing lights cutting through the gloom like shining daggers as it raced off to some calamity. A portent of what was to come. Of what could come.

FRIENDS AND ALLIES

Jane Badrick was no stranger to taking risks, but this was a risk she hadn't taken before. Not that it scared her, far from it. But relying on other people bothered her, and Anson Darby's ambition worried her more than she liked.

The morning brought with it a new day and a fresh start for the mayor. Jane Badrick appeared at her desk earlier than normal, unaffected by the several gins she'd quaffed the night before.

The Saturnalia festival loomed closer with every rotation of the clock. The anticipation of what she was about to achieve consumed every fibre of her body, making her feel stronger, younger.

She had come a long way since her days working at the reception counter of Drafford's Drapery. From secretary to someone who made policy and ran the town. If only those silly simpering girls at the drapery could see her now.

Jane sucked on a cigarette and stretched, easing the tightness nestling between her shoulders. With less than a week to get this right, her eyes glossed over the paperwork on her normally pristine desk. She should have been working late every evening to clear the backlog, but understandably her attention was elsewhere. Her plan had to work. Not that she doubted her success, but she needed to be extra careful. Nothing could be allowed to stand in her way.

As the day progressed, Jane couldn't shake the feeling that something was off. It was as if the unusual fog from the morning had followed her into the office, clouding her judgment. She could not put a finger on it, but knew it had something to do with Anson. He had been giving her the runaround, and today there had been radio silence from the man. And that was not good enough.

'Mayor? Do you need anything?' a voice called from the open doorway. Jane glanced up to see the gawky figure of Raymond Lamont, her erstwhile assistant, in the doorway.

Her assistant had been a godsend of late. Instrumental in keeping her plans from her husband Matthew's prying eyes, and involving the mayor's office in all aspects of Hexham's first Saturnalia festival.

'No, Raymond, thank you. I am just a little distracted today,' Jane replied, offering a weak smile.

'Is it about the festival?' Raymond asked, stepping further into the office.

Jane shook her head. 'No, the festival is going smoothly. It's something else.'

'Anything I can help with?' Raymond offered, puppy-like with his enthusiasm.

Jane paused, taking in the youthful eagerness in Raymond's long face. Maybe he could help. 'Actually, yes, there is something you can do for me.'

Jane leaned forward and lowered her voice to a whisper. 'I need you to do some research for me on Anson Darby.'

'The archaeologist? Consider it done,' Raymond replied, already typing away on his tablet. 'What exactly do you need to know?'

'Where is he? He is avoiding my calls, and that is unacceptable. I was expecting a report on the coins they found where I was carjacked. As a victim, I should be kept in the loop at every stage.'

Raymond nodded, his eyes wide with understanding. 'Of course. Consider it done. I'll get started right away.'

Jane watched as Raymond practically skipped from her office. She had a feeling that he would deliver like the Pony Express. All she had to do was wait for the information to come. With a renewed sense of purpose, she turned back to her papers, and picking up her favourite Mont Blanc pen, she signed the next document.

RAYMOND LAMONT PLANNED on spending his afternoon tracking down the archaeologist. He would do almost anything for the mayor, but he had a regular appointment to make first, one he had not shared with Mayor Badrick. One he never would.

'What is it like having her back in the office?' Apple asked as Raymond slipped into his usual seat at the meeting of the Hexham Supper Club, a collective of poets and poetry lovers, a club he had been attending for the past three years, alongside Apple Collings and a group of other Hexham odd bods.

'She has been pretty distracted,' Raymond replied. 'Actually, she asked me to hunt down Anson Darby, which is why I'm late. I was trying to track him down.'

'Anson Darby?' Apple asked.

'Do you know him?' his heart thumped a little faster. For three years he had been attending these meetings, promising himself every week that *this* would be the week he would muster up enough courage to ask Apple out.

'Isn't he the archaeologist working up at Ithaca Farm?' Apple replied, her pale eyes staring back at him.

'Mayor Badrick seems to be having trouble reaching him,' Raymond said, leaning forward in his seat, his eyes never leaving Apple's.

'Interesting,' Apple murmured. 'I might know someone who can help.'

'You do?' Raymond asked, his heart beating a little faster, and not because of the information about Darby, but more because Apple wasn't involved with the man.

Apple nodded. 'Lillian is a bit of an oddity, but I can introduce you if you like?'

Raymond grinned, his mind buzzing. If he could find Darby, he would be a hero in Mayor Badrick's eyes. And then maybe, just maybe, he would be brave enough to invite Apple to come to the Saturnalia festival with him. He might just be brave enough for that.

'Are we going to talk Roman poetry, or what?' asked another Hexham Supper Club attendee, a living caricature of a Victorian gentleman poet, complete with a gold-rimmed monocle.

As the group settled into their rowdy discussion of Virgil's Aeneid, Apple's laughter filled the room, her white blonde hair shimmering angle-like under the lights. Despite the scintillating conversation and repartee with his friends, Raymond felt sense of unease building. Why the mayor wanted Darby had started to niggle at him. He knew more about Mayor Badrick's activities than anyone else, and there was no reason she needed to interact with Darby, none that he knew of. The thing about her being a victim was true, of course. No one denied that she had been through a terrible thing. But that was the job of the police, to keep her updated about developments. Not Darby's.

As the evening wore on, Raymond found his concentration slipping more and more. His mind was consumed by thoughts of Anson Darby, and why the mayor wanted to know where he was.

After he failed to answer a fairly easy question about Virgil's ambition to rival Homer, he caught Apple staring at him, a frown on her beautiful face. His cheeks flushed hotter than lava spewing out of Mt Vesuvius. He had let her down. Raymond tried to swallow his rising panic.

Before he could recover his composure, the meeting drew to a close with the Hexham Supper Club members gathering their belongings. He had planned to linger, to ask Apple about her offer to introduce him to her friend Lillian, the one who might be able to help him locate Darby, but as he fumbled with his heavy jacket and scarf, Apple stepped up next to him.

'You weren't concentrating on the meeting, were you?' Apple asked, her eyes narrowing, the frown still on her face.

Raymond sighed, then the words tumbled out of his mouth. 'I'm still thinking about how I'm going to track down Anson Darby and why she needs to know.'

'She does not deserve your loyalty,' Apple said. 'Remember what she did to the poetry section at Hexham Library? That was the first load of books to be sent to the incinerator before we could save them.'

'So you keep reminding me. It was before I started working for her, otherwise I would have stopped it, or at least diverted them...'

She shrugged, her oversized jacket swamping her tiny frame. 'Closing the library was unforgivable. Destroying one of the best collections of poetry in northern England is the same as a bomb blowing up Westminster Abbey.'

Raymond nodded. 'She is the mayor and I have to do what she asks, but something feels off this time. I don't know why she needs Darby.'

Apple's expression softened. 'I understand your loyalty, Raymond. But sometimes we have to question those in power, especially if it feels like they are up to something.'

'I don't know what to do,' Raymond said, feeling lost.

Apple took his hand. 'Let me help you find Darby, but on one condition. We figure out what the mayor wants with him *before* we tell her where he is.'

Raymond thought his heart would burst with gratitude. 'I don't know what I would do without you,' he said that with complete sincerity.

Together they left the cafe, the cool night breeze on their faces, ready to uncover the truth behind the mayor's interest in Anson Darby.

WHAT TO WEAR TO A PARTY?

Lillian spent the night tossing and turning; sleep completely unobtainable. There were so many threads running through her mind that she couldn't follow one without tangling herself with another. And with the Saturnalia festival approaching, and no guarantee that she could even travel back in time, she did not know what to do.

Giving up sleep, she threw on her dressing gown and slippers, and tiptoed down the creaking staircase. With the heating off, and the fire out, the cold seeped into her bones, dampening her spirits, and making her question her decision to return to the past. And even made her question taking on something as big as Ithaca Farm.

As she sat at the kitchen table, sipping a freshly brewed cup of tea, Lillian's thoughts drifted towards Badger instead of Julius. Badger was here now. Living, breathing flesh and blood. So why would she throw that away? For what, for a phantom? Badger should be her focus, the safe choice. But Julius had risked his life to save hers. His life.

How could she make that kind of choice?

Lillian sighed, glancing out of the window at the darkness looming outside the glass. Saturnalia was less than forty-eight hours away. Would it work? It had to.

Badger was oblivious to Lillian's time travel. How do you explain that to someone without them locking you up?

She would have to tell him, somehow. Apple and Neumegen were both in agreement there. But it made her feel ill at the thought of his reaction. But she had a job to do, and they needed his help with his mother. Because it was not just Julius she was returning to save; it was an entire cohort of Roman soldiers, even the ones who had tried to kill her.

Pushing all thoughts of the two men out of her mind, Lillian finished her tea and focussed on her immediate problem — what to wear? There was no way she was returning to Roman Britain in the middle of winter in jeans and a white cotton shirt. She had nearly died of hypothermia once, and she wasn't keen on repeating the experience. Dressing for the Saturnalia festivities at the Bellingham Tea House needed to cover both the modern day expectations of the other guests, and still be hardy enough to carry her to the past.

Returning to her room, Lillian rummaged through the inherited wardrobe and drawers, hoping to find something suitable. Shopping for time travel appropriate clothing was not something you asked the womenswear clerk for help with at Marks & Spencer's.

She'd obviously never attended a Saturnalia festival before, but a distant memory surfaced, reminding her that Romans traditionally celebrated with lavish parties and feasts, and wore colourful, festive garments. Or at least, the BBC version of ancient Romans showed that to be true.

She needed something that could pass as both modern and ancient clothing.

After much deliberation, she decided on a long, flowing dress made of thick wool, in a deep crimson colour. Laying it out across the bed, the simple design meant it could easily pass as something worn two-thousand years earlier. To complete the look, she chose a simple gold necklace and tiny gold hoop earrings.

With an outfit chosen, Lillian felt a weight lifted from her shoulders. Paired with Julius' cloak in the wardrobe, the dress should prove enough of a disguise to see her through any chance encounter. The long thermals underneath, whilst not at all sexy, would keep her warm. For a moment, she forgot about the danger which lay ahead and revelled in the excitement of the adventure. Hobbits had nothing on the journey she was about to undertake. As a last-minute addition, she slipped the ruby ring onto her finger, the peacock intaglio as flamboyant as its namesake. And somewhere down the lane, the faint howls of a barking dog echoed across the barren fields.

TILLING THE SOIL

Fourteen people stood clustered around a table heaving with rusty toy cars, ancient soda cans, indecipherable coins and the metal detritus of nearly two millennia. At least half the group were in comfortable shoes with orthotic inners, their hand-knitted cardigans snug against burgeoning stomachs, whilst the rest of the group muddled about in various permutations of high street hoodies, camouflage trousers, Wrexham Football Club caps, heavy duty Doc Marten boots, and the odd pair of expensive branded leggings. The membership of Hadrian's Heroes Metal Detecting Club displayed an accurate cross-section of Hexham's population, as if someone had plunged a spade through several layers of the earth, digging up at least one representative from every background imaginable.

'Now that we've all had a look at this month's finds, we've got some serious business to attend to.' Clifton Beaufort stepped back from the table, his cheeks flushed. He knew full well that there was not a person in the room who did not already know what the serious business was that he was referring to.

As club president, he had a responsibility to do his bit to help the police. If even the merest mention of night hawkers made it into the papers, that would be enough to tar the club with the blackest of brushes. And Clifton Beaufort would not let that happen on his watch.

'Is it about what happened at Ithaca Farm?' asked Graham Ryan.

Clifton nodded, his plume of white hair bouncing beneath the unforgiving fluorescent light of the St Oswald Church hall.

'The police came to speak to me at work,' Clifton said, with all the seriousness of a BBC anchor announcing the death of the monarch.

A murmur flittered across the room. *Police.*

'Tell us more then,' pushed Graham.

Clifton acknowledged his long time detecting friend and lowered himself into a chair. The club's members followed, metal chair legs scraping against the already battered wooden floor.

'It's not just the police who've been to see me, but a reporter too. It's like something out of a novel at Ithaca Farm. And yes, there has been a filthy night hawker operating up there. So if anyone knows anything—'

The room erupted as thirteen metal detectorists decried their innocence.

Clifton appealed for calm.

'I know it's not one of you, as much as I know the difference between my deadly nightshade berries and me blueberries. Cause if I ever found out it was any of you—'

'We'd be stabbed to death with a trowel and buried in the spoil heap at Birdoswald,' Graham joked from the back.

'Quite right,' Clifton said. 'A blunt trowel, mind.'

The room laughed, the tension broken.

'From what I've heard, the filth might have found a cache of gold coi—'

He never got to finish. All hell broke loose after he uttered the magic word — gold.

Like Moses attempting to part the Red Sea, Clifton held up his dirt-stained hands, begging the club members to calm down.

'They've recovered several,' his voice dropped to a

whisper, 'gold coins. Until we've heard from the experts, we're to keep this to ourselves. You all know the rules around detecting in this area, so do not, and I'll say it again: do not run out with your machines trying to find more. The police have asked for our help to locate any coins the filthy cretin may have dropped, and I've volunteered myself and Graham, as the two most experienced members of the club. We'll be detecting under the direct supervision of the police, with the blessing of Historic England, if you can believe that for a tuppence.'

As the monthly meeting dispersed, Clifton and Graham stood in the doorway; two old-timers monitoring their flock.

'They're a good lot, but they're not going keep this to themselves,' Graham said. 'It's human nature to gossip.'

'You're right there,' Clifton agreed, running his hands through his hair. 'They might for a day or two, maybe till we've had a run over with our detectors. The Canadian, though, he'll tell his wife. Two peas in a pod, they are.'

'I don't think you can call him a Canadian anymore, not when he's lived here for nigh on twenty years.'

'He wasn't born here, though, was he?' Clifton said.

'She'll not share it, even if he does,' Graham replied. 'She's as trustworthy as they come.'

'So, what time do you want to meet tomorrow?'

'I've got to take the dogs for a walk first thing, so nine-thirty?'

'How's Pixie's hip?'

'She's as right as rain. They gave her an injection, and it's like she's a wee pup again.'

'Do they do injections like that for men like us?' Clifton laughed.

Like statues framing a temple, the men remained in the hall doorway, neither in any hurry to abandon the topic of the year or the decade.

'The mayor...' Graham started.

'Aye?'

'You said they found more coins near where she disappeared?'

'That's what they said.'

'Dropped by the night hawker?'

'Aye.'

'So he could come back?'

'He won't be looking for us. We're nout to do with him,' Clifton replied. 'Anything we find, we hand over. The police will be there, so no treasure payment this time. Not like with your ruby ring, the one the museum got.'

'Aye,' Graham said, his face a picture of sadness.

'Have they put that on display yet?'

Graham shook his head.

Clifton snorted. 'Come on, help me lock up and I will be at yours at quarter past tomorrow morning. Gives you plenty of time to walk those wee beasties of yours. Sorry for mentioning your ruby ring. Bastards.'

'Aye.'

MAGIC WANDS

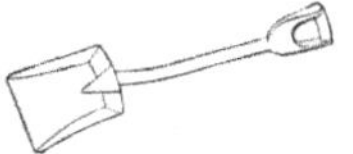

The two fully paid-up members of Hadrian's Heroes Metal Detecting Club, Clifford Beaufort and Graham Ryan, listened politely as the young police officer delivered strict instructions on how to operate their metal detectors around the area. They nodded and made all the right noises until the officer appeared satisfied.

'He's not even old enough to drive that thing,' Graham laughed as the officer returned to the safety and warmth of his truck.

Like a pair of physicists working on a nuclear reactor, they checked the settings on their state-of-the-art detectors and began to slowly comb the area. Both seasoned veterans of such searches, they were as familiar with the subtle nuances of their machines as they were with their wives at home.

'Bit of interference here,' Clifton said, adjusting his machine.

'The power lines,' Graham replied, his detector emitting a steady symphony of high and low-pitched beeps as he continued systematically walking forward, his movements strangely pigeon-like.

Clifford grunted in apparent agreement.

With the landscape shrouded in shadows, and the ground littered with the remains of centuries of human habitation, the men focused on their task, swinging their machines in mesmerising arcs, pausing to prick out beer tabs, and machinery parts, and car keys, and foil backed candy wrappers, and all manner of rubbish tossed from the windows of passing vehicles or dropped by weary travellers.

As they moved further into the field, Graham's detector began beeping with an increasing stridency, the sound nudging the officer from the confines of his truck.

Graham and Clifford paused, both holding their breath as Graham rested his machine on its edge and, with his entrenching tool, carefully dug a plug out of the ground. Clifford waved his detecting wand over the clod of earth. Another high-pitched ping.

'Careful,' Graham said unnecessarily.

Graham separated the dirt as Clifford waved his wand relentlessly, passing over each clump of earth, and then it appeared — a sliver of brassy yellow shining in the paltry light.

A gold coin.

'Your lucky day,' Clifford said.

'Our lucky day,' Graham replied.

'What have you found?' asked the officer.

Graham passed over the coin, brushing the last of the soil from the gleaming disc.

'It's heavier than I thought,' the officer said.

'It weighs about the same as a 20p piece,' Clifford said. 'but it's a damn sight prettier.'

'Everyone thinks gold weighs a tonne because of those Pirates of the Caribbean movies, but it's not that much different from a modern coin, just more valuable,' Graham said, with Clifford nodding along with him.

The officer looked doubtful. 'So, what now?'

Clifford and Graham exchanged confused glances.

'You're in charge,' Clifford said.

'Right, well, I guess if you just continue—'

'Continue?'

'Searching the field for more coins and stuff.'

'Do you want to put that in an evidence bag?' Graham asked, pointing to the coin in the officer's hand.

'Right. Yes. I will. In the truck. Good idea,' the officer said, as if someone had just suggested an unusual course of action for a piece of evidence.

'So wet behind his ears he'd need more than a cupboard full of towels to dry off,' Graham stage whispered to Clifford as the officer vanished into the warm interior of his truck, taking the coin and his puzzled face with him.

As they walked, Graham could not shake the feeling that they were being watched. He kept scanning the countryside for any sign of movement. But there was nothing more that the wind swishing through the hedgerows and the occasional baying of cattle in the distance. Even the roads were abnormally quiet for this time of day.

'What's wrong?' Clifford asked.

'Do you ever get the feeling that you're being watched?'

Clifford glanced around, his eyes darting from side to side. 'No, not unless it's the missus waiting to see if I'm going to take the dog out without her nagging me. Why?'

'I don't know,' Graham replied, shaking his head. 'It's just a funny feeling.'

'I've heard some detectorist's say that they've felt the presence of some poor soul, long gone from this earth when they've been out metal detecting.'

Graham scoffed. 'Ghosts? And you believed them?'

'They were all good people, not prone to fanciful talk. Sometimes the mind plays tricks on you, especially when you're out in the middle of nowhere with only your thoughts for company, and the crows.' Clifford said with a shrug.

'Next you'll be telling me that the fairy folk spread these coins all over the field because they're so happy with what our illustrious mayor has done for the town?'

Clifford started laughing so hard that Graham had to slap his back to stop him from choking on his own breath.

'The mayor! That's a good one,' Clifford gasped, trying to catch his breath. 'Oh, it's been a long time since I've laughed that hard. That woman...'

The two men carried on laughing.

'If she wasn't so utterly obsessed with thoughts of her own legacy, she might actually have done some good for Hexham. Some of her ideas weren't half bad in the early days.'

Graham rolled his eyes. 'You're pulling my good leg.'

'I am.'

And the laughing started afresh.

'Cup of tea?' Graham asked, wiping the tears from his eyes.

'Aye, then the rest of the field,' Clifford replied.

'Shall we offer some to the young copper?'

'His mammy probably doesn't let him drink anything with caffeine in yet. He's still too young.'

And with that, their peals of laughter kicked off again, drawing the puzzled attention of the police officer in his truck, and that of the motionless stranger hidden behind a crumbling stone wall, watching them through a pair of high-powered binoculars.

AFTER COUNTLESS FALSE ALARMS, sixteen bottle caps, a Dinky toy tank, two spent ammunition cartridges, and one rusted horseshoe, the sun began setting over the field, and Graham was ready to pack it in. His fingers were numb and his stomach growling, and the feeling of being watched had not dissipated. If anything, it had increased. He turned to tell Clifford that he was done when Clifford called out to him.

'Hey, Graham,' Clifford shouted. 'Over here.'

Graham jogged towards Clifford, favouring his recently rebuilt knee. His distance running days were now a thing of the past, and he only hoped that this new knee would perform well enough for him to keep detecting and beach combing, his two great loves after his wife and dogs.

'What have you got?'

Clifford was standing over a small patch of grass with

his detector in hand. 'It's a stronger signal than anything else I've had today. Deep though.'

The men began to dig, pulling up clumps of earth and tossing them aside, until Clifford whistled through his remaining teeth.

'Now that's a beauty.'

'It's got to be Roman, at this level,' Graham said.

'One-hundred-per cent.'

'Which period, though?'

'Post Hadrianic?' Clifford replied. 'What do you think?'

'What is it?' the officer called from the warmth of his car, barely visible in the failing light.

'It's past his bedtime,' Graham joked, his back to the officer.

'Aye, and his parents will send out a search party if he's not home soon. Come on, let's pack up and get this wee treasure into the hands of the baby copper. We can finish the field tomorrow.'

'Let me grab some photos first, for my file,' Graham said, pulling out his phone and slipping off the protective plastic bag.

Photos taken, the men trudged back to their cars, delivering the delicate artefact into the officer's waiting hands.

'Do you know what that is?' Graham asked the police officer.

The officer shook his head, a heavy lock of blonde hair falling over his unlined face as he stared at the piece of history in his hands.

'It's a brooch, a beauty too. You'll see that this gets recorded with the FLO?'

'Of course,' the officer replied, although his voice lacked any confidence that he knew what he'd just been asked.

'The FLO — the Finds Liaison Officer,' Clifford offered.

'There's an archaeologist assigned to this case, for the coins and the altar and the skulls and things,' the officer replied.

'I'll give the FLO a call in the morning,' Graham said,

motioning Clifford to just run with what he was saying. It was easier than trying to explain how things worked to the young lad who still only shaved once a fortnight. 'You pass this onto the archaeologist then, and that'll sort things out at your end.'

'What time shall we meet here tomorrow?' Clifford asked, thrusting the young officer further into distress.

'Tomorrow?'

'We haven't finished the field, laddie.'

'Oh, right, I'll have to check the roster,' the officer mumbled, his eyes darting between the two men as if he still wasn't sure what was going on.

'Call us when you know your timings. We'll be ready whenever you are,' Clifford said, before returning to his car with Graham in tow.

Graham and Clifford exchanged a knowing look before saying their goodbyes. They had seen it all before. Inexperienced officers sent to the countryside with a less than comprehensive briefing or any level of understanding of the task at hand. The world was a different place now than it had been when they were young.

Driving home, Graham still had the sense that he was being followed. 'You're being paranoid,' he said to himself, checking his mirrors and seeing nothing but an empty country road behind him. 'Maybe?' he said, unconvinced. 'But maybe not?'

JOURNALISTIC INTEGRITY

Jasper Fletcher may not have been the brightest tool in the box, but he had lived in Hexham his whole life and, as all reporters do, he had his finger on the pulse of the community. No closet remains shut with a small town reporter. And he could spot a deflection when he saw one, although it had taken him a bit longer this time...

Just when he thought he had stumbled across something, Pauline at the cafe had pawed at his sleeve, blabbing on about her grandchildren and her chickens. Christ, if he had to hear about her bloody chickens and their eggs one more time, he would wring their necks himself.

There was something more going on than just a cache of gold coins stolen by a rogue metal detectorist. Something involving the mayor. A good political intrigue story always sold papers, that and whatever those ex royals were up to in sunny California with their kale shakes and avocado body wraps. He had missed something, and he could not pin it down.

After losing sight of his prey in the coffee shop, he returned to his flat. As usual, the place was colder than the bottom of Loch Ness, but less picturesque. Wrapped up in his duvet, and in the safety of his lounge room with his coffee table papered with sticky notes, he tried to grasp the slippery tail of the common garter snake running around inside his head. His file on Hexham's mayor already filled three file boxes, but this was all new information, and was unrelated to the woman's previous dodgy dealings. He started a list:

- *Roman(?) coins*
- *Ithaca Farm*
- *Rewilding*
- *The mayor*
- *Metal detectorist/Night Hawker*
- *Car crash: where is the car??*
- *Lillian Arlosh and the old guy in the suit*

There, his pen stalled. Lillian Arlosh and Ithaca Farm — what did he know about her, exactly? Almost nothing. Perhaps that was where he should start, with the history of the family and of the farm. But how far back to go? That was another question.

The internet was some help. There had been an interview done as part of a series on farming families, one of the BBC's attempts to churn out something other than game shows, where they had interviewed William Arlosh about his famous ancestor, and Ithaca Farm. Conducted outside the farmhouse, with a view of the lush fields behind them, William Arlosh had answered questions about historical farming practices and whether James Losh — his eighteenth century ancestor — would recognise the place now. His answers may have given Jasper what he needed. Especially the line about how old the farm buildings were, and how James Losh would not only recognise the buildings but their contents too, before he'd suddenly guarded his words, and refused to answer any more of the reporter's probing questions.

What was in those sheds? Would Lillian Arlosh show him? It was worth a try.

THE CURATOR

Ryan Francis shuffled the papers on his desk. Another day, another crime, and another criminal who'd never be punished.

'Hey, Gem—'

'Gemma.'

A sigh escaped. As much as working with Gemma Dance inspired him, she was hard work.

'What do you know about Roman coins?'

'So you got the Caernarfon Museum file then?'

Usually files at the Art Loss Register were allocated based on the skill set of the investigator. But with the global recession, staffing numbers were half of what they had been before the pandemic, so their files were more of a potluck situation — coins, artwork, statues, even stamp collections. Today, Ryan Francis had the file for a 1969 theft from the Caernarfon Museum, just after the investiture of Charles the Prince of Wales.

'Tell me again why the file has been reopened?' Gemma asked, her head appearing around her side of the partition.

'They found a hoard of coins near Hexham in Northumberland, which might be from the Caernarfon Castle theft.'

Ryan smiled at Gemma's snort of derision. And knowing her track record, he would trust her instincts over any average police constable's opinion.

'I might head up there,' Ryan suggested. It had been far too long between trips up north. He had not been there since he and Emma had gone on an enforced break while she finished her studies abroad. And like most long-distance relationships, things had petered out. Perhaps a trip to Newcastle, for work, was the perfect foil for a catch up. A cocktail down at the new wharf development, perhaps?

'You aren't thinking of seeing Emma Humphreys again, are you?' Gemma asked.

How the hell did she know?

'I forgot Em was up there.'

'You're a terrible liar, Ryan. I knew the second you opened your mouth what your plan was. Let me guess, you're going to take her for a drink because you just happen to be in town for work?'

'It's technically true.'

'Ryan, it's over. Move on.'

'Did I ever tell you what she did for a job?' Ryan asked, prepping the ace up his sleeve.

'Does it involve the cosmetic counter at Harrods?'

Ryan ignored Gemma's dig. Emma wore the bare minimum of makeup and looked like a million pounds. Gemma knew the power of a fine mascara brush and was on first-name terms with her colourist and also looked a million pounds. They would never see eye to eye.

'She used to work for the Goldsmiths' Company in London, which is how we met. But since our breakup, she's been working for the Royal Mint as a coin designer.'

'We employ people to design our coins?'

'She does other stuff too, like medals and commemorative coins.'

Ryan listened to the furious tapping at Gemma's keyboard and awaited the inevitable fact check.

'The Royal Mint is a four-hour drive from Caernarfon Castle.'

'Not unsurmountable,' Ryan replied.

'You're an idiot. And she's not worth it.'

'And that, dear Gem, is where we disagree.'

***

Ryan ignored the green pastures whizzing by. Yes, the countryside looked as beautiful as a postcard, at least from the inside of his car. But there was only one beautiful thing on his mind, and she was not on the M1.

With the SATNAV directing him, Ryan mulled over the file. Stolen from Caernarfon Castle in 1969, the hoard had never been analysed by modern technology and the only photographs were grainy images in old souvenir books. The original negatives had been lost in a fire, leaving just one retired museum curator who had handled the coins before their disappearance. And it was this man who Ryan was meeting today.

With a population just shy of ten thousand people, it was not too difficult to find the home of Dafydd Wynne, the retired Caernarfon Castle Museum curator, especially as it was in the street running behind the legendary Black Boy Inn. No sooner had Ryan knocked on the curator's door than the curator was outside, pulling on his coat and dragging Ryan down to the inn for a pint or two to help "loosen his tongue".

The Black Boy Inn looked unchanged from its beginning four centuries earlier. Keeping its low-slung black beamed ceilings, uneven floor, scuffed doors, and a maze of narrow corridors. The only thing missing was the ghost of a woman, whose body had been discovered entombed in the inn's walls in the 1990s.

At a table in front of an open fire, and with a pint each, Ryan put on his most interested face and began questioning the octogenarian opposite him.

'Mr Wynne, what can you tell me about the coins?'

'It's been a long time, lad. I'm not sure how much help I can be.'

Ryan bit back his frustration. Dafydd Wynne had been more than forthcoming on the phone, assuring Ryan that he would share more information, but only face-to-face, in case the "government" was listening to their call.

'Shall we start with the day you last handled the collection?'

'Well, let's see. It was right before Charlie had his big day in the castle, and we were tasked with cleaning everything from the bloody spoons to the feathers at the end of the damn spears in the armoury. Couldn't get the smell of polish out of my beard for weeks.' Here he paused, taking a long slug of his beer. 'Security chaps were everywhere. There'd been some sort of threat, so there was always someone loitering about whilst we were cleaning. We ended up getting pretty chummy. Some of them even gave us a hand near the end. You know, pedal to the metal. I had everything in that armoury gleaming like the sun. I can tell you that.'

Ryan tried concentrating on Dafydd's words, but the dancing flames, and the warmth, and the beer, and the cosy atmosphere had other ideas, until Dafydd Wynne said something which jolted Ryan straight back to reality.

'Can you say that again?'

'Which bit?'

'What you just said about the coins disappearing and the cabinet still being locked?'

'See, I was the only one with a key. So how did they get in and take the coins and lock up behind them when my key was safe with me at home? My wife wasn't even in town, she was up visiting her old mam, god rest her soul, in Porth Penrhyn. Mind you, the police still interviewed her, and my mother-in-law.'

'Just to clarify, the hoard of coins were Roman?'

'As Roman as the Coliseum. We visited there, me and the wife, on our honeymoon. I wouldn't go back though, too many tourists. We've got everything we need right here in Wales. The most beautiful beaches in the world, and the best pints.'

'Did anyone do any tests on the coins before they went missing?'

'Tests? The boffins were shaving and drilling and weighing them like nobody's business before they made it into my museum. Gold, most of them, with some silver coins thrown in for good luck. I'll bet some poor Roman lad got a good hiding for losing those coins. I've still got one of them.'

Ryan choked on his drink.

'Pardon?'

'They gave me one coin to keep. They figured no one was going to notice one missing from the pile. It was one of the drilled ones. They didn't want that one going on display.'

'Do you still have it?' Ryan asked. If they could compare Dafydd's coin with the coins found near Hexham, and if they were a match, then his work would be done. File closed. And the insurers would live happily ever after.

'Well, now, that's a question, isn't it? Let me think. It was in the wife's box of jewels on the dressing table. She kept on at me about having it made into a pendant, but the funds were never forthcoming for frivolities like that. So it should still be in there, unless the daughter has taken it? She used to play with the wife's pretty things, lining them up to play shop. Of course, it made sense for her to get a job behind the counter at Siop y Plas. They're the jewellers in town. She's been there nigh on twenty years now.'

'Could we go back to your place to check the jewellery box? It would help with the investigation if we could run some analysis on your coin.'

'Aye, maybe, another pint first though, lad. I haven't even told you the most interesting part about when the coins disappeared. Oh, aye, you'll want to sleep with the lights on after you hear this story,' Dafydd said, pushing his empty pint glass towards Ryan.

Ryan had no choice but to take the glasses up to the scuffed bar and order two more pints.

'Old Dafydd bending your ear?' the bartender asked, pulling on the beer tap. 'He's in here every day. He's got no one since his old lady went missing. His high-and-mighty daughter never visits unless she wants something. So is that why you're here? Is it about his wife?'

'I'm looking into an old theft from the Caernarfon Castle Museum.'

'Oh, aye, that'll be the coins, I suppose. I remember

that. I'd just started here and the whole town was crawling with the police. Most of them were here for Prince Charlie, mind you. Those missing coins barely got a look see. They'd found another hoard of coins up north a few months earlier, so what difference did it make if one lot went missing? Coins are coins, eh?'

'How long ago did his wife leave him?'

'Leave him? She vanished, quick as a flash. Rumour has it she took off with one of Prince Charlie's guards. I never thought I'd see the day when Lizzie died and Charlie settled his skinny butt on the throne, with Camilla next to him. Mark my words, he won't last long—'

'Sorry, did you say she disappeared?' Ryan asked.

'She ran off and broke Dafydd's heart, and left him raising that girl all on his own. You'd have thought she'd show her old dad a bit more consideration than she does, given everything he did for her. Mind you, there were some who thought Dafydd might have done his wife in. I wasn't one of them. No, my money was always on her leaving him for a better life in London.'

Ryan frowned. The business with Sarah Lester back in London was still fresh in his mind, regardless of how he tried to forget about it. Dafydd's wife was just an odd coincidence, nothing more.

'Did Dafydd ever hear from his wife?'

The bartender shook his head. 'There you are, two pints. That's an award-winning drop that one.'

With the conversation clearly over, Ryan carried the drinks back to the table, rejoining Dafydd in front of the roaring fire.

'Ah, it's a good drop this, the Cwrw Braf ale.'

'Dafydd, when your wife left, did she take her jewellery box with her? Or is it still at your house? I'm only asking because testing that coin is pretty important, and obviously you'll get it back, and…' Ryan was making it up as he went. 'And we'll reimburse you for the effort.'

'Reimbursement, you say? Well, I don't know if the coin is still there or not. When Loretta… when she left, she took nothing with her. That was the oddest thing about it. Not that the police showed much interest. They put it down to a marital dispute.' The man wiped a tear from his rheumy eye. 'There was no marital dispute. We were happy.' He disappeared into his memories. With a jolt and a slosh of ale, he returned to the present. 'Anyway, I was going to tell you about when the coins went missing.'

Ryan screamed internally. All he wanted was the coin, and then he could be on his merry way, hopefully straight into the arms of the beautiful Emma Humphreys. He chanced a quick glance at his watch. Time was not on his side.

'Go on,' Ryan said. At this rate, he'd have to stay the night. At least the Black Boy Inn had an excellent reputation, so it was not all bad. And it was not like Emma was expecting him...

'Remember how I said that the cabinet was still locked? Those cabinets weren't like they are now, all temperature controlled and alarmed. Oh, no, they were a box knocked up by the local cabinetmaker, with a simple lock on one side. The lock would be easy pickings for any sneak thief worth his salt. But thieves rarely lock up after themselves, do they?'

Ryan shook his head, already confused about the direction of the story.

'Probably wasn't the first time they'd been stolen. That's probably the maddest thing about it. When those coins were first dug up and came to us at the museum, we all agreed that they weren't found in their original place of burial.'

'What?'

'You didn't read that in your files, did you? No, it was too tidy. No spillage from a shattered container, just one neat pile. As if someone had moved them there. A long time ago, mind you. But it was all a little too perfect. The man who found them had no idea. He wasn't an archaeologist, just a hobbyist; they're everywhere now. We had to chase them out of the castle grounds all the time. Anyway, I digress.' Dafydd took a long swallow of his pint, smacking his fleshy lips together, the sound reverberating through the near empty pub.

'The disappearance?' Ryan probed, barely containing his frustration.

'Right you are! We got them into the museum right quick, and into the cabinet. We had one spare, you see, and I had the only key. The place was swarming with protection officers, and they all wanted a touch. A touch of the coins, not me. I'm as straight as they come.'

Ryan choked on his beer. He'd never for one moment imagined a scenario where tough British Protection Officers were trying to cop a feel of the old curator, either now, or back in the 60s.

'But there was this one young lad, see. One night, the night the coins went missing, he was screaming like a banshee, and they couldn't shut him up. He screamed blue murder that someone was in the hall. We're old hands at seeing things, us. Even this pub has had its fair share of sightings. Mind you, those stopped when the builders found Flossie's bones in the walls a few years ago. Anyway, where was I?'

Ryan shrugged. He was tired. His backside was numb from the chair, and his beer was already warm in his hand.

'We hadn't noticed the coins were missing then. Everyone was running around looking for the fire because of his screams. That's what we thought it was, a fire, but of course there wasn't one. But this lad, he swore black and blue that there'd been a man in the hall, all dressed up like a Roman soldier. Well, those other guards, they laughed themselves silly, and from what I heard afterwards, they packed him off to the funny farm. They had to clear him out of the castle because of the investiture, you see. They couldn't have any shenanigans with all them royalty coming in. And that was when we saw that the coins had been stolen. Melted down for easy cash, that's my bet. And my money is on the lad. What do you think? They interviewed him, but his brain was up on the moon with those American astronauts. He was that far gone.'

Ryan finished his beer with a long gulp and wiped his mouth.

'It was probably him,' Ryan agreed, to speed up the process. 'Do you think we could look for that coin now? It's getting late, and I still need to check in and get myself sorted. I've got an early start tomorrow.'

'Oh, aye, I've got to be in for my tea. Gets delivered, see. My daughter does that, arranges my tea every night, rain or shine. Snow makes it difficult, though.' Dafydd laughed, the sound strange through his missing teeth.

The knowledge that Dafydd's daughter looked after her old dad, despite what the bartender said, made Ryan feel better about the man's daughter.

Once they'd pulled on their jackets and emerged into the winter night, the dusk shadows had already fled, leaving the stone buildings squatting like identical blocks on the ancient paved roads.

Dafydd kept up a consistent patter as they walked the seven hundred metres to Dafydd's terraced house. Ryan watched as Dafydd opened the front door and wandered inside. The man had left the place unlocked. What century did he think he was living in?

Ryan followed Dafydd inside, he elderly man bypassing all the light switches until he reached the kitchen, where he turned on a lamp. The cost of living had hit hard up north.

'If you wait here, I'll pop upstairs and bring down Loretta's jewellery box. I suppose I should have given it to Joyce. That's my daughter. But I've held on to it, you see, for when Loretta gets back. She'd be right cross if she found out I'd given it away, even if it was to our wee Joyce.'

Ryan thanked his stars that the man had held onto the box. Finding a coin from the hoard was a longer shot than winning the trifecta at the Grand National races. If everything panned out, he'd have a coin which was a perfect match to those found near Hexham. And then, he could profess his undying love for the young Miss Humphreys.

He was still daydreaming about knocking on Emma's door when Dafydd appeared, a mirrored jewellery box in his hands.

'You'll have to go through it. I don't think I can bear to look at her pretty things,' Dafydd said, a catch in his voice.

Ryan shelved his thoughts of Emma out of the way and took the box from Dafydd's wrinkled hands.

'How about a cup of tea?' Ryan suggested, giving the man something productive to do whilst he pawed through Dafydd's wife's precious things.

With the boiling kettle proving a distraction for Dafydd, Ryan scoured the contents of the jewellery box for the Roman coin. Costume clip on earrings from the 50s, gaudy brooches — most of which were missing several shiny paste jewels. An ostentatious carnival ring, wooden beads, delicate silver bangles, and a souvenir charm bracelet — the tiny charms rubbed clean of their gilt. Of the Roman coin, there was no sign. Ryan slammed the lid of the box, a little harder than he had meant to.

'There's no coin here, Dafydd.'

'Well, that there is a surprise. To think that she must have taken it with her. That's the only way it'd be missing, hmm?'

'You don't think that maybe your daughter has it?'

'Joyce? No, not her. I can't recall the last time she's been upstairs at mine. Not since she moved out. I can ask her the next time I see her?'

Ryan had to stop himself from yelling at the old man. He had places to be, and things to do, and he did not want to have to come back to Caernarfon unless it was to return the stolen hoard under the glare of a media frenzy.

'Do you think you could give her a ring now? It's just that it's such a long drive from London.'

Dafydd looked surprised at Ryan's request, but did not argue. Instead, he shuffled over to the old wall phone, its rotary dial an anachronism in the modern world.

'Hello, love, it's your old man here ... Yes, I'm well ... Yes, the meals are just what your mam would have made. Love, look, I have a tricky question for you ... No, it's not about the internet. It's about your mam's jewellery box. Can you remember seeing an old coin in there since she left? I didn't have any reason to look for it, and there's a man here from London who wants it ... No, he's not a scammer. You don't need to come here. He's an investigator from London, looking into the missing hoard of coins from the museum ... You were too young, you wouldn't remember ... No? You don't remember it either? I didn't think so. I'll tell the boy, and maybe you can pop around one day soon? Well, when you have time, then. I'm always here ... Okay. I love you too.'

Ryan had already drained his tea before Dafydd relayed his daughter's side of the conversation. What a waste of time this visit had been.

'She's coming back, you know,' Dafydd said.

'Pardon?'

'Loretta will be back. That's why I've kept everything the same, save for Joyce's room. She wanted it painted for her sixteenth, and when I said no, she painted it herself when I was at work. I'm sure Loretta will understand. I hope she does.'

'Why do you say she'll come back when she's been gone for so long?'

'I've seen her.'

'What?'

'I've seen Loretta watching me. She's trying to come back, I know that, but something is stopping her. I don't know what, or how, but she's close, always is. That's why I've waited for her. It's not like I didn't get offers from other women. Throwing themselves at me, they were. But Loretta is the only woman I've ever loved, or ever will. Other than our Joyce, of course.'

'Can I ask you something crazy?' Ryan chanced, well aware that he was drifting into a weird, weird territory.

'Do I think it was the coins?'

How did he know?

'It's ludicrous, and I'll lose my job for even asking. But there have been things I've seen...' Ryan said, thinking of Sarah Lester and the Old Curiosity Shop.

'Aye, like old Flossie in the Black Boy Inn. People thought it was a marketing gimmick, saying that the place was haunted. Folks seem to like that sort of thing, especially the Americans. They were laughing on the other side of their beers after they found her bones. She'd been trying to tell us where she was for years. You'll be fine sleeping there tonight. Flossie doesn't disturb anyone now that she's at rest in the cemetery. And maybe that'll be my Loretta one day, except that she's not dead. She just can't get back.'

A tear trickled down Dafydd's wrinkled face. And Ryan felt his heart constrict at the man's loneliness.

'Dafydd, I truly hope that this hoard belongs to Caernarfon, and if it does, I promise you I'll be the one to deliver it. Between us, maybe we can get Loretta back?'

The old man hugged Ryan at the doorway, harder and tighter than two men would in normal circumstances. For some undefinable reason, Ryan knew, with one hundred per cent certainty, that Dafydd's wife, and the missing coin, and the rediscovered hoard up north, were all connected. How he knew, he could not explain. But he would do whatever he could to help this man find his wife.

TWO SIDES TO EVERY COIN

The Black Boy Inn creaked like a Spanish galleon in a hurricane, and although Dafydd Wynne had assured Ryan Francis that the ghost of Flossie had vanished once her bones were removed from her untimely tomb inside the walls, he'd still spent a sleepless night tossing and turning and jumping at every noise, before relenting and switching the bedside light on as if he were a child of eight, instead of a grown man.

Over a decently large breakfast, complete with perfectly runny eggs and a gallon of tea, he contemplated his options for the day. A long drive to the Royal Mint (not *just* to see Emma Humphreys, regardless of what Gemma thought), or a drive to where the coins were found, and a chat with the numismatic experts at Tyne River University? He knew which one was more appealing. He had known that before he had even left the Art Loss Register's London offices. Emma would win, any day, in any lifetime.

The long drive, through some of the United Kingdom's most stunning landscapes, provided more than enough time for Ryan to mull over what he knew about the coins, and the possible explanations for how they had turned up near Hexham. It wasn't his job to decide what happened with the horde. He merely had to, literally, follow the money. Just like they did with Al Capone and Donald

Trump, and with every hell and brim-fire TV evangelist around the world.

There were too many things which couldn't be explained on paper. Things which only he and Gemma Dance could talk about since their experience with Sarah Lester and the Old Curiosity Shop. His suspicions weren't something he could write in a report or share with a client, otherwise they'd be forced to lock him up in the secure wing of the nearest mental hospital. He could share his thoughts with Emma, maybe? There had been a time when they'd shared everything until they hadn't. And that had been the darkest part of his life. Gemma hadn't understood. She had made it quite clear that she had never warmed to Emma, and that she saw no reason why Ryan should still be mourning the end of their short-lived relationship. Could he trust Emma enough to tell her all about what had happened in London at the Old Curiosity Shop and the stabbing at Christies and everything else? For the first time, he hesitated. Ryan wouldn't say that Gemma's warnings had wormed their way into his mind... but that was exactly what they'd done.

Pah.

He'd know once he saw Emma in person whether their connection remained. He could only hope.

With the coordinates to the Royal Mint entered into his SATNAV, Ryan began the arduous journey. Thoughts of coins and counterfeits and disappearing wives and antique dealers, and even former Prince Charlie (now King Charles III), tumbled around his head. Not the normal ramblings of most commuters, he mused.

If the missing Caernarfon hoard had made it to a random farm in Northumberland, then he'd understand that. It actually made sense that a thief would hide their loot for a period, knowing that the coins were too hot a commodity to sell straight away, although thirty years was a long time to hold on to stolen goods. But then any sort of mishap could have befallen the thief — a wronged partner bent on retribution could have resulted in a lengthy prison term. Or there could have been an untimely death at the hands of a competitor. Or even that wanton leveller of the great and small, cancer, could have stopped the thief from returning to his hidden horde. Those scenarios made sense. Time travelling wives of Welsh museum curators did not.

Ryan scoffed at the complete fantasy of giving even half a thought to time travel. He didn't want to put into words his thoughts about what had happened back in London with Sarah Lester — the owner of the Old Curiosity Shop and her missing parents, and the thing with the knife and Richard Grey. That situation was nothing like this one. No, this was a simple case of stolen Roman coins turning up in a field in Northern England. Theft, pure and simple. And a wife who had had enough of her husband, and was probably living a new life in Hackney with her lover. Simple, sensible, and lacking any hint of science fiction whatsoever.

PULLING up to the sprawling monstrosity housing the Royal Mint, Ryan's cheeks reddened as he start regretting his decision. Maybe he should have rung ahead? Maybe Emma was on annual leave, sunning herself at Spain with her closest girlfriends and a glass of Pinot Grigio by her side?

After gathering what little courage he had, he entered through the less ostentatious side door, thereby avoiding the busloads of tourists clamouring for a selfie with the odd coin-shaped sheep sculpture at the entrance to the busy visitors' centre.

Once inside, he handed his card to the receptionist and asked to see Emma Humphreys. He'd just started biting his nails to offset the anxiety welling inside him, when a steel door at the end of the corridor opened, and Emma Humphreys emerged, her face a picture of beauty and confusion.

'Ryan?'

Ryan cleared his throat, hoping for the power of speech

to return, and flashed her a brilliant smile, forever grateful that his parents had saved enough to get him braces in his teenage years.

'Hi.'

Hi? Was that all he was capable of?

They joined in an awkward hug, the gaze of the receptionist laser focussed on their interaction.

'Come through to the meeting room,' Emma suggested, escorting him out of sight of the bulldog-like receptionist.

'Are you allowed to be alone with me?' he asked, pointing back towards reception. 'She looks like she could crush me with her little finger.'

'She's like that with everyone, even royalty. You should have seen her when the Queen did a tour. We half expected Glenys to ask the Queen for photo ID before letting her pass.'

Emma led him into a small, windowless room, furnished with a table and a handful of designer, but terribly uncomfortable, chairs. Ryan took a seat opposite her, his heart pounding. *Christ, it was like he was fourteen again.*

'So?' she said, her hands clasped together on the table. 'What brings you to Wales? It has been a long time.'

Ryan tried to steady his nerves. 'I know, and I'm sorry for that. The truth is, I've been thinking about you a lot lately. I know I messed things up between us, and I'm not here to try and make thing right—'

Emma's eyebrows disappeared into her hairline. 'That ship has long since sailed.'

Ryan winced. 'I wanted to apologise, again, and I know you made your position clear years ago, but I need your expertise, and so I thought it would be better if I came to see you, rather than to try apologising over the phone, and—'

'You drove from London to Wales because you needed my help?'

'Well, not—'

'You didn't drive from London?'

'I did, but via Caernarfon, and we thought—'

'We?'

'I, *I* thought I should come here to ask for your help, and to apologise, and I feel awful about how we left things, and I haven't stopped thinking about you, and then this case came up, and it really seemed like too good an opportunity to not give it a go.'

'Give what a go?'

'Us. You and me. To make things right.'

'There isn't a you and me, Ryan. Have you forgotten why? Because I haven't.'

Ryan shook his head. 'I know I hurt you, Emma, and I regret it every day. I just wanted to see if there was a chance for us to... you know, maybe start over?' Ryan watched Emma's eyes flicker with something that looked like anger before they softened, as they so often had in the past.

'You broke my heart, and that's not something that gets wiped clean with an apology, no matter how many times you try.'

'I know,' Ryan said, his voice cracking. 'I messed up, but I'm willing to do whatever it takes to make it right. Just give me a chance to show you that I'm not that same person anymore.'

'What is it that you need my help with?'

Ryan's pulse settled. Despite Gemma's predictions that Emma couldn't let him in the front door, let alone entertain his apology, Emma's true colours shone through, as always. She was far too good for him. 'It's about a cache of coins found up by Hadrian's Wall.'

IN A SMALL MEETING room at the Royal Mint, Emma Humphreys leaned forward, her interest piqued. 'Go on,' she said to Ryan.

Ryan pulled the Art Loss Register file from his bag and pushed it across the table towards her. 'Originally, we thought that these coins were part of a Roman treasure trove, but there are some who think that they're the coins stolen from Caernarfon Castle. We need your expertise to authenticate them.'

Emma began flipping through the pages. 'Where did you say they were found?'

Ryan hesitated, then decided there was no point in holding anything back. They were using Emma as a subject expert, and he trusted her not to run to the media with the information. 'They were found at a farm near Hexham, alongside a newly discovered Roman altar, and a group of human skulls.'

'Skulls? Old ones or new ones?'

'I doubt that they ever danced to an Elvis song,' Ryan said, a smile teasing at his mouth. 'So not recently deceased.'

'Not cool, Ryan. They probably died horribly violent deaths, if you only found their skulls.'

'Sorry.'

Ryan remembered too late how serious she was about stuff like that. 'I didn't dig them up myself.'

'I realise that.'

Joking was definitely off the cards then.

'It gets a little more complicated,' Ryan added.

'Go on.'

'There were more coins found, but at another location. The coins were found at the same time as Hexham's mayor disappeared. Gemma tells me—'

'Gemma? She's still at the Art Loss Register?'

Shit. That had been the wrong thing to say. The two had never got on, although there'd never been any romantic rivalry as far as he knew.

'Apparently, the mayor turned up again, with no memory of what happened. A car jacking, they think, by night hawkers looking for more gold coins.'

'Night hawkers?'

'Metal detectorists, who do their detecting in the dark, without permission, and usually in places that they shouldn't be, like along Hadrian's Wall.'

'You know I can't do any analysis without the actual coins? I mean, the photos are great, and I can make a partial assessment against what's been recorded about the Caernarfon Hoard, but it seems pretty unlikely that they're the same coins, when you add in the skulls, and did you say, an altar? Surely the coins were from offerings made to whomever the altar was dedicated to. Do you have that information yet?'

'No.' The whole thing didn't make any sense to him. How could a cache of Roman coins found in the late nineteenth century, which were stolen in the 1960s from a castle in Wales, now be turning up in two different places near Hexham in England in the twenty-first century? Some god somewhere was having a laugh, that was for sure.

Emma leaned back in her chair. 'It does seem unlikely that they are the same coins, especially with the addition of the skulls and the altar. Without seeing the actual coins, it'll be difficult to make a proper assessment, even with any analysis they'll be running on them at Newcastle.'

Ryan sighed, running a hand through his hair. 'I know. But we need to know the truth about these coins. If they are the Caernarfon Hoard, then what a major media coup to recover them. If they aren't, then it could be a major archaeological discovery.'

Emma nodded. 'I understand, but I can't promise anything until I've had a chance to examine the coins myself.'

'Thank you,' Ryan said, relief flooding through him. 'I appreciate it more than you know.'

Emma smiled. 'Don't get too attached to the idea of us working together, Ryan. This is strictly business.'

'I understand,' Ryan said, unable to hide the disappointment in his voice. He had hoped that this time with Emma might lead to a reconciliation, but that was looking unlikely. He would have to content himself with working as colleagues, and maybe things could progress from there.

Emma stood up. 'Let me check with my boss about coming with you to Hexham.'

'Wait, what? You're going to come to Hexham?'

'How else am I meant to examine these coins? Besides,

I was already booked to do a Royal Mint roadshow next week, so I'll just pitch it as starting in Hexham this week instead.'

'How was Hexham even on your list of places to visit? There's nothing there?'

'It's been voted as the happiest place in England for the past two years, so of course we were planning to stop there. Short of going to Disneyland, where else is a girl meant to find true happiness?'

With that, she slipped out the door, leaving Ryan to analyse the unspoken meaning, and accusation, behind her words. He deserved the castigation, of that he was certain.

EMMA LEANED against the cool corridor wall, with her eyes clenched tight, and her stomach in knots.

'You will not let this man derail your life again,' she told herself, her breathing threatening to morph into a panic attack.

It had been over a year since she'd last had anything to do with Ryan Francis. A year of counselling, and many, many nights of sobbing into her wine glass to the increasing frustration of her girlfriends. She'd moved cities and jobs and flats until finally she was in a safe and happy place.

Yet the second he'd walked through the door, it had taken every ounce of self control to not throw herself at the man who'd stolen her heart all those years ago, before breaking it into a million tiny pieces.

'He is not worth the pain,' she chastised herself.

His image burned behind her closed eyes. Dark hair, strong jaw, his smell.

'Stop it. It is over. Do not go there again. You deserve better.'

She tried all the counsellor's words, yet none of them could quench the feelings she'd thought she'd discarded. He smelled so good — a mix of musk and sandalwood that she'd only ever noticed with him. And his smile. It was the kind that lit up a room and made her feel like the most special person on earth.

Emma took a deep breath, clearing her head. She couldn't let him distract her. It was time to put on her professional hat and get to work.

With one last deep breath, she wiped her eyes and pushed off the wall. She had a job to do, one she was damn good at it. And maybe, just maybe, she could prove to herself that she was over Ryan Francis once and for all. After all, she was only going on a drive to Hexham to look at some coins. What could go wrong?

ADD TO CART

Jane Badrick leaned against the canvas sports bag, using her weight to force it into the remaining cavity in the Defender. With any luck, the door would still close, disguising the contents of the car from any prying eyes. Fortunately, her past shopping habits had meant there had been no raised eyebrows or unseemly questions from her husband as to the quantity of courier packages arriving at the house. Although it was unlikely that her husband would ever have thought to show any interest in her activities. Not unless it involved long dead peasants or pre-reformation clergy and the designs of their toilets.

In two more nights, she would not have a husband or son. The husband had been a mistake from the very beginning. And so had the son, but she had at least grown to love him, even if he was consorting with the wrong sort of people. But soon his poor life decisions would not be her problem. She no longer cared if he got into a good university, or knew which fork to use at a formal dinner and married a girl from good stock. Those ideals were of no use where she was going.

She wondered if she might meet someone new and fall in love. But then again, more often than not, love ruined things. No, it was better to focus on her goals — power and wealth. Whilst fame had once been the plan for her life, it did not feature now. The most powerful people in the world had those positions because they flew under the radar, not because they posted pictures of sunsets and dogs on Instagram, gathering thousands of followers and false likes. Influence did not pay for custom-made shoes. But what a relief it would be to be away from the poisoned chalice of the online world. Away from the judgement of those too useless to step forward. With her knowledge and skills, there would be no limit to the opportunities open to her in the new world. In the past.

Her phone rang.

'Mayor Badrick?'

Christ! Was it so very hard to get a moment's peace in this world?

'Could whatever it is not wait until I was in the office? Did you consider that before ringing me, Raymond?'

Jane's jaw pulsed as she listened to her assistant on the other line.

'I'll be there in fifteen minutes. Offer them coffee and do what you can to distract them until I'm there. But whatever you do, do not let them into my office.'

While driving into town, Jane's thoughts were consumed with all the things that might go awry. She had meticulously planned every detail of her escape, but there was always the chance that someone would ruin it but not doing what she'd asked, or by talking out of school.

By the time she had parked outside the council building, she had convinced herself that the police were there to arrest her for the possession of an unlicensed firearm, among other crimes. Crimes she was, of course, guilty of a thousand times over. Not that any jury would convict her, of that she was certain. She just did not need this now. In two days' time, when she was gone, then they could comb through her financial accounts, and click on the files marked private on her laptop.

'Where are they?' she barked at Raymond.

'In the meeting room.'

'Tell them I'll be five minutes,' she directed, unlocking her office and closing the door behind her.

The sensible thing to do would be to shred everything. Let the forensic accountants try and piece that together.

Don't panic, she told herself.

From behind her desk, Jane's eyes scanned the room for anything incriminating. Her gaze fell on a photograph of her and Andy on the desk. Initially placed there more for decor than any other reason, she was surprised at the guilt washing over her when she realised she was leaving him behind. It was too late now, there was no going back. Especially now that the police were here.

A knock on the door.

'I said five minutes, Raymond.'

'They're asking to see you now. They saw you come in.'

'Did you explain to them that as the mayor, my time is valuable, and that they should have made an appointment?'

She just needed five more minutes.

'Mayor Badrick?'

Jane looked up to see Chief Inspector Kevin Readdie in her doorway.

She plastered a smile onto her surgically enhanced face. 'Inspector, so sorry to keep you waiting.'

'Chief Inspector.'

'What? Oh, yes, your recent promotion, well done. I presume that was because of the work you did with the Matheson Industries case? Terrible about what they were doing. Congratulations on uncovering that.'

'Thank you, but we're not here to discuss my promotion or the Matheson Industries case,' Readdie said, his expression grim.

Jane felt a knot form in the pit of her stomach at the tone of the Chief Inspector's voice.

'Then what is this about, Chief Inspector?' she asked, her voice betraying a hint of nervousness.

'It's about the coins we found at the scene of your car jacking.'

That was why he was here? He was here about some stupid coins found on the side of the road? She laughed.

'Coins?'

Readdie's expression turned serious. 'Yes, Mayor. The coins are identical to those stolen from the Caernarfon Museum.'

'Caernarfon? Isn't that a castle in Wales? I don't understand the link between the two?'

'Neither do we, so that's why we're here.'

'Couldn't you have emailed to ask me these questions?' Jane asked, desperately trying to steady her breathing. How had the coins ended up beside her car? The car she had left in Roman Britain.

'I am, of course, happy to cooperate, Chief Inspector,' she said, forcing a smile. 'But I know nothing about any stolen coins. And as I told the young constable you sent to interview me in hospital, I have no recollection of what occurred in that laneway. The whole evening is a blur. One minute I was driving, and the next I was braking for a man standing in the centre of the road. What happened after that is something I'm still waiting to find out from your investigation. An investigation, I might add, which appears to be lacking in forward momentum.'

Readdie's eyes narrowed, and Jane braced herself for the worst. But instead of pushing her further, he leaned back in his chair and let out a heavy sigh.

'Mayor Badrick, I understand that this situation is... complicated,' he said, appearing to choose his words carefully. 'We want to work with you to understand what happened that evening, but we need your full cooperation. We need to know everything you remember about that night, no matter how insignificant you think it might be.'

The mayor forced a smile. 'Of course, Chief Inspector. I'll do everything in my power to help your investigation. There's nothing I'd like more than for whomever was responsible for my accident to face the full force of the law.'

Readdie nodded, and a sense of relief washed over Jane. She was rehearsing the conversation she would have with Darby once the police left. He should have given her a heads up about the coins well before the police appeared. How could the Roman coins found where her car disappeared be connected to a historic theft from a Welsh museum? And what was the likelihood she would be able to get her hands on them now?

Not for the first time, she cursed Anson Darby, the Northumberland constabulary, everyone in her office, and her husband, for existing.

UPON SAYING her goodbyes to the Chief Inspector, Jane came to the realisation that she would have to make substantial modifications to her plan. Wasting no time, Jane summoned Raymond and began barking orders. 'Get Anson Darby on the phone. I don't care if he's busy digging up King Tutankhamun's cousin from the shores of the River Tyne.'

'WE'VE GOT A PROBLEM,' Jane said as soon as she heard Anson's reedy voice on the phone.

'What kind of problem?' Anson asked.

'The police were here. The coins they found at the scene of my carjacking match those stolen from the Caernarfon Museum. I should never have been put in this situation, Darby. Surprises are not something I enjoy. Explain yourself.'

'The Caernarfon Museum, in Wales?'

'Is there another one?'

'How did they match them so quickly?'

A SEED FOR THE FUTURE

Previously, Apple's happiest hours were time spent on her own communing with nature, listening to the bird life and the hidden rustlings in the undergrowth. She was just as satisfied sitting quietly as butterflies settled on her outstretched fingers as she was hiking over the undulating hills of the countryside. This, however, was all new to her — the happiness of a table of friends together in an overheated cafe, half quaffed coffees at their elbows, and a plate of pastries waiting to be eaten. There were no lazy flies at this time of the year. They were a summer curse. Curse was an apt word given the circumstances. And one that she had grasped with both hands. Rarer than a beaver in the wild, or a fox who knew no fear, a curse could be a blessing. And for Apple, that is exactly what it was.

'Have you got the coin?' Apple asked.

Neumegen shook his head. 'Soon.'

Apple thought he looked older than when he'd first arrived. She fidgeted in her seat. *Soon* was not an answer.

'I worked out where Darby is,' Raymond Lamont volunteered.

'Let me guess, he's not at Ithaca Farm excavating the altar?'

Lamont shook his head, his cowlick falling over one eye.

Apple almost reached to push it back, but that seemed

too intimate, so she stayed her hand, selecting a pastry instead.

'He's at the university, bothering the lab techs. I've a friend there who said he's asking them to test some coins. Which would be okay in normal circumstances, but these aren't the coins from where they found the altar…'

'What?' Neumegen's head shot up faster than a rabbit running from a farmer's gun.

'His coins are different. Still Roman, but more Celtic in origin I think. My friend couldn't be certain as Darby had demanded no one else be told what was going on.'

'Celtic in origin?' Neumegen repeated.

He did that a lot, Apple thought; repeating words and phrases in his unusual cadence. As though he were hearing them for the first time.

'It doesn't matter where the coins are from,' Lillian added, 'just their age and that they are in his possession. There's something about him having them and the mayor wanting to know where he is that doesn't feel right.'

'And then there's Pramod, and his whereabouts,' Neumegen said, a note of melancholy in his voice.

The table fell silent. The missing librarian thrust back into their minds.

'We'll find him,' Apple said.

Neumegen nodded. 'I just hope we're not too late.'

'Are we all ready for Saturnalia? Has everyone got their outfits ready?' Lillian asked, breaking the solemn silence.

Apple appreciated her for that. If she'd tried to change the subject like that she'd… Odd. Apple found that she didn't know how she'd be perceived. This was all so new to her — being included and appreciated, instead of being ignored, or worse still, being treated like an idiot. As if the percentage of melanin in someone's skin determined their intellectual capabilities.

The assembled group nodded, and everyone described their assorted costumes for the Saturnalia festivities at the Bellingham Tea Rooms.

'One more night to wait,' Apple announced, as if the timetable wasn't at the top of all their minds.

'She's going to be there, isn't she?' Lillian asked.

No one needed clarification about who she meant. The mayor.

'If she has a coin, she will be a risk to you on the night,' Neumegen predicted.

His warning was one they had already discussed at length.

'I can stop her,' Badger offered, his eyes staring at Lillian.

Apple recognised that it wasn't every day a son would offer sacrifice his mother. But then, this was not an ordinary day, and Badger was not an ordinary son. She'd have to ask Lillian later how the conversation with Badger had gone, the one where Lillian explained the whole time travel thing. But she'd noticed the way Badger looked at Lillian, and realised Lillian could have told him that the earth was flat and he would have believed her.

'It would be foolish for you to get involved now. Lillian has to be the one to stop her,' Neumegen said.

'And me. It's my grandfather who is going to be the one she fights,' Apple said, her hands flat on the table, her mouth set like concrete.

'Your grandfather is almost two thousand years old,' Neumegen replied.

Apple shot him a look designed to wilt the leaves on an otherwise healthy plant.

'My great grandfather seventeen times over.'

'Are we talking about the governor of Roman Britain? The albino?' Badger said.

'The person with albinism,' Apple corrected automatically.

'Her familial link to Decimus Clodius Albinus may be correct, but it is still irrelevant. She can't go back. Fate has already determined the fate of Albinus, and he doesn't die in England,' Neumegen said, a hint of exasperation in his tone.

'But isn't that what might change if the mayor goes back? The whole timeline of who becomes the next Roman emperor?' Apple argued.

'I'll put in another way. You are not going back. Lillian goes, as do I. You don't.'

Apple's pale eyes narrowed. People had underestimated Apple her whole life. Whether it was because of her family and their inherited albinism gene, or some other reason, she didn't know, but no one would stop her from warning her own ancestor about the threat to him, and their entire history. The history books were clear about what happened to Decimus Clodius Albinus, and his fate did not lay at the hands of the Mayor of Hexham and the Iceni warriors under her command, if that's what the deal was.

'Fine,' she replied after a moment, 'I'll stay.'

Apple could not wrap her head around the supposed rules of time travel, but even she questioned Neumegen's inflexibility as to who could and could not travel back with Lillian. Was there anything more exciting than the prospect of going back in time? What was the risk of her going? She had no dependents or responsibilities. And it wasn't as if Hexham offered anything remotely as exciting, unless you fancied a lifetime of working at the Tesco checkout. True, she could become a harried mother to the national average of two-point-five children, or an overworked doctor at a local general practice, verging on the cusp of suicide at the tidal wave of patients with nowhere else to go. But the prospect of travelling back to the time of Roman rule over (most of) Britain was beyond her wildest dreams, and now her greatest desire. Lillian could not do it on her own, and there was no way Apple would let her newest friend travel without backup.

'I think Badger's right though. He should do what he can to stop his mother from returning. If only to give Lillian a better chance to stop whatever it is Jane Badrick has put in motion. Can't you feel the change in the air now?' Neumegen asked.

The group paused in their deliberations. To the casual observer, life in the cafe seemed unchanged. The atmosphere remained tinged with the scent of burnt coffee grounds and sour milk, mixed with designer perfume and perspiration, wood smoke and something else, something earthy, old even. The rest of the cafe patrons looked no different — a mixture of old and young, heavyset and fashion magazine skinny, well dressed and dressed for comfort. Walking shoes, velcro-strapped hiking sandals. Doc Martens. Nikes. Everything appeared as normal, and yet there was something undefinable permeating every breath. Every tinkling laugh. Every transaction at the counter — a counter heaving with brochures for wall walks and tourist talks, osteopath treatments and an appeal for donations towards the Cathedral's roof fund. The same as last week, and the week before, and the one before that. But there was a heaviness to the air, a dark pall to the complexions of the cafe's patrons. An acceptance of a life not of their own choosing? But that could describe anyone in the modern world today. Tied to mortgages, to lives lived on credit, on borrowed time, on preservatives, imbedded within a prison of concrete and glass and plastic. Watching whole species disappearing one by one and two by two. Noah would be aggrieved.

'There is something different,' Lillian said. 'Things are changing. I can feel it.'

Apple nodded. Of course Lillian felt it. She stared at the others, waiting for their thoughts.

'Nothing feels different to me,' Badger said.

It wouldn't, Apple thought, he was too much his mother's son, even if the desire to change was there.

'I felt it at the office. It's like when a new manager starts and wants to change the world on their first day,' Lamont said. 'There's a nervous energy, like we're all waiting for Father Christmas to arrive.'

'That's one way to describe it,' Neumegen agreed. 'We're waiting for the veil to lift.'

'The veil?' Apple asked.

'Between us and them. Between now and before.'

Between now and before. Apple did not know what came before, but she was certain it was better than now. Apart from Lamont and Lillian, and Neumegen and Badger. Her new friends. Her only friends.

'Where are we meeting tomorrow?'

'At my house,' Lillian said with a finality in her voice that Apple had not heard before.

Meeting at Lillian's house on the eve of Saturnalia before going to the party at Bellingham sounded like a good idea, but Apple wondered if Ithaca Farm might have other ideas.

'Let's meet at mine,' Apple volunteered. 'It might be safer given what's happened before. Yes?'

The group agreed, going their separate ways, each wondering what the future, or the past, might hold for them.

THE MORNING of Saturnalia arrived shrouded in mist, under the threat of snow, and throughout Hexham and its environs, the residents stirred. And whilst they were pouring their coffees and steeping their teas, the thinnest of veneers stretched between the past and the present. Pulsing. Probing. Rippling in the wildest of places, amidst the wild pennyroyal, and the roots of the corpse of the giant sycamore tree. Among the less trodden paths winding alongside tiny streams, long abandoned by man, and frequented only by squirrels and moles and foxes made timid by an unseen intruder.

Life continued as normal for the taxi drivers and the garden centre employees, for the plumbers and the help desk contractors working remotely from home. For others, the day settled on their shoulders like a coat the wrong size. It caught in their shoulders and pulled across the front, the fabric itching and stretching the wrong way.

Holly Corben peered through the mist blanketing the street beyond her house and felt nothing other than contempt for the people in the houses whose outlines pierced the fog. Pushing her thoughts further, her contempt extended past her road, creeping through gardens and laneways and shops closed for winter. Fools, all of them. Her thoughts lingered on Badger, the only boy of any value to her in the whole town. And he'd dropped her like a hot coal for Lillian Arlosh. For a farm girl.

Her contempt grew, only this time she stirred it with hate. With every brush of her long blonde hair, the hate festered, curling itself around every strand of hair, every fibre of her body. A hate that was as palpable as the scent of a fire out of control.

Badger would be at the Saturnalia party tonight, and she would show him exactly what he was missing and what he needed. And it was not some country bumpkin who had inherited a farm she had no right to. It was lost on Holly Corben that she had no legitimate claim to Ithaca Farm either, but her mind could not process that. Vines of hate twisted through her brain, pulsing with bitterness, leaving no room for natural thought.

Tonight she'd show Badger that he was hers. She would show his mother too. The mayor was on her side. No one liked the Arlosh girl and her ruinous plans for Ithaca Farm. Life had to stay the same, the same way it had for hundreds of years. Local boy marries local girl. She and Badger would be together. The cream always rises to the top.

And if it meant Lillian needed to be moved aside, physically, then that is what would happen. She held no qualms there. Enough strangers were in town that if Lillian disappeared, well… no one could place the blame on her doorstep. After all, she was Holly Corben, the beloved Miss Hexham for the past two years, and the runner-up in Miss Northumberland this year. The papers loved her. There had even been talk of her doing a weekly column in the Hexham Herald, although Mr Revell had gone quiet on that the last few times she had asked. A minor blip. She had her online followers. And her subscribers, who clamoured for more and more content. She was a woman of influence. An influencer. And if that meant taking some risks to maintain her position in life, she would. With a smile on her overfilled lips, she reminded herself that Lillian Arlosh was no one. Nothing. And no one missed a nobody.

ALL HANDS ON DECK

Competing scents filled every corner of the Bellingham Tea Rooms — hints of cinnamon and fir sap, burnt pine cones and glossy holly leaves, roasting coffee and baked cloves, furniture wax and fresh paint, freshly cut wood and the unmistakable tang of brass cleaner. Paige Spencer, the Bellingham Tea Rooms proprietor, added to the cacophony of smells with her perfume, the liniment on her sore ankle, and sweat. The sweat of a woman who had worked harder than God himself to make tonight a success, as well as the sweat of half a dozen workers still beavering away before the quests arrived.

One guest had arrived early, which Paige took as a personal affront. It just wasn't good manners, and the guest's poor timekeeping had left her flapping like a fish out of water. Paige had left the woman at a table in the corner, with the stranger promising that she'd stay out of the way, as long as Paige didn't mind her pulling out her crochet project. What could she say to that? There were too many other things to worry about than some middle-aged woman knitting quietly in the corner.

THE EARLY GUEST leaned back in her chair and took in the final preparations for the Saturnalia festival. The straining of time infiltrated every breath she took, and she had long ceased checking her watch. Time was an artificial construct which had no real bearing on her life, save for a number of dates peculiar to whichever century she found herself in. And Saturnalia had been good to her over the years, so what a treat it was to find it being observed once again, and so far away from Rome.

'Are you okay? Do you need anything?'

Loretta looked up from the half-finished crocheted doll laying dormant in her hands. 'Everything is perfect, thank you,' she said.

'Are you making a...?'

Loretta noticed Paige's question peter out. Bellingham's owner was being polite, and polite conversation was welcome at any time. Friendly conversation was a welcome change from being chased out of an inn, or hounded from a train for being a single woman, or turned away from a club for being the wrong gender.

'Toys, for the children's hospital,' Loretta offered. 'It's the one thing I'm good at.'

'Sorry for the mess.'

'Everything will be fabulous tonight. I have faith in you,' Loretta laughed.

'At least someone does. I'll leave you to your knitting then.'

Loretta watched Paige rush around, checking and double checking the workers, the napkins, the lights, the logs beside the firebox. She watched her twitch the curtains and rearrange the display of brochures four times, before her attention was caught by a shout elsewhere in the Bellingham. And Loretta smiled. None of these preparations mattered one iota. Time would take control regardless of the flower arrangements or the flavour of the meat.

Loretta retrieved her laptop from a battered leather satchel and powered it up. Two emails — one from her publisher and one from the Caernarfon Castle Trust. She stopped breathing. Even just reading the word Caernarfon brought tears to her eyes. Loretta trembled as she opened the Castle Trust email and she had to read it twice before she could breathe. The email asked if she would be interested in writing a knitting pattern book specific to the castle and its history. Not as odd a request as some might think, but the correspondence also asked if she could create a pattern for the hoard of Roman coins stolen from the museum during the investiture of Prince Wales at Caernarfon Castle in 1969.

1 July 1969 would forever be seared into her mind. It was the date her old life had ended and her new life had begun. A life she both adored and despised.

The email brought back memories of that fateful day and Loretta found herself wondering what her life would have been like if Dafydd hadn't given her a coin from the hoard. And if she'd found a way back home right at the beginning.

If things had been different, Loretta would be living in a small townhouse in Wales, within sight of Caernarfon Castle, surrounded by beautiful countryside and lifelong friends. On weekends, she and her husband Dafydd would go for long walks along the riverbank or explore nearby historical sites with their daughter. Loretta imagined reading in a snug little library corner; their bookcases filled with knick-knacks collected over years from family holidays. And every evening, they would enjoy a cup of tea on their plant-filled terrace overlooking the River Seiont.

But no, that was not her reality. Hers was one of constant movement and change, of hiding and running from things she could not control. She was a woman out of time. Someone who did not belong anywhere and lived nowhere.

Loretta shook her head to clear away the memories and to focus on the present. She moved onto the email from her publisher, scanning it quickly. They were pleased with the progress of her latest pattern book, and were asking her to make a decision on the Caernarfon Castle commission. A decision? She could barely focus on anything beyond the memories of her past, let alone decide about her future. Loretta always knew that at some point in time, she would have to face her past. She just hadn't pegged that time to be now, not when she was about to slip back almost two thousand years, back to her favourite time in history. Back to a time when the Colosseum stood proud, and Marcus Aurelius's shadow touched every aspect of Roman life.

One more trip back to Rome, and then she would decide. Her publishers were used to waiting. What was one more week?

'Hello?'

Loretta looked up from her laptop to see a head of bottle-blonde hair weaving its way through the workmen, causing a testosterone ripple through the room.

'*Ms* Spencer?' the young woman called, with a tart measure of emphasis on the prefix.

Paige Spencer appeared from the bowels of the Bellingham, with wood shavings in her hair and white paint on her chin.

'Yes?'

'Holly Corben.'

'Yes?'

It was satisfying watching the blonde woman bristle at the lack of recognition.

'Your little soiree tonight, my invitation hasn't yet arrived,' Holly said, her perfectly plucked eyebrows lifting at what Loretta assumed to be some expectation of a showdown.

'I issued an open invitation to everyone in town. You're more than welcome to celebrate Saturnalia with us. The more the merrier, especially young people such as yourself, and Lillian Arlosh and her friends,' Paige replied, her tone overly polite.

Loretta smiled into her laptop, closing it gently to enjoy the show.

Holly's painted lips thinned at the mention of Lillian's name, and Loretta watched with amusement as Holly's eyes darted around the room, clearly seeking any diversion from her mistake.

'Where are the decorations? The statue of Saturn?' Holly asked, her voice laced with disdain. 'I was told that tonight would be a true recreation of the Roman Saturnalia Festival, complete with all the bells and whistles.'

The Bellingham's proprietor bristled. 'I'm sorry if we're not up to your standards, *Ms* Corben. We've been working tirelessly to prepare the Bellingham for tonight. *We* are doing our bit for the economic recovery of Hexham.'

Loretta couldn't help but interrupt from her half hidden table in the corner.

'Where do you want these decorations?' she asked, lifting a randomly convenient box and walking towards the women.

'If you could start spreading them out over the tables, that would be amazing, thank you,' Paige replied, giving a small nod in Loretta's direction before turning on her heel and heading back to her painting.

Holly remained motionless, her face displaying sheer astonishment. Evidently, she wasn't familiar with being dismissed so readily. She shot Loretta a venomous look before hurrying out the door, her heels clicking on the cobbled street outside.

Loretta lowered the surprisingly heavy box, peering curiously inside. Beautifully hand carved wooden ornaments filled the box. Dozens of them. Ornaments that were more than a little familiar to her, but from a long, long time ago. A lifetime ago. There was no chance that they were carved by the same man. Was there?

Time holds many faces, and one of those belonged to Pramod Sharma. A man she had stumbled across in London in a time when she was passing herself off as a seamstress in one of the better parts of town. He had been delivering a package to her employer, staying for a moment to talk with the salon's owner. There had been a passing comment, nothing of vital importance, a simple observation about zipping up his jacket due to the inclement weather. A comment most would not have blinked at, but her hand had frozen mid-stitch. No one in the 1860s would ever have used that word, in that context.

The zip would not be used for clothing for another forty years.

She had tried persuading herself that she had misheard, but upon leaving for the night, and trudging home in the dark, wondering not for the first time why she did not just return to an easier time, Sharma had appeared at her side, offering to escort her home. It was then that she knew who he was. Or at least, what he was.

Time travellers are a rare breed, and it was always a surprise when she stumbled upon another like her. They all had different stories of how they began. Hers had started with the coin Dafydd had given her. Pramod had obtained his abilities through his father — Sanjay, a street urchin from Jaipur. He used his carved figurines as a way to facilitate his travel, and he had once carved a wooden figure for her as an aid for her travels. She had begged for a Welsh dragon to remind her of home, and to use as a key to return there one day. And that same figurine was nestled in a protective quilted bag in the bottom of her trusty leather satchel.

As she placed the wooden ornaments on the tables, she wondered if Pramod was still alive. She had not seen or heard from him in years, but then again, that was the way it was with time travellers. They could disappear for years, only to resurface when it suited them.

The candles flickered, casting a warm glow throughout the room, giving life to the wooden animals, who appeared ready to pounce upon the Saturnalia guests.

'Oh, they look perfect,' Paige said from the doorway, clapping her hands.

'The animals?'

'They look like they're about to leap off the tables and run around the room,' Paige said.

'They are exquisite,' Loretta agreed, running her finger across the back of a detailed elephant, its trunk raised triumphantly in the air. 'It's considered good luck for an elephant to have its trunk raised like this,' she added.

'We need all the luck we can get,' Paige said. 'Have you seen outside? This was not the weather they forecast.'

Loretta had been so consumed with her memories and the decorations that she had not noticed the deteriorating weather, which did not bode well for the Saturnalia celebrations.

'We'll make the most of it,' Loretta said with a determined smile, turning back to face Paige. 'You've got decorations and candles, and there are even a few Romans roaming around,' she said, pointing to some costumed guests tumbling from an idling taxi van outside. 'What more do you need?'

'A Christmas miracle?' Paige suggested with a grin.

THE GUEST LIST

Rhema Patel, the Hexham Herald's intern, adjusted the startlingly white toga around her body, shivering uncontrollably.

'Can you hurry up?' she said through chattering teeth. 'I'm freezing to death.'

'As undoubtedly many Romans did when they were here,' Jasper replied, readjusting his own toga.

'Yeah, but I'm not Roman am I? I'm from Bournemouth, and it never gets this cold there.'

'You know, everyone thinks you're mad for taking this job. It gets properly cold here.'

'Thanks, Sherlock. I'm beginning to realise that.'

Jasper laughed before locking the car and throwing a tatty blanket around the intern's shaking shoulders.

'How old is this blanket? It smells like death?'

'Steady on. It's not as old as the car.'

'And your car is at least twice my age,' Rhema replied, tugging the offending blanket tighter around her bare shoulders. 'I could be at home watching the Strictly Come Dancing Christmas Special.'

'And miss the fireworks?'

'There are fireworks?'

'A figure of speech. But knowing the guest list, let's just say that life is about to be as entertaining as dining with Caligula.'

. . .

PAIGE STOOD AT THE ENTRANCE, welcoming each guest and trying to hide her surprise at the number of people arriving despite the dreadful weather. The Bellingham was packed to the rafters, with people of all ages dressed in togas, or as Roman soldiers, with some even dressed as Julius Caesar himself.

'Most of them look a damn sight better dressed as centurions than they do at the bank,' she whispered to Loretta, who'd materialised at her side, smelling faintly of aniseed and cinnamon.

'Some of them though, you wouldn't want to come across in a dark laneway...' Loretta said, inclining her head towards a ruffian dressed in what appeared to be rags on top of rags on top of rags.

'That is a fine upstanding member of our local constabulary,' Paige said, laughing behind her hands as they both stared at Sergeant Bishop hovering awkwardly by himself, with a decidedly modern cellphone in one hand and a drink in the other.

'I'll ask him to give me a hand in the kitchen,' Loretta announced. 'He looks like someone who can only relax when they're busy,' she explained. 'And you have more guests arriving.'

RHEMA AND JASPER pushed through the Bellingham's doors into a room warmed by dozens of costumed bodies, and a roaring open fire.

'Is the mayor here yet?' Jasper asked.

Paige shook her head. 'Only her assistant. He's by the window with the others.'

Jasper looked towards the window, spotting Lillian Arlosh with Raymond Lamont — the mayor's assistant, and the Collings girl and the mayor's son, the one they called Badger. All four of them were dressed as though they'd walked in off the set of Russell Crowe's *Gladiator* movie.

'Should we join them?' Rhema asked.

Jasper nabbed two mugs of mulled wine from a passing waiter and shoved one into Rhema's hand.

'You go, I'll be there shortly,' he said. 'I've just seen someone I need to talk with.'

'I'll come with you.'

'No,' came his response, short and sharp. He missed the hurt look on Rhema's face as he strode towards the stranger, helping the caterers add the finishing touches to the feast fit for an emperor, complete with roasted meats, vegetables, figs and honey cake.

'You're Lillian's friend, right?'

The man laid down his wooden tray before turning towards him.

'Jasper Fletcher.'

'I know.' The man's voice held a hint of an accent that Jasper couldn't place. A tall man, with narrow shoulders and dark eyes, he seemed to stare right into his soul.

'And your name is?' Jasper asked, clearing his throat, the heat starting to affect him.

'Henry Neumegen,' the man replied, extending his slender hand.

Jasper took it, experiencing a sudden jolt of déjà vu which almost unbalanced him.

'So, what brings you to Hexham?' Jasper asked, trying to ignore the strange vibes emanating from the man.

'I am here for the Saturnalia celebrations, naturally,' said Neumegen. 'As are you, I suspect?'

'I'm covering the event for the Hexham Herald.'

'Yes, you're a journalist,' Neumegen said, his eyes burning into Jasper's. 'You must know many fascinating stories about this town.'

'I could tell you a few. But I'm actually more interested in hearing your story, and why you've been trying to source antique coins.'

Jasper watched Neumegen sip from a hand-carved cup, the cinnamon of the mulled wine sickly sweet in the turbo heated air.

Neumegen paused, his eyes scanning Jasper's face

before replying. 'You're quite perceptive, Mr Fletcher,' he said, a small smile tugging at the corners of his mouth. 'But I'm afraid my hobby isn't at all as exciting as you may think.'

Jasper raised an eyebrow. 'Is it related to the coins found at Ithaca Farm?'

'Ithaca Farm? If my memory serves me right, Ithaca is an island in Greece. Perhaps you confuse me with someone else? "Tell us of the peoples themselves, and of their cities —who were hostile, savage and uncivilised, and who, on the other hand, hospitable and humane." That is a short quote from Homer's *The Odyssey*. An unparalleled piece of work, which oddly enough, is about returning to Ithaca.'

Jasper took a sip from his own drink. The heat and the wine and the verbal gymnastics and the unnerving presence of Neumegen left him questioning his own train of thought. He shook his head, trying to get back on track.

'Interesting. And how did you come to find yourself in Hexham for the Saturnalia celebrations?' he asked, laboriously forming his words one by one.

He watched Neumegen's eyes flick towards the group at the window, where Lillian sat talking with Apple Collings, with Badger standing protectively behind them. 'Let's just say I have some connections,' Neumegen said cryptically. 'And I couldn't pass up the opportunity to witness such a unique and festive tradition. Not tonight.'

Jasper's heart skipped a beat as Neumegen's gaze settled on him. There was something in those dark eyes, something that made him feel like the man was reaching into his past, and shuffling through his secrets.

'Saturnalia is certainly a unique celebration,' Jasper said, his voice a little shaky. 'But it's also a time for secrets to be revealed.'

Neumegen chuckled, a deep, throaty sound that made Jasper's skin prickle. 'Secrets? What kind of secrets, Mr Fletcher?'

Jasper took another sip of wine to steady his nerves. 'Rumours are that the mayor herself has some skeletons in her closet, relating to the same Roman coins you're looking for,' he said, watching for any reaction from Neumegen.

'I do not know your mayor, save for what I have read in your newspaper. From all accounts, she seems to be operating just as a mayor should. Is that not correct? As for her penchant for old coins, that I cannot speak to.'

'Can't or won't?'

Neumegen's thin lips curled into a faint smile. 'Can't, Mr. Fletcher. I have not had the pleasure of discussing my hobby of collecting rare coins with the mayor, or with anyone else in this town for that matter, save for your very well-placed source at the pawn shop.'

Jasper prided himself on his ability to read people he interviewed. But with Neumegen, he was stumped. The man was enigmatic, with his words carefully chosen and his demeanour guarded.

'What is your connection to Hexham?' Jasper pressed, buoyed by the mulled wine and the absolute belief that the Roman coins were the key here.

Neumegen shrugged. 'I am a collector of antiquities, Mr Fletcher. I travel the world in search of rare coins, artefacts, and relics. Hexham happens to have a rich Roman history, and I thought I might find something of interest here.'

Before Jasper could respond, a commotion from the entrance drew their attention. The mayor had arrived, and all conversations ceased as she made her way through the parting crowd.

Jasper felt a hand on his shoulder, and turned to see Rhema, her toga already crooked, and a grin on her face. 'I think I just threw up a little in my mouth.'

Jasper returned his attention to Neumegen, but the man had moved away, and was now sitting with Lillian Arlosh and her eclectic group by the window.

'She's dressed as Boudica, the—' Rhema started.

'I know who Boudica is,' Jasper interrupted, 'and what she did.'

'Do you want me to take a photo for the paper?'

'You can try, but I don't know if Revell will let it run.

The most skin I've ever seen in the Hexham Herald was a photo of the crowning of Sally Spring as the Coal Queen of West Wylam Colliery Pit Yard in 1960, where she was showing her bare shoulders. You should read the letters to the editor about that photo. There was quite some uproar.'

'I think in this instance not taking a photo for the paper is a good idea. I know I wouldn't want to see that over my breakfast cereal,' Rhema laughed.

JANE BADRICK, adorned in a resplendent replica of Boudica's warrior regalia, strode through the Bellingham Tea Rooms as if she owned the establishment, and that the Saturnalia festival was her private function. The crimson and gold-trimmed cloak billowed behind her, revealing a barely there figure-hugging tunic, more Hollywood style than historically accurate. At least her leather sandals added an authentic touch, and as she moved, the clash of her ensemble against the traditional decor of the tea rooms created a visual spectacle — a blending of eras that made Jane the focal point of the festival.

Her air kisses sailed past Paige's ears, leaving behind them the strongest scent of alcohol and something else. Ambition. Unadulterated, pure ambition, almost Thatcher-like in its intensity.

A sight across the room caught her breath. What was her assistant doing sitting at a table with that Arlosh woman?

'Raymond, thank you,' she commanded, her voice cutting through the party atmosphere, and crashing across the tables heaving with fresh cut holly wreathes and candles and carved wooden ornaments, jostling for space amidst the wooden goblets and pewter trays of cheeses and olives and nuts and dried fruits.

Pausing to wait half a second for Raymond to join her, she made small talk with the people clamouring around her, camera phones clutched in their pathetic little hands. *Could their lives be so small that a photograph of their mayor became the highlight of their week?*

'What were you doing with that woman?' she asked, as Raymond appeared at her side, his shoulders hunched.

'Nothing. Talking,' he replied, his voice barely above a whisper.

'I saw you speaking with her. What about? Was it about the ruins on her farm?' Jane hissed, leaning in closer, the alcoholic fumes almost intoxicating in themselves.

Raymond shifted half a pace backwards. 'We were talking about the costumes people are wearing, just party talk, nothing else,' he offered.

'You're a smart young man, Raymond, and I've enjoyed having you work for me. Let's keep it that way.'

With that, she turned to greet the rest of the crowd, her attention already on the next photo opportunity, her smiles and well-rehearsed charm hiding her cold and calculating side.

THE MAYOR'S Boudica costume had indeed become the talk of the room, with none of it flattering. Some likened the heavy golden torque around her neck to a dog collar, whilst others made disparaging comments behind their hands about the shortness of her multicoloured tunic, and the authenticity of the cape around her shoulders, held together by an intricate brooch that shined brighter than the blazing firewood in the hearth. What they couldn't see was the disdain flooding through the mayor's body as she made her way around the room. By the end of the night, none of these people would matter anymore. Some would undoubtedly cease to exist, their entire existence snuffed out by the changes she was about to make to history. She amused herself wondering who would vanish and who would remain, and under what circumstances. Just as Jane was imagining her lawyer's fate in the new world, she noted John and Gail Revell's arrival.

The unbelievable nerve of the pair, she thought, her hand involuntarily flexing at her side, anticipating the touch of the replica Roman knife sheathed at her waist, hidden by the folds of her costume. No, not here, not in this time, she told herself. The Revell's would never amount to anything in her world, of that she was certain, and that was punishment enough for their debts to her.

As John and Gail pushed their way through the crowd towards her, Jane plastered a smile on her face, which didn't reach her ice-blue eyes. 'What a surprise to see you both here,' she said, her tone sugary sweet and dripping with acid, because, of course, the longtime editor of the Hexham Herald would have been invited to the official reopening of the historic Bellingham Tea Rooms.

To Jane's immense satisfaction, she saw John blanch at the candy-coated barb.

'What an adorable costume,' Gail countered, her own costume more demure than a vestal virgin. Gail wore a plain white linen dress, cinched at the waist by a length of hemp rope, and in her hand she carried a (now soggy) loaf of bread. Her husband cut an incongruous figure in his toga, held together with three safety pins at his shoulders, paired with sandals which were scuffed and worn at the heel, and a crown of fresh laurel leaves wilting on his head. Their costumes may not have been as flashy as Jane's Boudica homage, but they made them appear more successful than their financial situation suggested.

'Is Matthew joining us tonight?' John asked.

Jane couldn't have cared less if her husband had been served up on one of the many platters being carried around the party.

'He was called to an important meeting in Newcastle,' Jane offered, her reply sparse enough in its detail that she wasn't exactly lying. The last thing she wanted to talk about was the vicious argument that she had had with her useless husband before arriving at the Bellingham tonight, with Matthew threatening to leave her for good unless she sought help for her alcohol consumption. At least where she was going, there would be no one trying to control her, or her appetites.

'Mulled wine, Mayor?'

Jane switched her gaze from the tray of drinks to the man proffering them to her. Jasper Fletcher. He had always been a thorn in her side, with his newspaper articles often critical of her policies and actions, although she'd had Revell quash any that she considered too damaging, or too near the truth.

'Jasper, look at you. They let you come to the grownup's party.'

Jasper's smile in return was all teeth, and Jane felt a frisson of fear at this unexpected response to her underhanded insult.

'So, what do you think of my costume?' she asked, full of the confidence of someone who knew they'd receive only flattery and nothing less.

'It takes a lot of audacity to show up dressed as Boudica, given your track record with leading this town,' Jasper replied, his eyes glinting.

Jane laughed. 'Oh, you have always been such a stick in the mud, Jasper. This is all just a bit of fun.' Jane sipped her drink, confused at the lack of respect she was being shown. Had she misjudged her outfit selection? No, ignore the creep, she instructed herself. She shouldn't be wasting her energy on him or any of the other losers in town. Tonight was about later, about the past. And soon Darby would appear, coins in hand, and her time engaging with imbeciles like Jasper Fletcher would be over.

Jane continued to smile, her impatience growing with every second that passed.

'Are you waiting for someone?' Jasper asked, his head swivelling towards the Bellingham's ivy draped entrance.

'My husband,' she shot back, annoyed that he was still conversing with her. 'Excuse me, there are other people who need my time,' she said, her anxiety rising. Where the hell was Darby with her coins and her car?

OUTSIDE THE BELLINGHAM, the unexpected snowflakes continued tumbling to the ground, their dangerous beauty illuminated by the orange streetlights. Biting wind whipped through the streets, carrying with it a chill that made any late revellers heading towards the

Bellingham shudder in their finery. A treacherous blanket of snow now covered the ground, concealing a slick of ice underneath. Anyone foolish enough to venture outside now wouldn't last long. Even from inside the warmth of the Bellingham, the guests began to comment on the flickers of ice licking at their ankles and teasing the back of their necks.

'They've just issued a weather alert,' Apple said, pushing her phone in front of Lillian's face.

'It doesn't matter,' Lillian replied. 'I doubt that it's snowing like this two-thousand years ago.'

'One-thousand, eight-hundred and thirty years ago,' Apple corrected. When Lillian didn't reply, Apple tucked her phone back into the concealed pocket of her tunic.

'It's almost time,' Neumegen said, appearing at the table as silently as was his way.

He must have secured the coins he needed since being here, Apple thought. But from whom? She hadn't seen him talk with anyone other than the reporter from the paper, and she doubted he had a stash of Roman coins in his faux leather wallet.

Lillian drained her mulled wine, and Apple followed her lead. She needed all the liquid courage she could get if she was going to go through with her plan.

'What do we do?' Apple asked, as if they hadn't already rehearsed the plan a hundred times already.

'Don't do it,' Neumegen said quietly, leaning towards her, an inscrutable look on his narrow face.

He couldn't know her plan, Apple thought, dismissing his comment. 'It's only my second cup,' she replied, reaching for another mulled wine. A misdirect Neumegen seemed satisfied with, as he returned his attention to Lillian. Everyone underestimated her all the time.

A sense of recklessness washed over her, a sensation she was not familiar with, but one which made her feel alive for the first time. Whatever happened next, she was ready for the adventure.

'We wait for midnight,' Neumegen said, 'and as we exchange gifts, Apple will light the candle,' he said, pointing to the unlit beeswax candle in the centre of the table. 'Then I will hand Lillian the coin we need to pass through the veil.' Here he patted the tiny breast pocket of his waistcoat.

Apple nodded, the excitement in her chest growing. They were going to do this. They were going to send Lillian and Neumegen back in time to stop the slaughter of the Roman army. And her. She was going to go back, too.

As THE CLOCK ticked closer to midnight, the snowfall outside grew heavier, and the guests inside the Bellingham grew more boisterous, most of them happily consigned to an unexpected sleepover courtesy of the weather. But not all of the guests.

Jane Badrick paced the Bellingham's vestibule, her long cloak billowing behind her.

'Ring Darby to find out how far away he is,' she ordered, her own cellphone showing no service.

'My phone isn't connecting,' Raymond replied.

'Someone's phone must have service. Do what you have to, to get hold of Darby so I can leave this godforsaken building. We should have torn it down years ago,' Jane whined.

'People are looking,' Raymond counselled.

'Do you think I care about them?' Jane said, her volume rising.

Raymond started to reply, when the Bellingham's solid wooden door opened, and Darby stepped in through a flurry of snow.

'Finally, where have you been?' she asked, gripping his hand, her manicured nails digging into his skin.

'Sorry,' Darby said, his voice muffled with a snow encrusted scarf. 'The roads are dire.'

'You could have called,' Jane replied, her voice laced with irritation.

'How?' Darby shook the snow from his coat, a cloud of white dusting the floorboards. 'The phone lines are down, and half the roads are closed. It's total chaos out there, and it's only a matter of time before the power goes out too.'

'You were meant to have been here earlier, to take me to my car, like we'd arranged.'

The Hexham Abbey bells rang out, and the room fell silent as the Westminster chimes finished and the bells tolled the hour.

One, two, three…

'The bells never ring this late at night,' Jane said. 'Nine o'clock is the latest they're allowed to toll. Who authorised this?'

Four, five, six…

The overhead lights flared for a moment before winking out. The Bellingham's door opened, with the rush of cold air snuffing out the candles and plunging the room into a lingering darkness. The fireplace crackled as if in defiance of the power outage, its warm glow offering itself up as the only source of light and comfort.

Seven, eight, nine…

'Now, Lillian,' Neumegen said, 'and help me find my friend.'

Apple's heart raced and her palms grew moist as she realised the moment had arrived. She lit the candle on the table as they had rehearsed, and Neumegen reached into his pocket to retrieve the ancient coin.

Ignoring the disturbance, Neumegen handed Lillian the coin, their hands touching for an instant.

As Lillian's hand closed around a tiny wooden tiger waiting on the table, Apple mimicked Lillian's every movement, choosing an exquisitely carved eagle on the cusp of flight.

Ten, eleven, twelve…

Apple entwined her free hand in the folds of Lillian's cloak and with her breath in her throat, she pushed Neumegen out of the way.

BIRDS OF A FEATHER

As the bell's last toll echoed through the room, Neumegen picked himself up off the floor, wincing at the unexpected pain in his hip.

'It worked?' Badger asked, his face an absolute picture of surprise. 'Where's Lillian? Hang on, what are you still doing here?'

Neumegen did not respond, searching instead for another face in the darkened room — Apple.

'She's gone.'

'Lillian, yeah, I can see that,' Badger said. 'But why are you still here? What happened?'

'Your mother is missing as well.'

'What?' Badger stood up, his sudden movement extinguishing the last remaining candle. 'How?'

'The same way we did it. Saturnalia is the most powerful time of the year. Tonight had every element she needed.'

'But what if...'

Neumegen knew what the boy was asking. Was it possible that Apple and Lillian would appear at the same time and place as Jane Badrick? He'd never travelled back in time with another person, so he couldn't answer Badger's unspoken question, but it was a terrifying proposition.

'I don't know.'

'Why didn't you go back? You're the experienced time traveller. Why leave it to Lillian to sort out? We should have gone back with her. What were you thinking, letting her go by herself, with no protection—'

'She has Apple.'

'What?' Badger's head swivelled around the room, realisation dawning. 'Where's Apple?'

'With Lillian.'

Badger's eyes widened. 'You sent her back with Lillian, didn't you? You and her arranged everything without letting us in on your plan.'

'That is incorrect.'

Badger shook his head. 'This is insane. We could have all gone back, two men with two women, the perfect cover story.' Badger sat down in the chair, his head in his hands. 'I can't believe this is happening.'

Neumegen placed his slender hand on Badger's shoulder. 'They knew the risks going into this, and the rewards. We must trust that Lillian and Apple know what they're doing.'

'Apple has never even left Hexham,' Badger said. 'And you think she's competent enough to stop the slaughter of the Roman army in Britain? You're mad.'

'Well, we're about to find out.'

PART TWO

NORTH BY NORTHWEST

Pramod blew on his fingers, hoping that his warm breath would keep the threat of frostbite at bay. It was not that cold; he told himself, not yet. That cold would come next month. Then he would worry.

The escape from the fighting at Ithaca Fort to somewhere safe was not over, but at least he had Metella with him. Travelling as a group was proving to be a challenge, with the villagers they encountered wary of the four of them, especially the giant visage of Silas towing the cart holding Pramod. No one wanted an extra mouth to feed this winter, let alone four of them. Every minute required constant vigilance, least they be robbed of their cart, the women raped, and Pramod left for dead.

Pramod blamed himself for Metella's deep melancholy. Nothing could budge her from the deep well she had retreated to. He should have brought her back to the future with him when he'd had the chance, before he had fallen ill. But there was no use thinking like that when what he needed to do was to concentrate on getting better, before returning to the future with Metella. Silas could look after Carmella.

From his position in the cart, Pramod pondered the giant's back. Metella had told him little of Silas, of where he had come from, or what his connection was. But he had sensed that there was a lot more to tell. For some unknown reason she had not shared that information with him.

'How much longer?' Carmella asked from beside the cart.

They had been walking the best part of four hours, utilising what little daylight this time of year gave them.

'We keep going,' Silas said, barely breaking his stride.

Metella walked with her hand on the cart's side, her cloak clasped tight around her throat. He had once given her a beautiful brooch in the shape of a coiled serpent, with a ruby for an eye. He had not seen it since. Perhaps she had sold it? One day he would ask.

There had been little conversation, with the air too cold for speech, sapping whatever energy they had left from their meagre supplies. The last villagers they'd encountered had given them a dry loaf of bread, which was all they could spare. A common enough occurrence with the constant unrest in the region.

'Wait,' Silas commanded.

Pramod tried lifting himself to see what the delay was.

'Stay down.'

He did not need to be told twice, especially as Metella's hand snaked over the side of the cart, motioning him to stay down.

Pramod groaned as Silas dropped the cart. The great oaf usually showed more care.

A stranger's face appeared above him, angry eyebrows framing dark eyes filled with suspicion.

'Get up,' the stranger commanded.

'He can't, he's sick,' Silas grunted.

Pramod tried not to move. There were other reasons he wanted to stay in the cart. His lack of physical ability was the least of them.

The face disappeared, and Pramod listened for what was happening now. The stranger was not a Roman, which meant that they were a villager, or, and this was more concerning, a scout from one of the warring local tribes.

'Don't touch her.'

Metella's voice, clearly referring to Carmella.

Pramod started to rise, but a warning grunt from Silas stopped him.

'Where do you come from?' the stranger asked.

'Ithaca,' Silas replied.

'From the fort?' the stranger probed.

Pramod could see the back of the man's head now. Long grey hair, matted and woven with silver beads.

'The village. We run, like the others,' Silas elaborated.

A good ploy, Pramod thought, shifting uncomfortably in the cart's tray.

'What else is in the cart?'

Here it came. If the man was on his own, Silas would deal with him. If he was not, then what little they had left would be taken. And then their lives, if they were lucky.

'Just the old man and our blankets for sleeping.'

That was not all they had. Pramod was stretched out on the bags of Metella's coins, hidden away in case of events such as these. They had taken great pains to disguise the bags as bedding for Pramod, but the risk was there, every day and every night, that someone would discover the coins sewn between the blankets that cushioned Pramod's body in the cart.

'Show me.'

Silas lumbered to the rear of the cart. Metella's knuckles were white on the cart's wooden edge. Pramod could not see Carmella, but he knew she would not be far from Metella if she had a choice.

The white-robed man had joined Silas. 'What's in that bag? Open it.'

Silas nodded, and passed them a small hessian bag. They had rehearsed this a hundred times. The bag contained nothing more than wooden drinking vessels, a ladle, and four plates. But oddly it also held a crudely carved figure — a depiction of a god of some importance to Silas. The man prayed to the figurine every night, without fail. He normally kept the statue tucked somewhere in the folds of his clothes, but maybe the god had warned Silas, and he must have slung the wooden carving in the bag after their evening meal.

The stranger examined the figurine with a reverence Pramod associated with a lover. The druid returned it to Silas with a nod, before calling to his companion in a language unfamiliar to Pramod.

Silence fell as the stranger's footsteps faded away. The colour returned to Metella's knuckles, and he heard Carmella sigh dramatically before she flung herself onto the back of the cart.

'I thought that was it,' she announced.

'Hush,' Silas replied. 'They're still close by. We carry on.'

Carmella almost looked like she was about to complain, but hauled herself off the cart, before suddenly whispering. 'He's coming back.' She clambered into the cart, pulling her skinny knees up to her nonexistent chest.

'I have spoken to the druid, and he is pleased you are also a worshiper. But that man,' and he pointed to Pramod. 'He must stay here. The druid says that he is not...' The bearded stranger seemed to struggle for the right words. 'He is not of this place. He doesn't belong here.'

Silas nodded, and Carmella shrank back against Pramod, her eyes wide, her teeth chattering.

'You can't—' Pramod started, his voice no more than the flutter of a raven's wings.

'I understand,' Silas replied.

The stranger nodded, and Pramod watched him return to the side of the skeletal druid, who was now surrounded by a group of riders barely visible on the brow of the hill. The druid cast a last glance behind him before disappearing into the hillside.

Pramod did not dare ask what Silas had planned. Given his health, he had no more control over the decision making than a moth flying towards a flame. It was Silas and Metella, usually in concert with each other, who would dictate their... no, his, future.

OVER A SUBDUED MEAL of dry bread, unripe apples and roasted chestnuts, the group huddled around the small fire Silas had begrudgingly allowed. Metella massaged Pramod's hands as he practiced flexing each of his fingers, revelling in the incremental improvements only he could see.

'What did they want?' Pramod asked, his voice competing with the wind rushing through the bare branches above them.

'Information,' Silas replied, using a smooth rock to crack the hard chestnuts open. A constant staccato in the dark — *tap, crack, tap, crack.*

'On what?'

'The strength of the Romans at Ithaca.'

Pramod considered Silas's answer. Why would a local tribe be worried about the size of a minor Roman outpost?

'They travel with a druid,' Silas said, his words unusually emotional.

'A druid? But they were all...' Pramod stopped. The Roman emperors Tiberius and Claudius had suppressed the druid orders, meaning that the druids had all but disappeared by the second century. But if time travellers could exist, then so could druids. And who's to say that the history books were correct?

'How far from the coast are we?' Metella asked.

They were going north, were they not?

'We'll be there late tomorrow, and I'll find us passage to Gaul.'

Gaul?

'We can't go to Gaul,' Pramod said.

'We go to Gaul, then to Rome. You stay.'

Metella's head hung on her chest. Was this why Metella had been so sullen? She knew that they weren't travelling north as planned.

'No,' Pramod said. In order to travel home to his time, he had to stay near to his point of entry. That was Time Travel 101. Going north was enough of a stretch. But to cross to a different land mass was impossible.

'We go,' Silas replied, pushing out his solid chin. Petulance writ all over his face.

'Metella, you swore you would never return to Rome.' Pramod was powerless. And any explanation he gave to stop their travel to Rome would not be believed. It couldn't be believed.

'We aren't safe here. You told me that,' Metella said, finally meeting his pleading eyes. 'I was always going to face the consequences of my choices at some stage.'

'We can hide here until I'm stronger. And then you can come home with me. The way you should have years ago. I should never have left you.'

'She comes with me,' Silas said.

'She,' Pramod said, 'can make up her own mind. Metella?'

'What do we do?' Metella asked Silas, ignoring Pramod.

'I think now,' Silas said.

Pramod fingered the leather pouch hanging around his neck. He could try to return now to Hexham and his library, taking Metella with him, although he suspected he was not yet strong enough to survive the trip back. Death might take him, but Metella would be safe. By his calculations, being this close to Saturnalia might be enough to let them both slip through the veil of time together. Damn it all to hell. If only he were stronger.

'We stop here tonight and then we go on without you. The druid has only said what I already knew,' Silas shrugged, as if his words were law.

Pramod saw tears welling in Metella's eyes. How could she allow this, after everything they had been through? He only had this night to persuade her to... To what? To stay with him? Oppose Silas's decision? The man was a servant, a slave, what right did he have to demand anything of Metella? Regardless of the final path, Pramod knew he would probably die, so he really had nothing to lose.

A MOTHER'S LOVE

Metella shivered under the woollen cape Silas had draped around her shoulders. The sounds of Carmella's tears were a thousand nettle barbs piercing her skin as guilt enveloped her like a fog. She had tried placating the girl, but Carmella had pushed her away with an unearthly force, snapping at her with a throaty snarl until Metella had retreated to the furthermost reaches of the fire Silas. Silas now knelt beside Carmella, speaking in a low voice, holding her hands with his meaty paws, his knuckles still stained with the blood of their attackers.

Metella once again cursed their predicament. Some days she missed having someone to hold her hand, to reassure her that everything would be okay. Today was one of those days. Her thoughts drifted to her son, and grief threatened to overwhelm her as she thought of what might be happening to him at Ithaca Fort. She looked towards the cart where Pramod lay sleeping. At least they had let him be. Contenting themselves with assaulting Carmella before Silas had come to her aid, the blackness of the night disguising their attackers. Whatever, or whoever, had lured Carmella away from the cart could still be out there, biding their time, waiting for another opportunity to attack. It was sheer luck Silas had woken to Carmella's cries. He'd always had ears like a wolf, capable of hearing the quietest of whispers. His trade was in whispers, Metella realised.

She shook herself from her thoughts. She had to be strong for all of them. 'Carmella,' she called softly, 'crying does us no favours. At some point Silas will have to sleep, and we will be as helpless as newborn babes if their friends return to avenge them,' she said, gesturing to the two men Silas had ripped apart with his bare hands.

Carmella looked up at Metella, tears streaming down her face. 'We have no way of defending ourselves. The old man slows us down.'

'She speaks the truth. I told you, we must leave him. It's as the druid warned,' Silas said, his voice gruff but calm. An echo of Metella's father, a man she had not seen for longer than she cared to remember.

Metella nudged a crude sword from the stiffening hand of one of their attackers. 'Now we are armed, and we will not leave him.'

Silas raised a brow at her, his expression unreadable. 'And what good will that do us, woman?'

'It will give us a chance,' Metella said fiercely. 'I have not come this far to give up without a fight.'

Silas shook his head. 'He is dead weight. We should leave him here if we are to survive.'

Metella glared at Silas. 'He is a man, not an amphora of spoiled wine. He saved our lives back at the fort, remember?'

Silas snorted. 'We don't have the luxury of sentimentality. Survival is all that matters, and returning you to Rome.'

Metella stilled. Rome. She had left that life behind for a reason.

'I won't return to Rome without him,' she said, her voice echoing with conviction.

She watched his eyes narrow.

'If we bring him, you will return willingly? To your father's house?'

Metella nodded, her heart in her throat as the darkness of the night pressed closer.

'Fine. We take him with us, but we leave now, before their friends come looking for them,' he said, pointing to the bodies of the vagabonds who had chanced their luck, and had lost.

The trio quickly packed their meagre belongings into the cart, the tension palpable. Silas stripped the dead of their water skins and what little valuables they carried. No one wasted any breath on conversation. There was nothing left to say.

STANDING on a shoreline littered with the detritus of a battle won and lost by Metella knew who not, she waited for Silas to finish his conversation with the master of the ship. Metella's stomach churned. Not with the thought of the crossing, but with what awaited her on the other side.

Silas walked towards her, his face unreadable as usual. 'It's done,' he said. 'We have safe passage to Gaul.'

She turned to look at Pramod, leaning against a nearby rock, gazing at the expanse of ocean in the distance.

'Rome?' he whispered.

'Yes.'

Metella watched him struggle with the knowledge. He did not know the danger she would face upon her return. It had been well and good to bargain with Silas, but she could no more guarantee Pramod's safety in Rome than she could change the location of the rising sun.

'No, we can't go,' he said, reaching for her hand.

'It's the only way,' she replied.

THEY HAD SOLD the cart at the port of Arbeia, leaving them no means to transport Pramod. So as a temporary solution, Silas had strapped Pramod to a makeshift litter, the straps stiff and unforgiving, designed for transporting goods, not people, but it was better than nothing. As Silas dragged the contraption onto the ship, Metella saw him slip the master something extra to cover the addition of the disabled man. It was considered bad luck to carry someone like Pramod, a man frozen in his body. The gods had cursed him, and none of the crew wanted him on board. Metella feigned ignorance of the uneasy looks from the crew and could only pray that none of them took it upon themselves to divest the boat of the bad omen.

The torturous passage along the coast to Portus Rutupiae was worse than anything Metella could have imagined. Her original journey to Britannia, across the Oceanus Britannicus, had been in the summer, where the ship has been protected by the gods and the passage was only a summer day's outing. But this winter voyage was worse than being hunted by the barbarians.

Carmella spent the entire voyage hanging her head over the side. So unappealing was the scent clinging to her body that even the sailors kept their distance, the only silver lining to their journey, Metella mused.

As they disembarked at Portus Rutupiae, the air was thick with the stench of rotting fish and seaweed. The odour followed them as they passed numerous fishmongers, their wares laid out on rough hewn trestles. The shouts of the fishermen and the constant background noise of shouting, wailing, arguing, and bargaining filled the air. It was a far cry from the peacefulness of the town by Ithaca Fort, a town surrounded by rolling meadows and heather soaked hills.

Their goal now was to find some suitable accommodation until they could secure passage on a ship to Gaul and from there to Rome — a perilous journey, but one even more dangerous in the winter.

Silas led them through the bustling town, his massive form parting crowds like the prow of a ship as he dragged the litter behind him. Metella and Carmella followed, Metella's hand resting on the hilt of the sword she had taken from the dead man back at the campsite.

The town's inhabitants barely gave them a second glance — their group looked like everyone else in the Roman empire, a mixture of ethnicities and backgrounds, all seeking their fortunes in a harsh and uncompromising world. As they navigated the narrow streets, the scent of fish and salt clung to every stone block and hammered board. Metella could even taste the iron tang of blood in her mouth.

They found themselves outside a small inn on the outskirts of the port. An inn Silas seemed overly familiar with. The stench was less oppressive here, but the accommodation was barely passable — the rooms small and dingy, with filthy straw pallets for beds. It was nothing like the grand villas that Metella had grown accustomed to in Rome, and it bore none of the luxurious trappings she had surrounded herself with in her brothel in Ithaca, but it would have to do.

She had no illusions about their situation. They had nowhere to go but forward. Carmella had collapsed onto the nearest pallet and was already weeping. Silas had disappeared after depositing them in their room, ostensibly to enquire about passage across the channel, but undoubtedly he had other orders he was attending to. Orders from her father.

Ignoring the crying girl, Metella sat on the edge of her own pallet, and stared at the walls. The journey from here to Rome was long, and anything could happen between now and then, so Metella could only focus on the present. She refused to allow herself any thoughts of Julius, or her father's reaction to her return.

'Metella?' Pramod called from the litter. 'We cannot go to Rome,' he said. 'I have to stay here. *We* have to stay here.'

'I have no choice. We will make it work.'

Pramod shook his head, his movements getting stronger with each passing day. 'Rome is dangerous for you. Me, I don't matter, but you... You are everything.'

Metella covered her face with her hands, feeling Pramod's unhappy eyes upon her.

'I wish I could protect you,' he said, his voice straining with the effort of forming the words.

'I know,' Metella said again, her voice barely above a whisper. 'But you're sick, Pramod. You must focus on healing.'

'And I will heal, at home, with you. Please, we must leave while your servant is away,' he said, panic projecting his words.

'Shh,' Metella cautioned. 'Silas will return at any moment. And he's not my servant, not really. He is my father's man.'

'I don't understand?'

'My father. It's never been discussed, but my father sent him to bring me home. But Silas and I reached an understanding. He will also suffer the consequences of his decisions upon our return. This is not an easy journey for him either.'

The pair lapsed into silence as they each considered their position. The secret about Silas had been weighing on her, and she already felt lighter after telling Pramod a version of the truth. She still held one secret, the one about Julius. Would she ever tell him? Could she? Or were the risks too dangerous for them all for Pramod to know that he had fathered a child with her?

'Metella?'

'We have to go to Rome. I'm sorry.'

A PILGRIM'S JOURNEY

Pramod watched Carmella heaving over the side of the boat. There was no delicacy in the action. Any self respect she may have had, had disappeared within an hour of their departure, and he wondered whether it was the churning waves or her fear of the monsters under the waves which was causing her distress. Carmella had shared her fears about the threat of being eaten by sea monsters as Silas escorted them to the vessel he had secured for their crossing to Gaul.

'I am not going on that,' Carmella has sworn, backing away.

'We are, and you will,' Metella had answered, pushing the girl towards the boat.

From his position strapped to the wooden stretcher, Sharma had sympathised with the girl. A channel crossing was no fun even in the twenty-first century, let alone in the second. At least modern ferries had heated cabins, bar service and, usually, functioning toilets. This boat featured none of them. It did, however, have of a crew of suspicious looking sailors, who more resembled modern day people smugglers than fine upstanding citizens of Rome. Because of course they were not. They were dirty little Britons, operating under Rome's sturdy yoke.

'Sit with me,' he'd said to Carmella, patting the space

on the stretcher beside him, hoping to provide some comfort.

Carmella hesitated for less than a second before firing herself onto the stretcher next to him, grabbing onto his arm as the boat rocked violently.

'Have you ever seen a water monster?' Carmella asked, her voice barely loud enough to be heard above the waves.

'There's no such thing,' he replied automatically, forgetting that the girl had less education than a pack horse. The daughter of a whore, Carmella had been trained how to clean house and serve food. Metella had done her best with the girls under her roof, but educating them about the world had not been a priority.

'There is. I heard the sailors talking about them as we boarded. They say it has the head of a dog and the body of a giant fish.'

Pramod sighed. 'They're just stories, Carmella. Sailors like to tell tall tales, especially to scare pretty young women like you.'

Carmella shuddered. 'I don't like it here. I want to go back.'

'Back to the fort?'

'To my home. My friends.'

Pramod smiled. Isn't that what everyone wanted? Friends to rely on, who would always be there for you? Friends like Alfred Neumegen. He thought back to when he'd first met the pawnbroker. It seemed like a lifetime ago now, several lifetimes.

It had been at the Great Exhibition in London in 1851. He had just completed his apprenticeship as a silversmith and was eager to explore the wonders of the world, including the world he had left behind in Jaipur, India. He was captivated by the strange contraptions that filled every corner of the hall, but what he really wanted were stories of adventures in far-off lands. And Neumegen provided those tales.

How he stumbled across Neumegen amidst six-million other visitors to the exhibition still made his chest compress.

Tall and gaunt, with fathomless dark eyes, Neumegen's wardrobe only added to his mysteriousness — an odd combination of Victorian garb mixed with something which did not quite gel. It was as though he had been dressed by a costumer from the twenty-first century who assumed that they knew what a Victorian gentleman wore, and had done their best to make modern garb fit the bill. Unbeknownst to Pramod at that stage, was that Neumegen was so very new to time travel that he was close to death, and barely one step ahead of the law at the time.

Neumegen had been desperate for money to buy food, so much so that he was willing to steal from the other exhibition-goers. Having been in that position in his younger years, Pramod recognised the desperation in the other mans actions.

He had been paces away from Neumegen when the man keeled over, fainting in the summer's heat.

Sharma had been quick to act, catching the man before he hit the ground. He had dragged Neumegen to the side of the path, waiting with him until he came around. The first words from the stranger's mouth were, "No need to call an ambulance. I'm okay." To any Victorian passerby, his words would been nothing more than a jumbled word soup. To Pramod, they were a clear sign that the man was from another time. The word ambulance would not enter the English language until the Crimean War, in just a few short years' time. And "okay" wasn't in general usage yet outside of the city of Boston.

The hapless time traveller was in no fit state to be left on his own. Who knew what madness might ensue if he inadvertently broke all the rules? So Pramod had taken him under his wing. And they had become the best of friends. Two men with an ability they could share with no one other than each other.

The boat lurched to one side and Carmella let out a piercing scream, clinging painfully to Pramod's arm. As the sailors cursed, and struggled to steady the vessel, Pramod could not help but wonder what fate had in store for him now. He'd purposely steered clear of ancient Rome, choosing places in time which were less likely to kill him, or enslave him. Rome had a propensity to do both. But Metella had insisted on going to Rome, following a summons he knew nothing of, and now they would all pay the price.

Pramod looked towards the figure of Metella, leaning on the railings and staring into the distance, her cloak wrapped tightly around her figure, secured at the neck by a cockerel brooch Carmella had miraculously produced before they had left Britannia. The seller promising that the brooch would provide protection for their crossing. Whether it would be of any use once they arrived remained to be seen.

After an excruciating eight hours of being tossed about like puppets on a string, the ship docked at the port of Gesoriacum, leaving them at the mercy of Silas's arrangements. For things had been put in motion well ahead of their arrival and they were met by a group of armed men, men of a similar age and bearing to that of Silas. Ex army? Pramod thought so. Silas may have been playing the part of a subservient man servant whilst living under the shadows of Ithaca Fort, but he was far from being that man now.

'Come, we will go with these men. We will stay here one night, then we continue to Rome,' Silas said.

With Silas leading the way, two of his men carried Pramod's stretcher, with the other two following closely behind the women. Carmella was never further than a foot away from Metella, her head swinging like a horse's tail, taking in the bustling streets of Gesoriacum. With her eyes already wider than the Oceanus Britannicus, the sight of the towering lighthouse Tour d'Ordre had made Carmella gasp, and with good reason. Made up of twelve octagonal floors arranged in steps, the lighthouse bore more than a passing resemblance to a giant centipede stood on its head. Metella seemed not to care for the impressive view, spending her time scanning the crowds. Pramod wondered if she was looking for danger, or for a chance to avoid returning to her father's home?

With a journey of eight-hundred-miles ahead of them, Pramod had more than enough time to discover why Metella feared returning to her father. And why she had not turned Silas away when he'd first appeared in Britannia? And more to the point, why she had left him all those years ago. Wasted years. Years he could never get back. Not when he was so weak. And not without the help of Neumegen.

Even if walking twelve hours a day was possible, it would still take them nearly a month to reach Rome. But then factor in the weather, detours, illness or injury, bandits, rest, food, their journey seemed longer than a lifetime, and nigh on impossible.

'Metella,' he started saying, as the dawn broke over their first morning in Gaul.

'Not now,' she had replied. 'Later.'

So he had left it that day. And the next, and the one that followed. Metella seemed never to be alone. She either had Carmella whimpering by her side, or Silas sitting next to her. His large bulk blocking the wind, or any potential interaction with the silent warriors accompanying them. Of their companions, Sharma had tried engaging them in conversation, but they seemed not to understand his slurred speech. They would only nod and answer in the shortest way possible. He got no further information about them or what to expect upon their arrival in Rome.

The landscape changed rapidly as they made their way towards Rome, with the mild coastal weather giving way to driving rain and a wind chill colder than a midwinter night. Silas had performed feats of magic on their journey, buying heavier cloaks, blankets, even mittens for the three of them, for which Sharma was eternally grateful for. It would have been a terrible irony to regain the use of his hands, only to lose his fingers to frostbite. Accommodation was a different story. The four of them could have talked their way into any establishment, but together with the four horsemen of the apocalypse, no one wanted them under their roof. There was enough lawlessness without inviting it to share your hearth.

It was on the seventh day of their journey that Sharma sensed a new tension between Metella and Silas. After stopping for the night in a valley devoid of any buildings of any sort, they had made camp and were settled by a reasonable-sized fire when Metella snapped at Silas.

'Know your place,' she had said.

And Silas had slapped her.

Metella had leapt to her feet, her face red. She pointed a finger at Silas.

'Hades, take you from my sight,' she screamed. 'From my life. I never want to see you again. This was a mistake.'

It was only then that Metella seemed to see him, as if for the first time since they had boarded the ship bound for Gaul.

'What have I done?' she whispered, staring at Pramod.

'I can fix it,' he said. 'I promise.' And Sharma was left pondering what had just happened between Metella and Silas, and between Metella and himself.

THE PRODIGAL DAUGHTER RETURNS

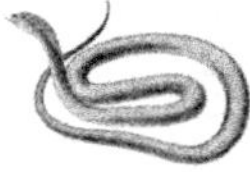

Metella marched silently behind the cart carrying Sharma and Carmella, who had fallen earlier in the week, leaving her slender ankle twisted beyond what was normal.

Together, the motley crew trudged the last few miles along the grand stone-laid Via Aurelia leading into Rome, and for her, leading towards perpetual servitude.

Silas lead the way, speaking only with the remaining former soldiers who had accompanied them for the entire journey. Metella had not uttered one word to him since her outburst nearly seven weeks ago. And she had ordered Carmella to do the same. At least the weeks had been kind to Sharma and his recovery. He would never walk without aid again, but his strength was returning. At least the cold of the journey had not plucked him from this world, nor had their encounters with bandits on their treacherous journey through the Alps. Silas and his men had efficiently dealt with the bandits, stripping their lifeless bodies of anything useful before tossing them down the precipitous cliff face as if they were nothing more than rotting carcasses.

Silas had used an official pass provided by her father, for them to stay at a variety of salubrious inns along the long route to Rome. Without the pass, they would have been forced to sleep in accommodation that she wouldn't have wished upon her worst enemies. It was the only time she embraced her father's influence, influence which hung above her like the sword of Damocles.

On one leg of the journey, across rocks which were nothing more than crystalline sheets of ice, they lost one of Silas's soldiers. In a moment of inattention the idiot slipped off the path and tumbled hundreds of feet to his death. His shrieks still rang in her ears when she closed her eyes, but she felt no emotion about his departure from her life. It meant one less mouth to feed and one less man to worry about when she and Carmella huddled together for warmth at night. Not that Silas would have allowed one of his men to touch her. He valued his own life too much for that to happen.

Metella had long since ceased counting the milestones. At the beginning of their journey, she had entertained Carmella by reading out every inscription, many of them more like political propaganda than distance markers. But now she'd lapsed into her own dark abyss. Carmella's life would not change much from what she had known at Ithaca. But Metella's would.

Metella had lived a life under her own rules, beholden to no man — husband or father. Yes, she had taken lovers until Silas had appeared at her doorstep, but ostensibly her life had been her own. She'd had a child. A secret son that she had paid dearly to legitimise in order for him to live the life he deserved — the life of a Roman citizen descended from a great family. But that link to her past was how Silas had tracked her down.

What a fool she had been to think that her secret would be safe.

As they entered Rome, the weight of her fears grew heavier with every step. By rights, she should be reclining on a litter, being conveyed to her father's home by his slaves. As it was, she felt every sliver of every stone beneath her leather sandals. Her arms ached from supporting Carmella's lopsided gait as they'd abandoned the cart upon arriving in Rome. If you arrived at the gates of Rome during the early daylight hours, carts or carriages were forbidden. They could have waited to enter, but

Metella was too proud to break her vow of never speaking with Silas to argue. So now she had to endure watching the man she loved struggling to navigate the paved roadway between Silas's thugs, whilst she followed behind with a whimpering Carmella at her side.

Memories flooded back. Memories of her father's coldness, of the arranged marriage she had rebelled against, of her flight from Rome. And now she had returned to a life she thought she had left forever. She shuddered at the thought of returning to the gilded cage she had once called home. But she was not the same woman who had fled all those years ago. Yes, she was older, and wiser, but this time she had something to lose. Someone. Her son.

As they made their way through the crowded streets, she caught sight of familiar landmarks — the soaring walls of the Colosseum, the Temple of Jupiter. But even those miracles of engineering seemed smaller than she remembered, more dilapidated. And everywhere she looked, the once-grand statues now sat weathered and cracked. Even the people seemed to have lost their vibrancy, moving about their business like shadows. Fear dominated their lives. Fear of inadvertently professing support for the wrong emperor, the wrong faction.

Upon reaching her father's estate, the thick external doors opened like magic, and the group made their way through the villa's halls, past the artwork Metella had once cherished, crossing familiar courtyards. Each step bringing her closer to her father's chambers. And with every step, her anxiety grew. Would he forgive her for leaving? For the shame she'd brought upon their house? Would he even recognise her after all this time?

Her escort deposited her outside her father's study, before bundling away Sharma and Carmella to elsewhere on the estate. She was truly on her own now.

She knocked, and opened the door before waiting for permission. Defiance was the only defence left.

The sight of her father behind his desk took her breath away. Here was the man who had terrified her. A man who had intimidated senators and emperors with his cunning ways, and his mastery of secrets. But now he looked old, almost frail. But that was just a front, for his eyes were as sharp as ever, and they bored into her with an intensity that made her want to disappear.

For a moment no one moved. Then her father spoke, his voice cold and clipped. 'Metella.'

She swallowed the lump in her throat, and the years fell away.

'Father, I am home.'

PUBLIUS SEPTIMIUS APER, rose from his chair and walked over to his daughter, his flesh made real, her face instantly recognisable, a mirror of his wife.

She made to kneel, but he bid her stand and embraced her tightly. 'I have dreamed of this day,' he whispered into her ear, his hand caressing her loose hair.

And then he slapped her.

The sharp retort echoed off the frescoed walls, down the elaborately decorated hallways, across the mosaic tiled courtyards, through the copse of olive trees and private fish ponds before petering out at the edge of the huge estate.

Metella didn't flinch.

'You have no apology for your father? For the shame you brought upon this household? Well? Speak, child.'

'I am no longer a child.'

'You are my child, mine. And you will do as I say.'

'I am a woman grown—'

'No, you are no different from the goods in my warehouses or the slaves who sleep at the end of my bed.'

'In your bed, Father. The slaves in your bed. You spoke wrong.'

Publius returned to his chair, his movements stiff. Age had found a chink in his armour, and was eating away at the former consul, as much as he tried to deny it purchase.

'You have cost me a great deal of money.'

'No one asked you to spend a single denarius on me,' Metella said. 'I see that my return hasn't dented your finances too much. Was this a gift from an admirer or from a reluctant debtor?'

Publius followed the direction of Metella's gesture, as she pointed towards a solid table hosting an ostentatious golden map adorned with intricate engravings depicting the vast expanse of the Roman Empire.

'Cast by the finest Roman goldsmiths, the entire surface is gold. See the precious stones? Each one of them marks a city of note in the Empire,' Publius said, his eyes gleaming with a fanaticism peculiar to the immensely wealthy.

Moving over to the table he pointed. 'See here, Rome, signified by the ruby — the beating heart of the Empire. There's Alexandria, representing the jewel of the East with a radiant sapphire. For Carthage, Emperor Augustus demanded an emerald. And finally, for Antioch, a brilliant diamond, worthy of its strategic location.'

'This map belonged to Augustus?'

'So I'm told. Regardless, it is mine now, to trace the journeys of my stock, and of my daughter.'

'I have no interest in your jewels or your gold. I grew up swaddled in them. They hold no value for me.'

'And yet you carry a bag of gold beneath your skirts?'

With satisfaction he watched Metella's hand stray to the bag concealed beneath the folds of her skirt. *She thought I didn't know*, he mused to himself.

'Why am I home, father? I am too old to be traded like cattle. There can be no family who would have me join them by marriage now? I am sullied goods. You waste your time, and mine, by continuing this farce which should have ended when I left for Londinium.'

'When you look at that map, what do you see?'

She stared at him, frustration writ across her face.

'The map? What do you see?'

'A gross abuse of public funds.'

Publius laughed. His laugh followed the sound of the slap across the estate.

'What you see, daughter, is your future, your destiny. Unless you deny it, and then what you see is your death, and the death of your son, my grandson, Julius.'

MUSICAL CHAIRS

Metella stirred from her sleep as the warm rays of the late morning's light filtered through the shutters in her bedroom. Stretching, she found Carmella already meticulously preparing her attire, whilst grumbling under her breath about the heat.

'By the gods, Carmella,' Metella huffed, 'stop complaining. There is barely any warmth to the day.'

Carmella ignored her, her fingers fussing with the folds of a stola more valuable than all the dresses Metella had owned in Ithaca, 'It feels like I've been transported to the mouth of the underworld,' Carmella mumbled.

Metella, a slip of a smile gracing her lips, replied, 'I know, Carmella. Britannia was far more temperate, but we must bear the heat. For now at least.'

Carmella, seemingly satisfied with Metella's non answer, continued her prattling. 'You would not believe the fuss the others made about the visitors last night.'

Metella's curiosity was piqued. 'What visitors?'

Too preoccupied with lacing up Metella's leather sandals to notice any intrigue in her mistress's voice, Carmella rambled on. 'They said that some of the men were former senatorial adversaries of your father but that they didn't recognise the woman with them. They spent the whole evening laughing and drinking.' She yawned. 'I barely got any sleep.'

'You must have heard more if you were pouring their libations?'

Carmella, now brushing Metella's hair with deft strokes, cast a furtive glance around the room before leaning in closer. 'They were discussing a plan for a new emperor.' Carmella said, unaware of the power of her gossip. 'A new emperor! When we've only just got a new one. How can that be?'

Metella's fingers sorted through the ornate jewellery on the table as she absorbed her slave's words, turning them over and over in her mind, sorting the facts from Carmella's make believe.

THE ROMAN SUN hung high in the clear sky as Metella prepared to meet her father for the midday meal. Now dressed in elegant stola, she descended the stairs, the ancestral masks watching her through empty eyes as she passed, her mind swirling with questions about the visitors who had arrived the night before. *Who was the woman?*

Her father had taken his traditional couch in the dining room, his expression unreadable. The slaves had laid a lavish feast, and the room was filled with the scent of roasted meats, fresh fruits, and wine. Metella suspected that the extravagant display was more about impressing her than anything else. But then again, she was not party to the news her father's guests had brought with them, so it may well be a celebration.

'Metella,' Publius greeted her with a smile. He waved her to take a seat on the couch across from him. 'You look radiant. Rome suits you.'

Metella seated herself and accepted a goblet of wine from a nearby slave. Her gaze never wavered as she addressed her father. 'Who arrived last night, Father?'

Publius chuckled, although the mirth did not reach his eyes. 'Curious, are we? Merely old friends and allies. Former adversaries turned confederates, if you will.'

Metella leaned in. 'Allies in what?'

'You have been gone a long time and my loyalties have shifted somewhat. Now that you are home, we must come to an understanding that you will support our cause to ensure our continued prosperity.'

Metella's eyes narrowed. The weight of her father's words did not escape her. 'I thought we were prosperous enough. What more could you want?'

Her father regarded her with a shrewd gaze. 'The time is ripe for a leader who believes in the *old* ways. Commodus had grown increasingly unstable, and the Empire needs stability. The question now is who best suits our needs.'

Metella frowned. 'You are a former consul, Father. You have no role in this decision.'

Her father smiled, his expression enigmatic. 'It is amazing what power a wife can wield, don't you think?'

The pieces of her father's game fell into place with her father's words. She had always known that her father was an influential man, but now the power of his connections became clear. Their family was poised to play a significant role in shaping the fate of the Roman Empire.

'And what do I get, Father?'

Publius leaned back, a contemplative expression on his face. 'Wealth, influence, and the assurance of protection for our family in the times to come. Our association with the rightful ruler will secure our legacy, and that of your illegitimate son. I presume that is his father you have smuggled into my home? I should have had Silas slit his throat when he first arrived, but now he lives and breathes under my roof. If you want him to live, you will do as I say. And you will marry whom I choose. That is my offer.'

The weight of his words crushed Metella.

Ignoring her tears, Publius continued. 'Tonight, we will host a party to celebrate your return. You will meet your groom — one of my closest associates. It is a match that will cement our alliance and secure our future. Then a date for your wedding will be set after consultation with the priests. But that date will not be more than one month from now.'

Metella's heart sank. She had hoped her age would have meant a reprieve from her father's marital aspirations for her, but now any escape from being subsumed by his political machinations would be impossible.

'LOOK HOW BEAUTIFUL THEY ARE,' Carmella said, fastening a heavy string of giant rubies around Metella's neck.

'They're just bits of stone from the earth, Carmella. Nothing more than baubles and no better or worse than the beads you wear around your wrist.'

'But they're a gift from your father.'

'My father is used to buying affection and loyalty. This necklace does not differ from the shackles the slaves wear at the market,' Metella said. 'You can have them after tonight.'

Leaving Carmella standing open-mouthed in shock, Metella walked the familiar path to the dining room, ignoring the judgmental looks of her ancestors from the niches in the walls. There was nothing they could do to help her now.

Metella pushed open the door and recoiled. *What had her father done?* The entire room was black. From the walls to the couches to the crockery and even down to the slaves hovering at the edges of the room. The table heaved under midnight black platters and marble slabs, where each guest's name had been inscribed like a tombstone. It seemed as if her father had invited death into his home with open arms.

Publius slipped into the room behind her, the flickering candlelight highlighting the smirk on his face. 'Doesn't it look marvellous?'

'What is the meaning behind this?'

'Merely some fun, Metella.'

Metella's horror grew as she noticed the hidden symbols of death subtly woven into every aspect of the decor — a skull and crossbones had been burnt into the wood of the chairs; flickering candles were held aloft in the mouths of carved wooden snakes entwined in a death thrall. A tapestry depicting Hades presiding above his dominion was strung across one wall. This event had been months in the making.

There was only one reason for this morbid imagery, and one alone, to make her father's guests believe that this could be their last supper on earth.

'What is the point, Father?'

He had no time to answer before the first guest appeared, their face a mirror of the horror infusing Metella's whole body.

As the remaining guests arrived and took their places, exchanging nervous glances with each other, Metella could only pray that they would consider the eerie decor as nothing more than a quirk of her father's eccentricity as opposed to the threat that she believed it to be.

The couch beside hers remained unoccupied, and Metella tried asking who it was for, but her father ignored her. Instead he clapped his hands and ordered that the dinner begin.

Slaves brought out extravagant dishes from every corner of the world — bowls of black olives, roast quail stuffed with dried cranberries, lamb steaks cooked in juniper berries and garlic, glistening platters of charred vegetables drizzled in olive oil. The smell of red wine filled the air as the glasses of the guests were constantly topped up.

For a moment, Metella allowed herself to believe that everything was normal, if you ignored the forced cheerfulness of the other guests, and the empty seat, and the blackness of it all.

Whilst her father had introduced her to the others, he had not indicated which of the aged senators he expected her to wed, and bed. For there was no one in the room younger than her father.

Then Pramod shuffled into the room, leaning heavily on his walking stick. Silas escorted him to the empty couch and Metella's stomach tightened as she looked from

Pramod to her father's jubilant face. It was only then that she realised that the pageantry of the night was not for the benefit of their guests, but that it was all for her. Her father's perverse way of warning her that Pramod would die if she did not obey him.

'Ah, our honoured guest, welcome, please I beg you to join us in this celebration. It is, after all, in your honour.'

Pramod seemed unfazed by the morbid atmosphere as he took his seat, his eyes flashing momentarily to hers, conveying all his love with one look. Words were unneeded.

Publius began recounting to his guests how Pramod had warned Metella about the imminent barbarian attack before falling gravely ill. And then he proposed a toast to Pramod's good health.

'A toast! May health and prosperity be your constant companions, for in the mosaic of life, every hue contributes to the richness of the masterpiece. Here's to Pramod Sharma, a soothsayer, and a resilient spirit. May the threads of our destinies continue to weave a tale worth remembering. Salud!'

Metella raised her glass with the others, toasting her lover under the watchful eye of her father.

Publius nodded towards her, before holding his hands up for quiet.

'Tonight we are doubly blessed — once for the safe return of my only child, and once for her betrothal.'

A surprised murmur flew around the room, and the wine turned sour in Metella's mouth. If the announcement was a surprise to the guests, then her betrothed could not be one of them. She stared at her father, waiting for more.

In the eerie ambiance of the blackened room, Pramod's eyes betrayed a subtle flicker of fear as Publius announced Metella's betrothal. Fate's web had led to this moment, and Metella, who was his beacon of solace in his time-travelling journey, was now entangled in its sticky threads.

He lifted his gaze and met Metella's for a moment — a silent exchange of understanding of the gravity of the situation and the burden they now both carried.

As Publius raised his hands for attention.

Time stuttered to a stop.

At the revelation of Metella's future husband, Pramod had just become a silent witness to history's changing path.

WEDDING BELLS

Amidst the opulent surroundings of the Roman villa, Metella found solace in father's gardens, a sanctuary of greenery and vibrant blossoms that masked the constraints of her impending marriage. The air was scented with the fragrance of the yellow winter jasmine, a burst of summer in December. The soft murmur of water from the elaborate fish ponds provided a calming backdrop to the chaos in her mind.

Pramod accompanied her with his walking stick in hand. They strolled through the manicured paths, a facade of normalcy concealing the depths of their pain. Slaves tended to the plants, their presence a constant reminder of the limitations to their discourse.

Seated by one of the ornate fish ponds, their conversation meandered through the intricacies of the villa's gardens and how Metella's father had commissioned the fishponds to emulate those of the Emperor Tiberius in Sperlonga.

'Do you know the names of the fish?' Pramod asked, staring at the darting shapes beneath the water's surface.

Metella pointed to a spear-shaped yellow smudge in the water. 'Those are lupi. If you watch them long enough, they'll put on a show seemingly just for you. I spent hours sitting here watching, waiting for them to leap out of the water. But I felt sad too, because maybe they were leaping out of the water to try to escape? Maybe they too were searching for something more for their lives?'

'Is that why you left?'

IT HAD BEEN in the heart of Londinium, the bustling hub of Roman activity in Britannia, where Pramod Sharma had first laid eyes on the young Metella. Her beauty, as yet untouched by the weariness of travel, captivated Pramod, drawing him like a moth to a flame.

He had observed her from a discreet corner of the tavern, where the air was thick with the scent of cheap wine and the lively chatter of locals and soldiers alike. Metella, clad in garments that spoke of Roman affluence, sat alone at a weathered wooden table. The wine in her cup had seemed to offend her palate, as her nose crinkled in disgust with each sip.

Intrigued by the contrast between her elegance and the gritty reality of Britannia, Pramod couldn't resist the urge to approach, something he had never done before on any of his journeys through time.

Embarking into unfamiliar territory, Pramod mustered the courage to approach Metella, the woman he now knew and loved. He had appeared at her table, a self-conscious smile on his lips.

'May I join you?' Pramod had asked, his voice a careful balance of friendliness and uncertainty.

Metella had glanced up from her drink, caution filling her eyes.

'Ah, the infamous Britannia wine,' Pramod remembered remarking. 'It takes some getting used to.' He had motioned towards the empty stool opposite her, his question hanging in the air.

Metella had managed a tentative nod. 'Getting used to might be optimistic. More like enduring,' she had replied.

Emboldened by the hint of humour in her reply, Pramod had seated himself at her table, striking up a conversation with a women who was as out of place as he was.

At the time, their conversation had remained resolutely at surface level, and as someone who always kept his past a secret, Pramod recognised that she was doing the same. Somehow that had made him feel closer to her. A person with secrets was less likely to want to know his. And so, for the first time in more years than he cared to remember, in a tavern filled with strangers, he had found himself at ease.

'YOU KNOW WHY I LEFT,' Metella said, waggling her fingers in the water. Ripples fled across the surface.

'But I don't know why you came back,' Pramod said.

Metella tried to ignore the plea in his eyes to look at him, to acknowledge his pain.

'My father needed me.'

The bells from a bronze wind chime hanging in the nearby arbour added a jarring note to the lie she had just told.

'We could have stayed in Londinium,' he said.

She shook her head, her jet black hair covering her face.

'I had to return.'

The air hung heavy with unspoken words, the weight of their shared history pressing down on them like an invisible force.

'There's something you're not telling me,' he said, his voice barely a whisper.

Metella's fingers, dancing on the water's surface, teasing the fish, delayed her answer. The decision to reveal the existence of their son, Julius, loomed like a storm cloud threatening to break. 'There's...' she began, her voice faltering, 'there is something. Someone.'

The wind chime echoed the unspoken turmoil between them, turning the air brittle with emotion.

Pramod's gaze intensified. 'What is it?'

Metella took a deep breath. 'We have a son,' she confessed, her eyes meeting Pramod's. The words, once released, shattered the false serenity of the gardens.

Pramod's expression shifted from confusion to shock. 'A son?' he echoed.

Metella nodded. 'Julius Stertinius Carpus. He's a centurion in the Roman army, stationed at Ithaca Fort.'

Metella watched Pramod struggle with her words.

'Why didn't you tell me?' Pramod asked, his voice full of pain.

Metella, her eyes reflecting the weight of her secret, sighed. 'You left.'

PRAMOD'S MIND flashed back to that fateful day in Londinium, a city caught in the throes of bustling life and still recovering from Boudica's destruction. He had travelled to the Roman temple dedicated to Jupiter, standing proudly in what is now Greenwich Park, taken there by his curiosity and another new friend. Another woman. Another time traveller.

That temple became the stage for his inadvertent separation from Metella.

'I never meant to leave,' Pramod began, his voice full of remorse. 'I was taken from you. From that moment.' His eyes focused on a distant point, reliving the inexplicable events that had unfolded. The marble inscription to Jupiter had drawn Pramod's attention, and in an ill-fated moment, he had touched the inscription. A subsequent surge of energy had then torn him from the temporal fabric of Londinium, propelling him into a different time, with no way of returning.

'I never meant to leave,' Pramod repeated, pain etched on his face. 'And I would never have left if I'd known... But I don't understand. Why would you leave Julius in Britannia and return to Rome?' Pramod asked.

Metella's fingers stilled on the water's surface. 'My father threatened Julius,' she confessed. 'He found out about our son, and used him as leverage to force me back.'

Pramod frowned, 'He threatened our son?' The idea seemed inconceivable, and yet he easily he could believe it of a man he had only just met.

A bitter smile touched Metella's lips. 'My father is skilled at manipulation and control. I rebelled against both, running away from the marriage he had arranged for me. I was just a child promised to a man old enough to be my grandfather. My father will never forgive me for that embarrassment.'

'Silas,' she continued, the name like venom on her lips, 'tracked me down. My father sent his loyal hound to fetch me back to a life I couldn't bear.'

Silas? The bear of a man who'd carried him, dragged him, defended him, fed him, and who had escorted them from Ithaca all the way to Rome? He was an agent of Metella's father?

'Silas is your father's man?'

'Silas reported every move I made to my father. And after he discovered my connection to Julius, he wrote to my father,' Metella confessed, the pain clear on her face. 'He then had the gall to apologise for telling my father. Because he'd given my father the ultimate bargaining chip. Through Silas, he threatened to harm Julius unless I return. You, however, were a complicating factor my father hadn't bargained on.'

'Why hasn't your father killed me already? What use am I to him here?'

Metella exhaled, the burden of her choices clear in the lines on her face. 'The condition for keeping you alive is that I will marry the man my father has chosen for me.'

'I can't let you sacrifice your life for mine,' he said. 'You have to return to Ithaca to be with our son. There must be a way to change your father's mind? To save you from a marriage you don't want?'

Metella's gaze softened, her fingers tracing absent patterns on his arm. 'My father is relentless. He holds Julius' life, and yours, in his hands. I have no choice but to comply.'

Pramod's gaze shifted to the horizon. He thought he had one more journey left. Would that be enough to save Metella and their son? The unseen chessboard of fate stretched before him, each move creating future consequences which would reshape the destiny of those he held dear. But so many things had already changed. What sort of future would he be taking them to?

'I will marry the man my father has chosen for me. That is the condition for keeping you alive,' Metella's words hung in the air, a cruel bargain that tied her fate to Pramod's existence. A marriage she did not desire, and a life she did not choose, all orchestrated by the puppeteer who held the strings of all their destinies.

Pramod's thoughts turned to the son he had yet to meet. The yearning to protect Metella and their child surged. There must be a way to change her father's mind. He searched for some kind of hope, but Metella's attestation that her father was relentless and the resignation in her voice made him feel like he was grasping at shadows. The price of defiance would be steep and yet, he knew he couldn't stand by and let her sacrifice her happiness for his sake. They had to go back to Britannia. And from there, home.

POWER PLAY

Metella reclined on the luxurious litter, her eyes tracing the columns of the Forum as her bearers navigated the bustling heart of Rome. The rhythmic swaying of the litter and the distant murmur of the city's life created a surreal backdrop for her thoughts. Carmella sat next to her, her eyes wide as she absorbed the grandeur of the imperial city and the tantalising aroma of unfamiliar foods wafting through the air.

'What do you think the emperor's wife will serve at the lunch?' Carmella asked, her mind easily swayed by the allure of lavish banquets, her gaze lingering on market stalls laden with delicacies she had never seen before in her short life in Britannia.

Metella smiled, her thoughts focused on a different feast — information, the currency of Rome. 'I'm told that Flavia Titiana is known for her exquisite taste. I will try to remember everything they serve. Will that make you happy?'

A smile split Carmella's face. 'I still can't believe that you are meeting with the emperor's wife.'

'Neither can I, Carmella. Neither can I.'

The litter wove through the crowded streets, passing statues of long-dead emperors and lively shop fronts which defined the vibrant soul of Rome. Metella ignored all the sights. Her mind was firmly anchored in the shadowy corridors of her father's power. Publius had orchestrated this lunch to extract any morsel of information which might reveal Pertinax's intentions and alliances. And Metella had to comply if she wanted to ensure the safety of her son, and Pramod.

As the litter reached the emperor's palace, Metella composed herself whilst Carmella fussed over her mistress's attire, ensuring every fold of fabric fell perfectly.

'Don't forget, Carmella, that I'm relying on you to remain vigilant. You, too, must remember every word you overhear. Do you understand? And not just for my father's benefit, but for my benefit too, and yours.'

The doors of the palace swung open, and the atmosphere inside the litter changed.

Two Praetorian Guards emerged, helping Metella from the litter before escorting her down a path adorned with fountains and mosaics. The air felt thick with the heady scent of palace intrigue.

Flavia Titiana — the wife of the head of the Roman Empire, stood waiting at the end of the path.

Metella took a deep breath and stepped onto the stage her father had prepared for her.

METELLA RECLINED on a sumptuous couch in the opulent dining chamber of the imperial palace, surrounded by other esteemed women of Rome. The air was thick with exotic oils and perfumes, and the room echoed with the soft murmur of feminine conversation. The women were adorned in flowing silken stolas, the rich hues of their garments catching the flickering light of the oil lamps adorning the chamber.

Flavia Titiana — the wife of Emperor Pertinax, wearing a gown of royal purple, presided over the banquet. Metella could not help but admire the sophisticated gold jewellery adorning Flavia's neck and wrists. She touched the gaudy rubies hanging from her own neck. Money could buy almost everything, except grace.

The banquet began with a ceremonial libation — a slave poured wine into a shallow bowl placed before Flavia, who then raised it in honour of the gods. The unforgettable aroma of spiced wine filled the air as the libation was followed by a costly selection of appetisers, including delicate figs stuffed with almonds, honey-glazed olives, and freshly baked bread with bowls of aromatic olive oil for dipping.

As the feast unfolded, slaves moved like shadows among the reclining diners, presenting an astonishing array of dishes. A platter of roasted dormice, glazed with a honey and wine reduction, elicited murmurs of delight over the rare delicacy. Succulent oysters, brought in fresh from the Mediterranean, were served on a bed of ice, their briny aroma reminding her of the oceans swaddling the shores of Britannia.

The main course featured a selection of meats: tender lamb roasted with fragrant herbs; a peacock adorned with its iridescent plumage, its flesh succulent and rich. Bowls of lentils, seasoned with cumin and coriander accompanied the meats, providing a flavourful contrast.

Carmella, wide-eyed and mesmerised, waited quietly in the background, her gaze flitting from dish to dish. Flavia's slaves, meticulously trained, anticipated every need. They expertly replenished goblets, offered steaming towels scented with lavender, and discreetly cleared away empty dishes.

Dessert soon followed. A symphony of sweetness with honeyed dates, stuffed with spiced nuts, served alongside platters of fresh fruit. A decadent honey cake, drizzled with saffron-infused syrup, provided a fitting conclusion to the lavish banquet.

Throughout the feast, the women indulged in spirited conversations, their laughter mingling with the gentle strains of lyres played by musicians in the corner. Praetorian Guards maintained an unwavering vigil at the door. The recent assassination of Commodus still spread an almost invisible pall over the festivities. Metella observed that the other women — all spouses of senators and consuls, each cast the occasional furtive glance toward the silent guards. Etched on their faces was the unspoken query — could they be trusted?

In a moment of subdued whispers, Flavia leaned in, her voice conspiratorial. 'Fear not, my dear, they are trustworthy,' she reassured. 'My husband has secured their loyalty and allegiance with funds from the treasury. The Praetorians are under our sway and no harm shall befall us within these walls.'

Although Flavia had meant to comfort her, Metella could not dispel the notion that an undercurrent of concern lingered beneath Flavia's reassuring words.

As they dined, Metella scrutinised Flavia with subtle precision. Nestled in the plush cushions of the dining chamber, they had danced delicately around the topic of their families and now their memories of Britannia. Flavia had accompanied her husband Pertinax during his governorship of Britannia, and so entertained the women with stories of her limited experiences in the distant province. Her farthest venture north had been to Eboracum — a city which had left her unimpressed with its cold climate and lack of entertainment.

'You can only imagine how much I missed the vibrancy of Rome with its grand festivals and bustling streets, the culinary delights, and the weather! Britannia simply could not compete. Surely you agree, Metella?'

Metella had spent time in Eboracum before moving to Ithaca and held only fond memories of the empire's newest city. Leaving Britannia hurt more than she would ever admit. She sipped her wine before asking, 'Could you not find anything in Eboracum to your liking? The landscapes are like nothing I've ever seen in here. And the baths rival those of Hadrian himself.'

Flavia's expression soured slightly. 'The cold and the isolation were unbearable. And the entertainment, or lack thereof, left much to be desired. Two years felt like an eternity.'

Metella mentioned her glimpse of Pertinax during his visit to Ithaca Fort. 'I recall when your husband visited Ithaca Fort, and I was told that the cohorts under his command held him in high regard, especially during his time as the commander of the Tungrians.'

Flavia brightened in agreement, a spark of curiosity in her eyes at the mention of her husband. 'Pertinax has always been a man of great character. His leadership in Britannia is still spoken of with reverence. Now, as emperor, he is steering Rome towards a new era, dedicated to ruling in accordance with the Senate's wishes for a harmonious governance.'

Metella pressed further, 'And what changes does he aim to bring about?'

Flavia's pride in Pertinax's achievements outshone her curiosity about Metella. 'He has already set in motion the minting of new coins featuring the two-headed Janus — the god of new beginnings, symbolising his commitment to a fresh start for the empire. He is determined to restore Rome to its former glory, and we are fortunate that he enjoys the unwavering support of the Senate in these noble endeavours.'

As the afternoon wore on, the conversation turned to more intimate topics. The women leaned in to share their secrets, emboldened by the mix of wine and female companionship. Flavia whispered to Metella, 'Do you know of Decimus Clodius Albinus, the current governor of Britannia? He cuts quite a striking figure, an albino hailing from Africa. Such talk of the size of his...' She paused for effect, a playful glint in her eyes. 'And the gossip from the games he hosted, where Commodus fought as a gladiator, is simply quite scandalous.'

'What happened at the games? Tales such as these rarely reached our ears in Britannia.'

Flavia's eyes sparkled mischievously. 'Oh, it was quite the spectacle. Commodus insisted on participating as a gladiator. The crowd couldn't decide whether to be amazed or amused as he brandished his weapon. Some say he looked more like a clumsy buffoon than a fearsome gladiator. Whispers and chuckles raced through the stands, and even the gladiators were laughing behind their masks. Albinus maintained an air of dignity, as did my husband, but I shall never forget the sight. They were right to rid us of Commodus. Madmen should never hold the reins of power.'

Metella nodded. She had overheard the soldiers from Ithaca Fort gossiping about the former emperor's erratic behaviour. But to openly discuss his assassination? That was a conversation for the darkest of corners in the blackest of nights, and not for the dining room.

Flavia continued, 'Although Albinus should never have let it get that far. He was close enough to Commodus to counsel against his appearance at the games.' Flavia dabbed at her mouth. 'Pertinax is also planning a series of games for the summer, with captives from Britannia. Northern barbarians I'm told.' Here she shuddered. 'I've seen them — giants covered in brutal tattoos, as if someone had upturned an ink bottle.'

Metella's blood ran cold. Were these the men her son had been fighting? 'They are already here, in Rome?' How had she missed this information? Why had her father not told her?

Flavia nodded gravely. 'They arrived not long ago. A formidable bunch, I must say. And the story of how they were captured is even more intriguing.'

Metella's eyes widened, 'Captured? How?'

Flavia's voice dropped to a conspiratorial whisper. 'There was a skirmish near the northern borders of Britannia. Reports suggest Albinus led a legion of soldiers against a tribe of fierce barbarians. The clash was brutal, but the Romans emerged victorious, capturing a group of the barbarians alive.'

Metella's mind raced. A battle near the Empire's northernmost border suggested Julius might have been involved. Anxiety gripped her. Had her father purposefully kept this information from her? There was no way she could inquire about Julius; the possibility of the emperor's wife knowing about the well-being of a single soldier was slim. But her father would know. He was playing a dangerous game with a mother's heart. And that was dangerous.

FIDDLING LIKE NERO

Pramod flexed his fingers and marvelled at the mechanics of his almost fully functional tendons and ligaments. Only a dragging left foot remained as a subtle reminder of his stroke. Metella's love and care had been instrumental in his recovery. And he would always be grateful that she had not cast him aside when he had appeared at her door in Ithaca. Although his stroke had delayed his plans to whisk her back to the future, and their journey to Rome was far from ideal, here they were. Together. And that was a triumph in itself.

Carmella's voice interrupted his thoughts from her spot in the doorway. 'Someone's coming.'

Pramod pushed himself up off the floor, sweat beading on his brow from the clandestine exercises he had been performing since their arrival in Rome. For some unknown reason he had kept his physical progress hidden, even from Metella. Only Carmella was privy to the full extent of his returning strength. Sometimes secrets needed to be kept.

Silas appeared in the doorway, and instinctively Pramod slumped in the corner his cot, as if he had no strength for anything else. The trust between them now seemed like a faint shadow of its former self. Whatever relationship the two men had formed during their perilous journey from Britannia to Rome had melted away to nothing.

'Silas,' Pramod said, adjusting his position on the cot with a wince.

'Publius Aper would like a word,' Silas replied.

Pramod felt his guts clench. 'Of course. Give me a few minutes and I'll be there. In his study?'

'I'll wait,' Silas said.

An audience meant it was time to put on a show — a skill he had honed over years of navigating foreign situations and times. However, Silas's unwavering stare unsettled Pramod more than it should have.

THE WALK to Publius Aper's study made Pramod feel like he was being marched to his death. Silas, normally a man of few words at the best of times, hadn't opened his mouth once and the tension between them thickened with every step. Pramod's mind raced with a thousand possibilities, none of them reassuring. As they approached the grand door of Aper's study, Pramod grew lightheaded, his heart racing. Was is possible to relapse after a stroke?

Silas, ever stoic, pushed open the door and Publius looked up from his papers.

'Ah, our house guest, do come in. I have been eager to speak with you.'

Aper's veneer of hospitality did little to ease Pramod's unease, especially given the absence of Metella in this little charade.

The room was more like a gilded cage than a place of conversation. As the door closed behind him, Pramod imagined walking straight into the lion's den.

Pramod took a hesitant step into the room, dragging his weakened leg behind him. The scent of burning incense mingled with the mustiness of parchment papers, both old and new. Flickering light cast long shadows on the woven rugs that softened the floor. Aper motioned for him to sit, his gaze seemingly predatory as he watched every move Pramod made. Silas remained by the door, a silent sentinel to the pantomime.

'Tell me,' Aper began, his tone casual yet probing, 'how did you find yourself in the company of my daughter?'

Pramod felt the weight of Aper's scrutiny as he lowered himself into a chair, taking a moment to construct a suitable narrative to satisfy the Roman's curiosity.

'I come from a distant land,' he began cautiously, 'far to the east of here. I was a trader who moved goods across vast territories. My work took me to Britannia.' Pramod shrugged, as if there was nothing more to his story.

Aper's eyes narrowed, his interest palpable. 'The East? India, perhaps? My wife once owned a string of beautiful red coral and pearls from that land. I have not yet had the privilege of visiting those shores, yet you have crossed the empire more than once?'

'I have been fortunate in my travels,' Pramod replied, keeping his voice steady. 'India is a land of rich treasures and vibrant cultures. But it was during my travels to arrange the trade of wood between India and Britannia that I encountered Metella.'

'A fortuitous meeting then — a young Roman woman *and* a trader from India? She must have been fascinated by your origins — you coming from a country renowned for the beauty of its gems and the allure of its landscapes. Oh, and the grandeur, which is unparalleled. Pray tell me more about your country.'

Pramod sensed Aper was playing word games with him. But time had set the stage, and he had to play his part. So he spoke of sprawling marketplaces, vibrant festivals, and the opulence of the Indian royal courts. He painted a picture of a land as enchanting as it was distant. Much of what he described had come straight from the History Channel. As the child of a time traveller, he hadn't been brought up in India, and knew it only as a tourist.

'And your initial journey from India to Britannia? Such a venture must have been costly?' Aper cocked his head. 'It would be fascinating to hear about how you financed such a thing. Wouldn't you agree, Silas?'

Silas nodded, betraying nothing more in his stony expression.

Pramod felt like he was being backed into a corner. Despite his experience with storytelling, he had little to draw on as the child of a former street urchin. How could he just casually explain that he'd been travelling through time since birth?

'In the beginning, I was an agent of another merchant, and it was exhausting work,' Pramod declared. 'The constant travel took its toll on my health, as you can see. In the waters of the Mediterranean sea, I encountered many fantastical creatures. There were violent tempests threatening the cargo I escorted on behalf of my employer. I traded exotic items across the Roman Empire from Athens to Hispalis and other distant lands. Exotic woods from India were my main commodity, but as they became harder to source, I set my sights further to Britannia. After severing my relationship with my employer, I struck out on my own.'

'Fascinating,' Aper said. 'Did you keep any souvenirs from your days trading? As you can see from my study, I too like to collect memories from my travels.'

What would it take to appease the man?

'Yes, of course,' Pramod said, his eyes scanning the room.

Where was this line of questioning going?

'And do you have any of those with you now?' Aper inquired, his gaze unwavering.

Silas shifted his weight at the door.

What? The question caught Pramod off guard. He had nothing to show for his travels. He wasn't like Neumegen, trading his way through history, delighting in the clever deal. For Pramod, it had always been enough to experience history. To live a different life.

'Sadly, no,' Pramod said, trying to keep calm. 'I have nothing with me.'

Aper leaned back in his chair, a half smile on his lips. 'That's not exactly true now, is it?' He withdrew Pramod's leather pouch from a drawer and plucked a denarius from the bag. 'It's curious what people keep as mementoes. Take this coin for example. It is a simple denarius. Useful for buying food, or wine, or women. But your denarius, this one,' he waved it about in the air, 'isn't for spending, is it?'

The denarius was just a coin. A hunk of silver weighing just over three grammes, impressed with the face of… Pramod stopped breathing. Whose face was impressed upon the coin? Which ruler?

Pramod rubbed at his throat, the act of swallowing almost impossible in the oppressive fug of incense and intrigue. His heart raced, faster and faster. Skipping beats. *One, two, skip, four, five.* No, this couldn't be happening. The items in his pouch were his lifeline for travelling back to Hexham. Losing them meant forfeiting any chance of returning home. There was no value to anything in the bag. Even the coin had little value on its own. Pramod kicked himself for ever removing the pouch from around his neck. How did Aper get his hands on his pouch? His eyes shifted to Silas, whose own eyes were fixed on the painted ceiling. He cast his mind back to when he'd last worn it — on the day of the black supper. On Aper's orders, Silas had dressed him in black and had removed the pouch from around his neck. *For the sake of appearances,* Silas had said.

THE FACE of Decimus Clodius Albinus stared out from the silver denarius, the face of a man who had yet to rise to power. 'The coin has no value,' he stammered. 'I keep it as a trinket, nothing more.'

Aper chuckled, his eyes gleaming, 'Oh, it has some value, but to whom?' He placed the denarius back in the leather pouch and tossed it onto the desk, his fingers lingering on the worn surface. 'You see, Pramod, I have a knack for ferreting out secrets. That's how I found Metella, and persuaded her to return, sans her son. But you have been more problematic. So tell me, what other secrets are you hiding, other than being Albinus' man? Am I harbouring a viper under my roof?'

Pramod tried breathing again, the short, sharp intakes

of breath barely enough to sustain life. 'The coin is a trinket. A folly—'

'No one mints coins as a folly,' Aper interrupted. 'I wonder, my friend, what you have been doing in the twenty years since you last saw my daughter? You are a ghost, unheard of until you appeared at my daughter's door. Silas should have thrown you out with the garbage. On that, we both agree.' Aper's tone sharpened.

Pramod's mind raced as he tried to think of a way out of this nightmare. He had to keep his secrets safe, but how?

'Tell me of Albinus' plans, or Metella dies.'

He'd threaten the life of his own daughter? The man was worse than Caligula.

Pramod couldn't reveal his true identity or the nature of his time travel, but now Metella's life hung in the balance. He felt his intricate web of lies unravelling.

As Aper's gaze bore down on him, he searched for a way to divert the man's attention without sacrificing Metella. And in that tense moment, he made a decision — a half-truth, a carefully crafted narrative that would satisfy Aper's curiosity without betraying the essence of his secret.

'I know Albinus plans to declare himself emperor before he marches upon Rome.'

'But we already have an emperor,' Aper said, becoming very still.

'But you aren't planning on having him for very long, are you?' Pramod chanced, trusting his memory of Roman history, and of the year of the five emperors.

Aper's expression hardened. The room seemed to shrink to a pinprick as Pramod prayed that his performance was convincing enough to protect both himself and the woman he loved.

FOLLOW THE LEADER

The flickering flames in the brazier lent an air of the underworld to the unfolding drama in the study. Aper's eyes bore into Pramod, assessing the value of the information he'd just laid before him.

'What more do you know about Albinus' plans?' Aper inquired, his voice a low rumble. He watched his daughter's lover hesitate, keenly aware of the power he wielded over the other man.

'I know he gathers support among the legions. There is discontent with Rome brewing, and Albinus aims to exploit it. He sees himself as the rightful emperor, a challenger to Severus.'

Aper's cunning smile returned, and no one could mistake the turning of the gears of his political mind.

Silas slipped silently into the study like a shadow, his presence clearly adding to Pramod's disquiet, just as Aper had planned.

'So he thinks he's more deserving than Severus? Interesting,' Aper mused out loud, his fingers tapping on his desk. 'And Albinus aims for the throne itself?'

Pramod nodded. 'He believes he has enough support, and once the other legions declare in his favour, he will make his move. But I know that he has already chosen a date, and that he will make his move during the festival of Lupercalia.'

Aper's eyes gleamed. 'This information suits us very well. Do you not think so, Silas?'

The enforcer, a man of few words but swift actions, nodded in agreement, deepening Aper's cunning look. Pramod's revelations were merely pawns in a larger game, a game where Aper dictated the rules and determined who were the winners and who were the losers.

'Thank you, my friend,' Aper said, leaning toward Pramod. 'Your insights align with information I have already received. Later, we'll delve into this in more detail. But for now, my personal physician awaits in your room. For my daughter's sake, we'd like to see you rid of your afflictions.'

As the door closed behind Pramod, leaving him to the uncertain ministrations of Aper's personal physician, the senator turned to Silas, his eyes glinting.

'Silas,' Aper began, his voice lowered to a conspiratorial murmur, 'Our new friend unwittingly provides us with a unique opportunity. The discontent in the legions can be used to our advantage but we must act swiftly.'

Silas's expression remained stoic. The loyalty etched in the lines of his face spoke to the years of clandestine dealings between the two men.

'Pertinax is performing beyond the parameters we expected, and his popularity grows. The puppet perches upon the precipice of becoming the puppeteer unless decisive action is taken,' Aper continued, pacing the room with a predator's grace. 'His fall must be swift, and soon.'

Aper approached a small table where a map of Rome lay open, his finger tracing the roads and landmarks as he outlined his plan.

'Pertinax presents himself as a new man, a good man, but even good men fall. A few well-placed rumours, some discreet manipulation, and any simmering discontent will erupt into open rebellion. We shall be there to offer Albinus as the alternative.'

Silas listened without comment. Aper's machinations

were second nature to both men, a dance they had performed in the shadows for years.

'We have allies within the Praetorian Guard,' Aper added, a glint of confidence in his eyes. 'Allies who are compassionate towards our goals. They will be the spark that ignites the flame. And when the time is right, Albinus will present himself as the saviour Rome needs. Rome does not need Septimius Severus.'

Silas finally spoke, his voice a low rasp, 'I hear the man enjoys a fine palate, and that he is partial to the local fungi. If I may be so bold as to mention it?'

Aper nodded, a smirk playing on his lips. 'A dinner it is then, with his family. A timely reminder to everyone that you have to be so careful when collecting mushrooms. Yes? And then the Senate will have to rally behind Albinus as the legitimate heir. The pieces are falling into place, my old friend. Soon, Rome will have a new emperor, and we shall have our man on the throne.'

Silas's eyes shone with approval as the room crackled with shared ambition and the anticipation of the impending upheaval.

'Subtlety is the cloak that must shroud our actions,' Aper said, his dark eyes gleaming with naked ambition, the air heavy with the scent of conspiracy. He was well aware that he held the fate of the empire in his gnarled hands. History would rightfully record him as the architect of shadows and the puppeteer of power.

Silas nodded, his gaze unwavering. 'I have contacts within Pertinax's household. Trustworthy individuals who won't invite any suspicion. The emperor isn't overly fond of banquets, but the Parentalia festival approaches, and he will be hosting a dinner for his closest family and advisers.'

Aper's lips curled into a sinister smile. 'It is too late in the season for fresh mushrooms, but dried mushrooms abound. Even those of the deadly kind. Have them poison the dish subtly. Let it be a taste of fate rather than an overt act. Make it appear as though the mushrooms were an instrument of the gods, hastening Pertinax's journey to the underworld. An accidental mishap, a rare misstep from the kitchen where an apprentice mixed up the different fungi.'

Silas inclined his head. 'It will be done. The emperor and his family shall dine together at their last supper, unaware of the hand guiding them into the shadows.'

Aper clasped Silas's shoulder with a firm grip. 'Remember, Silas, the puppeteer leaves no visible strings. This one act will herald a new era for Rome. Proceed with caution and let the mushrooms write the final notes of Pertinax's troublesome reign.'

THE KITCHEN of the imperial palace bustled with activity and the intoxicating aromas of an opulent feast in the making. Flames flickered beneath huge iron pots, casting a Hades-like glow over the faces of chefs as they prepared for the annual Parentalia festival — a celebration to pay homage to family ancestors.

In a darkened corner of the bustling kitchen, away from the prying eyes of the culinary chaos, Silas conferred with the head chef — a seasoned master of his craft who had danced in the shadows for years. The air was thick with the scent of secrecy, and the fragrances of aromatic herbs, including fresh basil and oregano, and savoury meats, soot and sweat, and fear.

Oblivious to the machinations in the corner, the rest of the kitchen slaves were busy preparing an array of Roman delicacies — roast boar seasoned with a blend of exotic spices and sizzling over open flames; platters of fish drizzled with garum — a fermented fish sauce, bowls of seasoned olives; honey-glazed figs; and pomegranates glistening like jewels, all destined to adorn the imperial table.

Amidst the chaos, no one noticed Silas leave, as the head chef prepared a simple addition to the menu — a patina fungi — a mushroom and cheese casserole made with eggs, milk, and spices. With a practised hand, he added a handful of Death Cap mushrooms to the harmless, and common, Caesar's mushrooms, transforming the innocuous culinary creation into an instrument of fate.

PRAMOD LAY on his bed exhausted. The intricate dance he had performed to protect his secret had lead him into a perilous alliance with Aper. Whilst that solved one problem, it had opened a Pandora's Box of others. As for the Aper's Roman physician, whilst he was undoubtedly more knowledgeable than some of the Elizabethan charlatans he'd met in his travels, the physician could no more cure the effects of his stroke than he could resurrect Julius Caesar himself.

In his dimly lit chamber, Pramod's thoughts swirled in a vortex of urgency and uncertainty. The imminent marriage of Metella, the woman he loved, loomed like a storm amidst the catastrophic upheaval to history if Aper's machinations were to succeed.

Of course, none of that mattered to him personally if he couldn't return to the future. If he were to die here, in 193, it mattered not one iota if Pertinax or Albinus were the emperor. Although it did pose an interesting question of whether an alternate Roman emperor would halt the assassination of JFK or Indira Gandhi. Would it change the outcome of Watergate, or save Princess Diana? If Caracalla never ascended to the throne, would the world ever hear the dulcet tones of Dame Vera Lynn or Lata Mangeshkar? Would the world see the art of Vermeer or the sculptures of Brâncuși? What would the world lose if the timeline changed?

Pramod's mind lurched towards the contents of Aper's study, more specifically to the contents of his leather pouch, which contained the keys to his freedom, and future. Retrieving the pouch was Pramod's singular focus, and filled every second of every minute of every hour.

One unexpected bright point in the chaos was Carmella's unintentional reinvention as a spy, akin almost to Guy Burgess or Kim Philby, part of the invisible slave network carrying the weight of Rome's secrets. Through the intricate tapestry of gossip that weaved its way through the household, Carmella had learned of Aper's reconsideration of whom he'd chosen for Metella to marry. Pramod had seized upon this information like a lifeline.

As if on cue, Carmella appeared in his chamber, slyly closing the door behind her.

'More news?' Pramod asked.

'The senator has had another change of heart.'

Pramod's pulse quickened. 'About Metella, or something else?' he whispered.

Carmella's gaze darted toward the doorway as if to ensure the shadows were their only companions. 'He has chosen a new suitor. But that's not all!'

How could there be more? Pramod thought. 'Who?'

'Aper sent word to Britannia that upon Albinus's arrival in Rome, he will have the senator's full support for his claim upon the throne. And the hand of Metella.'

'Word takes time to travel,' Carmella added, 'Albinus won't have yet heard. Things could still change…'

Pramod nodded. It wasn't the worst news he'd heard. 'It gives us more time.'

'Time to escape?' Carmella asked.

As Carmella's eyes gleamed with hope, Pramod realised the magnitude of his responsibility. His destiny was entwined with that of Metella and her father, but so too was Carmella's. A girl born into servitude who still yearned for Britannia; for the distant shores of the only place she knew as home.

He considered his words carefully. 'Escape? Don't you want to stay here and forge a new life?'

She shook her head vehemently. 'I want to go home.'

'You deserve a life beyond these walls, beyond the whims of Roman aristocracy. You deserve freedom, even from Metella.'

'I want to be with you and Metella. I want to go home.'

In the silence, Pramod grappled with the realisation that there was more that needed to happen before he retrieved his leather pouch and returned to the life, and time, that he'd come to love.

'I promise,' he said, and he could almost hear the wheels of fate turning, reshaping his destiny, and the destiny of all those he touched. He'd broken the one rule of time travel, and his world would never be the same.

PART THREE

173

AN APPLE A DAY...

Apple woke to a piercing headache and the biting wind. 'Lillian?' she called out, the dark wind swallowing her words. Then more frantically, 'Lillian?'

Of course, Lillian wasn't expecting Apple to be here. Lillian would have expected Neumegen to be by her side. And if he wasn't, then she would have found shelter without waiting. Apple's secret plan didn't seem like such a good idea anymore.

The air clawed at Apple's skin like razors, nipping at her face and snagging on the folds of the cloak in her hands. *Her cloak?* She hadn't been wearing her cloak at the Bellingham. Lillian was the one wearing a cloak.

'Lillian?' she tried once more, trying not to panic, her shaking hands wrapping the woollen cloak around her shoulders.

No answer.

Apple hesitated, not sure what to do now, or which direction to take. She needed to find shelter or she would die out here.

In the distance, the jagged ridges of hills cut marred the horizon while pristine snow blanketed everything — including the village nestled under the protective walls of a huge stone fort — Ithaca Fort, in all its Roman glory.

Beyond the fort, she spied the burning embers of a small campfire. To whom it belonged, she didn't know, but a chill ran down her spine as her innate sense of self preservation kicked in. Apple turned away from the pinpricks of firelight, towards the village, whose buildings were nothing more than indistinct masses under a blanket of snow.

The panic Apple had tried so hard to control rose as the fear of exposure drove her onward until exhaustion got the better of her and she slumped against a splintered tree trunk, her body shaking. How could she have lost Lillian? Her grip on Lillian's cloak had been tighter than a vice. There was no way that they could have been separated. What if Lillian wasn't even here? What if Apple had arrived alone, too late to stop history from changing, or too soon?

Tears welled as her shivering became more violent. Remaining hidden under the tree was an option, but one which would result in her death from exposure. She had to reach shelter. The village was her only choice, at least until she found Lillian.

Apple scraped her hands against the rough bark of the Hawthorn tree as she pulled herself to her feet. Trudging forward, the howling wind threw itself at her body, ripping at her hair, her cloak, and stabbing at her exposed hands, whipping her face like a lust-fuelled demon. Apple stumbled on, inching closer to the village, violent shadows threatening from every direction.

The cold hands of frostbite caressed her fingers as the village seemed to slip further away. Apple's body was almost ready to give in to the cold when she heard what she recognised as the gentle whinny of a horse coming from a snow shrouded structure ahead. Apple lurched towards it, alarming two belligerent mules as she pushed open the door, before she collapsed into the scent of hay permeating the stable. A smell of safety.

IN HER SLEEP, Apple dreamt she was in the barn at home, feeding her aged pony, Charlotte. She remembered her father teasing her for giving the pony a human name, but it suited the cunning beast. Charlotte had a mane of perfectly blonde hair, and although prone to biting anyone who came near, Apple was the only child Charlotte had ever accepted on her back. And so they had been inseparable, growing up together. Apple had not ridden her for years, but their bond remained. And so it was with a moment of confusion, and the remnants of a blinding headache, that Apple had woken in an unfamiliar barn, next to a pair of mules uglier than sin.

'Lillian?' she whispered, in the half light of dawn.

The mules snickered in response.

If the mules were awake and she could see shapes in the barn, that meant it was sunrise. And sunrise meant that people would be up. And people meant the potential for discovery.

Apple's stomach rumbled. To her, it sounded louder than a Spitfire warning up on a runway. The mules took no notice.

'It's okay for you, eating your hay. What am I going to eat, huh?'

Apple crept to the stable door, held shut by the flurries of snow the night before. Regardless of how much she pushed, the door would not budge.

'Can I get a hand here?' she asked the nearest mule.

No response.

Apple searched the stable for any other way in or out. For a structure built nearly two thousand years before the London Eye and the Gherkin, it was impressive in its construction.

'They didn't want you two getting out, did they?' she asked.

A simple overhead platform had been built to store the winter's hay, and Apple shimmied up the ladder. This is where she should have spent the night, cocooned amongst the prickly hay bales.

She froze as the sound of voices outside the stable door reached her.

Apple burrowed deep into the hay, her colouring and clothing helping her blend into the shadows this close to the roof. She silently thanked her lucky stars for climbing the ladder when she had.

The words of the two men below washed over her in a language she did not understand, but their tone was aggressive enough to make her heart race. She pressed herself tighter into the hay, held her breath, and prayed. She could not afford to be discovered now.

She did not know who these people were or whether they could be trusted, but she knew they would not appreciate a strange woman hiding in their stable. The last thing she needed was to be caught and accused of being a spy. Their heated discussion certainly made her wish she could quiet her hammering heart. Something was afoot, and it did not sound good.

As the men lead the animals from the stable, they left the stable door ajar, much to Apple's glee. As their voices faded into the distance, Apple took a deep breath and clambered down the ladder. Now to find Lillian, or Pramod. Given the tone of what she'd just heard, it sounded like trouble was coming.

Apple peered around the stable door to see a landscape still swaddled in a swirling morning mist which the winter's sun had yet to penetrate. She wrapped her cloak tighter around herself, shivering in the biting cold.

The landscape could have been carved from a single slab of marble. Everything stood frozen in place, implacable and immovable. The view was both familiar, in that the hills stood proudly where they'd always been, but different. There was an absence of things — an absence of buildings and roads and fences and sounds and people and smoke and planes and the sheer hectic pace of modern life. They were all missing from the world outside of the stable door. It wasn't that there was nothing outside, but everything outside had been stripped back to its purest form. Apple felt a sense of awe at the beauty of it all, mixed with a creeping sense of dread at what she knew was going to happen to the villagers, to the soldiers guarding the fort, and potentially, to the governor of Britain - Decimus Clodius

Albinus, her great-great-grandfather how ever many times removed.

With her stomach growling, Apple slipped through the doorway, pausing to get her bearings. Should she aim for the village or the fort? Who was less likely to kill her?

A decision made, she started trudging through the snow, her boots sinking into the fluffy drifts, her eyes sweeping from side to side, alert for any signs of life. Not that she knew what she would do if she bumped into someone. Although at the rate her stomach was trying to digest itself, she needed to source some food sooner rather than later, which would mean finding someone who would feed her.

As Apple navigated her way towards the village, her stomach growling louder than ever, she saw a figure in the distance. At first, she thought it was just a trick of the light, but the closer they got, the more she began to panic. Frozen in place, she waited, her heart fluttering as wildly as a bird caught in a trap.

But it was just a child no older than eight, with a wooden toy sword clasped in his ungloved hand, and a suspicious look writ across his tiny human face.

'Who are you?' the child demanded, pointing his sword at Apple, his voice ringing out like a warning bell in the silent landscape.

'I'm Apple,' she replied, holding up her hands as a sign of peace.

'Are you a barbarian?' he asked, his voice small but full of conviction. 'Because if you are, I will chop off your head.'

'Do I look like a barbarian?' she asked, scanning the countryside, willing the mist to lift. 'Are they nearby?'

'They might be, but you can't see them because of their magic.'

'Their magic? They don't have any magic, they're just very good at hiding,' Apple said.

'How do you know?' the boy said, brandishing his sword. 'You must be a barbarian if you know things like that.'

If the sword had been made of steel and not wood, and if he were ten years older, Apple might have felt threatened, but as it was she couldn't stop the smile which crinkled her pale eyes. Her stomach chose that moment to rumble louder than the boy's arguments, which stopped him in his tracks.

'Barbarian's stomachs don't make sounds like that,' Apple explained.

The child lowered his sword. 'Are you hungry?'

Relieved, Apple nodded. 'I'm starving, and cold, and lost, and I can't find my friend.'

The child seemed to weigh up her words. It was a complete mystery how the boy was able to understand her, but then so was how she was able to travel through time. So for now, she was just happy that the boy hadn't tried to run her through with his beautifully carved toy.

'Follow me,' he said and began leading the way through the snow, clambering over snow drifts with an ease that had Apple panting. She followed behind, her stomach rumbling so loudly she was sure the barbarians, and the Romans, would hear it before they saw her.

As they lumbered through the snow, the boy kept glancing back, as if worried that at any moment she would transform into a tattooed barbarian, covered in blue dye made from woad, with lime-washed hair. Apple couldn't blame him; after all, she was a stranger. She briefly wondered if parents taught their children about "stranger danger" or whether that was a modern phenomenon?

'Here,' he said, pausing at a circular stone hut. Stone which had been robbed from some older building lost to time.

As Apple ducked through the low entrance, the darkness enveloped her like a thick blanket. Apple blinked, trying to adjust her eyes, only just recognising the outline of a woman hunched over a low fire.

'Ma, look who I found,' the boy said, tugging on the hem of the woman's skirt.

The woman was already staring at Apple with a mixture of fear and apprehension.

Apple held up her gloveless hands to prove that she held no weapons and that the woman had nothing to fear.

Once again, Apple's rumbling stomach broke the ice.

'She's hungry,' the boy added, reverently laying his sword on a ledge carved into the wall, before passing the woman a wooden bowl — one obviously made by the same skilled carver who'd fashioned the toy sword.

'Thank you,' Apple said, as the woman ladled stew into the bowl and passed it wordlessly to her.

'She's not a barbarian,' the boy said from his stool on the other side of the fire.

'Who are you?' the woman asked, breaking her silence. 'Are you a Roman?'

'No,' Apple said, looking up at the woman, who was still staring at her with suspicion. 'My name is Apple. I came up here to join my grandfather,' she said, warming to her cover story.

Unable to deny her stomach any longer, Apple took a spoonful of the stew. She closed her eyes and sighed, savouring the flavour and warmth slowly spreading through her. Upon opening her eyes, she found the woman's expression softening just a little.

'Where did you come from?'

'I... from far away, from Londinium,' Apple said, not knowing how else to answer. They hadn't workshopped this scenario when they were preparing Lillian for her journey back to Roman Britain. 'I was travelling with my friend, but we were separated in the storm.'

'A friend?' the woman asked, her tone wary.

'A girl, the same age as me, but with dark hair and blue eyes. Have you seen her?' Apple asked hopefully.

'No, I haven't seen anyone like that. Two women travelling alone?' She shook her head, her hand reaching for a medallion hanging around her neck on a leather thong.

'She might have gone to the fort, looking for me?' Apple suggested, her voice cracking as fear settled in her stomach.

'Then she's made a terrible mistake.'

Apple's eyes widened. 'Why?'

The woman shooed the boy from the hearth, sending him outside with a flurry of unintelligible commands, before turning back to Apple. 'The fort is under double guard because of the attack from the Iceni warriors,' the woman said, her voice low. 'And their Iron Beast.'

Apple's heart skipped a beat. The Iron Beast had to be the Mayor's missing car.

'Have you not seen the heads atop of the fort's walls?'

Apple shook her head. She hadn't seen anything in the storm other than the inside of the stable.

'If they have her, they'll think she's one of the Iceni.' The woman spat into the fire. 'Those soldiers use you for their own purposes before discarding you like a piece of rubbish when they're done.'

The woman's words dripped with bitterness, and Apple wondered about her personal experience with the Romans. Perhaps one had been the boy's father?

Apple straightened her shoulders, returning the now empty bowl to the woman's rough hands.

'You can stay here with us until the weather clears,' the woman said, as if she could read what Apple had in mind. 'The help would be welcome.'

'Thank you, but I need to join my grandfather. He might be able to help me find my friend. Thank you for the food.'

'No one in their right mind would go out there now,' the woman said, 'not with the Iron Beast on the loose. And they have a druid.' Her hand strayed back to the talisman around her neck.

Druids? Apple tried to remember if Lillian had ever mentioned a druid. Hadn't the Romans wiped out the druids when they'd attacked the island of Anglesey, destroying the druid's shrines and their sacred grove? Had one escaped, only to be recruited by the mayor and her Iron Beast? Recruited and raised to a level history wasn't prepared for?

'Did you see this Iron Beast?'

'We ran and hid. Not even the Romans were safe from

the druid's magic and his beast. I heard it though. Screaming louder than anything I've ever heard.'

Apple tried not to scoff. Magic was nothing more than the stuff of children's stories. And the Iron Beast was just a car. And yet, if there really was a druid using some sort of dark power, then that changed everything.

Apple stepped outside the hut, the cold air hitting her like a slap in the face. She took a deep breath of the crisp air to steel herself for whatever came next. Lillian was in danger, and she had to find her. It was as simple as that.

APPLE MOVED like a ghost through the dense thicket of the winter woods, navigating the skeletal trees and frozen underbrush. The snow crunched beneath her boots, and the biting wind numbed her cheeks. She pulled her cloak tighter around her shoulders, its ragged edges blending seamlessly with the faded hues of the landscape.

Her wary eyes scanned the horizon for any signs of Roman scouts or the Iceni. Apple had learned the art of invisibility, not from any stealth training, but from a lifetime of avoiding the pointed stares of the curious back in the twenty-first century. It was a skill she hadn't expected to be a survival tactic in ancient Britannia, but here she was, depending on her ability to blend in.

Apple's unique appearance — her inherited albinism — was both a curse and a blessing. Her pale skin and white hair made her distinctive, but her lineage connected her to the very Roman she now sought — her great-grandfather however many times over. He was a powerful figure in these times, and his life was at risk whilst he remained inside the fort, which would now be an easy target for an army of Iceni warriors armed with modern weapons, and the power of hindsight.

Every decision Apple made had to take into account the potential risks and rewards of warning her ancestor and locating Lillian. Ensuring Albinus' safety was paramount, considering the imminent Iceni attack under the mayor's guidance. Yet, the uncertainty surrounding Lillian's whereabouts tugged at her heart. The battle between her responsibilities weighed heavily on her shoulders.

Ithaca Fort loomed ahead, a formidable stone structure in the snowy landscape. Lillian could already be inside, which added another layer of complexity to the situation. Apple had already spent hours pondering ways to infiltrate the fort, even going so far as to consider the idea of posing as a prostitute — a disguise which might grant her access without arousing suspicion, but which had the major drawback of potentially being forced to *prove* her credentials. She shuddered.

Concealed amidst the winter foliage, Apple fixed her attention on the fort's wooden gates. The rhythmic tramp of boots echoed as a group of Roman soldiers approached the fortifications, their collective breath forming frosty clouds above their heads.

As she observed the soldiers, she assessed the attentiveness of the gate guards. On the surface, they seemed absorbed in their duties, vigilant but possibly overly accustomed to the routine of the comings and goings. Apple's mind raced as she strategised her approach, dismissing at once the idea of posing as a prostitute. The more she watched, the more she considered instead the feasibility of entering under the guise of a nondescript local woman delivering supplies to the fort. A purveyor of wares, easily missed in the hustle and bustle of normal life.

The fort's gates swung open and revealed a glimpse of the inner courtyard as the guards admitted the returning soldiers, their identities barely visible above the ice-encrusted scarves wrapped around their faces.

A new idea struck her like lightning.

Apple's heart raced as she imagined sneaking inside disguised as a soldier. A fully fledged Roman soldier. And she knew that there would be at least a two locations outside of the fort where she might be able to source a uniform without having to resort to violence. Because violence was never the answer.

Slipping away from her vantage point, Apple ventured

towards the village nestled at the fringes of the fort's influence. Despite the weather, the vicus buzzed with activity, but Apple moved with the same stealth that had served her well in the modern world. She knew what she was looking for — a place where people happily disrobed regardless of the cold — either the public baths or a brothel.

Fortunately for Apple, the brothel wasn't hard to find. A talented artist had painted a series of erotic scenes across one external wall, leaving very little to the imagination. The best sort of billboard.

With her hood drawn low, Apple slipped through the brothel's unguarded entrance like a wraith. Inside, dim oil lamps illuminated the worn furnishings and not much else. Without Metella's oversight, it hadn't taken long for the brothel to morph back into the basest sort of establishment.

Apple waited to be challenged, but no one questioned her presence. From the floor above, she heard the sounds of rigorous activity. And from what she could hear, Apple trusted that she had sufficient time to search downstairs for any stray pieces of uniform.

As quiet as a whisper, Apple entered the makeshift changing area for the brothel's clientele, her heart pounding in rhythm with the ticking of time. A quick glance revealed a soldier's uniform cast aside in erotic haste.

Without hesitation, Apple shed her outer cloak, replacing it with the stolen uniform. The coarse fabric hung off her frame, and she adjusted the fit as best as she could. A gleaming helmet completed the ensemble. In a polished bronze hand mirror, she saw a transformed reflection — a Roman soldier, their face obscured by the helmet's shadow.

Confident in her makeshift disguise, Apple slipped out of the brothel and back into the icy embrace of the village. With her newfound Roman disguise cloaking her like a second skin, Apple made her way towards the fort's imposing wooden gates.

The shadows of the formidable walls reached out like fingers, threatening to rip away her disguise, and as Apple paused to adjust the helmet, the rhythmic clatter of hooves disrupted the day and a group of cavalrymen cantered past.

Apple pressed herself against the rough stones of a nearby building, her heart in her throat. The horsemen, their steeds exhaling plumes of frost, appeared to have stepped straight from the pages of Sir Arthur Conan Doyle as ephemeral spectres against the pristine snow. At the rear of the group, a figure detached himself, his eyes locking onto hers.

With a racing heart, she met the gaze of the horseman with her blue eyes. He was younger than the others, with dark hair that fell over his shoulders. He seemed to study her for a moment before a sly grin formed on his lips. Apple waited for the inevitable discovery, and wished that she'd been bold enough to steal the soldier's abandoned sword from the brothel, as well as his uniform.

She held her breath, the soldier's cloak wrapped tightly around her figure, but the man nodded, and carried on riding, his attention returning to the cavalry troop as they disappeared into the embrace of the fort.

Apple could never have known who she'd just faced. But Lillian would have recognised him. Marcus.

As the clattering hooves of his companions faded into the distance, Marcus's thoughts lingered on the pale apparition huddled beside the building they'd just passed. A flicker of curiosity and something more primal sparked in his eyes. Marcus had always been adept at sniffing out secrets. It was a skill he had honed with deadly practise.

The soldier struck Marcus as unfamiliar. He wasn't anyone he had served with before. Perhaps he was one of the governor's men? Marcus' instincts, honed by a life of deception and clandestine dealings, suggested caution. He filed away the image of the mysterious soldier to be considered at another time, and it wasn't until he'd passed the figure that he clocked the absence of the soldier's sword and shield. He threw one last look over his shoulder as he urged his horse on. A girl! A girl dressed as a soldier. A pale girl, with hair the colour of moonlight and eyes that you could fall into.

Marcus couldn't shake the image of the girl soldier from his mind, and he found himself riding towards the cavalry barracks consumed with the image. He couldn't explain why, but there was a familiarity of her that he couldn't place.

As he dismounted his horse, Marcus catalogued his options. He could alert the guards to the presence of the interloper, but that wasn't his first instinct. There was more to her appearance than met the eye, and nothing about her stance had sparked even the slightest sense of danger. Marcus trusted his instincts. But why was she impersonating a soldier? There could be only one reason, and that was to pass unchallenged into the fort.

He laughed. Someone, somewhere, was missing his uniform, which would end badly. But for whom?

Marcus leaned his spear against the wall and contemplated his next move. It was best to wait and let any trouble reveal itself in due course, and he would, of course, exploit it where possible.

'Yo, Marcus.'

A voice sliced through Marcus's contemplation. He turned to face the source of the interruption — Gaius, the oaf, with a perpetually amused glint in his eyes. A man who lived for the thrill of mischief, without giving the repercussions any thought.

'What's got you brooding on a day like this?' Gaius asked, his tone teasing, his expression expectant.

Marcus managed a wry smile, a master of keeping his thoughts guarded. 'Just my usual scheming, Gaius. You know how it is.'

Gaius chuckled, a low rumble that echoed in the close quarters of the barracks. 'Always scheming, that's our Marcus. Anything interesting?'

Marcus hesitated, his thoughts still lingering on the

pale figure. 'Nothing too exciting, just a pretty young thing I saw out on patrol. A mysterious newcomer who is looking for warmth in all the wrong places.'

Gaius laughed, slapping Marcus on the shoulder. 'Leave it to you to pluck the finest peaches when you're out on patrol, my friend. Now, speaking of mysteries, have you heard the latest?'

Marcus raised an eyebrow.

'The governor of Britannia is gathering his legions for a march to Rome,' Gaius revealed, his voice lowered. 'Including us.'

A shiver crawled up Marcus's spine. He hadn't anticipated any change to their posting, certainly not until he had orchestrated his disappearance from Ithaca Fort. He feigned nonchalance, his mind working furiously to adjust to this unwelcome development. 'What's in Rome?'

Gaius leaned in, his expression conspiratorial. 'Potentially a dead emperor.'

'You stupid oaf, stay your thick tongue, Gaius,' Marcus cautioned. 'The walls have ears.' Any trouble in Rome meant increased scrutiny, more patrols, and a disruption to the delicate balance he and Darius had established with their illicit dealings with the Iceni.

As Gaius switched his chatter to the minutiae about a disagreement he'd had with the supplier of his socks, Marcus's mind whirred with fear. New orders would unravel the carefully woven threads of his scheme. There was no way he'd allow himself to be ensnared in Rome's political web. Not after everything he'd already achieved.

After Gaius left to attend to his duties, Marcus pondered the implications of another new emperor, and what it might mean if that emperor was Decimus Clodius Albinus. How quickly life became unpredictable and threatened to wash away everything he had planned for his future out from under the Roman yoke.

Someone had to know more about what was going on.

Leaving his horse to the ministrations of his slave, Marcus wandered the fort, until he reached the infirmary, where he found Julius checking on the men injured in the last Iceni attack.

'Julius, my friend, I hear our illustrious governor is planning a journey to Rome,' Marcus said, his face a mask of nonchalance.

Julius stiffened and shot him a suspicious glance, his dark eyes narrowing. 'Friend is a step too far, Marcus. I am not privy to the governor's plans. Why do you need to know?'

'Call it curiosity, Julius. I have made plans with a divine young lady, and I'm concerned that the governor's trip might impact negatively on them. You know what young women are like when they are left unattended? They can cause trouble.'

Marcus tried not to squirm under Julius's steel gaze. There was something simmering under the surface of Julius that he couldn't quite read, but it made him regret his initial boldness.

'I swear on Mars himself that she shimmers like the moon, and her legs—'

Julius held up a hand, the injured men tittering like women around a well. 'I don't need the details.'

Marcus hesitated, pretending to weigh his words. 'Just let me know if we're expected to travel with him, so I can adjust her, ah, expectations...'

The infirmary erupted in laughter and Julius stared at him, his mouth a thin line. 'You do know that all leave has been cancelled?'

Marcus leaned in and lowered his voice. 'Not for all of us, my friend.' He winked. 'I just need to know when he's leaving. You know how it is? I'll be in and out faster than a fox down a rabbit hole.'

Julius seemed immune to Marcus's legendary charm. 'I'll find out,' he said.

Marcus grinned. 'Just remember what I said about how beautiful she is. You wouldn't deny a man a last moment of happiness now, would you?'

As he left the infirmary, Marcus felt a new sense of purpose wash over him. Their new orders made his clandestine escape plans riskier, and he needed to find Darius to tell him of the governor's impending departure, and to set the wheels in motion for the Iceni's next attack, one he wouldn't be here to witness.

Marcus's thoughts circled back to the pale figure in the woods, the mysterious albino girl dressed up as a soldier. What would happen to her when the Iceni attacked? Oddly, he found himself worried, which was not part of the plan at all.

AS SUPPER APPROACHED, Marcus found that he hadn't needed to ask Julius, as the news of the governor's impending departure, so soon after his arrival, ran through the fort like a flood. Titus Caelius Castus, the fort's commander, had issued orders to his centurions to whip the garrison into shape for the governor's inspection in two days' time, whereupon half of the legion would depart for Rome alongside of Albinus.

Marcus pretended to be engrossed in his food, the conversations around the fire supplying all the details he needed. The fort's defences were to be reinforced, the barracks cleaned, and extra patrols had already been assigned. The tension within the ranks was palpable. Usually anything different at this outpost at the arse end of the empire was worthy of celebration, but not this. Not a forced march to Rome to claim a throne not yet empty.

Marcus still hadn't located Darius, his dimwitted accomplice. One who had almost outlived his usefulness, apart from one last job — to convey a message to the Iceni about the governor's departure.

Marcus excused himself under the guise of needing the latrine. The shadows concealed his movements as he searched for Darius among the various nooks and crannies where his friend usually sought refuge from the watchful eyes of their superiors, usually with a bottle in hand.

'Darius,' Marcus called, his voice a low murmur in the darkness.

Darius looked up, his eyes clouded with mild inebriation. 'Marcus?'

'Who else would it be?'

'Leave me alone, I'm off duty.'

'A Roman soldier is never off duty,' Marcus said, casting a glance around to ensure there were no prying eyes or ears. 'Listen carefully. The governor is leaving in two days—'

'The governor? Of Britannia?'

Marcus had to stop himself from strangling the man. 'This is what you need to do. Find Gar, the Iceni chieftain, and tell him that the governor is leaving in two days.'

Darius blinked at the depravity of Marcus' words. 'Why would we betray the governor?'

'Mars, give me strength,' Marcus muttered. 'Rome begs this of us. They need to have the false emperor dethroned before he can gather the legions behind him and march to Rome. Now, find Gar and tell him everything. This is our duty.'

Darius nodded, an alcoholic mix of uncertainty and determination in his eyes. 'I'll do it, Marcus, for Rome.'

'For Rome.'

Marcus watched Darius stumble into the night on a mission that held consequences far beyond his comprehension. Marcus knew that the impending chaos would serve as the perfect cover for his own disappearance from Ithaca Fort, and from the only life he'd even known.

A GOOD WIFE

Lillian hadn't fared much better than Apple, or Jane. She had woken with a similar headache, but inside the walls of Ithaca Fort, without her cloak, shivering uncontrollably.

She frowned, remembering that the cloak had been around her shoulders at the Bellingham. She'd been too hot with it on but too scared to remove it, not knowing when, or if, their plan would work.

Light filtered through cracks in a nearby door, allowing her to identify the faint outlines of a small room filled with wooden shelves heaving with paper scrolls. As well as a desk and a handful of sturdy stools. An office perhaps?

Sounds outside the door interrupted her thoughts and Lillian shrank back into the shadowy corner, her heart racing at the prospect of being caught. She just needed to find Julius to warn him of what was coming. After that, nothing mattered. But being caught now would be a death sentence, and not just for her.

The sound of footsteps faded. Lillian took a deep breath and crept over to the door, lifting the latch and peering through the minuscule gap. The door opened onto an empty corridor punctuated with identical closed doors, illuminated by smoky oil lamps nestled in small cavities along the stone walls.

Lillian slipped out of the office, hugging the stone walls as she tried to orientate herself. Torchlight danced on the walls, casting eerie shapes that seemed to reach for her. With her heart pounding like a battle drum, Lillian crept forward, her breaths coming in short, shallow gasps.

'Come on, Julius. Where are you?' she thought. Her racing heart was not entirely down to the fear of being discovered.

Heavy footsteps jolted Lillian from her thoughts. Panicking, she slipped through the shadows of the nearest doorway. As the heavy wooden door swung shut behind her, she found herself in an opulent chamber adorned with vibrant murals. And seated on a plush divan, sat a woman, her eyes red and swollen and her cheeks stained with tears.

'Who are you?' the woman demanded, her voice wavering between anger and fear. 'What do you want? Guards!'

Much to Lillian's astonishment, not a single person came rushing in, not even the lowest of slaves. The woman was alone.

'Please, I mean you no harm,' Lillian implored, raising her hands. 'I'm looking for Julius.'

'Julius Stertinius Carpus?' the woman's eyes narrowed. 'What do you want with Julius?'

Lillian hesitated before replying. She was already on shaky ground, being a stranger in the woman's room, but sharing news of an impending attack would mark her as a spy. Instead, she tried a different approach. 'I have... news of great importance. Please, I must find him.'

The woman sniffed, wiping away a tear with the back of her hand. 'You and every other woman here. I am Claudia, wife of Titus Caelius Castus, the commander of this forsaken place. He'll not welcome the news that another of his men has fathered a child.'

The woman's words unnerved her. Had Julius played her for a fool? She'd never once felt that from him, but then again, how much did she really know about him?\

'I'm not pregnant,' Lillian said. 'That's not why I'm here.'

'You don't need to lie to me. I do not care who Julius has been with.'

'I wasn't. It's about...' Lillian tapered off. The woman's tears had started falling again. 'You're crying.'

'It's nothing that concerns you.'

Something in the woman's demeanour made Lillian press on. 'Can I help?'

Claudia's eyes flicked back and forth between Lillian and the door. But in the end, the desire to unburden herself won out. 'My husband brought me back to this place against my wishes. We arrived in time to mop up the Roman blood staining the roadway I was forced to travel down. The blood of soldiers who died fighting barbarians. Filthy animals who slip through the night like eels to slay good men in their beds. My husband is out there now, counting the bodies like a lowly scribe. For all I know, you could be one of them here to murder me. Hurry, I beg you in the name of the goddess Juno, for I cannot bear this life for one-second more.'

Lillian shook her head. 'I'm not one of them, I promise. I'm only here for Julius—'

'Julius, again? He is not one of the bodies out there. I checked myself. He'll be between your legs tonight. Have no fear.'

Lillian held her blush in check, but something else bloomed inside her. Something she could not give a name to.

'Of course, that could change tonight or tomorrow. We are outmatched, but my husband refuses to retreat. He would rather see his men die at the hands of the barbarians than ask for help or admit defeat. He wants to prove himself to the governor, whose men stand behind the walls of the fort and watch, instead of fight.' Claudia's voice shook. 'Our men are terrified. I have never seen so many offerings at the altars. But we have been undone by the magic of the druids. How can we win?'

A shiver ran down Lillian's spine. It was not magic they were facing.

'If you can just help me find Julius, I can help stop the attack,' she said.

Claudia laughed. 'You're a girl. There is nothing you can do.'

'So was Boudica,' Lillian replied. 'Look, there is a woman more powerful than Boudica leading the Iceni now. That's where the iron beast comes from. From her...' Lillian struggled to think of a way to phrase it without saying from the future or something equally obscure. 'From faraway. She can foretell the future, which is why you have to persuade your husband to attack the Iceni before Albinus leaves Ithaca Fort.' Lillian paused to gauge Claudia's reaction. So far the woman was listening to her. 'That's why I'm here. I've come from the same place as the witch leading the Iceni to warn you *and* Julius. He saved me once. Now it's my turn to save him.'

'How do you know Albinus is here?' Claudia asked, suspicion clouding her eyes once more.

Lillian felt the thin ice shaft beneath her. She had to convince Claudia that she wasn't a spy and was telling the truth. 'Albinus plans to proclaim himself emperor, and is gathering support for a march to Rome as we speak. However, the Iceni know this as well, and they're planning to attack the governor, and his supporters, whom I assume include your husband, and yourself.' Lillian made up the last part. History hadn't recorded what happened to the commander of Ithaca Fort. He was another name lost to time.

For a moment, Claudia stared at her. 'If you are telling the truth? If you really are from the same place as the Iceni witch, then you will know how to convince my husband of your truth.'

Lillian hesitated. How could a girl from Hexham persuade a Roman commander to change tactics? But there was something in Claudia's voice that made her want to try. Would Neumegen warn that this was messing with time? She didn't know, but she knew that it might just save the life of Julius. And that was all that mattered.

'I'll try.'

.   .   .

CLAUDIA LED Lillian through the corridors of the commanding officer's residence. With their hoods up, they exited the palatial building and ventured to the outskirts of the fort — the looming shadows conspiring with the walls to guard their secrets, until at last they arrived at the baths. The vestibule was empty, save for the steam swirling around them like spirits. The walls were adorned with mosaics depicting scenes of Roman grandeur — an oasis of luxury in the middle of the harsh northern winter.

'Why are we here?' Lillian asked. The building appeared empty. Was this a trap?

Claudia turned to Lillian. 'This is where you prepare yourself,' she said. 'You need to look the part to speak with my husband.'

Lillian felt Claudia's gaze upon her as she busied herself stripping off. Doubt had infused the woman's face as she watched Lillian remove her outer garments to reveal her underwear — items of clothing which bore no resemblance to anything a Roman matron of good standing would recognise. In her defence, Lillian hadn't anticipated anyone seeing her in her matching lace bra and knickers. A knot of fear tightened in her chest.

'Once you have bathed, I will ensure that you are *properly* attired for the meeting.'

Lillian noted a curious look on Claudia's face. Was it jealousy? Was she afraid of Lillian meeting her husband? In the absence of any other options, she had to trust the woman.

What Lillian couldn't know was that Claudia viewed her as a chance to change the trajectory of her husband's career, which would in turn provide Claudia with an escape from the life of drudgery at Ithaca Fort that she'd desired more than anything. More than Julius.

LILLIAN AND CLAUDIA reconvened in Claudia's private quarters where the air was thick with incense and the echoes of whispers from distant corridors. Claudia helped her don a dress of silk and fine linen, adorned with intricate patterns and vibrant colours. The transition from modern attire to the garments of ancient Rome jarred her, and she felt the weight of her borrowed identity suffocating her.

With every passing minute, the threat of the Iceni attack under Jane's control drew nearer. The future was unclear, but the course of history now hinged upon the actions of two women.

Claudia spoke in hushed tones. 'Titus takes advice from no one, but especially not from a woman.'

'Then we should speak with him privately, away from his men.'

'There's a small study adjacent to his quarters. He retires there when he wishes for solitude,' Claudia answered. 'And when he has certain *visitors* he doesn't wish me to meet.'

Lillian saw the look of pain in Claudia's eyes. 'I swear to you, Claudia, that I am not here for that reason. You do believe me?'

Claudia nodded, and Lillian began breathing again. 'Thank you. Now, how can you get me into his study?'

A FIGHT TO THE DEATH

Julius combed his fingers through his hair, wincing as he knocked the still fresh wound on his scalp.

'Leave it or it'll bleed like buggery,' said one of the other men, prostrate on the cot next to him. 'Is it bad?'

'I'm not dying,' Julius replied, swinging his legs onto the floor, the fresh rushes on the ground tickling his bare feet. 'I should find out what's happening out there.'

He could not believe that the Iceni had attacked a second time. Surely they must have seen the extra men arrive alongside the governor of Britannia? You could hardly miss him — an unnaturally pale man, trussed up like a gift for the emperor himself, accompanied by a quarter of his legendary legion. If only he'd brought his entire legion with him.

'Better you than me. At least no one is trying to impale me on a spike in here.'

'You might be next if we don't help the poor souls out there,' Julius replied.

'Have you seen the state of my arm?' The man pulled back his woollen blanket, revealing a blood-soaked bandage tied to his arm, which ended somewhere near his elbow.

Julius stammered out an apology.

The man laughed. 'You should see your face. I haven't had that part of my arm for the last six years. But this time

I got an arrow in my stump, and not even one of theirs. I fell onto one I was carrying for that lot out there.' His laughter filled the sickroom. 'Don't go thinking I did it on purpose. I tripped over some fucker who was less lucky than me.'

Julius's laugh petered out, with determination replacing the smile on his face. 'I need to find out what we're up against.'

He grabbed a broken spear and a shield — the only weapons he could find, and made his way out of the sickroom.

Stepping outside, he was met with chaos. Bodies littered the ground, some of them soldiers he had served alongside since joining the army. Julius gagged on the stench. He had been in battle before, but never when the stone walls of the battlefield pulsed with a miasma of sweat, death, and burnt flesh.

His head throbbed with pain, making it difficult for him to focus, but there was nothing wrong with his peripheral vision. Julius braced himself as a painted barbarian launched himself at Julius with a blood-curdling cry.

They tumbled to the ground, all arms, and legs, and teeth, and testosterone. Julius rolled onto his back, using his shield to block the savage blows from the barbarian's stout sword. The two warriors grappled, each struggling for the upper hand. The putrid stench of the barbarian's breath filled Julius' nostrils as the man tried angling his sword towards Julius' chest.

An opening appeared, and Julius kicked out, striking the barbarian in the shin, before pressing his advantage and plunging his broken spear into the barbarian's stomach, savagely twisting it from side to side until the light drained from his attacker's eyes.

His victory was short-lived. Another barbarian appeared around the corner of the granary, his sword raised high. Julius braced himself, ready to defend himself and his home.

Just as the barbarian was about to strike, a piercing whistle sounded from the top of the fort's walls. The barbarian hesitated for a fraction, looking up to see what the commotion was about, giving Julius the chance he needed. He thrust his spear forward. The half-naked man was nothing more than skin and bones, and so the spear encountered little resistance as Julius plunged it deep into the man's cadaverous chest.

A little cough. The widening of dark brown eyes. Then nothing. A dribble of blood. A life extinguished.

May Mars show mercy on his soul, Julius thought, pulling the spear free from its fleshy scabbard.

The whistling has been replaced with the sound of trumpets and shouts of glee.

Julius took a moment to catch his breath, before climbing to the top of the walls to see what had caused the sudden shift in the battle's momentum.

From the elevated viewpoint, he saw the polished armour of a group of Roman marching towards the fort — reinforcements summoned by the governor to handle the barbarian incursion. Their prayers had been answered.

And from the top of the wall, Julius saw the Iceni warriors melting into the landscape. Too many to count, and too adept at hiding to bother chasing down.

***

'How many dead?' Castus, the Fort's commander asked.

'Too many,' came the reply. 'Ten or twenty men?'

'Ten or twenty men? Is that the answer you would give to the Emperor if he were here?' Castus asked.

The man shook his head.

'Then give me a number, a proper number, not an approximation,' Castus said, his voice a quiet thunder in the still room.

The legionary scurried from the room, with the remaining men shuffling nervously under the commander's gaze.

'I want to know the numbers of wounded, as well as the dead. And if any of you imbeciles dares to mention the appearance of lemures, or blame what happened on the druids, I will have you nailed to a cross and hung upside down for the ravens to feast on your eyeballs. You have been warned.'

'There was an iron horse—' a centurion started, his face a bloodied mess.

Titus Caelius Castus, the commander of Ithaca Fort, held up a hand, beckoning the centurion closer.

'Is that your blood? Did you receive a blow to the head in the battle?'

'It is the blood of a barbarian.'

'So I can therefore assume that your hearing is unaffected, and that you retain control of your cognitive functions?'

'I...'

'Which means you heard my warning yet took no heed of my words?'

The men shifted uneasily.

'Speak, soldier,' Castus barked, his patience wearing thin.

The centurion swallowed. 'There was an iron horse. We tried following it, but it was too fast.'

'I warned you. I warned all of you. Do you know the punishment for insubordination?' Castus spat at the feet of the quaking soldier. 'Take him away. I've heard enough. Let the ravens feast on his lies.'

'Commander?' Julius said, stepping forward.

'You too, Julius?' Castus asked.

'He speaks the truth.'

A murmur of agreement went through the assembled men.

'And we can't afford to lose another good man,' Julius said.

'Out, all of you,' Castus ordered. 'Go clean up the mess outside. I want the patrols doubled, our defences assessed and any weak points repaired. He lives another day, but I want his pay docked.'

It was as if the men were carried from the room by a tsunami they scattered so quickly. Castus slammed the door shut behind them. What little self control he had left evaporated as he threw a Samian ware jug at the wall, where it shattered into hundreds of shards, soaking the freshly laid rushes.

He'd heard nothing so preposterous in his life, yet when he'd rode in with the auxiliaries from Eboracum, their scout had pulled up at the sight of tracks so unusual, they had spent nigh on an hour trying to analyse the marks. In hindsight, it had been an error of judgement not to send any of the troops to investigate. But he'd had his hands full with the arrival of the governor of Britannia.

Castus groaned. What would the governor think of the sneak assault on the fort? What should he say — that the druids had summoned a beast from the underworld and had burrowed their way into the fort? Or he could just not say anything about the iron beast, and hope that his men keep the secret too? But secrets were like fire. They smouldered unseen, consolidating their base before becoming impossible to control and devouring everything in their path.

He would face the governor's wrath soon enough. If he could produce this iron horse his men spoke of, things might go differently for him. But as it stood, he faced losing his command. And where would that leave him? There was nothing worse than what he had now — the command of a ragtag bunch of auxiliary soldiers at the arse end of the empire.

Castus rubbed his temples, the throbbing getting worse with every passing day. He could not go to his wife for comfort or advice. The only day she had pleased him had been their wedding day.

The thought of returning to his quarters made his headache even worse. There was only one woman who could caress the pain away — Metella. It had been too long since he had seen her. So that was what he would do. He would visit Metella and beg for relief before returning to his wife and her empty eyes.

'WHAT DO YOU MEAN, she's gone? Gone where, and with whom?' Castus raged at the cowering child in front of him. One of the various waifs Metella protected instead of casting them out of the filth they had been born into.

'Gone with Silas and Carmella, and another man.'

'A man? A Roman man? A barbarian? Be more specific, child. We are all men here. I have no time for your riddles.'

'Not a Roman, a stranger, with his body frozen like a statue. Only his eyes could move.'

'You are next to useless,' Castus said, his head threatening to split like an overripe plum. 'Iron horses, men like statues, next, you'll be telling me that the emperor himself is your father. Send me someone who knows something.'

The child scurried away, the movement of its scrawny legs reminiscent of a spider spinning its sticky web.

Castus sank onto the couch in the receiving room, his head in his hands. Metella had gone. But where? There was nowhere to go. If she had been travelling south, they would have met her on the road. There was nothing north but death. That left east or west. Going west at this time of year was akin to committing suicide, which left east — the direction of the mysterious iron horse.

Castus stood up. He needed Metella. How dare she leave the vicus without his permission? He was the commander of the fort, and he demanded that she return.

After marching out of the receiving room and into the street, he had to stand back whilst villagers carrying what little they owned scurried past, their eyes looking anywhere other than at him and his retinue.

Pushing through the mob of villagers, he mounted his horse and surveyed the scene from the higher vantage point. Odd that the barbarians had spared the vicus from their attack, he thought, watching as villagers returned from wherever they had taken shelter during the assault on the fort. Why hadn't Metella returned?

'Find her,' he ordered, his eyes searching the distant hills, 'and bring her back.'

STICKS AND STONES

Bricius warmed his hands above the fire. The flames were too small to do anything more than provide the barest of hints of warmth. They had taken a chance lighting it, but nothing banishes demons faster than an open flame and a polished sword.

'The iron beast won't move,' Iolo complained, his sharp cheekbones appearing even more skeletal in the flickering flames.

'And it won't,' Bricius commented. Why his chieftain Gar had saddled him with this fool was beyond his understanding. They were not of the same tribe. There was no affiliation, but for some unknown reason Gar had shown the druid Iolo the same level of deference that he would if Diviciacus himself were among them. But this man was a much greater fool than Diviciacus.

Bricius spat into the fire.

'You waste your vapours,' Iolo intoned, his voice as sharp as his anorexic body.

'Do not worry about my vapours. Busy yourself with reading the signs for the woman's return, so that we can prepare the beast. Is that not your role, druid?'

Iolo's response was to return to mumbling his unintelligible prayers, shuffling back towards the motionless beast hidden under the sweeping branches of the copse of willow trees.

Bricius imagined separating Iolo's head from his shoulders, a far better picture than the one which faced him now — a husk of a man dressed in robes of woven hemp, the scent of falsehoods clinging to him. But Gar trusted him, and Gar was his chieftain.

In Bricius' opinion, Gar's first mistake had been to trust Iolo. The second was to believe that the woman would return. For days they'd searched the countryside. Fanning out from the goddess Satiada's altar, Gar had sent his hunters east, north, west and south. But the woman had vanished just as quickly as she had appeared, leaving her iron beast behind. Regardless of the druid's incantations, or the application of the oxen's whip, the beast would not move. It mattered not. The Romans were scared whether they deployed the beast, or didn't. Bricius had witnessed the terror of the Romans and knew, in his darkest of hearts, that the time to attack was now.

And Gar's third mistake? Gar's mistake was that he had not listened to Bricius.

You win a battle before you fight it. Every warrior was taught that from birth, so Gar should have attacked when the beast was under their control, instead of retreating. Bricius poked a small stick into his meagre fire, followed by another. Winter limited their fuel, with the ground beneath them groaning under the weight of the snow. Still, this fire was larger than the fire in his chieftain's belly. Gar was a man besotted with a vision, and nothing more.

Bricius chanced another look at the druid, watching as Iolo hobbled his way around the beast, muttering his incantations. Perhaps Jane was nothing more than a vision conjured up by the druid's magic? The Romans were right to rid the land of the mischief makers. He spat in the fire, the hiss of the flames agreeing with his theory.

And far above, the stars continued their nightly dance, unfettered by the human concept of time. And it was to the stars that Bricius looked to for advice. Advice on how to deal with Iolo, and Gar's foolish decisions.

HIDE AND SEEK

When the power went down, Jane Badrick had been standing outside the Bellingham with Darby, the falling snow obscuring them from any curious eyes inside. Her last conscious memory had been Darby pressing a coin into her hand. Now all she could feel was an intense pain burning inside her head. A pain more excruciating than childbirth, coupled with a weighty pressure on her chest making it almost impossible to fill her lungs.

Coming to, Jane shoved the man off her chest, gasping for air, the bitter cold splintering her lungs.

'What's happening?'

Who said that? Darby? Had it worked? Had she returned to the Iceni? But why was Darby here talking to her? Darby wasn't meant to be here.

'Jane, what happened? Where are we? Jesus it's cold.'

'Darby?'

'My head,' Darby complained, his face as pale as the snow threatening to smother them.

It was not meant to be like this. Darby was supposed to bring her car to the Bellingham, leaving the coin on the passenger seat for her. A simple plan. But instead he'd passed her the coin outside the Bellingham's entrance. Why hadn't he just followed her orders? And where the hell was her car? The fool had ruined everything.

Jane slapped Darby's face.

'What the actual fuck?' Darby yelped.

'Be quiet unless you want to die,' she whispered, shimmying under the protective canopy of the nearest tree. 'Over here, you idiot.'

Darby followed, wobbling like a drunkard, rubbing the sting from his face.

'You slapped me.'

'Shut up,' Jane hissed, quickly adjusting to this turn of events. All her arrangements were ruined. Everything she needed to make an impression on Gar — the Iceni chief, was in her car — food, weapons, medication, all gone. Gone because Darby couldn't follow the simplest of instructions.

Jane squinted through the dense fog of whirling snowflakes looking for any signs of civilisation. 'We got lucky. I think we're close to the altar.'

'What fucking altar? The one at Ithaca? It that where are we? Christ, my head. I barely had anything to drink, either.'

Jane ignored his monologue as she tried to get her bearings.

'Do you have a lighter?'

'What?'

'Do you have a cigarette lighter in your pocket for that filthy habit you inflict on the rest of us?'

A tiny flame flared, and Jane snatched the lighter from Darby's shaking hands. At least she could make fire at the flick of her thumb. That alone should impress the crass barbarians she knew were tracking their every movement, despite the storm.

'Hey, that's mine.'

'Darby, shut up and follow my every direction, then we might both live through this.'

'Just ring your office and tell them to send a car. It's a fucking storm, not the apocalypse. The roads are bad, but it's not like we've slipped into a mini ice age.'

How could he not recognise that they weren't in Hexham anymore? What use were all his fancy degrees? They weren't worth the paper they were printed on.

'Where's my car?' she asked, completely ignoring his complaints.

'Your *car*? Someone's dumped us in the middle of the countryside, and you want to know where your car is?'

Jane sighed. 'Just tell me where my car is, and then I'll explain.'

'There was a small issue that I got caught up in at Ithaca Farm. I was going to use your car, but you'd packed for a polar expedition, so I had to use my own, which isn't designed for this bloody weather. I slipped into a ditch and had to get a tow out from some farmer. So yeah, my night hasn't exactly gone to plan, although I still got your stupid Roman coin to you, didn't I? Do you know how bloody hard that was? So now you have to keep up your end of the bargain and appoint me as lead archaeologist for the borough. And I'm going to need a lift home, cause there's no way my car is going to make it through this, and I've got stuff at my flat that I need to sort.'

Jane laughed. There was no going home.

'Sit down, Darby, and shut up, while I figure out what to do.'

Whether it was the tone of her voice, or the realisation that something wasn't quite right, but Darby sat down, wrapping his arms around his legs. At least the idiot was wearing gloves, Jane thought, as she pulled her sleeves down over her own bare hands.

Her headache was fading and the freezing wind had sobered her up, allowing her to assess the situation she was in. If only she'd thought to bring her tame archaeologist back with her in the first place, she could have skipped all that study of Roman history. Who was the fool now? Having him here wasn't part of the plan, but he could be useful. She just need to pivot and adapt. She had a degree in that.

'What do you know about the Iceni?' she asked, lowering herself to sit beside Darby.

'We're outside in the middle of a snowstorm. You just slapped me, and now you're asking me about a shadowy tribe of Britons? Well, they didn't hang around in

Northumberland in winter, sheltering under trees on the side of the road.'

'Are you saying that they weren't from Northumberland?'

'You're dressed as Boudica, so I assume you know something about her history?'

'She was an early British queen and killed a lot of Romans. But what history doesn't record is that after she died, her followers kept up their resistance against the Romans under new leaders. Stronger leaders,' Jane replied, confident in her personal interpretation.

She couldn't see Darby shake his head, but felt it. She braced herself for the incoming lecture.

'The Iceni tribe was based in East Anglia, so nowhere near here. What would the Iceni have achieved being this far north? They were too busy putting Londinium to the torch, so they weren't up here playing noughts and crosses with the Roman soldiers. I don't know where you're getting your history from, but after Boudica's death, the Romans routed everyone involved with the uprising. They put tens of thousands of Britons to death.'

Jane lapsed into silence. Who was Gar then, or had the history books got it wrong? After all, the victors wrote the history books, not the vanquished. Perhaps Dio Cassius's description of Boudica was more a male fantasy than fact?

'Can we please just go inside, I'm literally freezing to death?'

'There is no inside. Haven't you worked it out yet?'

'It's bloody cold, Jane.'

'Look around, you idiot. Can you see any lights? Any cellphone towers? Wind farms? Where's the top of Hexham Abbey? More to the point, where the hell are the roads, the power lines, the rubbish? Think about it.'

'We're in Scotland?'

Jane glared at him under the cover of darkness. 'Are you joking?'

'It's fine, I'll walk back to town,' Darby said, getting up and ducking under the overhanging branches. 'I know you like your booze, but I really think you've got a problem. I'll speak to you on Monday.'

'If you walk away now, you'll die, either from exhaustion or from an arrow in the back. It's your choice.'

Silence.

'Darby?'

Nothing.

Darby returned. 'There is nothing out there. Nothing.'

'No, not nothing, just nothing you can see. They'll find us soon enough unless you help me get back to the altar at Ithaca Farm. Do that, and I'll explain everything.'

Darby stared at her with eyes full of disbelief. '*They?*'

Jane felt a deep sense of satisfaction at the sight; Darby was out of his element and completely reliant on her. Poetic justice for the way he had looked down on her in the past.

'This is some sort of joke, right?'

Jane didn't bother replying. She had a rule in life not to argue with idiots.

Darby continued to stare, his face pale and drawn, his whole body shaking. Until a type of acceptance settled on his features. 'What do you want me to do?'

Jane smiled, a glimmer of hope warming her cold heart. 'You work out how to get us back to Ithaca Farm, and I'll take it from there. But we need that car.'

MASTERS OF THE UNIVERSE

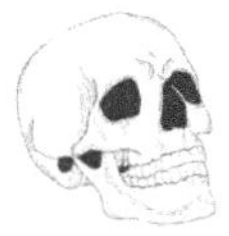

Jane Badrick straightened her shoulders, folded her arms, tapped her foot and waited. What she really wanted to do was to kick the useless lump, but for now he had his uses, so she silently commended herself on her restraint.

'What?' Darby mumbled, his eyes still as big as saucers.

'It's time to get moving.'

'I'm cold, and confused.'

'And you'll be cold and dead if you don't show me the way to Ithaca Farm from here,' Jane hissed, the words barely making it through her gritted teeth.

'Just follow the Stanegate,' Darby said, his head still swivelling as if he were waiting for Hexham Abbey to magically appear.

'Do you think I'd be asking for directions if I knew the way to the Stanegate? Come on, we need to move. Hopefully, I'm not too late.'

'Too late for what?' Darby asked, returning to the mediocre protection of the overhanging branch.

Jane didn't answer. She thought she'd seen something, a flash of movement in the distance. She could only pray that they hadn't already been seen.

'We just need to follow the...' Darby's voice petered out as reality sank in. 'What the... where are... Is that a mile marker? What's that doing here?'

Jane watched him run his hands over the smooth lines of a huge standing stone. Eight feet high, and twenty inches in diameter, the Roman milestone stood as straight as a soldier at attention, and was just as well presented.

'The text, look at the text,' Darby exclaimed.

The Latin text looked freshly chiselled by a master stonemason. Time had not yet weathered the stone, nor had the words been defaced by idle future hands.

'It's a stone,' Jane replied.

'It's a Roman milestone, and I have never in my life seen one is such good condition as this. It must be a replica, like those three altars at Vindolanda, but I don't recall reading anything about it. Did you do this, the council?'

'Do you think Hexham Council has money to waste on a folly like this? Are you really that stupid? Look around you, Darby, and tell me what you see? Yes, it's a milestone,' and she waved her hands in mock surprise. 'But surprise, surprise, it isn't a replica. It just hasn't been incorporated into a Christian monastery yet, or used as ballast in a ship sailing for the Americas. Don't look at me with such shock on your face. I know my history. You don't get to be mayor in a place like this without knowing history. But for god's sake, Darby, look around. We are *in* history today. In Roman Britain, hopefully sometime around 193AD, if everything went to plan.'

'To plan? What are you talking about? How much did you have to drink at the Bellingham?'

'Shut up and listen,' Jane snapped. 'You are in Roman Britain, in the middle of a time rift, where two different points in time converge. And while you're here with me, you will do what you're told, or we'll both end up dead.'

'You're insane, or drunk,' Darby said. 'Absolutely bloody, stark raving mad.'

A whistle in the air stopped them in their tracks, followed by the thunk of an arrow impaling itself in the trunk of the nearby tree.

'Get down,' Jane commanded.

'What the—'

Jane pulled Darby to the ground as a second arrow, and then a third joined the first in the tree.

'They've found us,' she whispered.

'Who?'

'The Iceni.'

Darby grabbed a rock, as if that alone could protect them.

'Don't be stupid. If they wanted to kill us, we'd be dead,' Jane hissed, knocking the rock from Darby's trembling hands. 'Just wait, and don't even open your mouth. They don't want to hear from you.'

Iceni warriors emerged like wraiths from behind the trees. Jane stood with her shoulders back, settling a veil of superiority on her face. She would *never* let these men see that they frightened her. She just needed to bluff her way through this setback in order to return to Ithaca Farm, and to her car, and then she would be ready to face Gar. Ready to betray him to the Romans in order to execute the next stage of her plan — entry into the highest levels of Rome.

Leading the warriors was a man on a black horse, an enormous bronze shield slung across his back as if it weighed nothing. His face was hard and chiselled, and his long hair streamed out behind him like smoke. Bricius, the second-in-command to Gar — the Iceni chieftain, had arrived.

Jane stared up at Bricius, who had not bothered dismounting.

'You return,' he said. 'But without your iron beast.'

'I have returned, yes.'

Bricius narrowed his eyes. 'Who is the man with you?'

Jane motioned towards Darby. 'My guide.'

Darby stood dumbfounded, his hands limp by his side.

Silence filled the space as the warrior appeared to process Jane's words. 'You return with a stranger, but without your iron beast and the magic weapons you promised Gar? How do we know he is not a spy? He looks Roman?'

For the first time, Jane took in Darby's outfit. Whilst she was dressed in a fair approximation of time period appropriate clothing, Darby was dressed like a modern day tripper, in a in a fleece-lined Barbour jacket, a heavy cable knit scarf and moleskin trousers, with a pair of sturdy steel cap boots on his feet. He stuck out like a sore thumb.

'He's my guide, from Londinium,' and here she thought quickly. 'My iron horse is nearby, but before it will let me mount it, I must make an offering to the gods. The storm turned us around before we could reach the altar. I have another iron horse for Gar, and my guide will ride it into battle for him.'

'She lies,' whispered one of the other Iceni warriors, a man who looked too much like Bricius for them to be anything other than brothers.

Darby had been staring at the Iceni, but when Jane mentioned her "guide" riding an iron horse into battle, he'd turned his attention to her.

'Like hell I will,' Darby hissed. 'Tell me what's going on here, Jane, or I swear to God I will smear you across every newspaper in the country.'

'I told you to shut up,' Jane said, her lips in a grim line, her eyes never leaving Bricius' tattooed face.

The warriors held whispered conversations from atop of their nervous horses. The beasts pawed at the frozen ground, tossing their heads and snorting as if they could sense the otherness radiating from Jane and Darby.

'Bricius, it's cold, and you know Gar will be displeased when he hears of your treatment of me,' Jane countered. It took every ounce of her willpower to stop her teeth from chattering and her knees from knocking.

'Jane?' Darby whispered.

She ignored him.

Bricius regarded her with his usual stoic intensity. 'You will come with me,' he said, 'and we will see if Gar believes your words. And if the gods agree, we will return you to the altar.' He turned his horse and rode away.

Jane's demands faltered in the face of Bricius' unyielding resolve. Her familiarity with power and control waned in the presence of a man whose time she could never possibly understand.

With swift precision, two Iceni warriors, their faces obscured by swathes of fabric, lifted Jane and Darby onto their horses. The moments that followed were a blur of galloping hooves, the subtle rustling of underbrush, and the heavy breathing of the riders navigating the almost invisible paths that led them away from the altar at Ithaca Farm. And away from Jane's ultimate goal.

TUCKED AWAY IN A DENSE FOREST, concealed by a thick canopy of leaves, lay the hidden campsite of the northernmost sub-tribe of the Iceni. Tents made from animal hides and woven branches formed a makeshift village in the centre of an ancient rainforest. The metallic rasp of swords being sharpened echoed through the ancient branches as the Iceni prepared their weapons for war.

As Jane and Darby entered the camp, they were met with the unwavering gazes of a people who had only ever known a lifetime of occupation. The campsite was more than just a temporary refuge; it was a space where the echoes of rebellion and the whispers of the past converged in a symphony of defiance.

Jane shifted uncomfortably on her horse as realisation dawned that every man there knew about her and her iron beast, but also of her abandonment of the Iceni in their hour of need. The judgement was clear on their faces. How *dare* she disappear when they had been so close to destroying the Romans? Uneasy mutterings followed them across the campsite towards the largest tent. Gar's tent.

After they dismounted, Bricius directed them into the large tent, where Jane promptly gagged on the smoke-laden air inside; air tainted with the smell of roasting meat, unwashed bodies, and death.

Gathering her bearings, she spied Gar reclining on a huge wooden chair at the far end of the tent, with the druid Iolo reclining beside him.

Jane moved towards Gar, Darby trailing in her wake. Jane's pride refused to allow her to cower beneath the chieftain's burning gaze. The strange tableau of past and present appeared frozen until Gar spat at her feet, and a rare smile bloomed on the druid's face.

'Have you been suckling on the teat of Romulus, witch?' Gar asked.

Jane paled, but lifted her chin defiantly, tidying her blonde hair with an air of studied nonchalance.

Darby nudged her, but she ignored him. She needed to plan her words carefully. Darby being here could be a hindrance, or a blessing. She hadn't quite decided how to use his presence.

'The gods took me,' she said.

Darby nudged her in the side. She moved half a pace away.

'The gods?' Gar asked, his head cocked to the side.

The smile on Iolo's face had been replaced by a sneer at the mention of the gods.

'Gar,' Jane said, her voice ringing with false confidence. It was strange how easy she found it to lie now. 'I bring you a guide to lead you into battle.'

Gar snorted, his gaze flicking over Darby. 'What use is he to me? I have braver women in my bed than this creature you offer.'

Jane stepped forward, holding Gar's gaze. 'He knows the strengths and weaknesses of the Romans. Their weapons hold no secrets for him, and he can explain how to destroy them. He...' She paused. 'He also knows when important Roman commanders will visit this area.'

'How could he know that? You said he was your guide,' Bricius argued.

'Why would you think I would tell you everything? Gar is your chieftain, or do you forget your place?'

For the third time, Darby nudged her, digging his fingers painfully into her side.

'Let me speak,' Darby said.

'No.'

'Your guide wishes to talk. Let him,' Gar commanded.

'I do not allow it,' Jane countered.

The entire campsite collectively held its breath.

Iolo leaned forward, his skeletal face stretched into a death grimace, his fingers dancing over the bones dangling from his neck. 'Let the man speak,' he said, his voice like the hiss of serpents.

Jane nodded, refusing to acknowledge the smug look on Darby's face as he stepped forward.

'Thank you,' Darby said, the quaver in his voice startlingly obvious. 'I know everything about the Romans in Britannia. I know when they leave, and who will lead them in the future. And I know what they fear the most.'

'And what is that?' Gar asked.

Darby smiled a twisted grin that made Jane flinch. 'They fear the wrath of the gods,' he said, his eyes lit with a frenzy that made Iolo nod in approval. 'They fear the power that the druids wield. And they fear that we are the ones who will bring about their downfall.'

We? Jane shuddered.

There was a murmur of agreement from the surrounding warriors. Gar leaned forward, his eyes drilling into Darby as if he were seeing him for the first time.

'And how do you propose we bring about their downfall?' Gar asked, his voice low.

Darby moved nearer, his eyes gleaming with a deranged insanity. 'We need a sacrifice,' he said, his voice low and urgent, 'to appease the gods and to unlock the full extent of their power. And I know just the person.'

Jane's heart thundered as Darby turned towards her with a look on his face which chilled her to her core.

'Darby?' Jane's voice faltered. Would this going to be the end of her story? Undone by a mediocre academic who had resorted to blackmail in order to procure a promotion within a stupid borough council?

'Do you know who is at the fort? Decimus Clodius Albinus — Britannia's governor, and a future claimant to the throne. If you strike him down now, Rome will quail before your power,' Darby said, his face alight with excitement.

'How do you know?' Bricius called out, his voice full of

disbelief. 'The Roman emperor is Pertinax, a freedman. Not Albinus.'

Jane felt Bricius' eyes on her as he asked his question. She needed to reassert her power before Darby usurped her. And for the first time, Jane's disdain towards the archaeologist turned to fear.

Perhaps it *was* time for a sacrifice.

BREAKING THE GLASS CEILING

Jane stepped forward, locking her gaze onto Bricius' doubt-ridden eyes. The thin veneer of control she had maintained in front of Gar threatened to crumble under the scrutiny of Bricius' piercing gaze.

'Because I have connections in high places,' Jane declared, her tone authoritative. 'I have my own sources of information, and I assure you, Britannia's governor is on his way. We can strike a blow which will echo throughout the halls of Rome. But you must act swiftly.'

Beside her, Darby grinned manically, oblivious to Jane's attempts to rein him in.

Bricius looked unconvinced. 'You return with a stranger who speaks of sacrifices and the downfall of Rome. But these are just words that even a child could speak. Would you have our great chieftain listen to the words of a child?'

Jane's mind raced as she sought a way to solidify her credibility. 'You may doubt my words, Bricius, but the governor's arrival is imminent. If you don't believe me, send your scouts out. I'm handing you a chance to strike a significant blow against the Romans. What have you got to lose?'

Gar nodded at her, and raised his hand, silencing the room.

Jane smiled, but her smile soon vanished with Gar's reply.

'If you deceive us, you will face the wrath of the gods, and our gods are not merciful. Bricius, send the scouts.'

With those words, the atmosphere in the tent shifted as the former tension lessened with the tentative alliance between Jane and Gar. Jane recognised the thin line she now walked and knew that the consequences of any missteps in the coming days would be dire.

Behind her Darby started mumbling, and she watched Bricius switch his gaze from her to Darby. Jane's breath caught. She really needed to find a way to control Darby's outbursts because her survival depended on manipulating the shifting sands of power, and Darby's interference threatened that delicate balance. Whilst he held an unparalleled knowledge of the Roman Empire, his opinions were tainted by history. Her view was all about the future.

Fortunately Gar's attention was elsewhere as he signalled to a group of Iceni warriors, and his silent command set in motion a flurry of activity as the scouts readied themselves for the task. Their faces painted with woad, weapons glinting in the dim light of the tent, they represented the spearhead of the impending rebellion against the Romans. One which would bring her closer to her goal.

As the scouts made their way out of the tent and disappeared into the shadows of the Northumberland winter, Jane turned her attention back to Gar. 'When might I be permitted to return to the altar, to make another offering to the gods?' she asked, moderating her tone to one of studied nonchalance.

'Why would you seek the gods again so soon? Are you not content with the favours you've already gained?' Bricius asked, suspicion dripping from his words.

Jane feigned a thoughtful expression. 'It is a matter of ensuring their continued favour, Bricius. The gods are fickle and I must maintain their goodwill to ensure the success of our endeavours. They await my return.'

Bricius' wariness was palpable, but another figure

appeared from the shadows, sucking the attention away from Bricius' concern.

Iolo's eyes gleamed with an unsettling fervour. A crooked smile split his lips, exposing chiselled yellow teeth, as his skeletal fingers recommenced their rhythmic drumming against the ancient bones strung around his scrawny neck.

'She talks of the gods as if she knows them. No one knows the gods,' Iolo whispered. 'Only the druids. Only I.'

Gar appeared mesmerised by the druid, and time slowed as his drank in Iolo's words. He returned his gaze to Jane, his pupils engorged with religious fervour. 'The gods will not be ordered about like a slave. You will be allowed to return when the scouts have returned,' Gar announced.

Returning to the altar was not about making an offering. It was her ticket back to the future. Back to a world of machines and modernity, to her car and its contents. She had to return.

'I need to—'

'Why do you need to return to the altar so soon?' Bricius interrupted.

'The gods have guided me thus far, but their ways are mysterious.' Here she chanced a glance at Iolo. 'I do not know the gods, but a humble offering is all I wish to present.'

The druid laughed, his disjointed bark echoing through the tent, the bones rattling around his neck. He turned to Gar. 'She seeks the altar but not for the gods' favour. She wishes to escape this realm and to return to one unknown to us.'

Jane paled in horror. How could he know?

Bricius turned to Iolo. 'And how do you know this, druid? Are the whispers of the spirits so clear to you?'

Iolo's bony shoulders convulsed with laughter. 'The gods speak in riddles, but I hear their warnings. This woman comes from fields filled with iron beasts who travel on rivers of stone, faster than fire from the sky. She craves power beyond our sacred traditions, and the gods will not suffer it.'

To Jane's surprise, Bricius looked just as suspicious of Iolo's words as he had of hers. Was there no love between the two men?

Gar remained hypnotised by the druid's words and the unfolding drama, until finally he blinked, and normality returned.

'You left us once before and that cannot be forgotten. Bricius will go with you when the scouts confirm what you have told us. If they confirm... Remember, your fate is intertwined with ours, and it will be judged by forces beyond our understanding,' Gar warned.

Gar may not have seen the look the druid gave her after his words, but Jane certainly did. The druid's unholy knowledge of the future was a threat, and she could not abide threats. He would have to be dealt with, sooner rather than later. Dangerously though, she suspected that he was well aware of what she was thinking, and Jane wondered how long she could continue playing the submissive supplicant to the Iceni while secretly plotting to denounce them to the Romans. The gods, the druid, and her shifting allegiances were making her headache worse, but as she rubbed her temples she knew she had to push through any discomfort to stay focused. Damn that fool Darby for disrupting her plans.

And it was then that she swore that she would not allow anyone to obstruct her quest for power, whether that be Bricius, Iolo, or Gar. Or Darby. No one.

THE ICENI SCOUTS moved with the silent grace of wolves stalking prey. The air carried the scent of damp earth and pine, and their breath hung in the frigid darkness as they descended through the rugged terrain. Each step taken in the velvety blackness was a cautious dance rehearsed through years of evading Roman patrols and navigating the treacherous winter landscape.

Their leader — a seasoned warrior with a mane of untamed hair, signalled for the group to halt as they reached a hidden vantage point overlooking the fort. Below them, the landscape unfolded like a tapestry of moonlit silhouettes. The scouts, their eyes trained for any hint of movement, waited in the stillness of the night.

As they settled into their silent vigil, a rustling caught their attention. Taut with anticipation, hands gripping the hilts of their weapons and they followed the source of the disturbance — Darius, the messenger sent by Marcus.

The scouts hunted Darius with an inhuman patience, their eyes glinting with animalistic hunger as they tracked their prey in the labyrinth of nighttime shadows. Every laboured breath by the Roman soldier brought his pursuers closer.

Darkness masked the scouts as they moved through the forest like phantoms. And in the eerie quiet, they encircled Darius, their collective breath quickening at the urgency of their mission.

The calm before the storm.

DARIUS GLANCED over his shoulder and caught a glimpse of a darkened figure. He froze. Fear clawed at the edges of his sanity and bile filled his mouth. Marcus had warned him that the Iceni would find him first. And now it appeared that they had.

Darius raised his hands.

'I am Darius,' he stammered, 'sent by Marcus with a message for your chieftain.'

The hardened scouts barely exchanged glances, and at a gesture from their leader, closed in, their weapons poised.

Darius shook, fear cloaking his entire body. He closed his eyes and waited for the first blows to strike.

In the tense stillness, a swift and brutal swing of a club sent Darius sprawling to the ground, screaming in agony.

'Hold,' commanded another voice. Bricius.

The scouts stepped back, their obedience absolute.

Gasping in pain, Darius curled into a ball, cradling his

shattered wrist. Snot bubbled from his nose as he begged for his life, his words barely audible.

'Yo, fucker of Romulus, tell me why my scouts shouldn't kill you?' Bricius spat. He had no love for the Romans. They'd wiped his entire family from the face of the earth, leaving him half buried under the stiffening corpses of his parents. But he had even less love for those who bore no loyalty to their own. Traitors deserved one thing, and one thing only. And that was death.

Darius shuffled awkwardly upwards, wiping his dripping nose on the back of his good hand. 'I come with a message from Marcus for Gar. Important information.'

'I will decide its importance,' Bricius replied.

'But the message is for Gar,' Darius whined.

The next blow stuck Darius from behind, filling the air with the sickening thud of metal meeting flesh, once again sending the Roman sprawling to the ground. Darius' cries reverberated through the valley.

'I speak for Gar here. The message?' Bricius asked again.

Darius groaned and struggled to sit up, clutching his broken wrist. 'The governor of Britannia will leave Ithaca with the Sixth Legion, Legio VI Victrix, in two days.'

Jane would have been happy to know that her information was correct.

'Good. Your message has been received. Now we will send an appropriate message for you to take back to your fort,' Bricius said.

Darius looked up, hope blooming his eyes, but ignorant of the disgust in Bricius'. Darius whimpered in pain as he watched the barbarian walk off. *How was he going to explain his shattered wrist when he returned to Ithaca Fort? Wait, why hadn't the Iceni scouts all followed the man who said he spoke for Gar? Why were they still here?*

THE ICENI SCOUTS grabbed Darius and dragged him into the depths of the thick forest the Roman army had yet to fell. And then the blows came with a relentless fury, each strike accompanied by the gurgled screams of Darius, until the beating rendered him unconscious. His body, a canvas of brutality, lay crumpled on the unforgiving ground lit by the indifferent moon.

Afterwards, the Iceni scouts surveyed their handiwork. The Roman would live, battered and broken, but alive. If he made it back to Ithaca Fort, then their message would have been delivered. If he died outside the fort's walls and was discovered later, then their message would also have been delivered. If he died in the woods and was only found after the spring thaw, then their message would have been delivered. War was a game. And Bricius was a master.

'SHE TELLS THE TRUTH,' Darius whispered in Gar's ear.

Gar smiled. 'Then we have much to do, and little time in which to do it.'

The druid leaned forward, his earthy stench filling the tent.

'She holds evil within her,' Iolo warned. 'Her essence tastes wrong. Like a fish left out of the water too long,' Iolo said, rattling the bones around his neck. 'Flesh does not lie, but she does. She breathes lies.'

'The Roman messenger confirmed the governor's departure,' Bricius repeated, struggling to hold his chieftain's focus with the druid's interruptions. 'The woman speaks the truth, at least in this matter.'

Iolo raised his voice. 'The woman's presence is a distortion in the weave of fate. The spirits are in disharmony when she is near. Trust not her words, for they are poisoned.'

Bricius felt his jaw tighten, his patience wearing thin. 'Iolo, the Romans occupy our land and we fight for survival. You of all people must recognise that? How many druids are left now? Just you? As much as I don't trust her, her information has been proven true. The governor will be vulnerable, so we must attack. Gar?'

Gar's eyes shifted between Bricius and Iolo,

contemplating the conflicting perspectives. 'This is a gift from the gods. We strike at the governor,' Gar declared. 'This is our chance to show Rome the strength of the Iceni.'

Iolo scoffed. 'That time is long gone. You walk a dangerous path, Chieftain Gar. The woman is a viper, and the only way to kill a viper is to cut off its head.'

Bricius saw Gar pause. The man was completely under the druid's spell. If the Iceni were to succeed, it was the druid who needed to lose his head.

'A sacrifice, that's what we need. We will cut the viper's head off, Iolo,' Gar said, his eyes blazing.

The druid's mouth widened into a rictus of a smile.

'The figural head of the Roman army in Britannia,' Gar continued.

Now it was Bricius' turn to smile.

Gar turned back to Iolo. 'Bring the woman and her guide here. It's time to offer the gods a sacrifice. We will appease them before we being our preparations for war. Their favour is our greatest weapon.'

Iolo's eyes gleamed with madness, his bony fingers already reaching for the sacrificial knife hidden within the folds of his robe.

'We don't have time—' Bricius started, but a cutting glance from Gar stayed his tongue.

Bricius's brother escorted Jane and Darby into Gar's tent, hovering nearby, his hand on his spear.

'Did you confirm my information?' Jane asked. 'Your scouts, did they confirm that the governor of Britannia plans to travel to Rome?'

Gar nodded. 'You were correct,' he said, 'and so you may return to the altar, but Bricius will accompany you. Leave your guide,' Gar directed, now staring at the druid. 'The gods demand blood, and blood they shall receive for their divine protection.'

'Leave me where?' Darby asked, his voice rising.

'My guide comes with me,' Jane demanded.

Bricius interjected, 'My place is with the warriors. Watching over her is a waste of my time. The altar is too close to the fort; it's a risk we cannot afford. Roman patrols will be out searching for their missing soldier and we can't expose ourselves—'

'I don't need a babysitter. My guide and I will go to the altar alone,' Jane insisted, her hand gripping Darby's arm.

Bricius watched the druid whisper in Gar's ear, before Gar's eyes moved between Jane and Iolo; between the woman who promised victory and the druid who foretold betrayal.

'Your guide stays,' Gar commanded. 'You go with Bricius, and you return with the iron beast, and the weapons you promised.'

The druid's influence over Gar was absolute, and whatever his qualms, Bricius could show no outward objection to his Gar's orders, but the time was coming where Gar would need to be replaced. As for Iolo, Bricius had no need for spiritual succour. Human sacrifices had not saved his parents, or anyone else in their village, and there had been plenty of sacrifices offered to the gods by the druids before the Romans had slaughtered them all.

Bricius stepped forward and took Jane's arm. He glanced at Iolo with disdain before guiding her away from the encampment. She looked back over her shoulder towards Darby but made no move to beg for his life.

'What will happen to him?' she asked.

'Don't talk of it now,' he hissed, pulling her away from listening ears.

'Will they kill him?'

'Does the sun rise every day?'

As Bricius pulled Jane from the camp, the sound of ritualistic chants followed them, raising the hairs on his arms. He could feel her urgency to reach the altar far more than he sensed any real concern about her guide. What was the man to her? She'd said guide, but that felt wrong. He shook his head to clear his confusion. There was no time for this now.

The path through snow-laden hills took what felt like forever as their horses struggled across the uneven terrain. Moss and lichen clung tenaciously to the bark of trees and rocks, their strident colours adding a touch of vibrancy to the otherwise monochromatic landscape.

'The altar is ahead. Be quick with your offerings so we can return swiftly. The woods have eyes and are restless.'

After dismounting from their horses, the crunch of their footsteps on the snow did nothing but amplify the risk they took in coming so close to the fort. As they neared the sacred site, a pair of midnight black ravens took flight. Their haunting calls echoed through the stillness and Bricius pulled up, his fingers digging into the woman's arm to stop her from advancing.

His furrowed brow betrayed his thoughts as he fixed his eyes on the snow around the altar. On the disturbed snow. *Someone else had been there.*

'Stop. The snow has been disturbed, and not by the wind or any woodland creature.'

He watched Jane turn as white as the snow, and felt her heartbeat quicken beneath his fingers. And his first thought was that she had lured him into a trap.

A CALL TO ARMS

All around them, the air flickered like a dying fire, its tendrils writhing and twisting around the altar, which stood as a silent sentinel, a bridge between worlds, blurring the line between reality and the dreams of gods.

Jane ignored his warning and fell to the ground, her painted fingernails scrabbling through the disturbed soil around the altar's base. She *had* to get home, or she'd end up like Darby. God save his soul. She needed her car and her guns and all the other modern magic to impress the Romans. And to save her life.

Bricius stood too close, almost breathing down her neck. 'What is it that you seek, witch? Be quick, because we're not the only ones interested in what's in this spot.'

She felt his eyes boring into her back as she pawed the ground searching for a coin, or a token, or anything which had the power to return her back to Hexham.

'It is unwise to trifle with offerings to the gods,' Bricius said, his displeasure a low rumble against the hallowed silence.

Jane looked at Bricius, 'I have no intention of trifling with your gods. I have my own.'

'The darkness is coming,' Bricius whispered to himself. And Jane herself felt his unease settling over her.

Her fingers scraped against the stubborn earth, her nails stained with the soil of centuries as she delved deeper, leaving Bricius's warning hanging in the air like a ghostly echo. The forest held its breath as the altar threatened to breach the boundaries of time itself.

As Jane continued her frantic excavations, the air around the altar came alive, tendrils of mist swirling and writhing like spectres in response to her quest.

A scowling Bricius cast wary glances through the mist, his sword raised in a defensive stance. 'Enough!' he hissed at her. 'You tarry too long. The Roman scum could be surrounding us in this mist and we'd never know.'

'Put that away,' Jane said, undeterred by Bricius' impatience. 'This would go faster if we both looked.'

'You waste our time,' Bricks muttered, his feet firmly planted on the frozen ground.

Jane's fingers grazed against a small, solid object, and she triumphantly pulled a coin from the soil. 'This is it,' Jane cried out.

The coin, featuring the visage of Emperor Decimus Clodius Albinus on one side and the stern countenance of the goddess Minerva on the other, seemed to glow in half light.

In Jane's outstretched hand, the Roman coin became a key — a small, unassuming artefact with the power to unlock the gates of time.

Bricius' grip tightened on his sword as an electric energy filled the air. 'Hand it over,' he demanded, his eyes never once leaving the mist. 'Hand it over,' he repeated, chancing a glance towards her.

Jane stood next to the altar with the coin raised high above her head, her eyes gleaming. The moonlight pulsed with an otherworldly hue and tendrils of mist twisted and turned, growing ever more chaotic until, with a sudden burst of energy, the air swallowed the pair of them whole, like the biblical whale consuming Jonah.

JANE AND BRICIUS materialised in a disoriented haze, the mist clinging to them like a cloak before dissipating into the brisk, modern air. The transformation was as abrupt as it was disconcerting. They found themselves standing in a field at Ithaca Farm, with Lillian's old farmhouse nearby.

Bricius gripped his head, his senses unable to operate beneath the agonising pain at his temples. The hum of modern life assaulted him from every angle, a symphony of sounds that he could not fathom. The metallic wails of monstrous metal chariots raced on invisible paths nearby, their roars reminiscent of the wolves who hunted in the wilds of his homeland. Overhead, a winged serpent bellowed through the sky, leaving behind a wake of disorienting echoes. And the formerly crisp clean scent of the countryside was now tainted with traces of exhaust from passing vehicles and decades of industrial pollution.

His knuckles whitened around the hilt of his sword, the antiquated weapon in stark contrast to the contemporary landscape, one adorned with wind farms and power poles. 'Where have you taken us, witch?'

Instead of answering, Jane pointed towards a small path leading to a nearby farmhouse. 'This way, we need to find my car.'

Bricius could barely open his eyes. 'Car?' he repeated, the word strange on his tongue

'My iron horse,' Jane clarified. 'If you want to beat the Roman's, then that's the key.'

As Jane marched towards the farmhouse, Bricius followed in her impatient wake. As they approached, a knot of anxiety bloomed in her stomach. She'd organised with Darby for her car to be left in the lay-by near the house at Ithaca Farm, but there was nothing there now apart from an old Starbucks cup, the foil wrapper from a chocolate bar, and a flap of yellow crime scene tape.

'Put that away,' Jane hissed at Bricius, who was still wielding his sword, ready for any attack.

'Where are we?'

Jane ignored him as she tried to make sense of the

situation. She had expected her car to be here, the key to her plan's success. But now... a flicker of doubt crept into her heart. This was all Darby's fault.

'I have to find another way,' Jane whispered to herself.

She turned and walked straight into the point of Bricius's deadly sword.

'I asked you once, witch, where are we? Now you will answer me.'

Jane held up her hands in surrender. 'We are not in your world anymore. This is not Roman Britain.'

'What trickery is this? You are a sorceress, I knew it,' Bricius said, his sword unwavering.

'No trickery, I promise. Please, put that down,' Jane replied in her calmest voice. 'I know this won't make any sense, but we have travelled forward in time, almost tw0-thousand years from your time. This is the future.'

Bricius's expression wavered between disbelief and confusion. 'Such things are not possible.'

'But they are,' Jane insisted. 'Look around you. The buildings, the metal beasts on the roads, the smells. This is not your world, it's mine. And in my world, people don't hold swords to other people's throats. So please,' she tried moving her head away from the sword's tip, 'please lower your weapon.'

Bricius squinted, taking in the unfamiliar surroundings. 'How?'

Jane took a deep breath, choosing her words carefully. 'I don't understand how it works, but it's the coin and the altar. They brought us here, and they brought me to your time. But something went wrong last time. My car, the iron horse, was supposed to come with me, just as I promised Gar. Darby ruined it.'

'Your guide?'

Jane tried to nod, the prick of the sword still tickling her throat.

'Time travel? This is beyond the realm of gods,' Bricius said.

'And yet, here we are,' Jane said. 'I need to retrieve my car and its contents, and then we can return to your time. If you help me, I will explain everything along the way. But pointing your sword at me won't solve anything.'

Bricius glanced again at the unfamiliar landscape before finally sheathed his sword. 'Explain, then. But make no mistake, witch, if you lead me astray, my blade will find its mark.'

As Bricius lowered his sword, Jane let out a sigh of relief. She quickly took the lead, striding toward the front of the farmhouse, leaving the disoriented warrior to follow as the modern world unfolded around them.

Jane didn't bother knocking. It was as if she expected the place to be empty as she opened the unlocked door and disappeared inside.

Bricius, still clearly grappling with his newly disorienting reality, followed cautiously, his eyes wide. If the outside world was a shock to the warrior, the interior of the old house at Ithaca Farm was beyond the power of his imagination.

'Close the door,' Jane directed.

Without thinking, Bricius closed the door, before jumping backwards at the sight of his reflection in the hall stand mirror. He stepped closer to the mirror, leaning into the polished surface, swaying from side to side, tentatively poking at his doppelgänger.

'Leave that, and get in here,' Jane called out, running the tap and filling the kettle over the sink.

'Where is the innkeeper?' Bricius asked from the doorway, his question dying on his lips as he watched the flow of water.

'This is a house, not an inn, and hopefully the owner is in hell,' Jane replied, plugging the kettle in and switching it on. 'Now, where's the phone?'

Ignoring the bewildered barbarian in the doorway, Jane lifted piles of papers — the detritus of a woman locked in a battle with bureaucracy, and searched unsuccessfully for the phone.

'The water...' Bricius started.

The piercing shriek of the boiling kettle made Bricius

clamp his hands over his ears, his eyes wide at the sight of the unnatural energy. 'What is this magic?'

Jane laughed. 'No magic, just electricity. It's as common as muck in my world. Now, I need to call my office and find out who moved my car. I'd ask you to make the tea, because God knows I'm dying for one, but I don't think you know what that is yet, and you won't until Mr Garway begins selling it in his coffeehouse sometime in the 1600s.'

Jane searched through the cluttered kitchen, moving and throwing aside items as she went. 'Does this woman not have a phone? Ahh, here it is,' Jane said, plucking the phone from the fruit bowl, where it lay nestled between two bananas well past their prime. Within seconds, she'd dialled, tapping her nails. impatiently on the rim of the bowl.

A voice crackled through the earpiece. 'Hello?'

'Raymond? Where's my car?'

A gasp echoed through the phone. 'Mayor Badrick, is that you?'

'Who else would it be?'

'Where are you?'

'Where's my car?'

Silence.

'Raymond, I asked you a question. My Land Rover?'

'There were some things in the back—'

'I am aware of what was in it, and I have my reasons. Is it at the office or at my home?'

'The police—'

'I don't care about the police, Raymond, and I don't have time for this pointless back and forth. My car?'

'The police have it. There were guns. *Guns.*'

Jane's frustration bubbled over. 'This is no time for games. I need that car now so you need to make it happen. I'll meet you at Ithaca Farm. And Raymond, I also need everything that was in it.' Jane slammed the phone down.

'More sorcery,' Bricius muttered, eyeing the phone as if it might bite.

'Christ on a bike, not sorcery, just technology,' Jane

shot back, her frustration with the man boiling over. 'While we wait for my assistant to bring my car, I suppose I should explain a few things.'

'Explanations are long overdue, witch. I demand answers.'

Jane rolled her eyes. 'First, that contraption over there is a phone. It's a device to communicate over long distances. No sorcery, just signals and wires.'

Bricius grunted in acknowledgment, his gaze shifting to the still steaming kettle on the stove. 'And that? Some form of alchemy?'

Jane sighed. 'No, an electric kettle to heat water for tea. A beverage we drink for pleasure, not necessity.'

Bricius frowned at the her attempts to bridge the vast technological gap between their times before the distant rumble of an engine reached their ears.

'He comes,' Bricius noted, his hand reaching for the hilt of his sword.

'No need for that,' Jane said, heading for the door. 'Put it away and stay in here out of sight.'

THE CAR that rumbled its way into the Ithaca farmyard was not a top-of-the line Range Rover, nor was it a middle-of-the line model. Instead it was a green manual VW Polo, which had seen its best days when David Tennant was the freshly minted face of the Doctor Who franchise.

'Lamont?' Jane Badrick barked, as the hatchback puttered to a stop.

Raymond Lamont climbed out of the car, his feet protected from the winter mud by heavy snow boots.

'Why are you at Lillian Arlosh's place?' he asked, his gaze travelling around the shoddy yard.

Jane tapped her finger against her pursed lips and glared at her assistant. 'That abomination is not my car,' she said, foregoing any pleasantries.

Raymond hesitated before answering. 'I'm afraid they won't release it, Mayor. They're treating it as part of a crime scene.'

Jane scowled. 'Crime scene? For what crime?'

'There were guns...'

'Guns that I had confiscated, which isn't in my role description at all. I shouldn't have to do their job for them. I'm the mayor, not bloody Scotland Yard. And you can tell them that. If they'd done a better job of keeping organised crime out of Hexham, then we wouldn't be in this situation.' She paused to take a breath. 'There are things in that car that I need, Lamont.'

'Exactly, and I anticipated that you'd want things put back right away,' Raymond said smiling. 'So I tried to recreate the contents of your car as best as I could. You know, like the food, the camping equipment, the notepads, everything.'

The mayor's ice-blue eyes narrowed. 'Everything?'

Raymond shifted uncomfortably, his cheeks reddening. 'Well, the guns were a problem. I mean, I know you've got a licence but considering the situation, I thought it might be best to substitute them with flare guns. And, uh, I threw in my .22 hunting rifle for good measure. You know, in case you need protection or something. I wasn't really sure...'

Jane stared at him. 'What on earth possessed you to think a hunting rifle is what I need right now?'

Raymond scratched at the acne on the back of his neck, avoiding Jane's eyes. 'I... I thought it might be useful. You know, just in case, given everything that's happened so far. The gold coins, and you being missing, and the handguns you had in the car to start with.'

'In case of what, Raymond? Invasion by extraterrestrial rabbits?' Jane sighed, rubbing her temples. She tempered her tone because she needed his help more than he realised, and a hunting rifle was better than nothing. 'I appreciate your efforts, honestly. You've gone above and beyond, even if the rifle is somewhat of a surprise. As I said, the guns in the car were from an earlier incident and I had every intention of handing them into the police.' A little white lie, but one Lamont wouldn't notice. 'Did you tell anyone you were coming to see me?'

'Of course not. Who would I tell?'

'Your friends from your poetry group, or whatever it is you call it.'

Lamont's eyes widened, and Jane smiled. The boy thought she didn't know what he got up to when he wasn't running her errands. Of course she did. She knew everything that went on in this town.

'Raymond, whilst Im impressed with what you have done for me so far, I'm only going to say this once. Get me a car or find yourself another job.'

Lamont flinched like a beaten dog. 'You can use my car. It's fully packed, like I said. I even put in 200 rounds of ammunition for the rifle. That's all I had at home.' His skinny arm snaked out of his parka pocket, his keys rattling in his hand.

Jane all but snatched the keyring from him.

'How much fuel is there?'

'I fuelled up on the way here. How much do you need? Where are you going?'

'Never mind that, you wait here until I—' she stopped as she clocked Lamont's face changing from scared to terrified. Jane spun around, knowing full well what she would see.

A figure stood in the doorway, his hair wild, his eyes wilder still, with a sword clenched in his hand.

Jane's grip on the keys tightened.

'Another iron beast,' Bricius said. 'Smaller than the last. A baby?'

'I told you to stay inside,' Jane hissed.

'Who's that?' Lamont asked, taking two steps back towards the car he no longer had keys for.

'See, he trembles beside the beast,' Bricius said.

Jane stepped forward, positioning herself between Lamont and Bricius.

Bricius pushed past her with a mixture of curiosity and disdain. 'I am Bricius of the Iceni tribe,' he replied. 'The witch says you bring weapons. Show me.'

Lamont's eyes darted between Jane and Bricius, his face pale. 'Mayor?'

'Lower your weapon before someone gets hurt.'

Bricius stared at her, his stony face challenging her command.

'I said, lower your sword.'

Bricius slowly relaxed his grip and lowered his sword.

'Thank you,' Jane nodded.

'Is this the man who kidnapped you?' Lamont asked, a quaver in his voice.

'It's time for you to go,' Jane replied. 'Don't tell anyone that you saw me. I'll explain everything later. But really, please know that you are doing a great service to Hexham and the country.'

Jane didn't wait for Raymond to leave before ushering Bricius toward the mud-splattered VW, her grip firm on the keys. It would have to do and she didn't have time to dally any further. The longer she stayed here, the more likely it was that someone would see her. And that just wouldn't do.

'Get in,' she ordered, opening the car door and sliding into the driver's seat, gesturing for Bricius to do the same on the other side.

The interior of the car reeked of cheap aftershave, stale takeaways and damp, courtesy of a leak in the rear window that Raymond hadn't got around to having repaired yet.

Jane fumbled with the unfamiliar key as Bricius awkwardly lowered himself into the passenger seat, his sword clanking against the gear shift.

The engine roared to life, and the car jerked forward, prompting a startled exclamation from Bricius. Jane focused on the steering wheel and the sticky clutch as the VW Polo bumped and jolted across the undulating pasture, carrying its unlikely passengers toward the altar.

Bricius squinted at the scenery, which was both at once foreign and familiar to him. 'How?' he asked, waving his arm across the hills, which had changed little in the millennia between his birth beside the banks of the Caw Burn, and today.

Jane ignored his question, because what she really wanted to do was to ditch him. The idea had come to her while she was still in Lillian's ancient kitchen. A kitchen so far removed from her own aesthetic that she couldn't breathe, surrounded as she was by mismatched crockery, stained bone handled knives, chipped platters and wooden chairs that were only good for the annual bonfire night. How could people live like this?

It was in the kitchen that she realised that Bricius now knew too much. Sure, he didn't know what he knew, but the shine of her magic had been tainted, and the way he was starting looking at her... she didn't need him undermining her mystique with Gar upon their return.

The car jolted over bumps and tufts of grass, with Jane manoeuvring the VW as if it were an all-terrain vehicle. Parking next to the tarpaulin-covered altar, she pointed to the sheet of plastic flapping in the wind.

'Take that off.'

Bricius frowned. 'You want me to do your bidding?'

'If you want to go home, remove that tarpaulin from the altar, and be quick about it.'

Jane's heart raced as Bricius fumbled with the unfamiliar door handle and stepped out of the iron beast, twisting his thick neck to look back at her. The distrust was clear on his scarred face.

'The tarpaulin,' she said, pointing to the tarp. 'Take the cover off the altar, so we can return to Gar. To glory.'

BRICIUS' expression hardened at the command, but the compulsion to get home overrode his gut instincts, and he ripped back the plastic tarpaulin, leaving it to puddle on the ground like a wrinkled elephant skin.

As he stood beside the altar, the silent landscape was split by the roar of the iron beast.

He stumbled backwards. 'What is the beast doing?'

Bricius saw the witch stretch her arm out towards the altar as the iron beast slowly moved closer. As he opened his mouth to... to what? To yell a warning? To stop her? He knew not.

Before he'd uttered one syllable, she'd placed the gold

coin on the altar's mossy surface, and in that instant, time contorted.

In the fraction of a second it took for him to realise what was happening, a blinding light engulfed the beast and the witch, and they disappeared. Leaving him standing in the empty field, his sword raised uselessly above his head.

THE SACRIFICIAL LAMB

With Iceni warriors prodding him forward with iron tipped spears, Anson Darby stumbled through the dense thicket, leaves and branches tearing at his clothes. Confusion flooded his face as he tried to make sense of the situation. He chanced a quick glance behind him, but in his heart he knew Jane had abandoned him. It shouldn't have been a surprise, but the certainty of her betrayal hit him like a blow to the gut and his steps faltered as raw panic clawed at his chest.

Darby finally emerged into a clearing. And there in the centre, bathed in an unnatural light, stood Iolo, his skeletal fingers clasped tight around a wooden staff as tall and as slender as he was.

'What's going on?' Darby demanded, his voice shaky. *None of his lecturers had ever covered this scenario in any of his Iron Age papers at Tyne River University.*

Iolo turned to face him, his eyes nothing more than empty pools. 'The gods demand a sacrifice,' he intoned, his voice scratching at the edges of the glade.

'Sacrifice? What are you talking about?'

Surely this was a joke?

Iolo raised his arms, as if gesturing to the heavens. 'A soul must be given to restore the balance disrupted by your presence. It is the only way.'

Darby took a step back, his heart pounding. 'You can't be serious? This is madness.'

A cold smile played on the druid's bloodless lips. 'Your willing sacrifice will sate the gods' hunger and ensure that we *will* prevail against the invaders.'

Four Iceni warriors stepped forward and threw him to the moss-covered ground, pinning him to the earth. Iolo began chanting in a language long forgotten to time whilst drawing symbols in the air with his gnarled staff and walking in complex patterns around the thrashing man.

IN THE AFTERMATH of the sacrifice the air hung heavy with an eerie stillness, disturbed only by the distant calls of unseen birds and the rustling of hidden creatures burrowing in the ancient grove. With eyes devoid of emotion, the Iceni arranged Anson Darby's severed head amongst Iolo's other recent sacrifices, forming a grisly circle of skulls around the weathered stone altar.

The altar bore the scars of countless ceremonies with its surface stained with the remnants of offerings made to appease deities long lost to the mists of time. Moss clung to the rough-hewn stone, and only the worn engravings still whispered the names of ancient gods.

Iolo moved with deliberate precision, his robes billowing as he circled the altar, assessing the placement of his most recent offering to the gods.

The warriors stood motionless, unaffected by the rich stench of death, as they awaited the druid's next command.

Darby's face, once sporting a supercilious countenance, now mirrored a mask of terror more at home at Madame Tussaud's Waxworks Museum. The grotesque display was yet another testament to the unnecessary brutality unleashed in the name of religion.

As Iolo completed his final circuit around the altar, the rhythmic cadence of his chants reached a crescendo and the grove pulsed with unseen energy.

The vacant eyes of the severed heads remained fixed on the desolate grove — a place where the past and present converged in a dance of blood and shadows. Their eyes appeared to follow Iolo as he left the grove to return to the Iceni camp, his blood-stained robes trailing behind him, the air thick with the scent of ritualistic offerings and the lingering weight of ancient magic.

THE GUARDS PARTED to allow the druid back into the Iceni camp, carefully avoiding Iolo's fanatically shining eyes, and Darby's still-warm heart and liver dangling from a leather belt around Iolo's waist.

The rhythmic dripping of blood created its own grisly melody as Iolo approached Gar, the chieftain reclining on his wooden throne.

As Iolo presented the dripping heart to Gar, the organ appeared to still pulse with the last remnants of Darby's short life. 'This is the key to our victory,' Iolo said.

A look of reverence crossed Gar's face. 'The gods have been appeased,' and he reached out to accept the organ in his calloused hands. 'To victory,' Gar declared, and with no further ceremony he sank his teeth into the warm flesh.

Iolo, his eyes reflecting a zealot's fervour, watched as Gar consumed the heart. 'The gods are with us,' he proclaimed, the echo of his words resonating through the camp, before his own sharpened teeth ripped into the warm liver of the moderately successful archaeologist formerly known as Anson Darby.

SNOW WHITE

The biting cold of the Northumberland countryside seeped through Apple's makeshift uniform as she shivered in the snow-covered landscape. Hunger gnawed at her insides, a persistent ache which intensified with every step. The warm stew was a distant memory.

The snow-laden fields and barren trees offered little in terms of edible vegetation, and Apple's stomach grumbled. She remembered episodes of survival shows she had watched in the past, contemplating what could be foraged in the wild. But with no fire to cook, her options were limited.

Her eyes fell on a cluster of bushes, their bare branches dusted with snow. Crouching down, she brushed away the snow with gloved hands to reveal the frozen berries clinging to the branches.

Despite their shrivelled appearance, Apple's hunger didn't discriminate, and she stripped them from the branches, hunger urging her forward. She popped one into her mouth, the icy burst making her wince. The taste was bitter, but then again, so was hunger.

She'd almost give her life for one of Pauline's perfectly flaky pastries and a strong cup of tea. At this point in time, handing herself over to either the Romans or the Iceni might be better than dying of starvation.

. . .

'HUNGRY, LITTLE ONE?' The voice cut through the crisp air, startling the pale apparition. Marcus leaned against the trunk of a large oak tree, one which would soon be devoured by the insatiable appetite of the Roman army. Resplendent in his armour, and stunningly handsome, Marcus' eyes met hers.

Marcus had been deployed as part of the search party looking for Darius, with Castus now worried that Darius was the Iceni spy.

Marcus had planned on resolving the thorny issue of Darius himself, if he'd found him first, but instead he'd found this vision in the snow, ferreting under fallen logs and stuffing blood-red berries into her pale pink mouth.

As APPLE STARED at the Roman soldier, her vision blurred, and the snowy landscape transformed into a chilling scene of the Roman, standing over a fallen man, the glint of a blade in his hand. Apple's breath caught as she witnessed the vivid image of him cutting the other's throat. Was it a vision of the future or a manifestation of her fears?

'Are you hungry?' the soldier repeated, a twisted smile playing on his lips, his dark eyes assessing her huddled form in the snow. Apple instinctively clutched the foraged berries against her chest.

'I'm not going to hurt you,' he said, kneeling beside her, his leather armour creaking softly. He produced a small bread roll and a flask of wine from his bag. The still warm aroma of the bread wafted to Apple's nostrils, intensifying her hunger.

'You're resourceful. I'll give you that,' he remarked, his tone betraying a hint of admiration. 'Out here, survival is a game, and not everyone plays it well. I am Marcus Aurelius Julianus, at your service.'

He extended the bread and wine toward her, a benevolent gesture that clashed with the danger in his eyes. Apple hesitated, her gaze flickering between the food and Marcus. Survival instincts warred with distrust, but hunger won out. She accepted the provisions, tearing into the bread with a voracity that surprised even her.

As she ate, Marcus studied her, his eyes narrowing. 'You bear a striking resemblance to someone I know,' he mused, a dangerous undercurrent underscoring his words. 'The newly arrived governor of Britannia, to be precise.'

Hunger hadn't released her from its grip, but Apple stopped eating, lifting her eyes to stare at the soldier.

He chuckled at her response, the sound low and menacing. 'And here you are, in the middle of nowhere, scavenging for scraps.' He leaned closer, his breath warm against her ear. 'You, a common thief, impersonating a Roman soldier, but with such a likeness to our leader. I wonder, do you have the same goals as him? Should I run you through with my sword right now? It could save us all a lot of trouble.'

With the hard bread providing some relief to her gnawing hunger, Apple wiped the crumbs from her mouth and stood to face the formidable Roman soldier.

'I am Apple,' she declared, her voice steadier than she expected. 'And I am not a thief.'

'That uniform suggests otherwise,' Marcus mocked, his eyebrows lifting. 'Apple? An interesting choice of name for a thief.'

'It is a name, and it is of no consequence,' Apple retorted, a spark of defiance gleaming in her eyes. 'Unlike Decimus Clodius Albinus, soon to be Emperor Decimus Clodius Albinus—'

Marcus burst into laughter, the sound echoing through the wintry silence. 'You're either mad or delusional. Decimus Clodius Albinus is a loyal servant of Rome. Your hunger has eaten away at your senses.'

'It's no fantasy,' Apple insisted, her voice unwavering. 'But he is at risk from the Iceni uprising.'

Marcus snapped his mouth shut and eyed her with newfound uncertainty.

'And why would you, a thief, know anything about the governor's ambitions? Or the Iceni?'

'Because,' Apple declared with conviction, 'I am his

granddaughter, and he awaits my return. You will take me to him.'

Marcus's eyes narrowed, searching hers for any sign of deception. 'You expect me to believe you're the granddaughter of the governor himself?'

'It doesn't matter what you believe. Take me to my grandfather, and all will become clear. Refuse, and you will find yourself on the wrong side of history,' Apple said, warming to her story, her gaze unwavering.

Marcus, torn between suspicion and an unsettling chill, hesitated. The notion of a common thief making such audacious claims was preposterous, yet Apple's confidence was undeniably believable. 'You're either a remarkable liar or utterly mad,' Marcus finally said.

Apple met his gaze with unyielding resolve. 'Take me to my grandfather, and you will be rewarded.'

As Marcus hesitated, Apple felt a sudden surge of power within her, a connection to something beyond the icy landscape and the looming Roman soldier. The vision hit her like a sudden storm. A pile of Roman coins spilling out of a bag onto the snowy ground next to an ancient altar. The coins glinted in the pale light, and Marcus stood over them.

She stumbled as the vision cleared, Marcus grabbing her to stop her from falling.

'Are you feeling ill?' he asked, his face a picture of genuine concern.

Her focus returned to Marcus, and her voice, though tinged with anxiety, held a thread of determination. 'My vision showed me what you've done with the coins,' she said, her words measured. 'Which is why you need to escort me safely into the fort. We're not the sort of family you cross, but I can help you if you take me back.'

Marcus's amusement faded, replaced by a hardened glare.

'Your imagination runs wild, little thief,' Marcus said, his attempt to dismiss her visions revealing a hint of unease. 'Visions are the delusions of the weak-minded.'

Apple took a step closer. 'I may look weak, but I am not

blind.' She had seen the tiny drops of blood which had fallen from Marcus' sword, and knew in her heart that the blood was recent, and didn't belong to his enemies.

A tense silence settled between them, broken only by the whisper of the wind through the wintry trees. Apple's heart pounded in her chest, but she refused to give in to her fear.

The standoff continued, both figures locked in a silent confrontation, until Marcus finally stepped aside.

'Very well,' he said, 'but know this, little thief. If this is a lie, you will not live to see the morning. But first you need to remove the uniform,' he said, turning his back with practised nonchalance. 'It's a bit of a giveaway that you're a thief if you walk into a military fort wearing another man's uniform.'

As Apple shed her disguise, Marcus wiped the blood from his sword with a scrap of cloth, skilfully concealing the evidence of his earlier actions. He re-sheathed the blade with a fluid motion.

The air filled with distant shouts as the rest of the search party drew nearer.

'Stay close and silent,' Marcus ordered, 'and don't think for a moment that I won't hesitate to silence you permanently if you say anything about this.' He waved his arm around the glade, the threat lingering between them.

As the sound of the search party grew nearer, Marcus gestured for Apple to follow. He guided her through the shadows with the skill of a seasoned predator until they emerged from the undergrowth to await the others.

THE SEARCH PARTY converged upon Marcus, their faces etched with grief as they struggled under the weight of Darius's lifeless body on a stretcher. A sombre air hung over the group, the fallen soldier a reminder of the dangers at the edges of the empire.

Questions tumbled from the lips of the search party, their eyes flicking between Marcus and the snow-coloured girl, who stood behind him. 'Who's this?' one demanded.

Marcus remained tight-lipped, his gaze cool. 'What happened to Darius? Is he dead?'

'They slit his throat, not far from here. He must have been trying to return to the fort. His body was still warm,' Gaius replied.

'We should have started the search earlier,' Marcus declared. 'This is on the head of Castus. He delayed us. Darius may still be alive if we had left when his absence was first noticed.'

'They're out there, watching us,' Gaius warned. 'We need to return before they attack,' he said, his eyes scanning the surroundings for potential threats. 'Unless we too want to be gutted like fish.'

To the side of the search party stood Julius, his gaze intense as he stared at Apple. 'And the girl? Is she one of them?' he asked, suspicion filling his words.

'She's why Darius was outside in the first place,' Marcus said, deciding on a plausible explanation for Darius' unauthorised absence.

'What?' Gaius exclaimed, his thick brows furrowing in confusion.

Marcus continued, maintaining the façade. 'Darius knew the governor's granddaughter from his youth. He was out here looking for her.'

Julius, still staring at Apple, looked unconvinced. 'Is she the—'

Gaius, not known for his astuteness, scratched his head and interrupted. 'The governor's granddaughter, eh? I never knew Darius had it in him.'

Julius never finished his question. He just stared at Apple. Switching his attention between the girl, the dead soldier, and Marcus.

The rest of the soldiers, indifferent to the details, exchanged worried glances. The complexities of Darius' personal life were inconsequential in the face of a potential Iceni attack, and they were desperate to return to the safety of the stone fort.

'Come on, I'm freezing my balls off. And since Darius is dead, he won't be needing his anymore, but I plan on using mine tonight, so let's get a move on,' Gaius said, hefting the weight of the stretcher in his huge hands.

THE SOLEMN PROCESSION continued until fort's gates opened with a creaking groan that echoed the heaviness in the hearts of the soldiers, each step weighed down by the loss of a comrade.

Apple's thoughts turned to the deception she and Marcus now shared. How would Marcus navigate his web of lies once they reached the governor? Would he actually present her to the governor, or was this all a ruse to cover his tracks? Apple wondered if Marcus had any intention of taking action against the threat of the Iceni, or if his motivations were purely self-serving.

The uncertainty gnawed at her as the gates closed behind them. Because deep in her heart, she knew the answer.

IT'S TOO LATE

As Decimus Clodius Albinus and his retinue had journeyed north, the landscape underwent a dramatic transformation, evolving from the bustling marketplace of Londinium into a realm of untamed beauty and stark contrasts. The biting winter wind, a sculptor of snow-dusted hills, had moulded the terrain into frozen waves. Skeletal branches of ancient trees extended like gnarled fingers against the pale winter sky.

Navigating the treacherous conditions of the season meant the journey had been slow, and doubts crept into Albinus's mind about the wisdom of consolidating support in these northern regions.

Albinus's horse whinnied impatiently as the Governor paused, fixing his steely gaze on the horizon. Small groups of red deer, their winter coats thick, grazed on patches of exposed vegetation, their pelts a crimson omen of the impending bloodshed Albinus envisioned. The news from Rome of Commodus' death, and the freedman Pertinax's ascension to the throne, had reached him like the chilling gusts of the northern wind. The wind, slicing through his cloak, mimicked the cold touch of steel on skin, but it did nothing to extinguish the flames of his ambition, and the emperor's throne beckoned across the vast expanse of the empire.

Albinus shifted his gaze northward. His visit to Ithaca

Fort was not a mere military exercise; it was a calculated step in his grand strategy. The timing of this tour couldn't have been more perfectly executed, even if he'd orchestrated the Iceni attack on Ithaca Fort himself.

With a decisive nod, Albinus issued orders to continue. His retinue, a legion of seasoned fighters, bore the weight of his ambition. As they marched, the red deer scattered, fleeing like Albinus' enemies — both in Britannia and Rome. 'Run as fast as you can, but there is nowhere to hide,' Albinus thought.

As the sun dipped below the horizon, the legion hastened to make camp. The wind in the skeletal branches overhead mimicking the sound of ghostly footsteps.

'Did you hear that?' whispered one soldier, his voice trembling.

'Hear what?' replied another, attempting to mask his fear.

Fear spread through the ranks like a creeping mist. 'We should turn back,' urged Felix, a scrawny Gaul who'd barely learnt how to shave. 'This is madness.'

'You are Romans,' the centurion announced, clipping one soldier across the back of the head, his voice echoing through the stillness. 'We are not afraid of shadows and whispers.'

His words did little to quell the soldiers' apprehension.

As shadows lengthened and temperatures plummeted, a small group of soldiers huddled together, their voices barely audible above the howling wind. Their conversation painted a stark contrast to Governor Albinus' staunch belief in his own popularity.

'I've heard about the Iceni,' whispered Felix the Gaul.

'Aye,' agreed another, shivering. 'They flay their captives alive, sacrificing them to their gods.'

The mentions of the Iceni's barbaric practices sent a chill down their uneducated spines. Far from home, strangers in a hostile land and surrounded by an unfamiliar enemy, the fear was infectious.

'And then there are the druids,' added an older soldier, his uniform as slovenly as the pigs he'd once tended back in Rome. 'They call upon the spirits of the dead, unleashing curses and plagues upon their enemies.'

'We should never have come,' muttered Felix, his voice laced with fear. 'Not in winter. This is a land where nightmares come to life.'

As the morning dawned, scouts from the Sixth Legion had emerged from the forest's embrace, sleep still in their eyes.

With wraithlike magic, the group of Iceni warriors erupted from the landscape, their ferocious cries reverberating through the trees. The ambush was swift and brutal, as the barbarians, eyes blazing with the thrill of battle, closed in on the soldiers.

A hulking barbarian, his body a tapestry of scars earned in countless clashes, swung a massive axe with merciless precision. The weapon cleaved straight through the armour and flesh of the nearest soldier, unleashing a sickening spray of blood, painting the snow in gruesome hues of red. The fallen man's guttural cry was abruptly silenced as his body crumpled to the frozen ground.

Young Felix, still new to the rigours of battle, stepped forward to replace his partner, only to face a pair of barbarians armed with spears longer than he was tall. He parried their thrusts with his short sword, but the tremor in his movements betrayed his inexperience. A spear found its mark in his throat, and the young Gaul, wide-eyed with terror, clutched at the spear in his neck. As the Iceni warrior yanked it from his victim, blood gushed from the Gaul's mouth and nose as he sank to his knees, his life force ebbing away as he called for his mother.

A red-maned giant, eyes filled with bloodlust, charged at another Roman scout. Battle-hardened, the Roman met the assault with a swift, upward thrust of his sword, the blade impaling the barbarian's throat and silencing his war cries.

The forest clearing had transformed into a nightmarish scene of clashing steel and bloodcurdling screams. Despite their rigorous training, the odds against the Romans were overwhelming. Yet they refused to yield. Defeat would only bring dishonour.

At the sound of a haunting horn, the remaining Iceni warriors melted into the shadows of the forest, abandoning whatever prey that had just been trying to kill.

Alerted to the danger by a scout's hasty return, the rest of the camp had been roused from their slumber and was preparing for battle. Albinus had wasted no time and quickly saddled his horse, determined to examine the scene of the attack. The ground bore witness to the tragic toll of the skirmish, strewn with the lifeless bodies of both his scouts and their adversaries.

Fallen soldiers lay like forgotten pawns on the chessboard of war. The wounded groaned in agony, their pain a haunting backdrop to the bleak start to his ambitions. Albinus remained resolute.

Now Albinus faced a dilemma — whether to honour the fallen by giving them a proper burial or to press forward, leaving the corpses behind as grim markers of the day's tragedy.

He weighed the options, his mind torn between his duty to his men and the urgency of what was happening in Rome.

'We will not leave them behind to be desecrated by the northern barbarians,' he declared, a steely resolve in his pale eyes. 'We take our fallen with us. Prepare to march,' Albinus barked, his words cutting through the lingering cries. He could not afford to delay their march to Ithaca, and then onwards to Rome. He couldn't give his enemies any time to regroup. And his enemies didn't just include the Iceni.

The soldiers nodded, and the sombre task of collecting the dead began. It had been a macabre procession, as both officers and legionaries worked together to prepare the deceased for the journey. Each fallen soldier was carefully placed on a makeshift bier, which would later be adorned with the symbols of their rank and achievements. Silent witnesses to Albinus's ambitions.

The procession to Ithaca Fort was a slow and mournful one, with the caravan moving in respectful and vigilant silence, the only sounds being the creaking of wagons and the muffled footsteps of the soldiers.

As Ithaca Fort came into view, a detachment of soldiers emerged from the gates to meet Albinus and his beleaguered legion. The air was charged with an undercurrent of unease. Whilst Titus Caelius Castus had been spared the immediate horrors of the ambush, he had learned from his own scouts of the butchery inflicted by the Iceni on the governor's men.

The detachment halted, forming a disciplined line as Albinus approached. Castus stepped forward, his face a mask of authority.

'Ave, Albinus,' Castus said. 'Your presence honours us. Let me express my deep condolences for the losses suffered on your journey. The path to Ithaca Fort can be perilous, and the sacrifices made by your men will not be forgotten.'

Albinus, his uniform marked by the blood of his fallen men, spared no detail as he recounted the ferocious Iceni attack.

Castus struggled to maintain his calm facade as the reality of the ambush sank in, and Albinus' unspoken accusation of blame. They had all underestimated the Iceni, and in doing so, they had failed Rome. Although Castus doubted it would be the governor who was blamed for the attack. Shit rolled downhill.

Upon reaching Ithaca Fort, preparations for the funeral pyre began. Before the bodies were consigned to the flames, the legion gathered for a moment of reflection. Libations of wine, drawn from large amphorae, were poured near the pyre. The rich, red liquid flowed like a river of blood, soaking the ground — a symbolic offering to the gods who presided over life and death. And beside the pyre, soldiers placed small offerings of grains, fruits, and coins — tokens to secure the favour of the gods for their fallen brethren. In the hushed moment before the pyre was lit, the soldiers bowed their heads in collective prayer, seeking divine mercy for those who had sacrificed everything in service to Rome.

The flames danced skyward as the funeral pyre was ignited, and the scent of burning flesh filled the air. The soldiers stood vigil as the fire consumed the fallen, becoming a bridge between the earthly realm and the afterlife. A bridge Castus worried he would cross sooner rather than later.

LOVE WILL FIND A WAY

Lillian shivered under the heavy cloak around her shoulders. She'd been waiting for what felt like an eternity to speak with the commander of the fort. She'd been promised an audience, but for the past two hours, all she'd heard, or seen, were men running. None of whom paid her any attention. Her stomach growled. She couldn't remember her last meal. A fish dish of some sort? She'd never tasted anything so fresh in her life, and remembered thinking that this is what food should be like, instead of being tainted with micro plastics or fertiliser run off.

Then she heard a commotion down the corridor. She stood up before sitting down again, her pulse racing with fear and panic. Both were her constant companions. Every creak, every bang, could potentially to herald the Iceni attack. Lillian had to remind herself that she was safe here within the dressed stone walls of the praetorium — the Commander's HQ at Ithaca Fort.

A group of soldiers appeared at the end of the corridor, their faces like dark clouds, with a tiny pale figure walking between them.

'Apple?'

The group pulled up.

'Lillian?'

As the girls rushed to embrace each other, Julius and Marcus both stepped forward. Confusion writ across their faces. But before any embrace occurred. Before the two men could even start to interpret the situation, warning bells clanged throughout the fort.

'The Iceni,' Lillian whispered.

Pandemonium broke out. Pandemonium coupled with gunfire.

'Guns?' Apple asked, her eyes wide.

Seemingly forgetting the loss of their comrade, the soldiers rushed away to answer the alarm. But not all the soldiers. Marcus grabbed Apple by the arm, dragging her down the corridor.

'Lillian!'

Lillian lunged for her friend, only to be dragged by Julius in the opposite direction. Lillian struggled against his grip, her eyes darting back to where Apple was being whisked away by Marcus.

'Let me go,' Lillian yelled, her voice lost amidst the sounds of chaos both inside and outside the fort.

The eruption of gunfire echoed through the stone corridors.

Julius flinched and tightened his hold on her arm, his gaze intense. 'I need to get you to safety. Don't fight me.'

Julius pulled her through a labyrinth of hallways, the sounds of conflict growing louder with each step. The air was thick with tension as Lillian tried to process the surreal turn of events.

Gunfire, in Roman Britain?

Julius dragged her into a small chamber, momentarily shielding them from the mayhem outside. He closed the door behind them, lessening the noise of battle.

'This is safest place for you until I can find out what's happening,' Julius said, scanning their surroundings for any sign of danger. He released his grip on her arm, his face grave. 'I told you to return home. This time, listen to me, but stay here. I promise to come back for you. Do not leave this room.'

Lillian nodded, her anxiety palpable. 'I think that's gunfire outside,' she offered.

'The Iceni must have summoned their old gods,' Julius

replied, pressing his ear to the door, straining to decipher the unfamiliar sounds, his tension obvious from his grip on his sword. As if his life depended upon it. Their lives.

With a sinking feeling, Lillian realised that he had no concept of guns or their consequences. She had to explain it to him.

'Julius, those sounds are not from the gods. They're… guns. Weapons from my time,' she explained, her voice barely above a whisper, acutely aware of the fragile atmosphere between them.

Julius turned to her, his brow furrowed. 'Guns? I do not understand. What manner of weapons are they? Don't worry, I will protect you.'

Lillian appreciated his determination, even if the clash of centuries left him ill-equipped to grasp the full extent of the danger. The fort, once a bastion of Roman strength, now faced a threat that they were powerless against.

She tried again. 'Your sword can't protect us from bullets from a gun.'

Julius seemed not to hear her, and he paced the narrow space behind the door. 'I need to be out there, defending the fort.'

Trying to explain to him was pointless. Lillian reached out to touch his arm, offering what little reassurance she could muster. 'Go. I promise to stay here.'

As Julius began to respond, the door rattled violently.

'Julius?' a muffled voice called from the other side.

Julius tightened his grip. 'Who goes there?'

'It's me, Marcus. Open the damn door.'

The urgency in Marcus's voice cut through the air, and Julius opened the door.

As Julius swung the door open, Marcus pushed his way into the chamber, his armour clanging against the doorframe. Behind him, the distant echoes of gunfire mingled with the shouts of soldiers, creating a symphony of violence.

'The Iceni have breached the outer defences. They're everywhere,' Marcus panted, beads of sweat on his forehead.

Lillian stood in the corner, watching the exchange between the men. The weight of the situation pressed upon her, a silent reminder that her presence here had become a catalyst for unforeseen events.

Then Marcus saw her, and recognition dawned on his face. 'It's her. She let them in. She's a spy. Her and the white witch. You saw them together in the corridor. What fools we have been. It was never Darius,' Marcus accused, his eyes drilling into Lillian's. 'Tell him, viper. Tell him about your connection with the white witch,' Marcus demanded, his voice sharp.

'You're the spy and a thief. Don't listen to him, Julius. I saw him steal from the pay chest.'

Marcus scoffed, a bitter edge to his laughter. 'Lies. Don't play the innocent. You and that witch are barbarian spies. It is no coincidence that the Iceni are within our walls.'

Julius, torn between the loyalty to his heart, hesitated.

'She's just a girl, Marcus.'

'What have you done with Apple?'

'Apple? Oh, she's safe, and I will deal with her later,' Marcus replied. 'But I will deal with you now.'

Marcus drew his sword.

Lillian, her back against the cold stone wall, met Marcus's gaze with defiance.

Julius stepped between them, his expression stern. 'Enough, Marcus. This is not the time.'

Lillian felt the weight of Marcus' eyes boring into her, as if searching for what she knew. The chaos outside mirroring the turmoil within the chamber.

Julius, caught between his duty as a Roman centurion and the connection he had with Lillian, looked from Marcus to the girl.

'They know things, these two. They're in cahoots with the druids. The druids, Julius,' Marcus insisted, as the distant roars and shouts outside intensified.

Before Marcus could press further, a loud crash reverberated through the chamber, accompanied by the clamour of falling debris. The fort was under direct assault, and the trio was forced to reckon with the immediate danger.

'Save your accusations for later,' Julius commanded, his tone leaving no room for argument. 'We must defend the fort. You stay here. Marcus, we'll address your accusations after we've defeated the Iceni.'

'If we defeat them...' Marcus muttered.

LILLIAN FULLY PLANNED to follow Julius's instructions. But her worry about Apple outweighed her good intentions. The accusation from Marcus hung in the air, but her primary concern was finding Apple. After taking a deep breath, and arming herself with a shield embossed with a bronze roundel she'd found leaning against the wall, Lillian slipped out of the chamber. The distant clash of weapons and the flickering light of fires painted an apocalyptic scene. Using nothing more than instinct, she navigated her way through the fort, hoping against hope that she would find Apple unharmed. She still couldn't understand how Apple had come to be in Ithaca. The last time she'd seen her had been at the Saturnalia festival at the Bellingham in Hexham. There would be time enough later to ponder that further, but that time was not now.

Turning a corner, Lillian discovered another chamber, its door slightly ajar. Pushing it open, she found Apple trussed like a pig going to market, and gagged. A look of relief washed over her friend's face at the sight of Lillian.

Lillian rushed to untie Apple, working quickly to free her from the makeshift bonds. Once liberated, Apple pulled the gag from her mouth. 'I can't believe I finally found you!'

'Looks like I found you,' Lillian said. 'But never mind that. What are you doing here? No, never mind, we'll talk about that later, if there is a later. Right, we need a safer place to hide. And I don't just mean from the Iceni.'

'There is a lot to talk about. That guy Marcus—'

'He's who we need to hide from,' Lillian interrupted. 'Is there anything in here we can use as a weapon?'

They spent a fruitless minute or so searching the scribes' chamber for anything more deadly than a bone writing stylus.

'It's better than nothing,' Apple announced, palming the pointed bone stylus and pocketing another more ornate bronze stylus. 'In case the first one breaks,' she explained.

'Now we need to find somewhere else to hide,' Lillian urged, glancing around the chamber for an exit strategy.

Apple and Lillian, armed with makeshift weapons and a false sense of their own invincibility, slipped out of the scribe's chamber, their footsteps cautious along the stone corridor.

As they navigated the fort, Lillian considered their options. The cavalry barracks seemed like a logical choice. If the soldiers were engaged in the battle, the barracks might be empty, providing a temporary refuge. It was either that or the grain silos, and given the way the various fires were spreading, the granaries seemed like the least safe place.

Upon reaching the entrance to the cavalry barracks, Lillian pushed the door open slowly, revealing an empty interior with space enough for several dozen horses and their riders, all of whom were absent. Lillian and Apple exchanged glances.

'This might be our best bet,' Lillian whispered, leading the way into the barracks where the air reeked of leather, hay, and the lingering anticipation of war.

They sought refuge in an empty corner, hidden from any immediate view should any of the cavalrymen return. Lillian's mind raced, contemplating their next move. 'We won't stay here for long. Just long enough to avoid Marcus, and to wait out the attack.'

Apple nodded in agreement, her eyes scanning the surroundings. 'I still need to find my grandfather,' she replied.

Lillian stared at Apple in amazement. 'You do realise that he's not your grandfather?'

'He's the closest thing I have to one, and he needs our help.'

'Apple, you're mad. Someone out there is using guns. Guns, Apple. And you want to go warn a man who died nearly two thousand years ago?'

'And what if we don't? What's going to happen to history then?'

'He's going to die either way. What did Wikipedia say? That he dies on the 19th of February 197, with Severus riding his horse over his naked corpse. Very I, Claudius, if you ask me.'

With their argument laid to one side, Lillian and Apple huddled together in the corner of the cavalry barracks, their makeshift weapons close at hand as the sounds of battle seeped through the stone walls.

Lillian couldn't shake the surreal nature of their predicament. Two women, displaced from their own time, caught in the middle of an ancient battle which had never made the history books. Ancient warfare meets modern killing machines. There could be only one winner. She glanced at Apple, whose determination seemed unyielding despite the chaos surrounding them.

'Do you realise,' Lillian began, 'that altering the course of history will have consequences? Consequences that we can't possibly know?'

Apple met her gaze. 'I can't stand by and let someone die when there's a chance we can do something about it. Me telling him might not change the grand scheme of history, but it will make a difference to him.'

Lillian sighed. 'Let's focus on surviving tonight first, and once the chaos settles, we can figure out how to find your… grandfather.'

Time stretched in the cavernous barracks, each moment pregnant with uncertainty. As the minutes ticked by, a muffled commotion from outside the barracks made them burrow further into the hay-filled corner.

As if summoned by their fear, the heavy door creaked

open, revealing two bloodstained cavalrymen. Their armour bore the marks of battle, and the dim light played on their fatigued faces. Lillian and Apple instinctively gripped their makeshift weapons.

The taller of the two soldiers, his face etched with exhaustion, spoke in hushed tones to his companion. 'Word is the governor has summoned the rest of his legion to join him here instead of waiting for him at Eboracum.'

Apple and Lillian exchanged glances.

'The governor?' the other cavalryman replied, disbelief lacing his voice. 'And you believe that? He waited until the bastards had exterminated nearly all of us last time before he finally showed up. And now he's summoned up some extra men? It's a bit late.'

'I promise you, his reinforcements are coming. Because without them, we're all be meeting our ancestors tonight.'

The soldiers continued their whispered discussion, unaware of their hidden observers.

'If the rest of the legion are coming, we might have a fighting chance. We can push back the Iceni and restore order to this forsaken end of the empire,' the taller soldier mused, the weariness in his eyes momentarily replaced by hope.

'They'll be too late. We're barely holding on. The Iceni have magic on their side. And what have we got? Spears and swords. They don't work against sorcery.'

As the soldiers debated the rest of the legion's arrival, Lillian considered the implications of their presence in this timeline. How would the Iceni's fierce battle against Ithaca Fort and the governor would alter the course of history? Or would the mayor's influence be no match for the enduring power of history?

THE EMPEROR'S NEW CLOTHES

News of Pertinax's untimely death had only reached Albinus and Ithaca Fort the night before. Now ensconced in a meeting with his closest advisors, they urged him to make haste to Rome to proclaim himself emperor before Septimius Severus could, leveraging the support of the legions. Leveraging the support while he still had it, he thought. Half of his legion had remained in Eboracum. The small military outpost here would not have accommodated an entire force. His advisors told him it was prudent to travel light.

His advisors had been wrong.

Ithaca Fort was under attack.

Albinus and Castus weighed what little information they had. The druids had built their strength under the protection of the barbarian tribe, and now appeared unstoppable, bolstered by some ancient magic.

'Summon the rest of the legion,' Albinus commanded, his voice cutting through the mist. 'They must come to our aid. The Iceni must learn that Britannia belongs to Rome, and no insurgency will be tolerated.'

Outside the Commander's HQ, the clash of steel against steel reverberated through the mist. The Iceni, masters of guerrilla warfare, darted in and out of the fog, striking with lethal precision. The fort, once thought impregnable, was overrun, and there was fighting both within the walls and outside.

Albinus surveyed the chaotic scene. It was impossible to tell who was who beneath the moisture-laden mist. 'Damn you, Mars. Give us strength.'

As the fog thickened even further, obscuring the entire battlefield, a peculiar sound echoed across the hills—a hooting unlike any animal the governor had ever encountered, coupled with the flashing of lights from Hades' underworld.

The Roman soldiers and Iceni warriors alike turned their attention toward the unexpected intruder. Through the mist, a shadowy figure emerged, driving a metallic beast that roared with unnatural vigour. Lights from the beast's eyes cut through the fog, and the hooting continued, creating a hell-scape that momentarily silenced the clash of swords.

DRIVING the metallic beast was Jane Badrick. Her eyes determined, and gripping the steering wheel with a firm resolve, she struggled to navigate the car across the snow smothered terrain. Next to her lay Raymond's semi-automatic rifle, already loaded, the safety catch off.

With no hesitation, Jane drove toward the group of Iceni warriors, gathering for a final push against the Romans. At the front of the group stood Gar, who had raised his hand in acknowledgement of her arrival. Welcoming her to his cause. Their cause.

ALBINUS SQUINTED THROUGH THE MIST, trying to make sense of this magic. Had the druids summoned this beast from the underworld? Was it a monster from the depths of the ocean, made bold enough to walk the land?

'What is this magic?'

· · ·

GAR WAITED for the iron beast and the woman to join them. To aid them in their quest to rid the land of the Roman invaders, as prophesied by Iolo after sacrificing the woman's guide. She had returned, just as she had promised.

THE ENGINE of the VW whined as Jane pushed the small car to its limits over the snow covered landscape. Avoiding the scattered Roman soldiers, she bore down on the Iceni warriors, who were still cheering her on, waving their rough hewn spears and clumsily forged swords in the angry sky.

With the skill of Michael Schumacher, she spun the wheel to the left and slammed on the brakes. The tyres slid across the glassy ground, slamming into the painted Iceni men, collecting them like pins at a bowling alley.

As the car came to a final stop, Jane emerged from the belly of the beast, the gun in her hands. Her hip thrust out, and her feet firmly planted, she slid the bolt home and raised the rifle to her shoulder. The rifle's report echoed through the misty air, each shot expertly aimed at the barbarian fighters.

Horror crystallised on Gar's face as he watched Jane unleash the power of the semi-automatic weapon.

'You defy the gods,' he yelled above the sickening cries of the fallen warriors.

Jane swung to face him.

'I serve only one god,' she said, aiming for the Iceni leader. 'Myself.'

And just like that, darkness stood knocking at Rome's door.

PART FOUR

ONLY FOOLS AND HORSES

When Anson Darby had first tied her up in the barn, Nicole had fully expected Lillian to find her later that evening, untie her, and together they'd phone the police. She never expected to still be tied to a splintery wooden upright in a barn which had seen the both the descent into madness of King George III and the abdication of King Edward VIII.

Nicole struggled against the coarse fibres of the rope binding her wrists to the wooden post, but her efforts were futile. Her breath materialised in the chilly air as she shivered, burrowing deeper into the old hay, grateful that at least Darby had had the decency to tie her up amidst the remnants of ancient bales of hay.

In the daylight filtering through the gaps above the barn door, she searched for any sign of life. But there was still nothing but silence outside the barn Darby had stuffed her in.

The creaking of the barn's timbers and the scurrying of invisible rodents only magnified her sense of abandonment. Nicole clenched her teeth to suppress another shiver from her agonising thirst. How long could someone survive without water? She calculated that she'd been in the barn at least twelve hours. By rights, she should be at the Saturnalia party at the Bellingham.

Nicole sagged against the beam, giving up trying to

loosen her binds. Her wrists were raw and she just didn't have enough energy. She'd long since given up screaming for help. Screaming had only made the thirst worse.

As the minutes and hours stretched on into an agonising eternity, Nicole's thoughts turned to Mel. Would he wonder why she hadn't called? Why hadn't anyone come looking for her? Where was Lillian? And as much as she despised Darby, surely he would come back? He'd scared her beyond her wildest dreams. But did he really mean to leave her here to die?

The barn, the place where she'd helped Lillian move the hidden tranche of Roman altars, was now her prison. It was karma, Nicole decided. She should have told the police about the altars and gravestones. And now it was she who'd need a gravestone to mark her place of death. She'd really been looking forward to the curry with Mel. She smiled as she slipped off into a restless sleep.

Nicole's sleep was interrupted by a distant sound — a faint rumble that clawed its way into the quiet of the barn. Hope flickered as the vehicle's headlights sliced through the darkness, sending long shadows dancing across the hay-strewn floor, before winking out as the engine fell silent.

Outside, a car door opened, then closed. Oddly quietly.

'Help,' Nicole called, her voice barely louder than a timid dormouse. 'Help me.'

The barn door opened, admitting a cascade of cold air and revealing the silhouette of a man in the entrance. The unmistakable shape of a metal detector hung from his hands, its electronic display casting a ghostly green shade on the man's gloved hands.

'Please, help me,' Nicole whispered, kicking at the straw to draw his attention to the back of the barn.

But it was too late. The man had retreated from the barn, closing the door behind him, plunging her once again into complete, and utter, darkness.

LETTERS TO THE EDITOR

The storm left Hexham and its environs without power or phone service for what seemed like weeks, but was in fact only three days. Jasper spent all three days of shivering like a pauper in eighteenth century England.

Jasper adjusted the duvet and blanket until only his eyes and nose were visible. Even in bed, his flat was colder than the arse end of Antarctica but with no cute penguins or a pristine landscape to gaze at. The only things he had to look at out his poorly sealed windows were the graffiti soaked hoardings covering the old workhouse, which was owned by yet another unscrupulous London property developer, who would rather see the site decay than allow ten per cent of the planned houses on the site be put aside for social housing. Wanker.

With no electricity, there had been no point in going into work. Almost everyone from town was in the same boat. Most of the roads were closed, so it was unlikely that his barely roadworthy car could have made it. Not that being away from the office had stopped him from working. In the raw daylight hours, he'd almost filled two notepads with thoughts about what had happened at the Bellingham, editing and rewriting and paraphrasing and deleting and adding hundreds of words, all dripping with a faintly unbelievable cast of the absurd. He would never try pitching the story to Revell in the form it currently sat;

that would be career suicide. No, the story needed this time away from the Hexham Herald for it to find a suitable ending, as well as for him to uncover a kernel of truth. A truth that the readers would believe.

Knock, knock, knock.

Jasper's eyes flew to the door. He was not expecting anyone.

Fully clothed, Jasper threw off his covers and approached the door the way you would a rabid dog.

'Who is it?'

'Jasper, open up. It's bloody freezing out here.'

'Charley?'

'It's not fecking Father Christmas. Hurry up, my tits are about to fall off out here.'

With a comment like that, he definitely knew it was Charley Scott standing on his stoop.

After opening the door the bare minimum required, and then slamming it as soon as the force of nature that called herself Charley Scott had rushed through, Jasper stared at his former workmate.

'How did you remember where I lived?'

'It's my job, isn't it?'

'Do you want a cup of tea?' he asked, somewhat redundantly, because he had no electricity to boil the kettle, and he had emptied his emergency gas cylinder yesterday during a failed attempt at heating a tin of soup. Soup, which he'd had to eat lukewarm.

'Anything stronger?'

Now that he could do.

Jasper poured them both a nip of whiskey, then offered Charley a crocheted rug draped across the back of the couch, before he whipped the duvet off the bed and wrapped it around his own shoulders.

'Did you make this?' Charley asked, a twinkle in her eye.

Jasper wasn't sure whether to admit to his secret talent, or if he should claim it had been made by his mother.

'Because it's gorgeous. I wish I could make things like this,' she added.

That did it. 'My Nan taught me, and I kind of just carried on.'

'The things you learn,' Charley said. 'Cheers.' She raised her glass, as if toasting him and his crocheting prowess.

'Why are you here?'

'Trust me, Jasper, there are many other places I would rather be. Like Fiji, or Bali, or even New Zealand in summer. But here I am, in Hexham, and I need the inside scoop on Anson Darby.'

'The archaeologist, Darby? What about him?'

'Word is that the coins found by the team at Ithaca Farm have gone missing. And Darby is the prime suspect, except no one can find him.'

'They can't find him?' Jasper played dumb, his mind running a hundred miles an hour.

'That's not all. Someone got their hands on the DNA analysis of those skulls they found next to the altar and not all of them are old.'

'Someone?'

Charley shrugged, the colourful crocheted squares brushing against her ears.

'It helps to have friends in high places.'

'How old are they, then?'

'What's it worth to you?'

'Jesus, Charley, just tell me, and I'll tell you what I know about Darby. Because there's a whole part of the picture that you're missing.'

Charley's face lit up like a Christmas tree, her eyes immediately straying to Jasper's distinctive red-jacketed notebooks stacked beside his bed.

Christ.

Jasper wanted to slap himself. Why the hell had he said anything? He should have kept his mouth zipped shut. The girl had not even hinted that she knew anything about Darby's relationship with Jane Badrick. Now he'd have to say something good enough for her to, hopefully, leave off badgering him for more. Because it was the more that would probably make his career. Or break it.

'All the heads are male, aged between twenty and thirty-five, or thereabouts. Seven of the heads were dated to sometime between CE150 to CE250.'

'CE?'

'Common Era, it's what they use now instead of AD.'

'But there were eight heads found displayed around the altar?'

'Exactly!'

'So what about the eighth head? Are you going to tell me, or do I have to beg?'

'Begging sounds attractive, but I don't think it's your strong suit. Can I have a top up? You're going to need one too.'

Jasper unwound himself from his duvet and poured a decent couple of nips into both their glasses.

'I love a good pour,' Charley said, sipping the amber liquid. She shivered.

'Do you want another blanket? I've got more in the cupboard.'

'I'm not cold,' she said. 'It's more because it feels like someone's dancing on my grave when I think about those skulls. All eight were cleaved off with one blow. Probably with a short sword or something like that. The guillotine wasn't invented until sometime around the 1200 mark.'

'A guillotine, Charley? Was that the eighth skull from the time of Napoleon? Come on.'

'It would be better if it was Napoleon's head they'd found at Ithaca Farm.'

'Don't leave me hanging, Charley.'

'It's modern. Fresh. Like, literally a few months old, give or take. Decomposition had barely set in, although the happy little maggots had done a good job of stripping some of their flesh, and then the boffins think some hungry rats had had a go as well. I mean, waste not, want not, and all that. Did you see them when they found them, the skulls? Could you tell that one was newer than the others?'

Jasper shook his head. 'I never saw them in the flesh—'

Charley started laughing, and before long, Jasper joined in.

'In the flesh…' Charley said, her eyes running with laughter.

When their mirth had subsided, they both finished their drinks in silence.

'Another?' Jasper asked, already standing up.

'I either drink myself into a stupor at home by myself with no electricity, or do the same in your dingy flat, but with company, and someone decent to bounce ideas off. So pour away.'

Someone decent? Had Charley Scott just complimented him? Or was this her way of worming out of him all the information she needed for a killer story? Jasper brushed off his concerns, and set about refilling their drinks, and diving into his stash of crackers, cheese, olives and dips, about the only food he had in any great quantity which did not require cooking.

'Any clues about who the victim is?' he asked, his head deep in the fridge. He knew he had a punnet of expensive imported cherry tomatoes in there somewhere.

'That's the thing,' Charley said, her voice almost as quiet as the falling snow outside. 'They think it's Darby.'

MY KINGDOM FOR A HORSE

Sergeant Gavin Bishop peered into the back of Mayor Jane Badrick's car, his eyes widening at the arsenal of clandestine items expertly packed in the Land Rover Defender.

They'd discovered the Defender in the yard at Ithaca Farm, with no sign of the mayor or any clues to her disappearance, although officers searching inside the farmhouse had reported signs of a struggle. It made no sense whatsoever, as the mayor had last been seen at the Bellingham with the archaeologist, Anson Darby.

The sergeant's gloved hands delicately lifted a sleek handgun from the car's cargo space. A silent exchange of glances with his fellow officers conveyed the surprise at this unexpected discovery. Next to the weapon lay a meticulously organised cache of ammunition, hinting at something more akin to a covert mission rather than a weekly trip to Tesco.

Close by, a brand new rucksack was filled with pepper spray canisters, each promising immediate incapacitation. 'What the hell?' he muttered under his breath, cautiously emptying the rucksack into a large evidence bag.

Packets of winter thermals—thermal underwear, gloves, beanies, singlets, all with their shop labels still attached, jostled for space in the new car. It was almost as if the mayor was preparing for an Antarctic expedition.

Beyond the weaponry and camping gear, Bishop uncovered a trove of handwritten notes and maps detailing the borders of modern-day England, Wales, and Scotland, and photocopies of ancient maps detailing the same area.

As Bishop continued his inventory, a disconcerting truth emerged. The mayor, whose public persona conveyed a life of service to her community, appeared to be leading a double life, transforming Bishop's police notebook into the plot of a John Grisham thriller.

CHIEF INSPECTOR KEVIN READDIE examined the contents of the mayor's car, meticulously laid out at the Hexham station. 'So, what the hell is happening here with all this gear?'

Bishop scratched his head, still trying to make sense of it himself. 'Honestly, my first thought was that someone had stolen her car, and that the gear was theirs. I mean, otherwise, it's like something out of a spy novel. But no, I think our mayor has gone rogue. Handguns, ammo, pepper spray... And look at these winter thermals. She's kitted out for a wartime polar expedition, not a drive to the Cotswolds.'

Readdie's eyes narrowed. 'Do you think it's drugs?'

Bishop shrugged, his confusion mirrored in his furrowed brow. 'Could be anything, Chief. Drugs, maybe, but more likely people smuggling. Fits with the clothing. That I can see her doing.'

'People smuggling?' Readdie grunted. 'Either way, we need to find out, and fast. No telling what kind of mess we're stepping into here, especially with the woman still missing. Bring in her family again, and see if they know anything about all this.'

SERGEANT BISHOP GUIDED Matthew Badrick into the small interview room at Hexham station.

'What's this for, Gavin? Have you got news about

Jane?' the archaeologist asked, settling into the plastic chair. His eyes showed nothing but concern.

'Thanks for coming in, Matthew. We have some questions regarding Jane's car and the items we found in it,' Bishop began, his tone measured. His friendship with Matthew Badrick went back a long time, but he'd never once imagined he'd be interviewing his primary school friend about guns in his missing wife's car.

Matthew's gaze flicked to the table, where a series of photographs showcased the array of weapons, ammunition, and camping equipment, along with photos of the Land Rover Defender.

Matthew frowned, pointing at the photos. 'That's Jane's new car, but what's all that?'

'That is what we're hoping you can tell us,' Bishop replied, opening a folder containing a list of the discovered items. 'Jane's car was packed with handguns, ammunition, pepper spray, and camping equipment. Any idea why?'

Matthew looked genuinely bewildered. 'We've only just replaced it after the last one was stolen, you know that. We only had it a day or two before she disappeared. She's the mayor, for God's sake. None of that stuff is hers. Why would she need any of it? She loathes camping. Hell, if she can't blow dry her hair, it's like the four horsemen of the apocalypse in our house.'

Bishop leaned forward, fixing Matthew with what he imagined was a sympathetic gaze. 'That's what we're trying to figure out. But the thermals were purchased with her credit card, and there have been a number of large withdrawals from her account recently. Did you notice any unusual activity or phone calls recently? Anything that might explain why she'd be involved in this kind of operation?'

Matthew shook his head. 'No, absolutely not. Jane's work is all about the community. This,' he gestured to the photos, 'isn't her style.'

Bishop sighed, tapping his pen against the table. 'What about the cash withdrawals, Matthew? Surely you noticed those? Did you ask her about them?'

'Jane takes care of the money, always has. It's not in my wheelhouse.'

'Is there anything she might have said or done recently, anything at all which might help us understand what's going on?'

Matthew's eyes darted between the photographs and Bishop's expression. 'I wish I could help. The last time I saw Jane, everything seemed normal. We went to the Bellingham. Darby was meant to drive us, but he never showed, so we taxied. That annoyed her. But this,' he motioned to the photos again, 'I don't know anything about this. Although I can say that you're barking up the wrong tree. None of that is Jane's.'

When Matthew had mentioned Darby, Bishop had stopped writing. His eyes sliding to the mirrored window opposite, where he knew Readdie was sitting.

'Darby was meant to pick you both up from your home?'

'Where else would he pick us up from?'

Bishop shrugged, using silence to encourage Matthew to offer something more.

'I wanted to try the new beast out, but Jane was adamant that she'd already arranged for Darby to take us. She was helping him with some promotion, and, well, you know what she's like. When people want a favour from her, she does tend to take advantage...'

When Matthew had married Jane, Bishop wasn't the only one who wondered how she'd managed that match. She'd been punching well above her weight, but it hadn't taken her long to morph into someone who wanted others to believe she'd been born with a silver spoon in her mouth.

Bishop took a deep breath, choosing his words carefully. 'Matt, I need you to think hard. What do you know about Anson Darby, beyond his dealings with Jane?'

'Darby? We've worked together on some projects, but I wouldn't call him a close friend. Why? What's this got to do with Jane's disappearance? Do you think they're together?'

Bishop hesitated, gauging Matthew's emotional condition before proceeding. 'We've been looking into Darby's activities, and we think he might have been involved in something not quite legal. We need to understand his connection to Jane, especially considering the items we found in her car.'

Matthew's expression shifted to concern. 'What are you talking about, Gavin? Darby's a bit flashy, but I can't imagine him being into anything shady. And Jane would never stray from our marriage. Never. It'd be the wrong look for the voters to start with.'

'Our information is that he was conducting his own research on the coins found when Jane first disappeared. And now some of those coins have vanished.'

'Then that's an indictment on the lab examining them. Come on, Gav, you know as well as I do that Darby is okay. If some Roman coins have gone missing, then that's not the end of the world. Do you want me to show you the articles about the stuff nicked from the British Museum? Come on. Darby and some missing coins have got nothing to do with Jane or the stuff in her car.'

Bishop could only nod. This line of questioning was going nowhere.

'What about Badger?'

'Andrew? He doesn't even live at home anymore. That broke Jane's heart. You can write that down in your notebook. The boy can't see past the end of his cock, and that's me being generous.'

Bishop coughed, choking on his coffee.

'Were you going to interview him too? Like a criminal? Like you're doing with me now?'

'Matt, be sensible. No one is interviewing you like a criminal. We want to find Jane, just as much as you do.'

Bishop sensed the growing tension in the room, an invisible weight pressing down on both him and Matthew. 'Matt, we're just trying to piece together what's happened. The situation is more complex than it seems, and it's not adding up.'

Matthew leaned back, anxiety etched on his face. 'So

tell me, what does all this have to do with Jane? I want to know what's happened to my wife. And to be perfectly blunt, I couldn't care less about Darby.'

He hadn't wanted to share the information about Darby with his friend, but the papers had got wind of it, so it was only a matter of time before Matt would piece two and two together.

'We found Darby's skull up at Ithaca Farm. Which is why we need to understand how he's connected to Jane and what they were involved with. The more we know, the better chance we have of finding Jane, alive.'

Matthew's face paled. 'Darby's dead? How?'

'We're still working it out,' Bishop admitted. 'But the key now is to find Jane. So if you can think of any detail, no matter how small, it might help us.'

AS THE INTERVIEW CONCLUDED, Bishop stepped into the dimly lit hallway, where Chief Inspector Readdie awaited.

Readdie's gaze was sharp, questioning. 'What did you think?'

Bishop sighed, the weight of the case heavy on his shoulders. 'I'm pretty sure he doesn't know anything about the weapons in her car. And he thinks Darby is clean. I don't think Matt knows anything, truly.'

Readdie nodded, his expression grim. 'Keep pressing. We need to find the woman before things unravel any further.'

THE FOURTH ESTATE

In his dimly lit lounge, John Revell, stood in front of a roaring fire, feeding handfuls of documents into the inferno — turning a lifetime of stories, secrets, and sins into ash. Gail watched on in hushed trepidation, her eyes filled with a blend of concern and fear.

As the hungry flames consumed the evidence of years spent dancing on the tightrope of questionable deals and under-the-table payments, Revell's thoughts were weighed down by the ominous impending shadow of the taxman. Their mounting debt, combined with the intricate web of financial transactions, had left their accounts in a chaotic disarray. The once-prominent Hexham Herald had become a crumbling house of cards, and the reckoning was drawing near.

Revell knew that the mayor, with whom they had entangled their newspaper, was now under investigation, with the discovery of a cache of illegal weapons in her car casting a pall of suspicion over the once-respected figure. Now that the woman had vanished, again, the police would turn over every rock to find her, which meant he would be under the same microscope. Him and Gail both. All their business dealings would be scrutinised, every transaction. Their whole life would be upended because of that witch.

'What will we say when they ask where the files are?' Gail asked.

'We blame the accountant.'

She nodded, chewing on already decimated fingernails. An old habit revived once the money for weekly manicures had dried up like the Sahara Desert.

As the glow of the flames danced upon Revell's face, the price of ambition, deceit, and compromise became all too apparent. The legacy of the Hexham Herald, once noble, now lay in ashes.

'What will we do when they find her?'

Revell noted the edge of accusation in her wife's words.

'It had nothing to do with me. You saw her at the party, same as I did, her and Darby. They went outside, and that's the last we saw of them. We do nothing. And you don't speak to anyone about her, save for what passes as normal gossip in your circles—'

'I do not gossip—'

'Listen to me. We carry on as normal. Without her here to demand her pound of flesh every month, we might be okay. Might,' he reiterated, as the firelight illuminated the hope on his wife's face.

'What will you print? Won't she be angry when she gets back if you write about, you know, what the police found? All those guns and things in her car?'

Revell watched the last of the incriminating documents turn to ashes in the fireplace. He wiped the sweat from his brow and turned to his wife. 'We'll publish the story, Gail. It's time to remind everyone that the Hexham Herald is the voice of this community, and it's time we let it speak the truth.'

THE HEXHAM HERALD office hummed to life with the return of electricity, and as the roads into Hexham cleared, Revell was already hard at work. He had turned on every light, readied the printing presses, and organised the chaotic stacks of papers littering the newsroom, shovelling a few more handfuls of potentially incriminating invoices into his briefcase for disposal later.

The staff trickled in one-by-one, their expressions a blend of curiosity and astonishment at the editor's newfound enthusiasm for work.

'Where's Jasper?' he asked, needed his journalist a damn sight more than he needed Sue the receptionist or Tom the print manager.

Just as he asked, Jasper Fletcher arrived, slipping in through the heavy outer door, bundled up in layers of jackets, gloves, woollen hat, and a long scarf wound several times around his skinny neck. His entrance was accompanied by the soft thud of snow falling from his boots. Unwrapping himself from his winter cocoon, he finally looked up, and straight into the unwavering stare of his editor.

'Gentleman's hours?' Revell asked.

Jasper raised an eyebrow. 'Did I miss a memo?'

Revell could have wrung Jasper's scrawny neck. He'd dealt with that boy's attitude for far too long, and should have fired him years ago. But they both knew that Jasper was Revell's only half-decent journalist who hadn't yet left the Hexham Herald for a better job. So, for better or worse, they were stuck with each other.

'In my office, now. We've got a story to write.'

'I've got a story I want to run,' Jasper countered.

It was then that Revell noticed the stack of hardback notebooks clenched under Jasper's arm.

'I couldn't write it up at home. The power's not back on there yet. Couldn't charge my laptop.'

Revell marched into his office, fully expecting Jasper to follow. And he did.

'Sit,' Revell commanded, before he fell into his own leather chair, the springs squeaking ominously underneath him. 'Tell me what you've got.'

As Jasper revealed his findings, Revell leaned in, captivated by the potential implications of this revelation.

Jasper, his eyes ablaze with journalistic fervour, explained, 'The eighth skull isn't the same as the rest. It's like it was placed there, almost ritually, next to the ancient altar. An offering, maybe? But it's fresh. It's not Roman, it's fresh. My source says that the police are speculating that it could belong to Darby, the archaeologist. But we need to confirm that, and we need to know how the mayor is involved—'

'If she's involved.'

'Of course she's involved. Look what they found in her car.' Jasper checked his notes. 'The police found two semiautomatic pistols with ammunition; a bulletproof vest; six cans of pepper spray and a taser. And of course she had spare batteries for the taser, don't we all? And night vision goggles. I can't even buy decent reading glasses at the supermarket. Where on earth do you get night vision goggles?'

Revell ignored Jasper's side commentary. He had seen the same list come through from his own police source, and it had rocked him. He wanted to run the story, but part of him, a big part, still feared any potential fallout from Mayor Badrick if there was a reasonable explanation for the things in her car. 'If we can get our hands on DNA evidence to prove that it's Darby, then that changes everything. But we can't jump to conclusions. It's a rock solid story, Jasper, but we need facts, not speculation.'

[Front Page of the Hexham Herald]

Mystery Enshrouds Hexham: Mayor and Renowned Archaeologist Vanish

By Jasper Fletcher, Senior Reporter
Hexham, December 20th, 2023

In a turn of events that has sent shockwaves through Hexham and beyond, Mayor Jane Badrick and Newcastle archaeologist Anson Darby have vanished, leaving the community baffled and seeking answers.

This second disappearance of the Mayor, and now the archaeologist, has gripped Hexham in an atmosphere of uncertainty. Both were last seen on the evening of December 17th, at the Saturnalia celebrations at the Bellingham Tea Rooms. Their disappearance follows shortly after the unsettling discovery at Ithaca Farm of several human skulls. Analysis of those items is ongoing.

A police source, who was not authorised to speak publicly, has advised that a number of concerning items were found in Mayor Badrick's vehicle. However, the specifics of these items remain shrouded in secrecy as investigations are ongoing.

Although authorities have been tight-lipped about the items discovered, speculation has swirled that the disappearances may be linked to the cache of Roman coins, also recently unearthed at Ithaca Farm. The ancient treasure, which has ignited much curiosity in Hexham, may hold further clues to the disappearance of two well regarded Hexham residents.

We urge anyone with knowledge of the whereabouts of Jane Badrick and Anson Darby to come forward and assist in the ongoing investigation.

Amid these perplexing events, our community remains united and determined to uncover the truth behind these baffling disappearances.

Stay with the Hexham Herald for the latest updates on this case.

[End Story]

REVELL'S HANDS trembled as he held the freshly printed newspaper, the paper still warm from the press. He had taken a monumental risk, and he knew that Mayor Badrick's reaction, if she read the article, could spell the end of his career. And Jasper's dogged persistence only added to his mounting discomfort.

'You know, Jasper, things haven't been easy for the Hexham Herald lately. We're teetering on the edge financially. I don't know if I can afford to lose the mayor's support.'

Jasper, with a tone of unwavering conviction, pushed back, 'But you also can't afford to hide the truth.'

The gravity of the situation weighed on their shoulders, creating a palpable tension as they stood side by side. Jasper's inquiries hit Revell hard, compelling him to face his own ethical quandary.

'It's not that simple. We have to be cautious. There are consequences to consider, not just for us, but for the whole town.'

'What about the truth? Isn't that what journalism is supposed to be about? For years you've refused to publish stories about the mayor, and look where we are now? She had *guns* in her car. What the hell was she planning on doing with those?'

The reality of the situation blurred the lines between boss and employee. The Hexham Herald was at a crossroads, and the choices made now would have far-reaching consequences for both the paper and the town.

X MARKS THE SPOT

Clifton Beaufort and Graham Ryan, stalwart members of Hadrian's Heroes Metal Detecting Club, sat in the cooling car, the engine off, staring at the blanket of snow outside. It was a decision that bordered on madness, heading out to detect in such harsh conditions. But the police were insistent that they search for more of the elusive Roman coins that had stirred the town's imagination, and which the police now believed had led to the mayor's disappearance.

Graham shook his head as he muttered, 'Insanity, this. Can't believe they want us to go out in this weather. What ever happened to health and safety?'

Clifton nodded in agreement, his gaze fixed on the monochrome landscape outside. 'Aye, but the police are desperate to find more of those coins. And I think more evidence linking them to the mayor.'

'Did you read the paper this morning?'

'Aye, but it's what they didn't say which interests me the most,' Clifton said, tapping the side of his nose.

'Give off,' Graham laughed. 'You know nought about anything other than your plants and the coil size of the XP Deus and how to fiddle with the discrimination settings, which you always get wrong by the way.'

Clifton adjusted his flat cap and replied, 'It's true. I can tell you the Latin names of a dozen different rose varieties, but when it comes to the mayor, I know what a rat smells like. And I know how that newspaper man operates—'

'Revell?'

'He's been propping up Jane Badrick since the beginning. They're thick as thieves, those two. So if he's left the dark side, and is reporting information from sources, then you know something is up.'

Graham chuckled, 'Aye, we may not understand the world above the soil, but I do know that we're experts in uncovering what's hidden beneath it. Come on, let's get this job done. That snow won't melt any faster with us sitting in the car.'

IN THE BARREN winter landscape surrounding Hexham, Clifton and Graham ventured forth, their feet breaking the frozen crust of the snow-laden ground, a chorus of soft crunching beneath their boots. The winter's grip was unyielding, and the chill in the air cut through the layers of their clothing, a relentless reminder of the season's dominance. Their breath, visible plumes, mingled with the crisp, pristine snow.

Despite the discomfort, they persevered. Clad in heavy jackets lined with insulation and fur-lined hoods, they resembled Arctic explorers rather than hobbyist metal detectorists. Despite the gloves encasing their hands, their fingers were as they held their detectors, the machines surprisingly nimble, a far cry from the cumbersome tools they used to use, back before arthritis had raised its unwelcome head.

Overhead, the calls of winter-hardy birds — fieldfare and redwings, provided a haunting chorus of resilience in the face of the cold, with the constant hums and chirps of the two machines adding a moody backing soundtrack to the adventure.

With the occasional distant rumble of trucks on nearby roads reminding them they were not entirely isolated, and that the modern world existed alongside the edges of their historical exploration, they carried on sweeping their machines from left to right and back again. Over and over.

A solitary red-breasted robin danced in the bare branches of an ancient oak nearby, its clear trills filling the air, sadly unheard by either man beneath their headphones.

As they combed the frozen earth, their metal detectors began to shriek and wail. The men exchanged astonished glances, their faces illuminated by excitement.

Clifton shouted over the howling wind, 'These signals are going wild!'

Graham's hands trembled with anticipation as he nodded, his eyes fixed on the frozen earth. 'Aye, it's as if the ground itself is singing with history.'

The work was gruelling, the frozen soil reluctant to yield its secrets. Their spades and trowels bit into the ground, and inch by inch, they cleared the topsoil, waving their stumpy wands over the small plugs of earth.

Clifton's eyes widened in awe as he held a piece of a Roman armour in his hands, offering it to Graham for confirmation.

'Aye, it looks just like the pieces of lorica segmentata they found in Corbridge,' Graham confirmed, turning the curved segment of armour over in his gloved hand.

'Let's hope this doesn't go missing like some of the Corbridge hoard.'

'Don't even joke about it.'

'Do you think this is evidence of a battle?' Clifton asked, peering out over the expanse of the field.

'One piece of armour does not a battle make,' Graham joked. 'That's what Yoda would say if he were out here with us.'

'No one would be stupid enough to be out here, save for us and him in the car.'

They both turned to look towards their chaperone — a young police officer, safely ensconced in his vehicle, reading the Herald.

'Shall we keep going?' Clifton asked.

Graham responded by taking up his machine and resettling his headphones over his ears.

With newfound determination, they continued, their metal detectors sweeping the frozen earth with renewed vigour.

As the winter sun tried casting its feeble rays across the field, the tranquillity of the scene was shattered once more by Graham's detector emitting a sharp and insistent beep. Clifton and Graham exchanged glances and, without a moment's more hesitation, they plunged their spades into the icy ground. The soil reluctantly gave way, and as the hole deepened, the men paused. There, partially buried in the frozen ground, was a Roman spearhead, a silent testament to the struggle for survival in ancient Britain.

'That's a beauty,' Clifton said.

'Aye.'

'Do we tell him?' Clifton motioned towards the oblivious officer.

Graham ignored him. 'What you need to do is check your settings. There's more down there. Look at my machine.' Graham's machine was lit up like Regent Street.

Clifton checked his Visual Discrimination Indicator and fiddled with the settings, muttering under his breath. 'Like this?'

'Aye.'

Graham had barely taken five steps when his machine's alarm pierced the air again, sending the robin hurtling into the air, her red breast a bloody slash against the sky.

Together, Graham and Clifton teased two more spearheads from the frozen ground.

Graham weighed the spearheads in his gloved hands, a sense of reverence in his touch. 'We cleared this field, right?'

Clifton scratched his head, the puzzle gnawing at him. 'This very spot, just a week ago, with our police escort.'

Graham examined the spearheads more closely, taking note of their depth in the unbroken soil. 'And there's no way someone could have buried these here since?'

Clifton pondered for a moment. 'Look at how deep they

are. This soil hasn't been disturbed since some poor sod lost them here. We missed them, that's all.'

The men faced a dilemma: whether to continue their excavation or postpone it because of the weather and the risk of damaging the relics. Clifton voiced his concerns. 'Do you want to carry on? We should probably leave off until the weather is better. We could damage this stuff.'

Graham weighed the options, glancing at the growing collection of finds. 'Aye, you might be right. They've waited a fair few centuries. They can wait a bit longer. We'll need to report these regardless and get the experts in.'

'Well, it won't be Darby, will it?'

'That man is about as trustworthy as a fox in a chicken coop.'

'Or we could call in the reinforcements? The rest of the club would be here in two shakes of a lamb's tail if we asked,' Clifton suggested.

'Best we keep this to ourselves. Loose lips sink ships and all that. If we tell anyone about this, it'll be like Sutton Hoo all over again.'

'I'll let our minder know what we've found, and he can make a call.'

Graham watched Clifton limp towards the police car. The cold played havoc with Graham's knees as well, but things were easier now that one of his knees was more titanium than cartilage. Clifton was still on the public waiting list for his knee replacement. Poor guy.

THE THREE MEN stood over the growing pile of ancient weapons. The young officer had literally been hopping from foot to foot every time one of the machines emitted the smallest of squeaks. Graham had even let the lad have a go with his machine. He thought the policeman would faint when the detector gave a true screech, and then they'd located another half circle of burnished armour. The boy had the bug now. Metal detecting was like an addiction. It only took one good hit, and you were hooked.

'Who do we tell?' Sergeant Gavin Bishop asked, his face a picture of wonder.

Graham and Clifton stared at the young sergeant.

'Normally we'd let the FLO know, or the town's lead archaeologist,' Graham replied.

'But that doesn't seem like a good idea this time,' Clifton added.

'Aye, maybe you could give Newcastle a call?'

'Who's the lead archaeologist again?' Sergeant Bishop asked, his notebook poised.

'That'll be Matthew Badrick. The mayor's husband,' Clifton offered, his eyes on the growing hoard, and not the sergeant.

Silence followed.

'Right. I'll give the university a bell then.'

Graham was on the ground, his stiff leg held awkwardly out in front of him.

'What's wrong?' Clifton asked, lowering himself down.

'There's no record of a battle here, and we've been working these fields for years, and what have we found before this past month? A couple of third century coins, a broken fibula or two. You had that half candlestick with the maker's mark. That was a good one, and I had that gold and ruby ring, but apart from that, nothing else Roman. Nothing. Ever. Don't you think it's odd that it's all coming out now?'

'Climate change,' Sergeant Bishop said.

'Could be,' Clifton nodded.

'Aye, it's a possibility,' Graham said slowly, elongating his words. 'But I don't think so. These pieces of armour almost look brand new. I think someone is having us on.'

'Come on, Graham, you can tell when someone's pulling your leg on a dig. Like that time at the Carlisle Cricket Club dig, when Jess, that girl from Zimbabwe, you remember her? Well, remember when she hid those replica Roman coins in Norman's barrow on his birthday? At first glance, you and Norman both thought you'd hit the jackpot.' He laughed. 'But it only took you and Norman all of five-seconds to recognise the coins for what they were — cheap imitations of the real thing. These are not the same. These are a once-in-a-lifetime find. Mark my words, they'll be calling this the Beaufort-Ryan Hoard.'

'I just don't know how we could have missed it,' Graham said, 'But you could be right. It could be just pure dumb luck that we found the Ryan-Beaufort Hoard.' He winked. 'That's what they'll be calling it. Of that I'm certain.'

AN UNLIKELY ALLIANCE

Neumegen checked his pocket watch — an 18 carat gold half hunter by Russells of Liverpool in pristine condition and hummed a long forgotten tune. The minute hand had barely moved. Time passed so slowly, and yet sometimes it could go faster than a shooting star flaming to its death. He enjoyed imagining every minute of his life as different layers of skin, each a separate life lived in the shadows. It had taken years before he had finally found one which had fit, and leaving it never sat well with him.

'You look grim.'

Neumegen looked up from his watch and into the eyes of the woman he had seen knitting in the corner of the Bellingham.

'Time seems to pass too slowly in this town.'

'I'm told it's the happiest place in England,' Loretta Hambly said, taking in the proliferation of charity shops, the decrepit chain pubs and the cars clogging the ancient market square.

'I'm surprised you're still here,' Neumegen said, dredging his eyes away from the time.

'And I you, and yet here we are.'

He nodded.

'Do you miss it?' she asked.

'It?'

'Your old life?'

Neumegen stilled. Her comment could be taken a hundred different ways, yet he knew there was only one life she was referring to. Every time traveller had an origin story, not so unlike the Marvel characters, although his was not nearly as exciting as Wolverine's or Iron Man's.

As a child, his clearest memory was being put to sleep behind the stage curtains of a draughty country hall whilst his parents spent the evening setting up for the next day's antique fair, just another one on the Rotary calendar, each town promising exquisite and rare goods for the discerning customer. By the age of ten, he had been promoted from the back of the stage to helping the dealers unload on the Friday night and pack up again on the Sunday, pocketing the shiny coins they shoved in his hands. At fifteen, he had the dealers patter perfected, mimicking the sales pitches perfected by both his mother and father, flattering the old dears and engaging in banter with the men carrying wads of cash, eager to placate their wives, or girlfriends.

At twenty, he had had enough, with the draughty church halls losing their appeal and no longer promising riches for the canny seller and buyer. The stock of the other dealers had become repetitive in every way with their array of the same Royal Doulton plates, identical Lladro ornaments, antique fishing flies, wooden planes long superseded by power tools available at every DIY store, and jewellery tainted with the deaths of the previous owners. He had wanted more. More than driving around England in an old white van, his head on a different pillow every week, hanging out with the same people he had known since birth, their conversations never deviating. That was his parent's world, not his, not anymore. But what to do?

He had left with twenty years of savings, a bag, his passport and no plan. But in the end, that had posed no problems. Beginning in Paris, he had wandered the aisles of the historic Braderie de Lille flea market, his hands twitching in his pockets. Then he had taken the train to Brussels, where he had spent a week strolling the legendary Jeu de ball market, each day offering slightly different dealers and their wares. Then onto Lisbon to the aptly named Feira da ladra — the Thief Market. For a month he had rambled through Lisbon's streets, soaking up its history and culture, and tasting dishes he had never encountered in his life before. Then he hitched his way to the Frühjahrsfest in Munich, which was held in the same place as the famous Octoberfest. And still he kept his hands in his pockets, choosing to absorb the electric atmosphere between the dealers and their ever changing clientele.

He'd backtracked to Milan for the winter and their flea market, visiting every historic site and museum, and spending hours in front of art rescued from the clutches of Hitler and his murderous henchmen.

Oslo had proven to be a handsome city, but did not fill the void in his heart, with the Birkelunden flea market offering mostly retro furniture and homeware — beautiful to some, but it didn't give him any joy.

And in the April of the following year, he pulled into Amsterdam, and had stumbled upon the Vrijmarkt — the city wide flea market. Here there were no dealers, no trestle tables hauled out of the back of white Transit vans, and no crones with a thousand rings on their fingers haggling with punters over the price of a silver charm bracelet. The citizens of Amsterdam lay their wares outside their homes, on top of blankets or tables or hanging out of wooden chests older than some countries.

He had spent a whole month walking and looking and talking and laughing with different people every day, on different corners, in suburbs as different as the phases of the moon. And it was here that he'd first opened his wallet, his heart beating wildly as he spied a book carved from what looked like yellow amber.

'How much?' he had asked in broken Dutch.

'Ten guilders.'

Neumegen remembered swallowing nervously, before tipping a bundle of coins into the woman's wrinkled hands.

She had smiled at him as she wrapped the tome in a

piece of muslin, securing it with a ribbon frayed at both ends, before shuffling her wares to fill the gap in her display.

It felt like he was carrying a ray of pure sunshine. Excitement had radiated from every pore on the long walk back towards his tiny flat in the centre of town. Not even the sloth-like arrival of ominous clouds, painted in every shade of grey, could shake his excitement.

The clouds soon gave way to light showers, and then to driving rain. None of that bothered Neumegen because the package in his hand was worth more than his parents would make in a good year on the road.

Thunder boomed through old Amsterdam, echoing off the city's faded walls and flagstone paths. With dreams filling his head, Neumegen rushed through the weather, intent on one thing, and one thing only, unwrapping the package in his hands and soaking in the glory of the almost translucent amber antiquity.

Lightning flashed. And flashed again, electrifying the air. With his head down, and the package tucked beneath his overcoat, Neumegen didn't shelter with the other commuters under the cover of the nearest striped awning until the storm passed. He lurched his way home, his long legs fair skipping across the growing puddles, puddles which joined to form temporary rivers crisscrossing the historic Amsterdam streets.

The pungent chlorine-like scent of ozone wrapped itself around Neumegen moments before another lightning strike pierced the clouds, stabbing at the earth with a ferocity borne from the gods themselves.

The ground shuddered, and still Neumegen carried on, oblivious to the danger.

Lightning struck the city again, and again, and again. A hundred times over. Two hundred times.

Ahead of him stood his accommodation — a narrow stone building unscathed by the disastrous Allied bombing runs during the war, although the scars of the poorly executed bombings of the Fokker Aircraft Factory remained nearby, waiting to be rebuilt, but by whom was a question the city was still asking itself.

As he approached the entrance, a woman rushed in front of him, haste writ across her lined face, her headscarf sodden and her stockings flecked with mud. Neumegen had paused as she had fumbled with her house keys. He had not seen her before, but then his hours were hardly that of a wage worker as he ambled around the city on his own clock. He waited with his hand on the metal strut of the awning. A man with all the time in the world, until the lightning struck again.

And when the woman in the headscarf turned to hold the door open for the skinny young man behind her, he was nowhere to be seen. Neumegen's life would never be the same.

'No, I don't miss it, I never really had any other sort of life,' Neumegen replied to Loretta, the trip down memory tugging at the corners of his mouth. 'Do you miss yours?'

'At times,' she said, 'but this life fits now. I can't see me belonging to the local WI and baking cakes for charity, anymore than you'd be voted on as secretary of the local Rotary chapter. Am I correct?'

Neumegen laughed. He'd known that there were others like him out there, other than Pramod, but he had never sought them out. The only other time traveller he had encountered had been Sarah Lester. And although he had recognised her for what she was, they had never spoken about it, and then she was gone. And he regretted that.

'How many others do you know?' he asked.

As expected, Loretta had needed no clarification as to what he meant by that, but her answer left him feeling more than concerned.

'Not as many as I used to,' she said, shrugging.

'What do you mean?'

'Exactly what I said. Can we talk about your friends?'

Something told Neumegen to mind his words. 'My friends?'

'The young ones you sent back with no support.'

This time, he shrugged before checking his pocket watch again.

'When are you expecting them back?' she asked.

And that was the problem. He didn't know when they were coming back. Or where they would return. Time travel could be precise, if you had the right keys. But if you didn't…

'You don't know, do you?' Loretta exclaimed. 'Do they even know how to return?'

Neumegen stared into Loretta's incredulous eyes.

'What was the end goal here, some sort of time travel tourism? Girls playing dress ups and make believe?'

'They weren't both meant to go back. I was meant to go with Lillian,' he said, completely taken aback by the woman's outburst.

'So go back and get them.'

'I've tried, but the portal has closed.'

The weight of his confession settled between them like an unspoken verdict.

'Did you close the portal?' Loretta's voice carried a mix of disbelief and anger, her gaze boring into Neumegen's eyes as if searching for any trace of deception.

Neumegen sighed. 'Not intentionally. Something went wrong. There was a miscalculation, and now it won't open in either direction.' A flicker of remorse crossed his face, but disappeared as quickly as it had arrived. 'I didn't expect both of them to go. It was a mistake, and I'm trying to find a solution.'

Loretta leaned back, crossing her arms. 'This is more than a mistake. I can't even imagine what might be happening to the timeline. The ramifications. Holy, Jesus.'

'I know where they are, and when. But without the proper keys to get there, I'm just as stranded as they are.'

Loretta's expression softened, only to be replaced by a calculated intensity. 'Let me help.'

The ticking watch echoed like a metronome, each resounding tick a reminder of the irreversible march of time.

TIME WAITS FOR NO ONE

Loretta and Neumegen spent hours examining the documents they had found in Pramod's little library. A fruitless search without Apple or Lillian to talk them through what they'd initially found in Pramod's makeshift sleeping quarters. And with everything that was happening in town, the church had made overtures about closing the secret library.

'He should be back by now,' Neumegen said, for the umpteenth time that day, pacing back and forth across the room. His eyes darted between the stacks of books they'd already searched for clues that might lead them to Apple, Lillian, and Pramod.

Loretta filled the one armchair in the library, and held court above her crochet hooks, her hands moving with practiced ease. The rhythmic sound of her crochet needles resonated in the small library. 'He will return. He will find a way, just like we always have.'

'But Apple and Lillian?'

Loretta shrugged. 'They'll...' Her needles fell silent.

'What?'

Loretta's hands froze mid-stitch as she looked down at the creation taking shape in her lap. It was a rendition of the emperor Septimius Severus, standing tall and victorious, but there was something wrong about it now.

'I'm not sure. It's as if the threads themselves are

telling a different story,' she said, staring at the threads in her hands. She looked up in horror. 'Something has changed. History has changed.'

Neumegen halted in his pacing, his eyes wide with apprehension. 'Changed? How is that possible? What have they done?'

Loretta shook her head, her hands trembling as she clutched the crochet in her lap. The rendition of Septimius Severus, once a symbol of Roman might, now resembled little more than a John Doe on the mortician's slab. 'I don't know,' she admitted, her voice barely above a whisper.

'If history has changed, what does that mean for Apple, Lillian, and Pramod? What does it mean for all of us?'

Loretta's gaze shifted from her hands to Neumegen, a shared unease etched on both their faces. 'The past influences the present, and the present shapes the future. If the past has been altered, it's a ripple that could reshape everything.'

Neumegen took a seat opposite Loretta, his eyes fixed on the altered crochet. 'Can we undo it? Can they undo it? Reverse whatever has been changed?'

Loretta's hands cradled her creation. 'I don't know if it's possible.'

As they contemplated the altered course of history, a new fear gnawed at them — the unpredictability of a future shaped by unknown forces.

At that moment, the library contracted for a second before settling back upon its ancient stone base. Forever altered, the change impossible to see, but still there.

To Be Continued

Read Ithaca Found - the final book in the Ithaca Trilogy to find out how it all ends...

ITHACA FOUND

In the final chapter of the *Ithaca* trilogy the past and present collide in a desperate attempt to rewrite history

Jane Badrick weaves her lies to ascend to the highest echelons of power in the heart of Rome.
Meanwhile, Neumegen races against the clock to save his friends from the clutches of time.
Will the heroes rewrite the tapestry of time, or will the mayor reshape history?

Read Ithaca Found, the final book in the Ithaca Trilogy

REVIEW

Dear Reader,

If you enjoyed *Ithaca Lost*, I would love it if you could please leave a rating or review on your favourite digital platform. Or post about it online, or even ask your local library to order in a copy for others to enjoy.

Thank you.

Kirsten McKenzie

CAST OF PLAYERS

THE ITHACA SERIES

Lillian Arlosh, owner of Ithaca Farm

Andy 'Badger' Badrick, Friend of Lillian
Matthew Badrick, Badger's Father, Archaeologist
Jane Badrick, Badger's Mother, Mayor
Raymond Lamont, Jane Badger's assistant

John Revell, Editor, Hexham Herald
Gail Revell, wife of John Revell
Jasper Fletcher, Reporter, Hexham Herald
Sue, Receptionist, Hexham Herald
Tom, Print Manager, Hexham Herald
Damien and Jan, Advertising team, Hexham Herald
Rhema Patel, Classifieds Intern, Hexham Herald
Lorna Milroy, BBC London Reporter
Charley Scott, Newcastle Reporter

Darren Saunders, Lawyer
Seb Arlosh, Friend of Badger's
William Arlosh, Seb's Grandfather
James Losh*, 18th century ancestor of William Arlosh
Lola Cassidy, Councillor
Jesha Martin, Friend
Apple Collings, Friend

Holly Corben, Girlfriend of Badger
Paige Spencer, Bellingham Tea Rooms Proprietor
Anson Darby, Archaeologist, Tyne River University
Ayla Raposo, Portable Antiquities Scheme
Sergeant Gavin Bishop, Hexham Sergeant
Chief Inspector Kevin Readdie, Newcastle Inspector
Clifton Beaufort, Hadrian's Heroes Metal Detecting Club
Graham Ryan, Hadrian's Heroes Metal Detecting Club
Pete Savin*, Photographer

Nicole Pilcher, Antiques Dealer
Pramod Sharma, Librarian
Henry Neumegen, Pawnbroker
Ryan Francis, Art Loss Register
Gemma Dance, Art Loss Register
Emma Humphreys, Royal Mint
Dafydd Wynne, Retired Curator
Loretta Hambly Wynne, Dafydd's Wife
Joyce Wynne, Dafydd's Daughter

Julius Stertinius Carpus, Roman Soldier
Marcus Aurelius Julianus, Roman Soldier
Darius, Roman Soldier
Gaius, Roman Soldier
Titus Caelius Castus, Commander of Ithaca Fort
Claudia, Castus' Wife
Metella, Brothel Keeper
Carmella, Metella's Servant
Silas, Metella's Manservant
Gattus, Healer
Caelius Apicius*, Roman Recipe Book Author
Decimus Clodius Albinus*, Governor of Britain
Publius Septimius Aper, Father of Metella

Gar, Iceni Chieftain
Bricius, Iceni Warrior
Iolo, Druid
Diviciacus*, Druid

Satiada, Celtic Goddess worshipped in Roman Britain
Meditrina, Roman goddess of health, longevity and wine
*Genuine historical figures

1. What was your favourite part of *Ithaca Lost*?
2. Who would you have aligned yourself with in Roman Britain?
3. Which scene has stuck with you the most?
4. Would you want to read another book by this author?
5. What surprised you the most about the book?
6. *Ithaca Lost* goes back 1,900 years. Where and when would you like to time travel to?
7. What is one question you have for the author?
8. What would you role have been in the *vicus*, the Roman village next to Ithaca Fort?
9. Which characters did you like best? Who did you like least? And why?
10. If you had to trade places with one character, who would it be and why?
11. How likely do you think it is that someone like Mayor Jane Badrick exists, and would behave the way she did?
12. How did the setting impact the story? Would you want to read more books set in this world?